Books by Roz Bailey

PARTY GIRLS

GIRLS' NIGHT OUT

RETAIL THERAPY

POSTCARDS FROM LAST SUMMER

MOMMIES BEHAVING BADLY

Published by Kensington Publishing Corporation

Mommies Behaving Badly

Roz Bailey

KENSINGTON BOOKS
http://www.kensingtonbooks.com

KENSINGTON BOOKS are published by

Kensington Publishing Corp.
850 Third Avenue
New York, NY 10022

ISBN-13: 978-0-7582-0927-6
ISBN-10: 0-7582-0927-4

First Kensington Trade Paperback Printing: September 2007
10 9 8 7 6 5 4 3 2 1

Printed in the United States of America

Contents

PART III: AFTER THE FALL

PART IV: NEW AND IMPROVED MOMMIES

Part One.

The Mommy Track

1

Almost Famous

So far it had been an odd business lunch, as difficult to maneuver as my favorite Manolo Blahnik heels, the slender ones with the delicate ivy leaves trailing up the ankle straps—shoes of a goddess—which, I'd discovered this morning as I tried to put them on, now were adorned with miniature pine cones that had been glued to the toe strap. Undoubtedly the work of six-year-old Scout, who'd face her mother's wrath just as soon as I got her home from school today.

Forced to adopt Shoe Plan B, I dangled my boring black pumps under the table in one of New York's four-star dining rooms, relieved to have my friend and agent Morgan O'Malley beside me to interpret the musings of the graying stuffed shirt who'd been beating around the bush throughout the meal. Morgan had warned me that Oscar Stollen, president of the most powerful romance publishing company in the world, liked to throw his weight around. I just hoped he was prepared to position that bulk beneath his cavernous suit into a book deal and offer me a big, fat brand-new contract.

"Bring us a round of caramel machiatos," Oscar ordered the white-jacketed waiter, then sat back in his thoughtful posture, index finger to square chin.

I suspected that his insistence on ordering for everyone at the table was just the beginning of Oscar's power trip. Oscar had been ordering for us since the waiter snapped a white linen napkin into my lap. I couldn't remember what was in a caramel machiato, but then I'd used up my quota of questions during the lunch, daring to ask what was in the foie gras, what were pancetta, carbonara, gruyére—and what, remind me, was the difference between radicchio and arugula? Cocking an eyebrow at Morgan, I relaxed and settled in for a caramel mucky-mucky. Oscar was a windbag, but I was well aware of the silver lining here: I was being served free food, and so far no one had spilled a drink, asked me to cut their meat or initiated a snarling slap fight. Having been a single parent this last week with my husband out of town, I didn't mind sucking up to Oscar in return for some culinary pampering.

Morgan's mouth curled in half a frown, her message: "I'm behaving for the moment, waiting on his offer."

His offer. If only it was that simple.

If we'd been able to lunch with my editor, Lindsay McCorkle, we would have covered business in the first ten minutes, tasted each other's entrees and shared child-rearing updates. By this part of the lunch we'd have our shoes off under the table as we doubled over laughing about office politics and anecdotes. Unfortunately, Lindsay had told Morgan that "the big guy" wanted to handle this negotiation himself, much to Morgan's dismay.

"Oscar's such an odd duck," she'd told me over the phone. "It's just going to cast a pall over what could be a fun occasion."

We'd already suffered through Oscar's high ick-factor menu of potted suckling pig, sea urchin that reminded me of my ninth-grade biology dissection and foie gras that brought to mind my twenty-month-old's favorite picture book about a fluffy duckling looking for its mama. ("Mama! Mama!" I would quack, much to his wide-eyed delight. "Are you my Mama?") Dylan would be crushed to discover his mommy had allowed bad men to keep the fluffy duckling in captivity, then kill it so that she could consume its fatty liver. But here I was, trying to make a book deal, not wanting to offend the lunch host.

In for a penny, in for a pound . . . or a few pounds, actually. So much for my diet. I could forget about the skinny, sexy black sparkle dress I wanted to wear to my husband's company Christmas party this month. But Oscar was insistent, and I didn't want to say no to the man who was going to offer me the big bucks. I fantasized at how high this next advance might be. Six figures? S-s-s-seven? That was crazy talk, an unheard-of advance for a series romance writer like me.

But a girl could dream.

For the past decade I had written approximately three romance novels each year, earning a reasonable income that barely faltered with the birth of my three children. My friends couldn't imagine how I did it. My mother worried that I'd sold my intellectual soul for steady money. My neighbors didn't have a clue that I was actually working holed up in the basement room in our bedroom community of Bayside, Queens. And the other moms at school assumed that I couldn't be doing anything, since I appeared at dismissal each afternoon in jeans and a down jacket, instead of pulling up outside the school door in a huge Suburban wearing a Dior suit and cashmere coat with a cell phone pressed to my ear. They tried to rope me into the PTA, the first-grade show, volunteer playground duty and box-top snipping, but I fended them off, content to hole up with a cup of herbal tea at my computer and click out my five to seven pages a day.

I enjoyed weaving the stories of my near-perfect people, teasing my characters through their crises and wrapping things up with a neat, heartwarming Ruby Dixon ending. But lately, I'd started craving more of a creative stretch, wishing for a chance to write something that actually made a statement. What that statement would be, I wasn't quite sure, but one night in a fit of inspiration I launched into the proposal for what my agent called "a big book," a longer, more candid story that pressed beyond the pat romance formula. My new story was about a hot-shot business executive, Janna Pearson, who suddenly gets a flash of the ruthless bitch she's become. She has a breakdown, which zeros out her career but leads her to rediscover the things that stir her soul . . . like making chocolates. Add in a dozen of the juiciest sex scenes I'd ever written, scenes that would make my husband wince, and there you have it. Entitled *Chocolate in the Morning*, the proposal was now being shopped around to various publishers, including Hearts and Flowers Romance, where my editor Lindsay told me she'd read it but had been pressed to keep mum on her response so that Oscar could "handle it."

Funny, but Oscar hadn't mentioned *Chocolate in the Morning* yet.

As Oscar and Morgan chatted about the firing of some publishing giant I didn't know, I straightened the napkin on my lap and wondered if I could get away with wearing these, my favorite black pants, to Jack's event. Since I'd turned thirty, I'd decided that black was the new everything. It hid a wealth of stains and it looked pretty good against my gold-brown hair that was now highlighted to cover the gray sprouting around my part. Black ruled, and these pants were the king. The woven black knit was wrinkle-proof and so comfortable and slimming, and the beauty of black pants was that you could dress them up or down. I plucked at a dark thread on the outer seam of my thigh and felt a tickle as the seam gave way slightly.

A hole. I'd just picked my favorite black pants open, revealing pasty thigh underneath.

Fortunately, neither Oscar nor Morgan seemed to notice, however I would need to devise a tactful means of escape once lunch was over. Perhaps I could keep my purse pressed to my thigh as I walked, like a vapid handbag model. Or maybe it would look more natural to throw myself into the arms of one of the smarmy faux-French waiters and ask him to deliver me to the cloak room, *s'il vous plaît*? After all, I was a romance writer; I might as well live up to that slinky satin reputation.

With my palm pressed over the tear near my thigh, I suddenly woke up to the conversation as Morgan made her move.

"Shall we get down to business?" she asked, her almond-shaped, unpolished fingernails gripping the table inches away from the untouched coffee drink placed before her. Morgan is a straight-up java girl, which she would have told Oscar had he bothered to ask before he ordered the cups placed before us, their mounded whipped cream drizzled with caramel sauce. I felt glad that my agent would be negotiating without whipped cream on her upper lip. I, however, wouldn't mind a dive into decadent dairy splendor.

"It's time to negotiate Ruby's new contract," Morgan said, rubbing her hands together like a gleeful miser. "And I'm so glad you've stepped in, since you've got the authority to toss us the big bucks. What say you, Oscar?"

"We're very happy with the way Ruby's books have been performing for Hearts and Flowers," he conceded.

Morgan nodded profusely. "Yes, yes, yes. She does very well for you." I always got a charge out of the way Morgan swung a deal, rubbing her hands together and repeating words for emphasis, fast as a rapid-fire machine gun. "Looking over her last royalty statements, I'd say that upping her advance by ten thousand is a no-brainer. You could even double it and probably still have the books earn out. No problem. Not a problem at all."

I tried to suppress a grin as my brain made quick calculations. Although I never excelled in math, it was clear that Morgan was pushing for me to get thirty thousand dollars a book. At three books a year, that would be ninety grand, but what if I wrote faster, signed up to write four a year?

Despite Oscar's dull presence and his sweaty upper lip, I was beginning to feel all hearts and flowers for Hearts and Flowers, Inc.

"Thirty is doable," Oscar said tentatively.

Thirty. My heart be still. I was tempted to jump up on the table and perform a victory dance, but I didn't want to spill our caramel coffees.

Oscar paused a moment to drain the white china cup, replace it on the saucer and push it away. "But then there's the issue of the new manuscript. What's it called? *Cocoa for Breakfast?*"

"*Chocolate in the Morning,*" I supplied, my pulse quickening at the thought of even more money and a shot at something I could sink my teeth into.

"The chocolate book. Thank you." Oscar nodded. "I think you know the policy of Hearts and Flowers when it comes to sharing our authors with other publishers. We don't like it. Our feeling is, we've put money, promotion, support behind your books and your name, and it's not fair to allow a competitor to cash in on the Ruby Dixon name, a franchise in which we've invested so heavily."

Morgan was nodding rapidly. "Got it. So we'll let you have *Chocolate.*" Her fingertips slipped away from the linen edge of the table as she sat back and grinned. "For a big, fat advance, of course. Lindsay told me she loved it."

Oscar pressed his lips together and blew his cheeks full of air. Unless he was auditioning to be the Stay-Puft Marshmallow spokesman, the expression didn't strike me as a good sign. "I hear that it's quite the read," he said, "but unfortunately, not for us."

My heart stopped beating.

Had there been an ambulance available, I believe the paramedic would have pronounced me clinically dead—no heartbeat, no pulse, no breath. Just stunned and blue-lipped.

Fortunately Morgan jolted me back to life with her telltale candor. "You've got to be kidding me," my agent said with her melodic New York brassiness. "Haven't you heard the buzz about *Chocolate*? That manuscript has been generating more chatter than *The Da Vinci Code*." A stretch, I know, but you gotta love Morgan for defending me.

"Popularity with editors is nice, but it doesn't guarantee a bestseller," he argued, "and this chocolate story doesn't fit into our publishing program. It doesn't speak to our market."

"Okay," Morgan said. "If you're sure you don't want to publish it, we'll take it elsewhere. Ellen Engle at Mission Books is in love with it, and Simon and—"

"It's not that simple," Oscar interrupted. "We don't want *Chocolate* to be published. Not by us or any of our competitors."

One of Morgan's brows arched as she murmured a restrained: "Remember the Stones's song, Oscar? You can't always get what you want."

"I never liked that song." He leaned over the table for emphasis. "And I know how to get what I want, Ms. O'Malley. When people don't cooperate, I fire them."

Morgan shot me a cross look. "Aren't we lucky that we don't work for Oscar?"

I shrugged, in a near panic, wanting to remind her that, while I might not be on the full-time payroll, Hearts and Flowers was my bread and butter. They paid for my life: everything from lattes to my son's Pull-Ups, to my daughters' juice boxes to my car and its ridiculously high-priced New York insurance. I needed them.

Morgan leaned over the table, as if ready to share a secret with Oscar. "This is Ruby Dixon we're talking about." Morgan pressed her finger onto the white linen tablecloth, jabbing the point home. "A strong track record, a broad fan base. She's never missed a deadline and we know she outsells every other romance published in her month."

"We're delighted to have Ruby Dixon on our list. We'd like to keep her. Writing short romances."

"She needs to grow," Morgan said. "Show us that you want to grow with her."

"Financial growth is a very good thing," Oscar said, "but Hearts and Flowers has a very specific market."

Morgan was shaking her head, frowning in dismay. "I think you're making a mistake here—"

"We know our readers; we can't take the chance of putting them off with this chocolate book and—"

"So *Chocolate* is off the table," Morgan said.

My eyes did laterals as they kept interrupting each other. This was juicier than I'd expected. Hard to believe it was all over me.

"Let's focus on the other deal," Morgan said.

"You seem to be missing the point," Oscar said, drawing himself back so that he could fold his hands in a little pile on the table. His fingers were small and pudgy. Putty fingers. "Unless you take *Chocolate* off the market, there is no other deal."

"What?" Morgan's voice snapped. "That's insanity!"

"It's done all the time," he said. "If you want to continue publishing with Hearts and Flowers, you must give us an exclusive on the Ruby Dixon name."

"You can't own her," Morgan said. "It's her real name!"

"It is," I added, as if this needed verification.

"We don't buy the person," Oscar said in a deadly low rasp reminiscent of a serial killer in a film, "only the name."

"Not this name," Morgan hissed. I saw my short, sweet writing career flash before my eyes as she tossed her napkin onto the table and stood up. "This writer is not for sale."

Oscar's body was stiff as a statue except for his eyes, brown shiny marbles that followed Morgan as she rose from the table. The man was cold, like one of those frosty December mornings that stings the lungs.

"Ruby . . ." She turned to me, her dark eyes earnest. "I can't in good conscience advise you to accept this deal with the Devil, not just for the big bucks."

In a flash I was beside her with less aplomb, my napkin tumbling onto the top of my sensible black pumps, my favorite black pants gaping open to reveal a silver dollar of pasty thigh. Inspired by Morgan's line "This writer is not for sale!" I wanted to toss off my own powerful protest, something with the passion of "Make Love, Not War" or "We Shall Overcome!" Unfortunately, the best I could do was, "I'm outta here." I picked up the fallen napkin, snatched the torn seams of my pants together and started to exit behind Morgan.

Halfway across the dining room, I paused and turned back, noticing Oscar's stone figure slumped in the chair. "But thank you for the lunch," I called cheerfully.

My career might be over, my livelihood dashed, but really, is that any excuse for bad manners?

2

Cowboy Hats and Hemorrhoids

"I can't believe you thanked him for lunch," Morgan said later as we recapped the contract debacle over the phone. I was plugged into the headset of my cell, edging the car home from the Long Island Railroad station amid the usual bumper-to-bumper flow of Queens traffic. Our little attached row house was less than a mile from the station, and yet it took fifteen minutes to get home amid the traffic, lights, pedestrians, and four-way stops that most New Yorkers took as a competitive signal to bear down and floor it.

Morgan was still at the office, thinking out strategies over a cup of orange-twist tea. "Oscar Stollen is a raving lunatic control freak, trying to make you his indentured servant," she said, "and you thank him for a slab of suckling pig?"

"People just aren't polite anymore," I said. "Manners may be the only thing that separates us from other species in the animal kingdom. Thanking him was a show of my behavior, not his." I had to remember that Morgan's kids were older, in college. TJ was off at Penn majoring in biology, and Clare was studying at the Fashion Institute of Technology in Manhattan while working part time for a furniture designer and hating it—"but at least she's working!" Morgan always said. Morgan didn't need quiet mommy time anymore, hence our luncheon with Oscar was not a break but business as usual for her.

"Well, honey, I'm just sorry I didn't see that one coming. I've always known Hearts and Flowers to ask for exclusives, but I never heard of them demanding them. Creating their own socialist publishing empire. It's like those think tank deals where you sign away all your creative thoughts. Remember Penelope Glitzman?"

"Penelope . . ." She was a former romance editor who'd left the company to work for a book packager, a sort of book-idea think tank where a prerequisite to employment was to sign your brain away. The packager paid Penelope top dollar, but also demanded that she sign over her ideas in an agreement stating that all concepts generated while employed there were the creative property of the packager. The book packager banged out half a dozen bestselling series while Penelope was in its employ. When one spun off to a TV series, Penelope moved out to Los Angeles to become its executive producer. Until the book packager filed a law suit, claiming to own Penelope's work on the series. Her ideas were their "creative properties." Pretty appalling. My situation was a little different, of course, but close enough to scrape the paint off my toes.

"You're right about this," I told Morgan. "No question about it. I can't sign my creative life away to Hearts and Flowers, no matter how big the advance is. I just got a little mesmerized back there by visions of dollar signs dancing in my head."

"Those dollar signs are a very real concern for all of us." Along with her share of woes, Morgan had a hefty mortgage on her Manhattan condo and some whopping credit card bills to pay down. Nine or ten years ago her husband, Jacob, a successful litigator, had flown to Chicago to ride with his biker buddies to a rally in South Dakota, never to return. Apparently Jacob, now Jocko to his biker buddies, was trying his hand at rustling cattle and taming a wild little redhead in Wyoming. When I met Morgan at a romance writers' convention, talk of Jocko the Urban Cowboy was all the rage. Of course, I didn't hear any of it, being out of the loop, more focused on my writing than on agent/editor scuttlebutt. So when I wrangled a meeting with Morgan and, by way of small talk, asked: "Are you married?" she laughed till there were tears in her eyes and told me I was refreshing.

Although he was the father of her kids, who were in junior high when their dad left, Morgan had never talked about Jocko much. She still didn't mention him much, aside from the occasional short-hand barbs in e-mail, things like "What do I know, he always hated redheads." and "Maybe there's some *Brokeback* lawyer thing going on." Along with the appropriate joke: "What do cowboy hats and he-morrhoids have in common? They're both worn by assholes!"

Since Jacob's desertion I'd seen Morgan through two minor surg-eries. She'd eaten her way up to a size 14 then dieted down to a ten, given up smoking and thrown herself into her career, which had meant a boost for mine. She'd become a great agent and a better friend. She helped me maintain my sanity when the kids and hus-band tore it to shreds, I helped restrain her from hiring a hit man to go after Jocko.

So in light of our relationship, I knew it would kill us both to have that jumbo, megacontract snatched away.

"We both need the income," I said, thinking aloud. "Not to be a downer, but even if *Chocolate* sells, I've got to keep writing ro-mances."

"Of course, of course, and why wouldn't you? You're so good at it, and it earns you a nice chunk of change. Don't you worry about Oscar. We'll get you a contract for more romances. Trust me, honey, trust me. This will work out over the next few months. If Oscar wants you that much, another publisher will want you more."

"It would feel strange not to be writing for Hearts and Flowers, not to be working with Lindsay."

"I know, I know. But in the meantime, you still owe them one ro-mance, and you've got *Chocolate* to write." We had already decided that *Chocolate* would be a stronger sell if Morgan could dangle the complete manuscript before the noses of a few editors, and so my work was cut out for me. "If I put my mind to it, I'll bet I can get you a fat offer to ease your worries. Once *Chocolate* is a hit, Oscar will come crawling back to us, whimpering like a suckling pig."

Christmas . . . ouch. Without a new contract, I'd have to think twice about getting Jack that new set of golf clubs he'd been drop-ping hints about. Of course, there'd be no cutting back on toys for the kids, or holiday trimmings, but I'd learned that the things that mattered most to the girls, like decorating cookies or reading Christmas stories under the tree, cost very little. In fact, without a new contract I'd have plenty of time to be the perfect Christmas mom. I'd delay delivery of my last book in the contract and spend my time decking the halls, organizing caroling parties, decorating cookies, building the gingerbread house the girls had been pining over . . .

"Of course, this is all the more reason to get *Chocolate* written, quick as the wind," Morgan said, rattling my vision of an idyllic Christmas. "How fast can you get it finished? That would help me sell it, to have a complete manuscript."

I tried to do a mental calculation of my calendar as I vacillated between turning right onto Northern Boulevard to pick up the girls from after school or heading straight home to the relative quiet of the house with just the sitter and Dylan. It was only four thirty and I could probably squeeze in another hour or so of work, but the December days were getting shorter and the sudden invasion of night in the afternoon always filled me with a haunting desperation to retrieve my children and see them safely tucked away at home. Funny, on a July night I could work until seven without guilt, but encroaching winter somehow tugged on my maternal instincts. I turned right, toward after-school care.

"Are you there?" Morgan asked. "Can you hear me?"

"Just dodging traffic."

"So finish *Chocolate* ASAP. Put Oscar's last book on the back burner, okay? We'll talk tomorrow."

"Got it. Bye!" As I hung up I realized that someone would have to tell my editor, Lindsay, our side of the story, and I wasn't sure about sharing any of this with Jack until things got settled. We'd connected briefly after the big lunch. I'd stood ducking the wind in a storefront above the tracks of Penn Station to get cell phone service. But I'd downplayed the meeting with Oscar, and Jack seemed to forget all about it, caught up in the office politics at Corstar Headquarters, in Dallas where CJ and Hank and Desiree were bemoaning the fact that they'd been passed over for promotion and the big bosses had seen fit to recruit a division manager from outside the company, hiring a woman named Terry Anne, aka Tiger.

"What do you think about Tiger?" Jack had asked. "Sound like trouble to you?"

"Be glad you're not part of the Dallas office," I'd told him. "Where there's a Tiger, there's bound to be prey."

Of course, I hadn't met any of these people, though I enjoyed following their trials and victories vicariously through Jack, similar to reading a soap opera summary at the end of the week—all plot, no emotion. And for now, the Dallas drama would keep Jack distracted from my lack of a new contract. Despite my rising contribution to our household income, my husband had always worried that one day the bottom would drop out of my chosen career, and I didn't want to give him any inkling that his worries might be coming true. Besides, things were tense at Corstar Corporation, where Jack had recently been given a promotion to management at the New York affiliate TV station, along with stock options that might, one day, knock us into the upper class if all went well. But getting kicked upstairs had given Jack an eyeful of the inner workings of Corstar, and firsthand knowledge of the sordid underbelly had been keeping him awake at night ever since. Promotion—good; underbelly—bad. I figured my news could wait until it turned into good news. That was me, the Can Do! Girl, Little Miss Silver Lining all the way.

"Hi, Ms. Nancy," I said as the petite woman opened the door of her home.

"Becca doesn't drink her milk," she said glumly. "I don't like to waste it. You tell her, next time, she drink it."

How's that for an end-of-day greeting? I thought as my smile froze on my face. "I don't force her to drink it at home," I said. "Maybe her tastes will change, but until then . . ."

"She need milk for strong bones and teeth," Ms. Nancy said wisely. I wondered if her parents had forced her to drink milk when she was a kid. Wait, milk in China? No, but rice—she'd told me about that, how her parents had warned her that each grain of rice left in her dish would be a pockmark on the face of her future husband. Amazing the twisted way we raise our young.

"I didn't ask for milk," Becca said, looking up from the table as we swept into the kids' playroom—a converted sunporch. Ms. Nancy ran a tight ship, the toys taken from their bins one at a time and all homework completed before play could commence. I loved her for that, for instituting the discipline that I never could seem to enforce in my own home. "Mom, you said I don't have to eat something if it's going to make me sick, and I said I didn't want it." That was my eldest daughter, eight going on eighteen.

I rubbed Becca's shoulder. "You know I'm okay with that."

But Ms. Nancy was shaking her head in disapproval. "All my children drink their milk."

Not wanting to take on Ms. Nancy, who, I admit, sometimes frightened me, I asked about homework, and Becca assured me it was all done, except for her reading, which she insisted on doing with me every night. A child of ritual, Becca valued our reading time, and sometimes, as I dozed off to the sound of her mellifluous voice, I worried that she didn't know how to read in her own head. Then again, Jack said I worried too much about Becca.

When she was born, Jack had been so smitten with her that he'd immediately wanted to get going on creating a second child so that Becca would never have to be alone. I worried that Becca subconsciously longed for those days when she was the only one—the object of all our affections. A first child leaves an indelible blueprint on a family, the entire pregnancy experience, when a mother is so hyperaware of movement inside her, careful and vigilant about diet, weight, exercise. I'd been taking prenatal vitamins before I even conceived Rebecca, though with the other two I remembered vitamins every other day or so. Jack came along to the doctor's office for checkups, marveled at the little alien bouncing on the ultrasound monitor and even read the parenting magazines in the office. Jack left work early to attend Lamaze classes with me and we read each other the more inspired passages from *What to Expect When You're Expecting.*

And then, the big-deal day, those first twinges of discomfort, similar to the onset of a menstrual period. The rudeness of the nurses when they learned I'd come to the hospital without being dilated enough, the walk back to the parking lot to get my coat, an interminable journey that took years off my life, I swear, as people looked on in horror, mothers pulling their children away when I had to lean against a cement pillar, and breathe with tears rolling down my cheeks.

"This sucks!" Jack said as he helped me back along the crosswalk to the hospital.

"Take me back upstairs," I sobbed. "I think my water broke."

A few contractions later, I was being eased into the dignified stage of labor and delivery, toted along on a gurney and an epidural of pain candy. Aaaah, the beauty of the epidural, the chance to give birth, to enjoy it and not hate the little dumpling whom you've been planning and prepping for so intently for nine months.

Our first daughter was born with a shriek of annoyance, a very clean baby, which she maintained through life, never drooling, rarely spitting up. I remember the smart set of her rosebud lips as the nurse placed her in my arms. Becca's steely-gray eyes stared up at me, and although the childbirth info claimed that babies could not focus because of the silver nitrate drops put in their eyes, our Becca was quite focused, her stern gaze demanding answers. *Who are you?* she asked as she stared carefully at Jack and me. *What am I doing here? How did I land with the two of you as parents? Do you really know what you're doing?*

Of course, we didn't.

But we did our best to fake it. I will never forget the high anxiety in the car as Jack and I drove our first baby home. I kept turning to the back to check on her, sure that her silence meant she was sleeping, but Rebecca was awake and alert, eyes open as the world flew past her windows and the grill of a truck loomed in the back window, which she faced. "I can't believe we're taking a baby home," I said to Jack.

He turned toward me, looking as if he'd never met me before. "What do you think is going through her head? I mean, what's she thinking?"

"Rosy, warm thoughts, I'm sure," I said. If I was correct, those rosy thoughts faded the minute Jack pulled into a parking spot across the street from our house. Becca started fussing and crying, her little head twitching and writhing in her car seat like an imprisoned nonagenarian. By the time we crossed the threshold, she was in a howling jag that didn't stop for four months except for the occasional break to nurse or pass out from exhaustion.

"I read that the average newborn sleeps sixteen to eighteen hours a day," Jack said. "Becca seems to be crying more than she sleeps. What's up with that?"

"Is it colic?" my mother asked me one day when I was pacing the floor with the baby, reducing her bloody-murder shriek to a disappointed howl.

"The pediatrician said that colic only occurs in twenty percent of babies," I answered. "Not that it would matter, as there's no real treatment for colic, anyway." Short of earplugs for the parents. And I mean those heavy-duty earphone types that you see the crew wearing at Monster Truck events. Although our baby Becca would nap in the morning and come alive with flirty eyes and cooing in the afternoon, she shriveled into a wailing wench by the dinner hour, crying and shrieking inconsolably until well after midnight.

"What's her problem?" Jack asked me one night, genuinely concerned over our baby's discomfort.

I just shrugged, feeling inadequate because I didn't have an answer. I had researched the proper dimensions of crib bars and the most stimulating mobile colors for infant brain development (black and white), but I'd never anticipated having a baby who was less than content and blissed out. Jack signed us up for a newsletter that would teach us about the stages of development Becca was going through, and we studied it like budding behaviorists, sure that the answer to our inadequacies would be explained in the cheerful articles on gross motor skills and cognitive development. "Soon your baby will be grasping at things," we were assured, even as another writer extolled the benefits of "tummy time for your baby." Based on Jack's reading we had Becca tested for gastroesophageal reflux, baby heartburn. Negative, of course. I knew it couldn't be that easy.

By three months, Becca had taught us a few things. We learned that she didn't like being too hot, that she hated being wrapped tight in a blanket, that she didn't want to be cradled in our arms like a baby. I realized she cried less on days that she got out more than once, so I made it a habit to take her to the grocery store or the bank with me, to walk her in the stroller even on the coldest of days. But I still kept her out of restaurants during the witching hour—dinnertime. Jack was the first to figure out that Becca didn't like staring up at the ceiling and devised a new baby hold that only he could manage, holding her face out with her bottom cupped in one hand, her back and neck supported by the other. Similar to the Popemobile or the Batmobile, Jack had devised the perfect touring vehicle for Becca, all in his hands.

By four months, the steady hours of shrieking faded away, and Jack was smitten by her all over again. Her googly eyes and generous smile had erased all memory of nights spent cringing from her howling cries, walking her around and around the living room, trying to dance her around to Hootie and the Blowfish. Becca became the light of his life, the reason to slip under the covers naked with me to try and make a sibling for her.

Recently I'd thought that the misery Becca had experienced those first few months had made her especially empathetic to other people. She tended to reach out to kids left out of the group and suffered when she saw news stories of famine in Africa or areas destroyed by natural disasters. When terrorists struck the World Trade Center, two of Becca's classmates lost their fathers in the North Tower. One of the men didn't even work in the building but was visiting for an early-morning conference. Devastation was all around us, but I couldn't turn my focus from these little children, six years old. While other classmates had pulled away, Becca had wanted playdates and tried to organize games to distract the two.

That was when her insomnia began.

She worried that Jack would go to work and never come home, like Lydia and Andrew's dads. She worried that one of Jack's flights to Dallas would crash into a building. Mostly, I think, she was haunted by the knowledge that the world is not always a safe place, and as her mother, although I could promise that Jack and I would do everything to keep her safe, I couldn't guarantee that bad things wouldn't happen to her. In fact, I knew she'd have her share of heartbreak.

And so, we often lay together in her bed, Becca staring at the cracked plaster ceiling while I fought sleep, trying to save myself for a short conversation and a crime show with Jack.

"I'm just saying"—Ms. Nancy's crisp voice brought me back to the milk crisis—"a girl your age need to drink her milk."

"She eats lots of yogurt at home," I said in Becca's defense. "Plenty of calcium." I moved over to Scout, whose head was bent intently over her pencil sketch. Her smooth, dark hair stuck out between the weave of her headband. "Hey, honey! I came to pick you up early," I said in my most cheerful mom voice.

"But I'm not done." Scout didn't look up from her pencil sketch. "I can't go yet. Mommy, can't I stay for awhile?"

Nancy shrugged and gestured over the children—Raj building quietly with LEGOs in the corner, Tyanna working a puzzle. "All children love it here," she said, as if she possessed a mysterious gift that eluded the rest of us. Ms. Nancy could be quite the salesman.

"You'll be back tomorrow," I told Scout. "Right now, we need to get home."

"But I can't," my daughter said without looking up. "Ms. Nancy said that if I finish she'll mail my list to Santa."

"Everyone make a Christmas list today," Nancy said proudly. "Your Rebecca has very small list. Only one thing she wants for Christmas." She nodded approvingly at Becca.

I drew a blank. If it was one thing, it had to be big. "What's on your list, sweetie?"

"Mom, you know." Becca's delicate brows pressed dimples into her forehead. "I want a puppy."

Ugh! Not the dog thing again. The last thing I needed was another little baby to take care of, though I'd nearly caved last Christmas when Jack and I realized that having a puppy in the bed might bring Becca some comfort at night. "Santa doesn't bring live animals," I said quickly.

"I've seen him bring puppies in cartoons," Scout said.

"And Alexa Vallone got a Bichon Frise for Christmas," Becca added.

"Becca, you need to think of something realistic," I said. "Santa doesn't bring gifts that parents don't approve of." I had always warned my children that there would be no furry animals in our house anytime soon. With three children, one still in diapers, the last thing I needed was a fourth responsibility, especially one that shed and would never master its own bathroom skills.

"Scout, get your coat on. You can finish your list at home," I said firmly, realizing that Scout was creating an illustrated list of toys she wanted from Santa. This task was right up her alley. In the past two

years Scout had become intently focused on creating the perfect
Christmas through compiling the perfect list that would lead to receiving a mountain of toys. Every year I felt anxiety at her potential
disappointment, but each Christmas morning she seemed delighted
with whatever display of toys and books and clothes I had concocted.

"If I take it home, Ms. Nancy won't be able to send it to Santa,"
Scout complained.

"I'll send it to Santa," I said with authority, feeling impatient. There
was dinner to be made, e-mails and mail, laundry and bath time. Besides, I didn't give up an hour of writing time to stand around at
after-school care and watch my daughter draw.

"Come *on*, Scout." Becca boosted her backpack on one shoulder,
bundled in her jacket and ready to go. "You *always* do this. You *always* make us late." Most days Scout can do nothing right enough for
her older sister. I still remember coming home from the hospital
with Scout bundled up in a receiving blanket and Becca snubbing us
both, as if the wispy-haired infant was a rude visitor and I the traitor
with the audacity to let her into the house. I still shudder when I remember the way she folded her arms and squinted up at me as if she
didn't recognize me at all. To this day, I don't think Becca has gotten
over the ruination of our quiet family of three.

"One minute," Scout said insistently. "I just need to finish this
rocket."

I glanced down at the elaborate contraption she was drawing, a
cartoonish aircraft with people in Santa caps riding on the wings.

"Don't look!" she squealed, glaring up at me with a flash of silver
eyes—her father's eyes.

I folded my arms, turning away. "Getting in the Christmas spirit, I
see. And I noticed today that you started decorating the house.
Glued some pine cones onto my shoes, did you?"

"I told her not to," Becca said.

"Am I in trouble?" Scout asked without looking up. "Or did you
like it?"

"You're not allowed to touch my clothes without permission, remember?" I spoke quickly, glancing over my shoulder to see if Nancy
was listening. Sometimes I sensed that she didn't approve of my system for disciplining the girls, loose though it may be, and it made

me second-guess myself. Fortunately, she was off in the next room, setting up a video for Tyanna. "But we'll talk about it later. At home. Let's go, honey."

"But I'm not done," Scout whined, still drawing.

"We really do have to go, sweetie. Finish it at home."

"Now you made me make a mistake." She erased something in the corner of the page, then handed me the paper and scooted her chair back. "Hold it for me, but don't look."

I was already saddled with her backpack and my purse, my hands gripping car keys and Scout's jacket. I snatched the paper, annoyed at my own impatience. "Fine. Jacket on. Got your backpack? Hats? Mittens? Come on, let's go."

Two blocks from home, I slowed the car and put the girls on the alert to holler if they spotted a place to park. Our modest, two-story row house did not come with a garage or driveway, and street parking was getting more and more difficult in a neighborhood where most households now had two or three cars: one for mom and the kids, one for dad and one for the teenaged driver. The upside to our location was that we were surrounded by lovely single-family houses with their own garages and driveways—ample room for their cars. The downside was that most Queens homeowners filled the garage with junk and parked in front of their house, despite the high rate of auto theft. In Queens, it seemed, you were safe in your house, but watch out if someone flags down your Jag. We'd even had a car stolen years ago—Jack's old rust-bucket Honda from college—and though the car was recovered the day it was stolen, we weren't enlightened until two weeks later, when we received a bill from a junkyard charging us storage for those two weeks. Apparently, the city's archaic system for recovering stolen autos allows the owner of the auto wrecking yard a chance to capitalize. When we went to claim the dented Honda with its shattered window, I felt angry and hoodwinked that we had to pay a storage fee although we didn't even know the car was there, but Jack had shrugged it off. His head and heart were already vested in the sporty new Miata we'd bought as a replacement vehicle. So with congestion and theft, you'd think people would be happy to squirrel the car away in the garage. Instead, residents felt a sense of entitlement toward the parking spot directly in front of their house, a fact that I'd been reminded of by more than one neighbor.

"You gotta protect the spot in front of your house," a dumpling-esque woman whined at me in a shrill voice my first week in Bayside. We hadn't even moved in yet; I was unloading a few plants and paper goods from my car when she waddled over and delivered the edict. She pointed to a wooden barricade blocking the street two doors down. "You need to save it or you'll never get to park there."

I blinked at the barricade. "I thought a construction crew was setting up there," I told her. I resisted the temptation to suggest that the walk from her car might actually help chisel away a few pounds; I was new to the neighborhood and I didn't want to tarnish my rep just yet.

"That's my spot, in front of my house," she said slowly, as if instructing a kindergarten class. "And welcome to the neighborhood," she added. "I'm Bawb-rah." That would be the Latin Barbara with a heavy Queens accent.

"Uh . . . thanks," I told her, ducking inside to call my then-boyfriend Jack to report that we were moving into a lunatic neighborhood. Being a Queens boy, Jack was aware of the unwritten laws of parking. Being a rebel, he'd always defied them, even, as a teenager, going so far as to crash into neighbors' garbage cans with his dented Chevy. Oh, that man I love! Sometimes I marvel that he never did time.

Jack and I decided not to buy into the parking-spot entitlement program, a decision that I occasionally questioned now that I had to circle for spots, double back, wedge my Honda in against someone else's bumper, and lug groceries, baby and children down the block, holding hands and limping under the weight of a gallon of milk.

We arrived home to find Dylan asleep, a lump on the living room carpeting beneath his favorite red corduroy blanket. Despite his angelic smile, I felt a twinge of annoyance. A nap this late in the day would probably give him a bout of insomnia tonight, not to mention the fact that Dylan never napped when he was home alone with me. Why was that? Was I so overstimulating that my kid couldn't doze off and give me an hour or so to work at the computer or tidy up the house?

Of course, the nap ended abruptly when Scout and Becca burst in and knelt over him, cooing and calling to him, touching his nose lightly and trying to make him twitch. Dylan uncurled himself, his face a mask of peace until it crumbled into the roar of a hibernating baby bear.

"Leave him alone," I said, then turned to Kristen, an energetic college student who watched the baby in our home a few hours a day while the girls were in school so that I'd have a shot at getting some work done. Most days I was around to see her in action, making up games and activities, sitting on the floor with Dylan, meeting him on his level. Her major in school was early childhood education, and I was grateful to have a sitter who liked kids and didn't sit around watching *All My Children* while the baby munched Cheerios. "How'd it go today?" I asked.

"Fine." She closed her fat textbook and straightened from the couch, a marvel in cable-knit sweater and tight jeans that hugged her girlish hips. College . . . ah, the days of tight young butts and un-limited potential. "But the Dill-man's not himself," Kristen added. "We walked up to the playground, and he just about fell asleep on the swings. He didn't eat much, either."

"Ear infection," I guessed.

My son was prone to them, and my mind raced ahead to the chance of catching the pediatrician and getting Dylan seen today, snagging a prescription and getting it filled, all while tending to the girls and dinner and my now-fledgling professional life.

Kristen slipped on her coat, a shiny black waist-length jacket, short enough to show off her outstanding denim form. "He tried to have fun, but he just passed out, head against his truck when we got home."

"I wonder if I can get him an appointment." I went into the kitchen and grabbed the phone. "Do you have plans tonight?"

"I've got a class." She appeared in the doorway. "Sorry. Is Mr. Salerno still out of town?"

I nodded as I speed-dialed the pediatrician. "He's back in two days. And thanks for everything. See you tomorrow?"

"Sure." She said good-bye to the kids and let herself out. Just then someone answered the line and punched me on hold, which was still better than getting the answering machine. As I waited on the line, I ran through the new agenda for the evening. A visit to the doctor, if we were lucky, where I would lament to the doctor that they should give me one of those ear telescopes so that I could look inside Dylan's ear, pronounce an infection and write him a prescription. I'd have to budget an extra half hour to circle the pharmacy since parking was so tight at that shopping center. I'd lug the three kids into the store, then I'd cave and stop at some fast-food place and stuff my children with fatty French fries and blissful crispy nuggets that came with a cheap plastic toy to boot. After that, I'd corral them into the dark house and try to move the bath-and-homework program along as quickly as possible so that I could fall into my chair in the corner of the dining room and, while talking on the phone with Jack, go over my e-mails.

The mail and laundry could wait until tomorrow.

As I locked in an appointment with the pediatrician that would have me whipping along the Cross Island Parkway to see a doctor before their office closed, I realized that this level of activity would keep me so busy that I wouldn't have time to lament over the huge book contract I'd almost snagged this afternoon. No time to cry in my sherry, there were ear infections to cure, Christmas lists to illustrate, homework to finish. In a mommy's world, all's well that ends when your children pass out in bed.

Rushing to collect coats and shoes and kids and get them out the door, I passed the day's untouched newspaper and grabbed a section to read in the doctor's office. One headline caught my eye:

IS THE MOMMY TRACK A DEAD END?

Ha! Was this another writer telling me I couldn't have my cake and eat it, too? Those naysayers drive me nuts, even if there is a grain of truth in their message of doom. In the big picture, I'd gotten everything I'd planned for: a fulfilling career, a thoughtful husband, a home in New York City and three adorable children. Bliss was right at my fingertips.

So why was I sponging up spilled juice, wiping my son's nose and yelling at Scout to get her coat on?

The Mommy Track wasn't a path at all. It was more like a treadmill on the edge of a cliff teetering over suburbia.

3

Can Do!

"There he is!" I crowed as my husband walked in the door, looking darkly handsome in his black overcoat, his suit bag slung over one shoulder. "Daddy's home!"

The children stopped what they were doing and ran to the door amid cries of "Daddy!" "Yay!" and, from Scout: "What did you bring me?"

With a twinge of creaky muscles I pushed myself up from the floor, where I'd been trying to build a tower of Duplos in pink and white, having to beg some blocks from my son, who claimed to need them rattling around in an old shoe box. Kids . . . They ask you to play with them, then they don't want to share the damn blocks.

"Look at you all! I swear, you sprouted a few inches in the past week." Jack kissed the crew, then pulled me close. "Hey, Rubes." He kissed me on the lips, his gray eyes smokey. My private heaven was in his arms.

"Welcome home," I said, loving the way I still fit into the crook of his arm. Jack's five-day trip to visit a few affiliates had stretched out into two weeks when he'd been summoned to Corstar Headquarters in Dallas, simultaneous with Morgan turning up the heat on my getting her the complete manuscript of *Chocolate* and Lindsay calling to tell me they moved up the deadline for my next romance novel. My "Can Do!" attitude had nearly undone me this time, causing me to get up before dawn to write, then finish off the day at the computer in Dylan's room, the keyboard clicking away under the dim glow of the monitor. "Am I glad to see you," I told my husband.

"Oh, yeah?" He grinned. "Single parenting not for you?"

"Mommy lost her marbles!" Scout reported, her gray eyes sparkling studiously. "That's what she told us. Do you have marbles, Daddy?"

He touched Scout's shoulder and lowered his voice confidentially. "I lost mine years ago."

The connection that flickered between them made me grin. When I'd been pregnant with Scout, Jack had come to me to confess that he worried about bonding with the new baby. "I love Becca so much, I just can't imagine feeling that way about another kid."

I'd promised him that he'd acquire a unique attraction for Scout, that the capacity for loving was not a finite thing. "I mean, you love a good T-bone steak, but when my mother brings us lobsters back from Maine in the summer, it doesn't diminish your love for steak, does it?"

"Are we talking kids or entrees?" he'd asked, folding me into his arms for kisses. "You're nuts, and I love you."

And I'd been right. When Scout was born, Jack was through the roof with delight once again. And since Scout was a calm, sensible infant who understood the beauty of eighteen hours of sleep a day, our newly acquired parenting skills were more than sufficient. Suddenly, it became my role to school two-year-old Becca in speech and manners while Jack buddied up with Scout. At last, he had a baby of his own, and this one didn't cry or shriek as if she had a knife in her belly. Mellow, dough-faced Scout was happy to doze off in Jack's arms while he read the paper, happy to take a ride in the stroller, happy to cruise along with Jack while he ran out for milk or to the car wash.

Six years later, I was glad to see that their bond had only deepened.

"We've got your favorite," I told Jack, who tugged on Becca's ponytail, "chicken cutlets for dinner." Simple, breaded chicken breasts was one of the few meals we could all eat and enjoy. Of course, Jack's mother, Mirabel, would insist on slathering them with tomato sauce—gravy, she called it—and then melted thick slices of Parmesan cheese on the top. And, according to Jack, no one makes gravy like Mamma Mira. I think Mira is still a little horrified at my lack of old-world cooking skills.

"And we made sugar cookies for dessert," Becca said proudly.

"Sugar cookies!" Jack ran a hand over her cinnamon-colored hair, giving a gentle yank on her loose ponytail. "You know I love those."

"We'll help you unpack, and you can show us all your souvenirs from Dallas." Scout teetered on the stairs, trying to carry up his bag. "Like key chains and cowboy hats . . ."

"Dylan wants a hat!" He pressed his fingers to the top of his head as he fell up the stairs behind Scout. *"My* cowboy hat."

Becca leaned over him, hands on his shoulders. "If Dad got me one, I'll let you wear it," she said sweetly.

"No! *My* hat!"

"No hats this time," Jack said, stepping over our son gingerly to grab the luggage before it came sliding down the stairs. "But I may have *something* for you, if you were good for Mommy."

"Are you kidding?" I grinned. "They were little monsters the whole time you were gone."

"Mo-om!" the girls moaned, well accustomed to our little joke that played out every time Jack returned from a business trip, which seemed to be a frequent occurrence these days. Part of his job at one of the network television stations in Manhattan was to keep the affiliates happy, which meant traveling to their various cities to wine and dine them. Add on the fact that Jack's station was headquartered in Dallas, which required a trip to the second biggest state in the union about six times a year, and it meant my husband was a very busy, very scarce man. He loved his job and was well suited to the requisite schmoozing. "The beauty of my job is that I don't really have to work," he always said. "I just have to get in lots of face time." I wholeheartedly supported my sweetie in doing something he loved, but I hated losing him to Dallas and Phoenix, Portland and Detroit.

"Why do you always go away?" Scout asked Jack as she trailed him up the stairs.

"I have to travel for my job," he said smoothly, though from the dark look he cast over her head I could tell her question cut him deeply.

That night after Jack supervised baths and played a giggling round of "Spank Your Fanny," a game the girls had fashioned with him out of idle threats, he tucked the girls into bed and joined me on the living room couch where I was snuggled under a fleece blanket, the TV muted as I waited for one of the millions of *Law & Order* spin-offs to come on. We watched the show together and tried to guess "who done it" before the TV detectives put it all together.

"We saw this one," Jack said as he picked up my feet and sat down. "Remember? It wasn't a robbery at the jewelry store, but the clerk's ex-girlfriend was angry because she found out the ring he gave her was fake."

"I never saw this one, and thanks for ruining it."

"Ah, you did, too, Rubes," he insisted.

"Nah-uh. You must have seen it one night in Dallas."

"No way. I was here. You saw it."

"Nope. You were lounging in bed in your boxers, surrounded by silver-domed room service plates and a passel of belly dancers."

He pulled my heels onto his lap and began one of his expert foot massages. "Make that a squad of cheerleaders and we're in business."

I wanted to sling a witty rebuttal back at him, but I'm a sucker for a well-placed thumb in the instep. It was during a picnic dinner in Central Park with friends who'd assembled to see opera at Met in the Park that I'd first learned of Jack Salerno's skill with foot massage. My friend Gracie moaned and squealed as he caressed her feet. "Get a room," one of the other guys joked, and I admit, it did seem quite intimate. But since I knew Gracie had a huge crush on someone else on the picnic blanket, I didn't hesitate and was next in line when Jack finished with her feet.

Although I held back my moans and sighs, I admit that that first massage was nearly orgasmic. I've had an exclusive on Jack's hands ever since . . .

"Scout's out," Jack said. "I told Becca she could read in bed for a few minutes, since she's not tired." Becca needed time to unwind, while Scout had an enviable ability to conk out soon after her head hit the pillow.

"Becca should sleep well tonight, now that you're back." I had told Jack about our oldest daughter's tears at night.

"I just feel so scared. Can we leave the light on?" she would ask me, though I'd noticed that the nighttime tears came only when Jack was out of town.

"No tears tonight?" I asked him.

"No tears." He stared at the TV screen as his thumbs worked the arches of my feet. "I feel bad about that. No kid should be scared at night because her old man is on the road. Sometimes I don't know why I don't jump off the old hamster wheel."

"I know why," I said. "It's because the wheel is a fun ride."

"Maybe, but lately I've been thinking about all the things I miss. The girls really do look taller than they were two weeks ago. And Dylan, he's lost that baby look completely. Those fat red cheeks? Gone. He's moving from toddler to boy, and I'm missing it."

I was glad to hear that Jack had noticed Dylan's growth. Though Jack claimed I was hypersensitive, I didn't think he paid enough attention to our son. By the time our third child was born, Jack was so caught up in vying for a promotion at work and managing the girls that he dealt with Dylan methodically, without joy or verve. "It's like your body is here but your mind and spirit are somewhere else," I'd told Jack one day when Dylan started crawling, the first time he'd made it from the living room to the kitchen. Jack had growled something back, but it was clear he was in denial.

"Our kids are growing up without me, Rubes," he said.

"You're just noticing these things because you've been away two weeks. That's a long time, honey."

"Exactly. And I don't want to go down as the absentee father."

I smiled. Maybe he had been listening all those times months ago when I'd complained about his parenting ennui. I pushed the decadent warmth of his hands out of my mind for a second to focus on the conversation. "What are you saying, Jack?"

"There's a position opening up at Corstar Headquarters. It'd mean a move to Dallas, but there's almost zero travel involved."

My smile faded. "Dallas, huh?" I humored him, knowing he hated it there—the warm weather, the oily twang. Texans didn't appreciate Jack, a wise-cracking New Yorker. "We could do that. Dylan would finally get his cowboy hat. What's the latest from Dallas, anyway? How are Desiree and Hank and CJ?"

Not that I'd met these people, but I'd heard enough about them from Jack to get a mental picture. CJ was a spunky goofball, Desiree a blonde bimbo with a vacant mind, and Hank was a boyish wisp of a thing who outsold everyone else at the station, maybe every one south of the Mason-Dixon Line.

"Oh, and Tiger. How's she working out?" Tiger was the new supervisor at Corstar, the parent company that owned the station where Jack worked. Her real name was Terry Anne Muldavia, but her nickname had made her a legend even before her first day of work.

"She should be nicknamed Shark," Jack said. "She's got the wide mouth of a predator, the sleepy eyes of a cold-blooded killer. She's always moving, cruising the halls, swinging her head back and forth in meetings."

"A charming young lady. It's a wonder she never married."

"You should meet her, really get to know the whole Dallas gang," Jack said, rubbing the back of his neck. "Especially if we're thinking of moving there."

"Hardy-har-har."

"You think I'm kidding? I could leave New York. The greatest city on Earth, the huge, stinking armpit that crushes us in its concrete embrace."

"Uh-huh." Dallas to me was no more real than the tourist sites I'd gone to while at a business conference there, back when I'd worked for an insurance consulting firm. My office buddies and I had done the JFK parade route, the Grassy Knoll and sampled just about every froufrou drink the Fairmont had to offer. Dallas was a lame fantasy. No one was going anywhere.

Although I grew up in the burbs of Jersey, Jack was raised here in Bayside, Queens, in a house about ten blocks away. After retirement his parents moved to Florida, but Jack had never roamed much farther than across the East River to Manhattan during a whirlwind period after college when he shared a two-bedroom apartment with three other guys.

I yawned. "Hand me the phone and we'll get this place on the market. We can start packing during the next commercial."

"So facetious." He shook his head. "I don't know where you get that."

"I live with the big kahuna of facetious."

"I sense you're not taking me seriously."

"What was your first clue?"

"You don't think I can leave New York, do you?"

"Honey, you've spent most of your life living in a ten-block radius. Being one of the Bayside Boys defines you. Nothing wrong with that."

"I could leave, you know." He turned away from me, staring at the television screen. "I'd do it for the kids. To be around for them. I mean, years down the road, do we want them in therapy talking about how their old man was never around? When the girls are sixteen they'll be dating men in their thirties, searching for a father figure. And Dylan . . . You know, last time I was home I caught him playing with your blush."

"My Estée Lauder? I've been looking all over for that."

"Is that the kind of son we're raising?"

"Blush without foundation? Appalling!"

"Rubes, you know what I'm saying." He tucked the blanket around my feet and reached for my left hand. "I've been thinking about this, really. With my job, and traveling, well, I don't want to screw the kids up. I could leave New York if it meant something better for the kids, for our family."

I swallowed back a giggle, trying to take him seriously. "Honey, it's too late for that. Between the two of us I'm sure we've already screwed those kids up for life. Damage done. Moving now isn't going to change that." And he was full of shit if he thought he could leave the Big Apple behind. Jack wouldn't be Jack without his New York persona, and as for me, I couldn't imagine leaving New York and relocating to some godforsaken place like . . . Texas. I leaned back on the couch and closed my eyes, giving myself a second to imagine driving around in a shiny minivan with a Texas license plate, my skin tanned, fingernails manicured, my kids answering a polite but twangy "yes, ma'am!" when I yelled at them to pick up their dirty clothes. An odd fantasy, but it wasn't me. Partly because I doubted my kids would ever pick up their clothes; I'd started warning the girls that they'd better pursue big-money careers so they could afford a housecleaning staff. And more to the point, I couldn't imagine living in a foreign land like Texas or Wyoming. Leaving noisy, cantankerous, pricey New York was out of the question. "Look," I said, "this place might be a looney bin, but it's home."

"Isn't home anyplace we're together?" he asked.

"That is just so sweet!" I gushed, squeezing his hand. "Sweet, but I'm not biting."

He shook his head and sighed. "This is what I get for marrying a woman who's smarter than I am."

I moved the tips of my toes along the top of his thigh. "Flattery will get you nowhere. I'm too tired for reunion sex."

"You can't be too tired for reunion sex." He grinned, a winning smile with straight, square teeth that I can only pray our children will inherit when their permanent teeth come in. "That's against the rules. There's no crying in baseball, and no calling off reunion sex."

Reunion sex had begun as one of those spontaneous "Gee, honey, I'm glad to see ya!" things and quickly solidified itself as a ritual. Not to be outdone by make-up sex, birthday sex or your-mom's-got-the-kids-overnight sex. I was, indeed, glad to have Jack home, but I'd been up late last night dealing with Becca's tearful insomnia, then Dylan had wrenched me from sleep twice with pain in his jaws that was either teething or a new ear infection or both. "I'd like to, but I feel like my body was hit by a Mack truck," I said in a fuzzy voice.

"Come on, Rubes. You're the Can Do! girl."

"I'm afraid my Can Do! is all done."

"Maybe I can help." He separated my legs at the ankles and leaned in between, massaging my inner thighs under the blanket.

I let out a muffled whoop as his hands moved up my legs. "That tickles." I caught his hands under the blanket, clamping down. "And you know it's been crazy around here with me trying to finish my book and write more of *Chocolate,* and Dylan being sick and Oscar going psycho." I didn't mention the fact that I'd had to cancel on Gracie twice, how I'd missed seeing *Wicked* with Harrison when two free tickets landed in his lap. I didn't mention the pressure I was feeling to get onboard for Christmas. When I wasn't stressed out it was one of my favorite times of year. I enjoyed all the trimmings, the decorated cookies, the familiar carols, the sparkling lights and packages wrapped in gold with fat bows. The spirit of the season made New Yorkers a little nicer, a little less likely to steal your cab or lunge for that last seat on a subway train. The kids had forced me to pull the boxes of bulbs and lights from the cobwebs of the crawl space in my closet, but we had saved the tree-buying ritual for Jack. "Give me a few days and we can combine it with Under-the-Tree sex. We've got to get a tree up, Jack."

"You can't combine two events." He leaned back. "I call foul."

I felt tempted to reply that right now there was nothing fouler than his wife who hadn't managed to squeeze a shower into her schedule that morning, but I wanted to defer the mood, not kill it. Tomorrow I would shower and exfoliate. At the moment, nothing could beat the irresistible lure of sliding under the comforter and burrowing my face into my pillow.

"The rain date is tomorrow," I said, thinking that I'd even slip on that red bustier that Jack so enjoyed peeling off. I pushed off the blanket, slid my feet down to the floor, leaned over and kissed my husband's beautiful hard jaw. "Good to have you back, Jack. Are you coming to bed?"

He reached for the remote. "I'm still on Texas time. Do you want me to do the morning run?"

Meaning, get up at seven, corral the kids out of bed for breakfast. Pack the girls' lunches, get them dressed and out the door. Although Jack had spent the entire evening with the kids, the morning run usually belonged to him. "That would be heaven," I said without a trace of guilt. Hey, I'd been doing the single-parent thing for the past two weeks.

I dragged myself up the stairs, heading for my stash of PM Sleep in the bathroom medicine cabinet and fantasizing about the warm glow of a good solid seven hours. If Dylan woke up, Jack would hear him.

My honey was home; I could dance in a field of poppies. Deedle-deedle-dee!

4

Tidings of Conflict and Joy

The first twenty minutes of Jack's company Christmas party reminded me of the receiving line of a wedding. As Jack called out names and shared warm shoulder claps with his colleagues, I was stuck as the outsider waiting to be introduced, smiling, nodding. How do you do? Nice to meet you. Heard so much about you. It's a little worse for women because some men don't think it appropriate to shake a woman's hand—especially a woman like me, the accessory, the wife of a corporate cheese. I hate that.

As if it isn't bad enough that I have to suck it all up and play Mrs. Jack. I don't know why, but somehow Jack's professional life sops up the bulk of our conversation, while mine is never discussed. Not that Jack doesn't value what I do; often he'll step up behind me while I'm whaling away on the keyboard and shake his head, saying: "I don't know how you do that, pull a story out of the air." I've given up explaining to him that it starts with an idea, then moves onto a three-page concept that gets banged out into a chapter-by-chapter outline that is the blueprint for each book. Each stage is reviewed by my editor, who guides me along the way, so I never experience that feeling of alienation or loss of direction, never that artistic panic of jumping off a cliff: "Here goes!" But writing is just that thing that I do. Jack's job at Corstar, well, it's like the path of our family's starship, the great shaman that sustains and guides our spirits.

With Jack's networking and the line for the coat check, we still hadn't gotten past the lobby of the Gorham Hotel, an old iron building with turn-of-the-century charm, now festooned with tiny white lights, fat red ribbons and garland filled with glittering red balls. With flames flickering in a marble façade gas fireplace, I felt a tingle of recognition of the many holiday parties, heartrending meetings and secret liaisons that had transpired in this building. Okay, I'm a romance writer.

"Jack Salerno, you smooth-talking hustler! How the hell you doing?" one silver-haired man shouted, embracing my husband in a huge hug. Turning to me, he added, "The last time I saw this man, I was working in Chicago. Next thing I know, I'm transferred to a two-bit station in Arkansas, and loving it."

"He's a smooth talker, all right," I said. "I'm his wife, Ruby."

"It's a pleasure to meet you, Ruby." Silver Hair looked from me to Jack suspiciously. "Wait! Jack and Ruby? Jack and Ruby. Jack Ruby!"

I nodded. "Easy to remember, right? And we didn't even plan it that way."

Jack flashed me one of those grins that still melted my heart. "It seemed like a bad omen, but I married her anyway."

Silver Hair insisted on buying Jack a drink, not getting that the booze was free tonight. I guess you don't get a lot of freebies at his station in Arkansas. "I'll meet you at the bar," Jack told Silver Hair as we finally moved up in the coat-check line. The temperature had dipped into the twenties the night before and though everyone was complaining of cold it was beginning to feel a lot like Christmas.

Jack helped me slide off my coat, then yanked his hand away. "Ew. What's that?"

Red goop on his fingertips.

"Something on my sleeve?" I checked the cuff of my new black dress, a waistless chiffon shift with rhinestones around the collar, simple yet elegant. At least, it would be elegant if it weren't for the SpaghettiOs on the sleeve. From Scout's last request as I left her with the sitter. "Dammit."

Jack swiped napkins from a passing waiter and handed me a few. "What do you want to drink?" he asked, wiping his fingers.

"Whiskey sour," I said as I backed toward the restrooms.

I spent a good twenty minutes in the ladies' room, scrubbing away at the orangey-red dots on my sleeve as the old commercial jingle "Uh-oh! SpaghettiOs!" chorused through my mind. Jack and I had taught the old ditty to the girls when they were toddlers, and we'd loved the way they'd popped up like little jack-in-the-boxes when they cried: "Uh-oh!"

Cute, sweet, sentimental . . . But the memory paled in comparison to the party going on outside in the ballroom, and I felt frantic to get back out there and replace a SpaghettiOs revery with hot hors d'oeuvres from wandering servers and the mellifluous croon of Harry Connick Jr. doing Christmas carols. "Out, damned spot!" I cursed as someone came out of the stall.

"Hi." The petite blonde, perfect from head to toe in a red suit trimmed with gold, spared me a friendly but demure smile. "You're Jack Salerno's wife, right?"

"Ruby. And you must be from the Dallas office."

"Desiree Rose." She chose the sink at the far end of the counter to wash her hands. "Did you spill something?"

"Sort of." I didn't want to share my mess.

A lemon-haired confection, Desiree certainly wouldn't understand the need to make SpaghettiOs on the fly while giving instructions to the sitter and grabbing clean Wonder Pets pj's from the dryer. Desiree struck me as one of those women who actually tried those beauty tips listed in magazines. Her nails matched her lipstick, which matched her fire-engine red suit. Her hair shone with gold-on-gold highlights, and her shoes—open-toed sandals—were dry and without a scuff from the streets of New York.

Desiree dropped the linen towel in a bin and turned to me awkwardly. "When you finish with that, come on out and visit at our table. Your husband's a hoot. We just love him down in Dallas, and I'm sure the rest of the folks from headquarters are dying to meet you, the woman behind the man."

That was me, the woman behind the hoot. "Gee, thanks," I said, wadding up the linen towel I'd used to lighten the orange stain. Although I usually avoided networking on my husband's behalf, I felt curious about the Dallas people, the names Jack had mentioned. I'd drafted a mental image of Elsa and Hank, CJ and Tiger and Desiree. Wouldn't it be fun to hang with them awhile, gather my own info and maybe insinuate myself with the group, all to Jack's surprise and horror?

"You 'bout done there?" Desiree asked me.

I smoothed out my sleeve and buttoned the cuff. "I've done enough damage here. Take me to your people," I said with an exotic accent.

Desiree gestured toward the door and led the way back into the ballroom like a real estate agent showing off a property. Granted, I envied her neatly sprayed, symmetrical hairstyle, the slightly feathered up-turned curls at her shoulders, but something about her walk was a bit stiff and formal. As in, "Ladies and gentlemen, let's hear a round of applause for Ms. Texas!" Inside the dining room Desiree sideswiped Judith Rothstein, the office manager of the station here in New York. Desiree excused herself. Judith seemed to hiss back.

Judith softened when she noticed me. "Ruby, bubbelah, how are you? The children?"

"All fine, Judith." I reached out and squeezed her bony hands. "You look fabulous, but I can't talk now. I'm on a mission." I nodded toward Desiree. "Meeting the Dallas in-laws."

"And why would you want to do that?" she asked bluntly. To her credit, Judith shunned all other branch offices of Corstar equally. A staunch Brooklynite, she knew no other city could measure up to New York, and thus the affiliates in other cities did not interest her in the least.

I shot a look at Desiree, who was beginning to disappear in the sea of people. "Let's talk later. I'll find you," I promised Judith.

The delay gave Desiree a minute to pounce on the table and warn the other people from headquarters that I would be joining them. By the time I squeezed behind two balding reps from other affiliates arguing market shares, all heads from Dallas were turned up toward me, eyes glazed, polite smiles in place. Elsa Wallace, a plus-sized gal apparently with stock in Revlon, dove into her role as office manager and introduced her crew. Besides Desiree there was CJ Williams, an African American woman with a bombshell shape and a handshake so strong I'd choose her first for my softball team.

The new head of sales, Terry Anne Muldavia, rose-dark and sleek, her long mane of shiny black hair cascading down her back as she sized me up with her dark, exotic eyes. She extended a hand, her talons the color of an eggplant. "Where's Jack?" she asked, as if I couldn't gain entry without him.

"He's shmoozing around here somewhere," I answered, wondering if that perfect tan on her legs was natural or sprayed on. Safe to say, Tiger and I weren't going to be sharing lattes anytime soon.

"So nice to meet you." Elsa placed her pudgy hand in mine. "It's Lucy, isn't it?"

"Ruby," I said. "An easy way to remember is Jack Ruby. Get it? Jack and Ruby?"

"Of course." Elsa withdrew her hand as Desiree let out a gasp.

"Is that supposed to be a joke?" Desiree asked.

I shrugged one shoulder. "Sort of black humor, I guess. I mean, it's a bizarre coincidence, don't you think? Not creepy enough to keep us from getting married."

Desiree shook her head in disapproval. "I'll have you know, that incident has marred our city's history. Half the tourists who visit Dallas take the Grassy Knoll tour. It's a tragedy I'd like to forget."

"Oh, get a life," Tiger snarled. "Were you even born when it happened? No. So back off." She sat down at the table and tore into a dinner roll, clearly giving up on the rest of us.

"Ruby?" Hank tried to change the subject. He was not the rangy cowboy I expected but a short, boyish chap with a pencil-thin moustache that made him look like a junior-high student impersonating a grown-up. "Ruby, I've got a question for you. I'll bet you meet lots of famous people, living here in New York. Have you ever met Liza Minnelli?"

"No, but I was in a writing class with a woman who fitted her for a costume once."

Hank gasped. "Oh, my stars. It must be something to live here in New York and be around famous people all the time."

"I'm sure it's not that different than living in Dallas," I said, enjoying Hank's giddy enthusiasm. "It's not like I have breakfast with Jennifer Aniston and Oprah each morning."

"Oprah's based in Chicago," Tiger said with such a tone of disgust, you'd think I'd plopped SpaghettiOs on *her* sleeve. I was beginning to see why people called her Tiger.

"Right. I was just flipping you an example." I pushed my chair away from the table and crossed my legs off to the side. Although my waist and hips may have softened with three pregnancies, my legs remained my strongest physical asset, and at the moment I was tempted to use them for a karate kick right to Tiger's prominent chin.

"Speaking of famous," Elsa said, her eyes wide in her chubby cheeks, "I understand we're sitting with a real, live author this very minute."

When the others looked around, she nodded at me. "Ruby is a writer. Romance novels, right?"

I nodded, pasting on the publicity smile. "That's right."

Hank gaped, clapping his hands frantically in mock applause. "Author! Author!"

"I can't imagine how you do that," Desiree said with a strangled gasp. "I could never write so many words."

You said it yourself. "I enjoy writing. I've been taking notes since my fingers were strong enough to hold a crayon." I recrossed my legs, trying not to appear smug. Most of the people in my world could care less that I was a published author; those who did care seemed to glaze over and salivate like a baby pterodactyl waiting for a meal. At the moment, everyone at the table had that baby-dinosaur look, everyone except Tiger, who was staring down at the floor, as if searching for a place to spit out a mouthful of aspic.

Hank clasped his hands together delightedly and fired off a barrage of questions. "When did you start writing? How many books have you published? Where do you get your ideas? Am I asking too many questions? Do you write under your own name?"

I laughed. "I write under my maiden name, Ruby Dixon, and I'm happy to talk writing with you, Hank."

"I've always been a writer, too," CJ said. "I write in my journal every day."

"That's a great—"

"You're running," Tiger interrupted me.

I squinted at her. "Come again?"

"Your pantyhose." She nodded down at my fair legs, where a hideous glare of pasty white shone through a run that shot up from my ankle along my shapely calf.

I groaned, quickly concealing the run behind my other leg. "Thanks." Not.

"Just take them off," Tiger ordered. "Pantyhose are passé, quickly becoming a fashion faux pas. Tights would have been okay, but it's a little late for that. You want to go to the ladies' room and get rid of them."

"Maybe I will." With as much dignity as I could muster I rose from the table, pretending that torn stockings and SpaghettiOs stains didn't matter.

"Ooh, Ruby! Don't leave us!" Hank begged. "We want to hear all about the life of a famous writer."

"I'll reconnect!" I promised, showering the love right back at him, over Tiger's head, of course.

Darting to the restroom, I caught sight of Jack lingering at the edge of the bar with his boss. He nodded as Numero Uno Laguno gesticulated wildly, her flailing arms nearly spilling her martini. Phoebe Laguno was probably half-crocked, but under the best of circumstances that woman was one olive short of a martini, anyway. Poor Jack, a party going on all around him and he gets stuck sucking up to Numero Uno Laguno. It looked like his evening wasn't going any better than mine was.

As I peeled off my pantyhose in a stall, I wondered why I was always feeling like my wardrobe and my life were held together by a broken safety pin. Here's one of the many ways in which I differed from the heroines in the romances I wrote—they were barely flawed women. A mechanic with dimples showing through the axle grease on her creamy cheeks who struggles to prove herself to the guys in the pit. A gourmet chef without an ounce of flab on her slender frame who fights to keep her restaurant open with competition from franchises. A magazine model who tries to dumb down her beauty but cannot hide her amazing beauty under hats, scarves and sunglasses.

Ha! I should have such problems.

Stuffing the ball of stockings into the trash, I smoothed the skirt of my dress and thanked God that I'd worn closed-toe shoes to cover my chipped pedicure. Okay, my pasty-white legs did not have the same sex appeal as they'd had in sheer black stockings, but the party was far enough along that no one, save Tiger, would remember.

Back inside the ballroom I tried to save Jack from Numero Uno. "Excuse me, Phoebe," I said. No one dared call her Numero Uno to her face. "But Jack and I haven't had a chance to dance tonight."

"Aw, that's so sweet. It is!" she gushed in her whiney Jersey accent.

"Great idea, Rubes." Jack set his drink on the bar and touched my arm.

"But we're talking business, right now," Numero Uno added. "So you need to disappear. Be gone! Off with you."

The desperate look on Jack's face made me pause, but I knew it didn't pay to argue with Numero Uno Laguno.

"Vamoose! Split!" Numero Uno went on, waving her arms to cast me off to distant places. "Scotty, beam her up!"

I tinkled my fingers at Jack and turned toward the cluster of familiar faces from the New York office. I was feeling alienated and needed a hometown fix. I took a seat beside Judith, hoping to absorb some of the intrepid mettle that oozed from her advice. In Judith's view, there was nothing she couldn't fix with a strong dose of chicken soup and a stern talking to. Decisive, wise and, okay, bossy as hell, this woman had kept the New York office grounded for nearly twenty years.

"You've got no stockings on," she croaked as I sat down.

"Tell me about it. Big run."

"You should think about self-tanning," she said. "I do it every Sunday."

Somehow, the image of Judith stripped down to her underwear and rubbing in tanning lotion was not going to help my lack of connection at tonight's party. "I'll have to add that to my list of things to do," I said. Right between "shop for Christmas gifts" and "scrub toilet."

"Really, dear. Just because you have little ones doesn't mean you can let it all go to hell. I know, believe me, I've been there. My two are grown, of course, but when they were little I refused to let myself go, and my Irving, God rest his soul, was never turned away."

I nodded, feeling more bedraggled and out of control than ever.

"But your skin is so lovely. Isn't it lovely?" she asked the rest of the table, where the sales team Jack worked with sat nursing scotches and leaning forward conspiratorially. I smiled at the crew, the high-energy, the highly agitated. Spokesmodels for anxiety medication. Jack said you needed to keep your edge to stay ahead in this business. "If you're not swimming, you're shark bait," he always told me. I tried to remind them that they were selling air. Air time. Commercials. If that isn't the Emperor's new clothes . . .

"Ruby is happenin'." Byron Smith held up a hand for me to give him a high-five. With his gravelly voice and Jelly Belly persona, Byron was definitely the coolest brother at the station.

I smacked his palm and leaned into the group. "What trouble are you guys stirring up now?"

"We're just taking bets on who's going to become Numero Uno's next scapegoat," said Britta Swensen, one of the two women who was doing a job share at the station. Blonde, and big-boned with crystal-blue eyes, Britta shared her job with a mother of two who commuted in from upstate two days a week.

"You're probably safe, Britta," I said. "Lucky you."

"Hey, I paid my dues," Britta said, glancing toward the bar where Numero Uno was still monopolizing Jack.

Two years ago, when Phoebe falsely accused Britta of being a cocaine addict, Britta rose to the challenge and emerged from the coffee room with her nostrils caked in white. Vaseline coated with Sweet 'N Low. Numero Uno went ballistic, calling in HR and security. When the dust settled, Britta lodged an HR complaint against Phoebe Laguno, and Numero Uno Laguno was sent off for job retraining at a spa upstate. Since then, Phoebe Laguno didn't mess with Britta Swensen.

"Oh, tell me it's not Jack," I said.

"He seems to be the flavor of the month," said Lyle, the office slut who would probably be voted most likely to step on his own dick. With spiky hair, buff body and puppy-dog eyes, Lyle was a real hottie. Too bad about the sex-compulsion thing.

The conversation shifted to a critique of the best restaurants in Manhattan, and names such as Le Bernardin, Per Se and Gramercy Tavern were tossed about. Britta said she refused to eat anyplace that wasn't five stars, and her job-share partner, Imani, complained that she didn't like having to make a reservation so far in advance. Lyle was a fan of steakhouses like Smith & Wollensky and Ruth's Chris and Peter Luger in Brooklyn. "I'm a red-meat man," Lyle said. Somehow, I was not surprised. And Byron and Nick argued that their clients liked places with excellent service, where the wait staff called them by name.

I listened in patiently, unable to add much since I so rarely had the chance to eat out anymore, and when I did step out with Gracie or Harrison we weren't dining at five-star restaurants. I would have put in a good word about Dish of Salt or the Russian Tea Room . . . or the margaritas at Arizona 206 and the view from Top of the Sixes, but these old stomping grounds of mine had closed down, making me feel slightly prehistoric. (Of course, if someone popped the question about where to find the best suckling pig, I was on it!) This was Jack's world, part of the job to wine and dine clients, while I was at home pushing Cheerios and downing a yogurt. It hardly seemed fair, but then again, while Jack was outside scraping ice and snow off the car, I was often home in my slippers sipping coffee at the computer.

The sales team then covered bars—everything from singles bars to historic bars and taverns to gay bars in the Village and the current hot bars to see and be seen. Again, my lips were sealed.

Fast-forward to Broadway shows they'd seen recently. Did it count that Harrison and I almost saw *The Producers* with Nathan Lane and Matthew Broderick except that Jack's out-of-town stay was extended and I couldn't get a sitter?

When the Broadway tableau was depleted, talk moved to the network's lineup this season: the sitcoms, sports events, reality shows and dramas designed to bring in high ratings shares and thus increase the price of commercial air time and boost station revenues. Familiarity with the network lineup was mandatory here. The sales staff needed to push the network shows and entice advertisers to buy into the dream. Which made it that much more embarrassing for me. I couldn't recall a single show I'd seen on the Corstar network this year. Actually, I couldn't recall any shows at all beyond the crime shows Jack and I watched after ten. I spent prime time giving baths, reading stories, and picking up LEGOs and dolls' heads. Jack and I had been talking about getting satellite TV with a DVR, but the prospect of learning a new system was overwhelming. What if we couldn't find *Sesame Street* for Dylan each morning, or *SpongeBob* for the girls?

I felt as if I should apologize to someone here, explain why I'd lost touch with Corstar's lineup, beg forgiveness for my ignorance of top-rated shows and rising sitcom stars and crushes from teen dramas.

Just then the music stopped and the sound of a spoon clinking against a glass cut through the ballroom. Everyone turned toward the stage, where lights now shone on a bald man at the podium. "What about Bob?" someone called, eliciting a ripple of laughter. No Corstar event was complete without a few words from CEO Bob Filbert.

If network programming was a religion, Bob Filbert would be the pope. This was the man who could offer me dispensation for my lack of devotion to the station. The corporate Big Daddy smiled down upon us all, proclaiming it a delightful celebration and a successful year for Corstar. "I know you've heard murmurings of the changes in the offing, and I'm hear to say that the rumors are probably true. We're going to be realigning our power here at Corstar. Moving the cheese, so to speak."

I squirmed in my seat, recrossing my bare legs under the table. Corporate-speak and I were not compatible. During the short time after college that I'd worked for that insurance consulting firm, I had quickly burned out on the insider's jargon, the anagrams and nicknames for procedures and contracts. When my boss had explained for the zillionth time that the pink copy of a requisition form was a pinky and the green copy a greeny, I had looked him in the eye and flatly told him: "I quitty." I have never been good with foreign languages and I just couldn't suffer corporate-speak gladly.

"Now, it's human nature to resist change. We all know that. But I challenge you to keep yourself open to revision and progress, and you'll be delighted with the new face of Corstar. No one says it'll be easy. We're raising the bar, expecting more."

I stifled a groan, knowing how Jack hated the "raising the bar" speech. "Fuck the bar," he always said. "If I were a trained dog, maybe I'd jump higher, but I'm not. Filbert can take his freaking bar and stick it where the sun doesn't shine." Without being too obvious I shot a look over to the bar where Jack stood tall, hands at his sides. While many of the men here tonight had rolls to hide under their suit jackets, Jack looked lean in his navy suit, and I longed to slide a hand under his crisp white shirt and run my palms down his firm abdomen, down, down, down. Maybe I would, as soon as we got home. I felt a secret thrill that he was going home with me—that handsome guy was my husband.

When Bob summed up his speech and announced: "Enjoy your dinner!" there was a mad scramble of the guests to tables. No one wanted to be stuck at a table with strangers or sitting beside the office black sheep. I walked to the bar, where my husband was ordering yet another scotch.

"I saved you a seat," I said, moving closer to whisper, "between me and Judith, far, far from Numero Uno."

He knocked back some scotch and let out a low rumble of pleasure. "Ah, Rubes, you sure know how to work a crowd."

I touched the smooth sleeve of his navy suit and gave him a squeeze. "Can do."

5

Ch-Ch-Changes!

"Ch-Ch-Changes! Bob will raise the bar. Ch-Changes. Don't want to take it in the ass. Ch-Ch-Changes . . ." My charming husband wavered at the corner of Fifth and Fiftieth, grooving to his own angry rendition of one of our favorite Queen songs. Amazing how that guy can hold his liquor so well in a business setting. Once out the door, he's just like every other loud, sloppy drunk.

"Got a little repressed anger there, palsy?" I asked.

"Barely repressed," he roared, spinning toward me, then lurching back toward the avenue. "We won't get screwed again! No, no!" he sang out, switching his parody to The Who.

I fastened the top button of my coat and looked up Fifth Avenue. No cabs in sight, yet. A group of us had taken a cab from the Gorham to Rockefeller Center to watch the skaters and see the Christmas tree, a beastly spruce that dominated the Plaza, colored lights blinking in its bobbing branches. Every year Jack and I talked about bringing the kids in to see it, and every year we talked ourselves out of facing the crush of crowds that thronged through Rockefeller Plaza on evenings and weekends. Besides, with a huge tree at the mall and a house three blocks from us strung with so many lights and illuminated inflatables that it resembled an amusement park, the kids would be unimpressed by the city's display.

"You know they'd never let you go," I told my husband. Everyone loved Jack, and he performed, a self-motivated man.

"I couldn't be so lucky to get fired. Besides, I hear that Bob has not only noticed me, he likes me." When Bob Filbert had joined Corstar last February, no one was sure which direction he would take the corporation. Bob had lots of experience as a CEO, but he'd headed up companies that sold mayonnaise or toilet paper or rental cars. Television was all new to him, but when Corstar's profits started dwindling the board had voted to try a leader who wouldn't be bedazzled by being in the entertainment industry.

"See! See, see! You work hundreds of miles from headquarters and the CEO still notices you and takes a liking to you. That, my friend, is an achievement."

"Numero Uno is secretly fuming about that." Jack folded his arms and tucked his hands away from the cold. "She wants to be top dog."

"Got to stay Numero Uno," I said, searching for a yellow cab in the onrush of traffic. "You didn't tell me Corstar was planning a reorg."

Jack winged his arm around, doing air guitar Pete Townsend. "I told you they want me in Dallas."

"We are not moving to Dallas."

He pointed his air guitar at me with a leer. "Worried about losing your cheese?"

I dug my hands deeper into the warmth of my coat pockets, not taking the bait. Like most corporations, Corstar had periodic in-training sessions that included everything from bungee jumping to figuring out who in the corporation would have to jump ship if they were on a sinking lifeboat. At one session everyone had been required to read the best-seller *Who Moved My Cheese*? The CEOs had appeared with cheeseheads, people role-played mice and men in a maze, and Jack and I had spent weeks arguing about who had the most adaptable personality.

"Bob's got all kinds of squirrelly plans," Jack went on. "If the board lets him get his way, he'll twist Corstar into a pretzel."

"Okay, that's two food metaphors in one breath. Are you hungry?" I spied a pretzel vendor with his cart across the street.

"Starved. That dinner was crap."

He was right. Jack's prime rib was dry and my salmon tasted fishy. Bad fishy. One of my rare nights out and the food had sucked. Welcome to my life as a wife and mommy. I crossed the street, moved into the musky smoke and bought us a large pretzel, warm from the coals. I wasn't hungry but it felt good to hold the warm pretzel in my hands.

As I looked up to cross back, Jack had his arm out in the avenue, flagging down a cab. I scurried across and dove in under his arm. The cab reeked of some kind of boiled root vegetable, a smell so strong I wondered if the driver had a Crock-Pot stashed under the front seat.

"Where to?" he hollered.

"Penn Station," Jack said, sliding onto the springless seat.

As he pulled away from the curb the driver cranked up his radio. I'm not sure what kind of music it was, but if I closed my eyes I saw a harem of belly dancers and a snake charmer.

"Give me that," Jack said, breaking off a section of the pretzel.

I leaned forward, not eager to have my hair and coat touch the seat of the skeevy taxi. Someone barked in the driver's radio in a foreign language. He answered back in rapid-fire staccato.

I turned to my husband, wanting to connect with him and shed this feeling of alienation, but he was staring out the window, miles away. I worried about Bob's speech. What would a reorg mean for Jack? He liked his job and was so good at it, but all that could change. I felt disappointed that my night out had been a bust. Jack was out all the time, dining at the Four Seasons, the W, the TriBeCa Grill. It was Jack who caught glimpses of JLo and Marc, Jennifer Aniston, Katie Couric, Ellen. When clients were in town Jack had to see Broadway shows he didn't even care about. At least he had the good grace not to rub it in. I didn't begrudge him these pleasures, but at the moment I wasn't too thrilled with being Mrs. Jack.

Before the party ended I did manage to hook up with the Dallas contingent again and finish off the conversation with CJ, Hank and Elsa. CJ and Hank were just so darned enthusiastic about my writing, about Manhattan, about my so-called life in New York. I was on the verge of offering to take them to my favorite places around town—a jazzy dark bistro in NoHo, the Frick Collection and an off-Broadway show that had been running for six years now—then I remembered with a jolt that I had three kids and a book deadline.

So sorry, kids, but Mrs. Jack has no time to play.

Fortunately, it was a short ride to Penn Station, where our train was already on the platform, the brakes angrily spewing out compressed air with a burst that always made me jump inside. The sour, greasy bowels of Penn Station sent a sting through my nostrils, reminding me that this was no way to end a romantic evening, and once again I wondered how an open chamber with trains rushing in and out all day could smell so pungently noxious.

We found an empty bank of three seats toward the back of the car and fell onto the vinyl upholstery. Once the train left, it would take thirty-three minutes to arrive in Bayside. We were close, but the mental voyage felt exceedingly long and wearying.

"What the hell are we doing here?" I mumbled.

Jack popped open one eye. "Taking the train home? Did you have one too many Lemon Drops, Rubes?"

"No, I mean, the big picture. What are we doing here, paying top dollar for real estate and racing the clock on this hamster wheel and struggling through each day?"

Jack closed his eye, his lips hardening in a straight line. "I was afraid of that. Honey, it's too late to grapple with a cosmic question."

"Do you know that if we lived in another city, on a night like tonight, we could get our car from a valet, a nice person who would bring it around to the restaurant so that we could ride home in toasty-warm comfort. No cabs and trains and deicing the car at the station. Door-to-door comfort in our own vehicle, which, though riddled with Cheerios, does not reek of some mysterious root vegetable."

"Whaddaya mean? We could have driven tonight."

"And paid seventy bucks for parking."

"So? You have to tip a valet."

I folded my arms. "That's not the point. What I'm saying is, we may live in the best city in the world, but we rarely take advantage of the good things, while the bad strike us down at every turn. We still haven't gotten the kids to the dinosaur wing of the Museum of Natural History, and each year, when the Tony Awards are given, I'm barely familiar with the shows that are nominated." My chest felt tight as I thought of my friend Harrison, calling earlier this week to offer yet another chance to see *Wicked*. Of course, I'd had to turn him down again, in the throes of finishing *Chocolate*. "All work and no play is making Ruby a very dull girl," Harrison had said.

He would know. We'd met in college, when we both signed up for an immersion-in-Broadway theater class. Stuck on the bus from campus to Times Square with bubbling sorority girls and football players looking for an easy A, Harrison and I had shared a seat and begun playing Six Degrees of Kevin Bacon. A relationship was forged, and despite the passage of heartbreak and boyfriends for both of us, we'd maintained our Broadway connection.

After college, Harrison got a job as an assistant with a small public relations firm—"a hellfire of yelling, contradictions and backstabbing," he called it. On the plus side, it helped him hone his skills, led him on to more corporate venues, and occasionally some fabulous tickets to Broadway shows landed in his lap. Still in public relations, his current account was a pharmaceutical company, where his biggest challenge was to get the word out that a drug that "put lead in your pencil" wasn't going to cause a heart attack, as one choice study had indicated. It was a living, but it was not a profile job that would put Harrison in places to see and be seen, and free theater tickets were not forthcoming.

But when he started dating Goldberg, suddenly gobs of free tickets started landing in his lap, courtesy of Goldberg's bank. The only downside was that you couldn't pick the night, which was becoming more and more of a problem for me. This week, when I'd had to turn him down again I'd apologized profusely, promising to go with him the next time. "Don't stop asking me," I told him. "I'm dying to go. It's on my list." He'd replied that I hadn't been able to step out for a show since Saigon fell—and he didn't mean *Miss Saigon*. "The thing is, I like the show, Ruby," he'd said, "but I may lose my enthusiasm by the sixth time, when you can see it with me."

In the artificial light of the train Jack was noticeably quiet.

"Think about it, Jack. We pay a premium to be in the greatest city on Earth, but we don't have time to enjoy it. I can't remember the last time I attended a gallery opening or shopped in Manhattan.

And you're in a rut, too. When was the last time you went to a concert or an opera?"

"*Opera?*" Jack nearly choked on the word. "Have you lost your mind? I'd rather stick needles in my eyes than sit through an evening with a bunch of big-mouth fat people."

His mean-street roots were showing. Sometimes it bothered me when Jack started culture bashing, but then I had to remind myself that I was the one who'd fallen for this decisive bad boy from Queens. "Big-mouth fat people?" I asked, stirring the pot. "The last time you had a poker night at our house, there were quite a few candidates for that category."

Jack let out a laugh. "God, you're right." The guys constituted a group of twenty-some men who had attended grade school with Jack—St. Rose of Lima Catholic School, here in Bayside. "We're all getting old, though if Gina Moscarella makes me compare hairlines with the other guys next time we get together, I'm going to tell her what I really think of her eggplant parm." Gina was the official leader of the unofficial Wives of the Guys Club, and she always ran the men through drills, comparing receding hairlines and measuring waistlines.

"Oh, you're not losing your hair, and I won't be derailed from my moment of angst. Maybe we made the wrong choice living here, Jack. You know I love being a part of the heartbeat of this city, but when the pulse is fading, you gotta let go."

He reached back and rubbed the back of his neck, a destressing gesture I'd always found endearing. "I'm sort of not getting where you're coming from. I mean, I'm the one who always says we should move, and you're the one who protests, and you always win. There's a certain balance there, Ruby, and right now you're screwing everything up."

"I'm just saying maybe I've been wrong, maybe we don't belong in this city." I leaned back and rested against his shoulder. "God knows, every time we take our children out in public we get that message. They're too noisy, too whiny, too active, too inquisitive, at least, according to the lady in the deli or the man waiting behind us in line at the library."

"Fuck them. Bunch of old farts," Jack said softly, consolingly.

"I just ignore them, but I find myself wishing that I could silence the kids, button up their childhood so that no one else is disturbed, and that's wrong. It's evil. I'm an evil mom."

"Yeah, well . . . nobody's perfect." He pressed his lips to my temple and slid a hand inside my unbuttoned coat, where his palm smoothed over my waist, pulling me closer to him. It was an innocent gesture, but somehow it seemed secretive and erotic on the Long Island Railroad. Of course, the car was half-empty, and no one could see unless they left their seat and walked up the aisle.

I reached a hand up to his jaw and pressed my fingertips over the bristle there. "Are you trying to distract me?"

Inside my coat his hand smoothed over my rib cage, tickling a little. "Is it working?"

"For the moment."

His eyes glimmered with the satisfaction of conquest. "Good." When his lips moved down to meet mine, I was ready to kiss him, breathless and hungry for connection. The lights flashed off for a moment as the train dashed through the tunnel under the East River, and I pictured us as characters in a film noir, two lovers kissing as their train rushed off into the distance.

Unfortunately, this train was bound for three noisy kids and a sink full of dirty domestic bliss. I calculated quickly. Kristen would drive herself home. The dishes could wait, and with any luck all three children would be asleep and not crying about some life-threatening malady. With our cranky old heating system, our bedroom would be stone cold, but we could warm the sheets fast. I crossed my fingers behind my husband's back. With any luck, I'd be dancing the horizontal mambo with Prince Charming before the clock struck midnight.

6

We Wish You a Manic Christmas

December sped up like a tape of Christmas carols played on hyperspeed—Alvin and the Chipmunks singing: "We Wish You a Merry Christmas," the disco version. We got the tree up and decorated, but Dylan seemed to think those shiny balls were his for the picking, and he didn't understand why Mommy hyperventilated when he tried to roll the blown glass Santa head she'd gotten from her grandma down the stairs. Becca auditioned for the church play and got the part of an angel, much to her delight until she realized that Shant Kevalian and Alexis Sanford from her class would see her onstage.

Scout kept revising her Christmas list, adding impossible, not-yet-invented toys like rocket boots that could shoot her over houses and yards and land her right in the schoolyard—"No waiting at traffic lights, Mom!" she beamed. She also wanted a hovercraft that could carry a handful of friends to fun places like the bowling alley or out for ice cream, and she'd recently added a shape-shifting device to spoof your friends and avenge bullies. In a sweat, I stared at the emptying shelves of remote-control cars and talking robots at Toys "R" Us and tried to think of what to say to Scout to ease the disappointment of not getting anything on her list.

All along I did my best to appear to be in the game, squeezing in batches of cookie-baking sessions, caroling with the Sunday

School classes, and running around the house like a fiend plugging and unplugging Christmas lights at dusk and dawn. I was a merry-old, jolly-old elf, but I was mentally vacant, my mind on the work that kept me at the computer each night until three A.M. or when I faded off, whichever came first. In my mind I like to compare writing under deadline to accepting a mission on a nuclear submarine that takes a dive and stays deep in the ocean for months at a time. I also like to think that in some ways writing is harder since you're not completely cut off from the outside world, which demands that you participate and contribute and bake twenty-four nondenominational holiday cupcakes for your child's first-grade class, which is not having a holiday party but a publishing celebration that just happens to be falling in December near Christmas and Chanukah. Whatever.

Knowing I'd be working at odd hours, I'd moved my PC out of Dylan's room and set it up in the center of the dining room table— the only space available, though I'll admit that glowing screen definitely detracted from our Christmas decorations.

"Where in the world are we going to eat dinner?" Rebecca asked, throwing her hands up and reminding me of my eighty-three-year-old grandmother.

"We'll eat around it. Or in the kitchen," I said, not allowing dining etiquette to waylay my efforts. *Must write book* . . . Besides, half the time the kids ate in a daze in front of the television, especially when Mommy was under deadline. I'd read all those articles that warned how it was unhealthy, but one look at them, half-stretched out and dropping grapes into their mouths as if they were sultans surrounded by harem girls and, well . . . I'm a sucker for relaxation.

Must write book . . .

I told myself that I didn't mind working through the holidays because this book was for me. After years of writing to format, I was having some fun writing characters who were more like me. Janna, the main character of *Chocolate,* was pushing forty, an age that would be considered rode hard and put away wet by most romance publishers. One of her friends was a single mom. Some of her relationships didn't work out, even after she slept with the guy. I was breaking some rules and enjoying it, and by doing so my story came alive for me. When it was time to string popcorn with the girls, I was there in body but my mind was wrapped around my main character and the choices she would make leading to the climax of the book.

One week before Christmas, Jack was summoned to Dallas. He came home early from work with a look of resignation and a ticket on a flight that night.

"Oh. My. God! Tell them no!" I knew I was arguing after the fact, as Jack was already tossing balls of clean socks into the pocket of his suit bag, but I had to state my case. "You've got three little kids, and Christmas is a week away."

"Don't get so emotional, Rubes. I'll be back the day before Christmas Eve." He kept his eyes down as he packed, as if to avoid facing my wrath.

"But you're missing the season. Christmas isn't just a day, it's the whole buildup of expectation, the excitement of the kids. Honey, it's such a short window that they believe in Santa. Dylan's almost two and he doesn't really get it yet, and I suspect Becca's got it figured out at seven. Don't miss Christmas because of some trumped-up emergency."

"Calm down, would ya? I won't miss Christmas, I promise. And I couldn't say no. Apparently Bob asked for me by name."

"Summoned by the pope. I guess you should be flattered." I sat on the bed, refolding his undershirts.

"Yeah, well, flattery can be a pain in the ass." He hung a clean suit inside the bag, still not making eye contact.

"Honey, I know you're under a lot of pressure. We both are." *Must write book . . .* I would miss him at night, freeing me up from baths and bedtime stories. But I was getting close to finishing, Christmas was bearing down on us, Jack had been handpicked for a task by the company's CEO—events slammed toward us like a runaway train, and I had learned that sometimes it's easier to go with the momentum than to stop the train.

"I'm sorry." He looked up from his travel kit, his silver eyes flashing with concern. "This really isn't fair to you."

I grabbed a ball of socks and launched it toward him. "Just promise me you'll work fast so you can get your butt home."

"I'll do my best," he promised, handily catching the socks.

* * *

Having Jack out of the house did have its advantages. I didn't have to pick up the trail of clothes he left on the way into the shower or rinse and load dishes and mugs left in the sink, half-full of water and floating crumbs. Jack didn't mind doing housework, but his cleaning sprees came in spurts in clear opposition to my drive to clean up immediately, at least in the kitchen. Also with Jack gone I wouldn't feel obliged to take time off from working to have an abbreviated adult dinner with him; once the kids were fed I could get them set up in front of the television or at the kitchen table for homework and cruise through another page or two of the manuscript while scarfing down wheat toast.

One of the downsides of being a single parent was the dreaded homework. Becca managed her own work but worried about making mistakes, so she insisted that I check everything over. Scout had been placed in an advanced reading group, and although she could handle the reading on her own, she needed help composing written answers to the comprehension questions.

One evening, when I was hot into a love scene, my fingers flying over the keyboard, she appeared in my doorway with a book in hand. "Mom, can you help me with this?"

"Read the story, honey, and I'll help you answer the questions."

"But I can't read the story. It's filled with something very inappropriate for kids."

Must write book . . .

I tore myself away from the computer and motioned her closer. "What's this?" The book she was reading was called *Mrs. Piggle-Wiggle,* an anecdotal account of a woman who helps parents get their children to behave. "Sort of a *Nanny 911* from old times," Scout had said last week when she started the book.

"This chapter . . ." Scout handed me the book, squirming. "The boy's name, I can't say it. I can't even say it to myself in my head."

I took the book from her. The boy's name in this chapter was Dick.

I hid a smirk. "I see." Scout and Becca had encountered only a handful of forbidden words, most of them spotted in graffiti on the back of the school. This was one of those words.

"You know, it's short for Richard," I said. "Why don't you change it in your head when you see it? Call him Rick. How about that?"

My six-year-old daughter scowled at me. "Are you kidding me? I don't have a computer brain."

"Okay, then." With a sigh I pushed the laptop closed, settled back into the old chintz chair and made room for Scout. "I'm going to read this to you with a new name," I said.

She settled in beside me, and I read the story, editing as I went along. When I was finished, she thanked me and headed back downstairs, calling to Becca: "Guess what? The kid in this story is named Penis!"

Must write book . . .

By turning off the world, writing at night and paying the sitter to work extra hours, I managed to get within striking range of the end of *Chocolate* three days before Christmas. I had been e-mailing the manuscript to Morgan in five-chapter installments, and we planned to meet today for a working lunch to go over her notes and revisions so that I could smooth and polish the entire manuscript and have it ready for her to messenger to editors January second when they returned from vacation, fresh and fat and still feeling generous with holiday spirit. I felt flattered that Morgan was giving me so much time and attention, grateful that she'd pushed her flight to Detroit back by one day so that she could meet with me today and pull it all together.

As luck would have it, Dylan had chosen the previous night to wake up in crying fits, moaning of pain in his teeth. By the time I flopped down the stairs in my fluffy robe and started making peanut butter sandwiches while I held for the pediatrician, a dull pain twisted at my forehead and my mouth felt dry and sour. I felt hungover without any of the glory of the night before, hit by the Stress-monster. I popped two Tylenol capsules and washed them down with black coffee as Scout scampered down the stairs and clicked on the TV.

"Good morning, sweetie," I called over SpongeBob's cackle.

"I'm not going to school today," she warned me.

"Oh, yes you are. Today is your last day before Christmas vacation." And my last chance to grab a few free hours to kibbitz with Morgan.

"Some kids are already on vacation, from a hundred days ago. It's not fair."

"You'll get your share of vacation," I promised her as Becca came down and gave me a kiss, then gave out a little whimper that she was sick of taking peanut butter sandwiches for her lunch. Which launched us into the lunch discussion of how the girls always demanded one lunch item, like peanut butter sandwiches, for two months straight—until they were sick to death of it.

"This is the last school lunch for two weeks," I said smoothly, trying to avert a major disaster on this day of days; I was so close to the finish of my book I could taste the happy ending, and nothing would deter me. "Tomorrow you can have Easy Mac, or fish sticks or a yogurt parfait."

"Yuck." Scout's nose wrinkled, her face puckered. "Yogurt parkways are gross."

But I just smiled at her as I dashed up the stairs to wake Dylan with kisses and the promise of a trip to the doctor to help him feel better. I managed to coax them all through breakfast, get them dressed and shepherd them past the frost on the ground and into the car, where I strapped Dylan and Scout into car seats. Unfortunately, the frost was thicker than I'd realized, and I had to scurry around the car, scraping windows and windshields, much to Dylan's delight. Then the girls bellowed that they'd be late for school, but I didn't care. I knew the wicked witch of a principal had to let them in the door, and so they were dropped off in the nick of time so that I could work my way through stoplights and past double-parked cars to the pediatrician on the other side of Bayside.

Thirty minutes in a stuffy waiting room of howling tykes revealed Dylan needed an antibiotic for his ears, and so I headed to the pharmacy, wishing they had a drive-thru window. Wonder of wonders, there was a spot right in front, though I had no quarters for the meter. I decided to chance it, bundled my son in my arms and raced down the aisles of the pharmacy, scraping tissue boxes and toilet paper displays in my haste.

While the prescription was being filled I tried to get change for the parking meter, but the cashier told me no quarters could be given out. She said this, pointing with annoyance to the Laundromat across the street, as if they were robbing her of silver. I bought a pack of gum and, chewing like a cow, strolled to the car to drop a quarter in the meter. Three cars behind me a man in a brown uniform, a so-called brownie, was writing a parking ticket for an expired meter, and I felt like the luckiest gambler in Vegas as I dropped my quarter into the slot and cranked the knob. But instead of registering twenty minutes, the red EXPIRED flag remained in place.

"Dang it!" I shifted Dylan to my other arm, fished for the other quarter and fed the meter a second time. Again, without success.

I glanced up at the parking policeman, who was now circling the car behind mine. "Did you see that? I put two quarters in and neither of them registered."

He stood beside the other car and stared through me, as if trying to assess whether he could get away with not answering me.

"This meter is broken," I said. "I just put two quarters in it and nothing happened. Didn't you see me?"

At last, he let his eyes meet mine from nine feet away. "You can't park at a broken meter," he said.

"But how am I supposed to know it's broken before I lose my quarters in it?" I demanded, my temper flaring.

"I'm just letting you know, the policy is, you can't park at a broken meter."

"But I put two quarters in, and I'm waiting for my son's prescription to be filled in the pharmacy." I yanked a thumb toward the pharmacy door and hitched Dylan up in my arms as he let out a little whimper. There. That'd win the sympathy vote.

But the brownie wasn't having any of my pity stew. He stepped toward the store, making a wide arc around me, perhaps to stay out of reach. He went up to the meter beside my car, twisted the knob and nodded.

"See? Broken?"

He flipped his ticket book open.

"It's broken," I shouted louder, thinking maybe he hadn't heard me.

"Says expired."

"Oh, for God's sake . . ." Burning with righteous indignation, I unlocked the door of the car and proceeded to strap the baby into his seat, all the time muttering like a crazy person. "You try to pay for the damn parking, but no! You can't! You can't park at all! Unless you want to pay a forty-five dollar ticket!"

Burning with fury, I pumped the gas and my car shot out of its spot with a squeal of wheels. I had the mad desire to smash my car into the brown traffic cop's, repeatedly, until his car was squashed into a toy car the size of a sardine can. Then I could kick it aside with my boot and swoop up *his* spot on the street.

But no. I stopped at the red light like a good citizen. I flipped on my blinker and turned right, kicking myself for not getting the brownie's name and badge number. Like that would have mattered. Like anyone would answer my complaint to the City. I circled and circled and circled in a wider arc until I found a place to park in the surrounding neighborhood. By that time, Dylan had fallen asleep and I was sorely tempted to leave him in the car and let him rest. But it just wasn't safe. What if he woke up, panicked and tried to get out of the car on his own? Or what if someone stole my car with him in it? I unbuckled his car seat and tried to hoist him into my arms as gently as possible.

It's not easy to walk three blocks with a shifting thirty-pound weight. I braced myself, imagining that I was in the final paces of the gold medal round of the Olympic Baby-Carrying Competition, set to bring home the gold for mommies across the U.S. My arms and upper back ached, but this one was for the mommies, dammit!

By the time I got home I was exhausted and it wasn't even ten yet. By some stroke of good fortune Dylan remained asleep, so I shifted him to his crib, stripped my clothes off in the hall and raced into the shower, hoping, for once, to be ready for my meeting with Morgan by the time Kristen arrived.

With my hair in a lather I felt a twinge of remorse over the situation with the traffic cop. It was rare for me to act out that way, but the man was ruining my quality of life and it was all just so . . . so *wrong*. That was a tight area for parking, but then so was most of

Queens these days. Should I drive out to Nassau County to get my prescriptions filled? Just thinking about it had me tugging knots from my hair, so I stepped back into the hot spray and pushed the topic off till later . . . another day, another month or year when I wasn't under deadline, pressed, stressed.

Wrapped in a towel, I checked Dylan. Still asleep, his downy lashes looking impossibly dark on that chubby cheek. A wave of tiredness doused me and I had to resist joining him in sleep, the steady ebb and flow of our breaths the only sound in the house.

Resist! The angry whir of my hair dryer in my ear cut short that dream.

Forty minutes later I began to worry about Kristen, my incredible, reliable babysitter who was now ten minutes late when, ironically, I was all made-up and blown dry and ready to go. Kristen had said she was finished with finals, hadn't she? Had she forgotten about today? And why wasn't she answering her cell?

The phone rang and I bolted for it, nearly turning an ankle in my Jimmy Choo boots.

"Hey, Rubes, how's it going?"

"Fine," I lied. "Except that Kristen's late, not here, and if I don't get out of here in the next ten minutes I'm going to miss my train. But anyway, how's tricks in Texas?"

"You've got your meeting with Morgan." He remembered aloud, and I was sort of surprised that he remembered at all, since my schedule is secondary to the calendar in Jack's Blackberry. "I'll let you go then. It's just that I had some fast-breaking news and . . . never mind. It can wait."

"What?"

"You go, finish getting ready. We'll talk later."

I could hear the pent-up tension in his voice. "What's going on?"

"Well, the good news is that I've been offered a promotion," he said. "Assistant general manager of a station. Turns out I was right about Bob taking a shining toward me. He likes me. He really, really likes me."

"Assistant GM? That's great!" It was the position Jack had his eye on, though we'd speculated that the current assistant GM, Byron Smith, would never leave the job. "So where is Byron going?"

"That's the snag. The job isn't at the New York station. They want me to relocate."

My puff of happiness rapidly deflated. "To Dallas."

"Actually, they want me in Portland."

"Maine?" Images of fat red lobster tails and inky blue lakes sailed through my mind like an "I Love Maine" commercial.

"Oregon."

"What?" I laughed, feeling as if someone had pulled a chair out from under me. "That's way out West, isn't it? Cowboy country?"

"Uh, more like lumberjack land, from what I'm hearing. Though apparently they have cowboys, too. Rodeos in the summer. Starbucks and Nordstrom and Nike."

"Well, we wouldn't have to give up coffee or shoes."

"And lots of rain."

"Like Seattle," I said, thinking aloud. Seattle was the only thing I could picture from the Northwest, and that was thanks to the sitcom *Frasier*. Perhaps not the most accurate image. "Did you tell them thanks but no thanks?"

"I didn't give them an answer. It was so out of the blue, I wasn't expecting a promotion, and I'm certainly not planning to uproot my family and leave New York."

His words placed me back on steady ground. Leave New York? Ha! Like that was ever going to happen. "Okay, now I can admit I'm relieved. I suspect your distinctive New York charm won't play well in lumberjack land, though it sounds like your day is going better than mine." The doorbell rang and I hurried down the hall, heels clacking on the wood. "Maybe you can parlay this into a position you want. I mean, if they're offering you assistant GM you're definitely GM material."

"Spoken by my biggest fan."

"You rock, honey. Kristen's here, so I have to go."

"Go catch your train. We'll talk tonight."

"Love you." I hung up as Kristen stepped in the door, shaking out her muffler.

"I am so sorry! Some of the students from my sociology class got together at Starbucks for a finals-over thing, and I lost track of time."

"No problem." I threw on my coat, grabbing an umbrella when I noticed the wet shoulders of her coat. "Dylan's asleep. He's had his meds. His ears again."

"Oh, poor baby." She slipped off her Diesels, which seemed amazingly white and clean for a New York winter, and padded to the stairs. Turning toward the door, I flashed back to those twentysomething years, a time when I had some fashion sense, a budget to support a style and a lifestyle to maintain a wardrobe minus drool stains and spills. "I'll go check on him," she said. "Good luck at your meeting."

"Thanks!" I called over my shoulder, ducking into the rain and fumbling to balance my leather satchel fat with manuscript as I opened the umbrella. The sky was stained a deep pewter gray and raindrops bounced on the wet pavement. I headed to the corner where I'd parked the car, pausing at the sidewalk as a big American car thundered by. Its front tires plunged into a pothole filled with water, which sprayed up in my direction.

With a squeal I jumped back, too late. My pants and coat were streaked with muddy water. Great, just great. Thank God I was meeting Morgan and not some stiff publishing mucky-muck.

The toes of my designer boots grew dark with cold saturation as I crossed the street to the corner. Fumbling for my keys, an unsettled feeling came over me as my heel crunched on the crumbling ledge of curb. The Volkswagen Bug on the corner belonged to one of my neighbors, as did the aging Impala behind it. I traipsed on through the rain, disconcerted.

Wait. Where was my car?

I swung around, checking the corner, the cross street.

No sign of my Honda.

The car had vanished . . . But my heels crunched on a spray of glass clotted with mud by the bumper of the VW Beetle.

Someone had stolen my car.

I hitched my bag onto my shoulder and cradled the umbrella as I slid out my cell phone and speed-dialed Jack.

"It's raining in New York, I'm going to miss my meeting, my car's been stolen, and Portland is looking better by the minute," I said in a voice so calm it surprised even me. "Let's get the hell out of here. How soon can you start in Portland?"

7

One Shrimp, Two Shrimp . . .

My second call from that rainy street corner was to the NYPD, whose dispatcher told me to return to my home and they'd send a car over to take a report. "But the last time I had a car stolen, I had to come into the precinct to make a report," I said. Having had two other cars stolen, I knew the gig, and I didn't want this anonymous phone voice to screw things up.

She assured me that the system had changed, which made sense. I mean, you lose your car, and now you've got to take the bus into the police station? Is that not the ultimate indignity? I headed back toward the house and called Morgan.

"Your car was stolen!" Morgan gasped. "What kind of Scrooge goes around stealing cars three days before Christmas?"

"An agnostic car thief? Let's face it, in that profession you don't get holidays off."

She let out a raucous laugh. "You seem to be taking this well."

I stepped around a puddle on the sidewalk. "I figured grace under pressure was preferable to throwing a tantrum in the street, especially with the pavement being so wet and this being the first time I've worn this Yves St. Laurent scarf. But I don't think I'm going to make it in today." Jack's car was parked at the airport, and although I could take a cab to the train station I needed to stick around to fill out that useless police report.

"No worries!" Morgan proclaimed. "You just take care of what you need to do with the car and the baby and all."

"But what about your notes? I mean, if I'm going to get this all done by the first of the year, I need to get going, and you're flying out tomorrow."

"Can you do it over the phone?" she suggested. "I can imagine you're having a terrible day and I hate to push, but I'd love to have a juicy manuscript to send round in the new year."

"You'll have it," I said, stopping short of saying: "Can Do!" I didn't want Morgan to see me for the total suck-up that I am.

Inside the house, I told Kristen about the car as I pulled off my boots. Upstairs, I reconnected with Morgan on the land line, settled in at the laptop and dove into her notes, blocking out all distractions. I didn't tell Morgan about moving to Oregon, knowing that it would waylay our conversation for quite awhile, and that it would make it all seem real, which I wasn't quite ready for yet. Right now it was sort of a fantasy of vengeance, as if to say: "You can't steal my car, because I'm taking it away—clear across the country! So there! Nanny, nanny foo-foo!"

That night Jack called to let me know that everyone in Dallas was thrilled for him. Of course, he had yet to face the wrath of Numero Uno Laguno and the rest of his team at the New York station, but whatever their reaction, he was outta there, leaving them in his dust.

"You okay?" I asked. He sounded like a kid who'd lost his favorite teddy bear.

"Are you sure about this move? I mean, it's a big one."

"And the farthest you've ever gone is across the East River," I teased him. In truth, I wasn't sure at all, but the thought of moving felt like a leap—some sort of movement—even if that leap was off a cliff.

"I'll always be a Queens boy at heart."

"You can take your Queens heart with you, but it's time to take some chances and shake things up, don't you think? You don't want to spend your whole life living in two houses in Queens."

"I don't know why not. It's New York. What's not to love?"

Car thieves and traffic, pollution and overpopulation . . . I could have

gone on all night but I didn't want to bash Jack's homeland. I leaned
into the glow of the computer, drawn to photos of towering green
Douglas fir trees and royal blue lakes. I'd been researching Oregon,
excitedly nesting. "Your roots are showing," I said. "Besides, this is
the path to promotion. You're going to be a GM someday, and you'll
look back and say that it all really started with this move, the fact that
you were willing to go out and take some chances."

"You're right. Management is thrilled with me right now."

I could hear the little zing of pleasure in his voice. Workplace
kudos always gave Jack a shot to the libido, turning the power trip
into a pleasure trip, and I was happy to come along for the ride.

"I wish you were here," he said. "We could order room service and
fuck all night. This bed is the size of the playground at P.S. 188."

The thought of a giant-sized bed made me think only of the sleep
I could enjoy there—days of sleep—but I didn't want to burst Jack's
bubble. "Ah, those were the days," I said, scrolling down a website
that showed me average standardized test scores of school districts
in the Portland area. "Have you ever heard of Lake Saranac? Or
West Green? They're both south of Portland, commuting distance to
the city but good schools."

"It just seems so random. Like some giant thumbed the globe and
jabbed a finger at Oregon."

"We should go check it out," I said, thinking aloud. "That will
make it real. Eyeball the towns, the traffic patterns, the locals . . ."

"Find a house," Jack said, ever the practical one.

The excitement of exploration tugged at me even as I felt the
weight of my book deadline holding me back. *Must write book . . .* I
really couldn't go anywhere until I hammered out this ending, but I
was getting close.

"So book a flight for after Christmas," Jack said, making it sound
all too real. "You probably want to take the girls, ease them into it."

The girls . . . I hadn't really anticipated their reaction to moving. I
decided to put that conversation off until after Christmas.

That Christmas I felt full of hope and excitement, sure that in future Christmases our family would be more relaxed, less harried,
leaving us more time to eat together and participate in family activi-

ties. Although I had no idea what those activities might be out in Oregon, I composed a placid family portrait in my mind: Jack with a fishing rod, me in worn blue jeans that fit at the waist, the kids in yellow slickers and rain boots right out of the Land's End catalog. Next year we could buy them bikes since they'd have a place to ride them in the wide-open spaces. Next year we could try skiing at Mount Hood, and this summer we'd rent a houseboat or take the girls white-water rafting.

"White-water rafting?" Jack asked dubiously one night as we rattled through plastic bags, trying to assemble as many toys as possible. "Sure. And I'll grow a beard and start eating tree bark and you can call me Grizzly Jack."

"Don't crush the dream, and can you figure out where the batteries go?" I asked, handing him a robot Scout had resigned herself to when I warned her that she couldn't count on Santa to deliver rocket boots or a hovercraft or any of her other new inventions this year.

By Christmas day our little town house was bursting at the seams under the weight of holiday gifts and decorations. Before we'd even had coffee and cinnamon rolls Scout's robot had knocked over a vase Becca had made for me in Girl Scouts, and Dylan had cut his foot on a twisty tie wire from a toy package. But I didn't sweat it, knowing that this would be our last Christmas in cramped quarters. We would probably have to sit for more than an hour in bridge traffic to make Christmas dinner at my parents' house in New Jersey, but I refused to get annoyed and packed a deck of cards to distract the girls with.

If Christmas Eve with the dysfunctional Salernos hadn't blown my resolve, nothing would.

Jack and I had stayed up for an hour early this morning, raking over the coals. Jack's mother had insisted we stay for course after course of verbal abuse and heavy foods—the appetizer, the antipasto, the pasta course, the fish course, the dessert platter. I didn't let myself get annoyed over Mira's bossiness or worried that we were keeping the kids up till midnight on Christmas Eve. If this was going to be our last Christmas in New York, I was determined to suck it up and make it a merry one, even if it meant playing the long-suffering daughter-in-law, though Mira nearly undid my resolve with a single platter of shrimp.

"Did you see Grandpa's fish?" Mira asked the children, pointing them into the den, to a mounted cod on a plaque, a small Santa cap perched on its head. "Isn't it hilarious? Press the button. Go on, press it!"

Becca followed her instruction and the cod's mouth opened and closed as it growled out the carol: "We Wish You a Merry Christmas!"

Mira clapped her hands to her cheeks in hilarity. Becca nodded politely, but the rest of us seemed unfazed.

"We've got one of these at home, Grandma," Scout pointed out. "We got it for Daddy last Christmas."

"Oh, really?" Mira's smile went slack as she spun toward Scout. With the aura of scotch hanging over her I worried she might fall on my daughter, but Mira righted herself, hands on hips. "And I suppose yours is better?"

Scout blinked, clearly uncomfortable.

Stepping in quickly, I put my hands on Scout's shoulders reassuringly. "It's okay, honey." I pulled Scout against me, as if the need for a hug had just come over me. "The fish is very funny, Mira. That's why the girls bought it for Jack. We howled when we first saw it in the store."

"I suppose," Mira said, but her movements were icy as she turned and headed back to the kitchen, mimicking my daughter. "We have one at home!"

It's not a competition, I wanted to call after her, but I held my breath, having covered that ground with Mira before, to no avail. Mirabella Salerno wanted to be the best, the prettiest, the funniest, the richest, and she didn't even have the refinement to mask her quest for self-aggrandizement beneath a more subtle façade. The daughter of Long Island's self-proclaimed mattress king, Mira's childhood had been chock-full of material splendor. I'd seen photos of the white baby grand piano, the pony, and the catered birthday parties with magicians, clowns and candy shops on wheels. Since her parents had died before I came into the picture I was never quite sure if these treats were reinforced by genuine love and affection. In either case, the goodies had stopped when the IRS clamped down on her father for nonpayment of income taxes while Mira was in high school. Her "good life" went down the drain and she'd been unable to pull herself back up into the privileged social strata. I sensed that her marriage to Conny had been a concession, with baby Frankie coming along a mere seven months after the ceremony. "He was premature," Mira always claimed. "You should have seen him—a scrawny thing." Despite her pride over the grown Frank, who'd revitalized the mattress dynasty, I sensed that Mira had settled when she married a mere transit worker. Over the years Conny had moved into the family business, but he never became the Mattress *King*.

Although family fortunes dwindled, Mira never lost her sense of entitlement and vanity. According to Mira, she was the best woman golfer at the Little Bay Club, the smartest player in her bridge club, the youngest-looking grandmother in all of Queens. I would agree that her home, a contemporary minimansion right at the edge of Little Neck Bay in Malba, was among the most breathtaking in New York City, though the cavernous great room and cold hardwood floors seemed to cry out that beauty is meaningless in a home without human warmth and compassion. In that way, the house was an accurate reflection of Mira's personality—a stark, expensive showplace with no tolerance for liveability.

"What do you think my parents are going to do in that house?" Jack had asked when construction was under way some ten years ago. "Did you see the house? It's huge!"

"Well, I suspect they'll start by having sex in each room," I had answered flippantly. "And then they'll strip off their clothes, run naked down to the water and shout: 'We're queen and king of the world!'"

Jack had been sorry he asked, though he laughed despite himself, despite the lingering pain that tugged at him whenever his parents entered his periphery. Apparently it hadn't been easy growing up in the Salerno household, son of Constantine and Mirabella. I didn't meet Jack until we were both in our twenties, so I can only go on his stories of the horrors of coming home at age eight and not knowing what to expect. A good day would be when his mother would pour him a glass of milk and remind him to clean his room and get his

homework done. A bad day? Well, they ranged from inebriated
Mom dropping whole jars of garlic powder into the spaghetti sauce
to Mom passed out on the floor, her face bloody and bruised from
the fall. It always broke my heart to hear Jack recollect these stories
so calmly, to picture the young Jack, close to Rebecca's age, picking
up his mother, dabbing at her wounds with a damp washcloth and
helping her back to bed, all the while worried that she might come
alive and lash out at him, spewing out accusations and curses in her
drunken state. "She wasn't always that way," Jack would tell me
calmly. "But not knowing, the anxiety of wondering as I walked
home from school what kind of mood she'd be in, that was the worst
part."

"And where was your father when this was going on?" I'd asked
dumbly.

At work, driving a train for the MTA. Or taking Jack's older
brother Frankie to a "go-see" in Manhattan, since Frank's success at
age seven in a TV commercial for bandages had the whole family
hot for Hollywood. Or coaching Frank's baseball team to victory
(though Frank was warned to duck fly balls to protect his money-
maker from disfiguration). Or carousing with his buddies down at
the Town Tavern. Or ushering the eleven thirty mass each Sunday—
one of the great ironies in my mind. Like it's okay to let your wife
drink her life away and your kid to be emotionally abused, but don't
be late for passing the collection plate for Sunday mass.

"My father was very reliable," Jack always said. "You could set your
watch by his coming and going."

Although, I pointed out, there was a difference between having a
set schedule and being reliable and responsible. But that didn't
seem to help Jack undo the damage of the past or relax in his current relationship with his parents, which was fraught with suppressed
rage on all sides, dashed with guilt and suppressed anger.

After the singing-cod incident, I settled the kids into a back room
with some videos, handheld computer games and a small bowl of
crackers. From holidays past I remembered that tonight's menu was
definitely not kid-friendly and had plied the children with chicken
fingers, applesauce and macaroni before we left the house. "No

crumbs on the floor, please," I admonished in a low voice, knowing Mira would have me whipped and tied for smuggling a snack onto her plush white wall-to-wall.

"We'll be careful," Becca promised, both girls nodding solemnly while Dylan's runny nose threatened to drip on the carpet. I gave it a quick wipe and returned to the party, where Frank had arrived.

"There she is, Long Island's next star!" Frank held out a hand to his mother and she twirled into his arms. "Ready to shoot your big commercial, gorgeous doll?"

Feeling as if I was watching a failed dance sequence on *American Idol,* I dared ask: "Are you doing another mattress ad, Mira?"

She air-kissed her oldest son on each cheek. "Frankie insisted on it. He said sales shot up after the first one aired, so I couldn't say no, could I?"

"Still a beauty, my Mirabella," Conny said from his favorite leather easy chair. "You wouldn't believe the number of people who recognized her after she did that last commercial. One woman came up to her, right at the supermarket. She comes up and says, 'You have the most exquisite skin.' Exquisite, she says. And I say, yup. That's my bride."

Frankie winked at me over Mira's shoulder, an indecipherable gesture. Did it mean the sales increase was all a lie, or was that just his way of saying Merry Christmas?

"We'd better watch out or producers from *Project Runway* are going to be calling. They'll want you on the show, Ma."

Talk about buttering the goose!

Mira rolled her eyes. "Get out! What can I say? Success is sweet, though I do wish my sister was here to enjoy all this with us. I do miss her at the holidays." She turned to me, as if I hadn't heard it all a million times before. "Died of ladies' disease. You know." She gestured awkwardly toward her shoulders, which I had learned was her way of designating breast cancer since she couldn't bring herself to say the "B" word. According to what I'd gleaned from Jack, his Aunt Angela had contracted breast cancer before the days of selfexamination and regular mammography.

"Very sad. I'm sure you miss her," I said, trying to sound sympathetic.

"I do," she cooed, "every day."

I felt for Mira, really, I did. But it seemed to me that she might focus on getting back the loved one who was still retrievable, the daughter who'd fled this madness years ago. What about Gia? Why didn't anyone ever mention her—a phone call, a childhood anecdote? *"Why would anyone want to bring her up?"* Jack would counter when I asked about his sister. *"She didn't get along with Ma at all."*

Was that any reason to banish the poor girl from the family?

Frankie rubbed his pudgy hands together. "What delicious morsels have you concocted this Christmas, Ma?"

Thank God for Fat Frankie, able to change the subject if it meant a segue to food.

"Shrimp, anyone?" Mira set the platter of pink curls down on the coffee table, and Jack leaned forward to snatch one and dip it in sauce.

"Delicious, Mom," he said, and I realized the poor man probably hadn't eaten since breakfast, as I'd had him locked in the basement closet for most of the afternoon, assembling a tricycle for Dylan. He reached for another, but his mother smacked his hand away from the platter.

"Leave some for Frankie," Mira snapped. "It's his favorite."

"I like shrimp, too."

"No, you don't," his mother retorted tartly. "Remember when you spit it into your napkin at Aunt Lucia's anniversary?"

"I was like, five, then."

"Still, it never agreed with you."

"Frankie is the one who always loved shrimp," Conny added, launching into the old family yarn as if we hadn't heard it a hundred times. "I remember when he was really little, just a tiny thing. Most kids wouldn't go near seafood, but there was Frankie, powering it down, cocktail sauce and all—the whole nine yards." He pointed the remote at the fireplace and a gas flame burst over the fake logs.

I felt the temperature rising in the overheated room. Or maybe that was the heat of my anger.

"Ma, I love shrimp," Jack insisted.

"Jack, please. Don't start with me."

"I'm just saying, I like it." He reached for the platter and grabbed two pieces quickly, on alert for a second slap.

Mira sucked her teeth in disdain. "I *said* save some for your brother. You never listen. Some things never change." With a sigh, she picked up the platter and moved it to the piano, where Frankie was leaning with a tall glass of Dewars and water, mostly Dewars. "Shrimp, Frankie?"

"Thanks, Mommy." He dipped into the red sauce with a coy smile.

Ooh, how I hated the way Frank still called her "Mommy," and the way they showered him with adulation while Jack received sloppy seconds. I wanted to overturn the platter, dump the cocktail sauce in Frankie's lap, or, better yet, smear it into Mira's white carpeting with the slick soles of my designer heels.

But no. I clenched a handful of Mira's ivory velvet pillow and sucked in a cleansing breath. No, I would not be moved to physical violence by shrimp. The shrimp incident was just the latest in a lifetime of unfairness and abuse that Jack had endured. If he could survive an alcoholic mother, a neglectful father and a prodigal brother, surely I could endure a few social irritations to keep the peace.

Endure, yes. Forgive? That was another story. Watching the way Jack's parents mowed over him on Christmas Eve, I coddled our secret, vengefully glad that we were leaving them behind and sure that they'd miss us, miss having Jack to kick around, miss manipulating the grandkids. Ha! Wouldn't they be sorry when they no longer had Jack as their scapegoat.

I pictured future Christmases with just the three of them huddled by the fire, the toothless grins of Mira and Conny gloating as Frank stuffed his mouth with shrimp, shrimp tails littering the floor and red sauce staining Frankie's polo shirt covering his growing belly.

Ironically, this morbid fantasy brought me little consolation, knowing that family members had faded into obscurity, never to be discussed again. After all, Jack's older sister Gia now worked for a technologies firm somewhere in California—where, no one was sure, as they'd "lost touch," as Jack put it, soon after Gia graduated from high school.

"Promise me you will never give up on any of our children," I told Jack the few times we'd discussed his missing sister.

"Of course not!" He always seemed indignant that I'd lump him in with his dysfunctional family. "Anyway, they didn't really give up on her. More like they drove her away."

"The same thing, or worse," I said, hoping he understood how important it was to keep in touch with our children and let them bond among themselves.

Oddly enough, when I married Jack I thought I was saving him from his dysfunctional family, that I was the one person who could bring stability and love to his rocky world. When I had expressed this theory to my friends, they were quick to point out that I was attracted to Jack because he was a tormented soul.

"You like him because of his fucked-up childhood," Gracie told me. "There's something sad and dangerous there, the bad boy on the edge of losing it, the orphan child to comfort."

"Ridiculous!" I insisted.

"Totally true," Harrison corrected me. "If his life weren't so darned bad, you wouldn't like him so darned much. Bad boys are hot, I tell, you! Hot, hot, hot!"

I vehemently denied the bad-boy attraction, though in my heart I knew there was a scintilla of truth to it. Certainly, Jack's Lost Boy quality had some appeal for me, but I was equally attracted to his sensitive side and the vulnerability he kept hidden from his family. I didn't want his dysfunctional family, but I was very interested in the boy who had survived those dysfunctions.

On Christmas Day we went to my parents' house in Maplewood, New Jersey, where all seven of the grandchildren were given free reign over Mimi and Papa's house. For the first time in weeks I felt free to enjoy a drink and adult conversation. As I laughed with my sister and brother over some old family photos, I felt relieved that none of us had slipped into self-inflicted alienation in some distant state.

"Another Christmas and still no sign of Sis?" Amber asked. "That's just fried."

When Jack and I were in the throes of wedding preparations word about his "missing" sister had slipped out, and though my sister and I had fought like demons through childhood we suddenly seemed to be shining examples of sisterhood.

"Well, after last night I'm beginning to think Gia had the right idea." When she shot me a curious look, I just shook my head. "Don't ask. It's a wonder Jack survived those people."

Amber put her empty glass on the end table and stretched like a cat on my mother's jade green sofa. Although she's got two kids and a career as a full-time mommy in New Jersey, she hasn't lost the ability to relax.

"The Salernos are a tough bunch. Compared to Jack and Frankie, you and I look like the Olsen twins."

I held up my hand with a laugh. "Ooh! Can I be Mary-Kate?"

My brother Sam popped into the living room to deliver a fresh batch of whiskey sours and tease us about abandoning our children.

"Don't get up," he told Amber, who was prone on the couch. "I'll just start an IV line and drip this one in for you."

She sat up and reached for the drink. "Smart-ass. Be nice to me or I'll go off to California or Alaska, never to be seen again."

I smiled, feeling the glow of Christmas and sibling affection.

He pointed toward the family room. "As long as you take those two screaming monsters with you."

I felt a twinge of emotion, knowing I'd be the one moving off to a distant state soon, though my departure wasn't like Gia's. There'd be family visits and phone calls and e-mails. I closed my eyes, picturing a house with a guestroom big enough to put up Amber or Sam and their families when they came to visit.

"How are the kids doing in there?" Amber asked.

Sam lifted his drink to his lips. "Tyler just bit Scout. Didn't break the skin, and she did punch him first. Otherwise, it's one big love fest."

The love fest grew louder when the food started coming out of my parents' huge refrigerator. Shrimp was not served, but my father had smoothed sour cream to concoct a fish shape out of layers of caviar, hard-boiled egg and red onion. It was delicious, and although caviar has always been a favorite of mine, Jack was allowed to eat as much as he wanted.

8

Jack: A Very Merry Dysfunctional Christmas

We are driving home from Ruby's parents' house, rolling ahead slowly in a glowing trail of taillights that twist ahead as far as the eye can see, under an overpass, up a hill and snaking toward the tollbooths of the George Washington Bridge.

"Throw in a little green and the lights would actually be festive," Ruby jokes, always putting a positive spin on things.

I don't know how she does it. She seems patient and content to sit listening to Scout mutter a twisted form of "Jingle Bells" in the backseat, while all I want to do is pull onto the shoulder and put pedal to the metal, shrieking ahead of these morons, violently surging away from all this traffic and holiday madness.

Not that it was such a bad night with her parents. Kat and Peter always put out a nice spread. They seem to be genuinely crazy about the grandkids, and I've always felt welcome in their home. Weird, those Dixons: Sam, Amber, their spouses, Ruby . . . They all seem to like each other. Kind of a nice thing for a family. A concept that eludes my side of the family.

Once when Ruby and I were still dating we were entwined on the old couch watching reruns of *Saturday Night Live*, one of the episodes shot during the Christmas season, and the sketch reduced me to tears. At the time she thought they were tears of laughter, and so I faked it, pretending that my choked sobs were caused by overwhelming hilarity. It was a family scene in front of a Christmas tree and they were trying to sell a Christmas album of dysfunctional family carols, like "I Saw Mommy Screwing Santa Claus" and "Grandma Got Drunk and Ran Over a Reindeer." There was some song about the *SNL* mom suffering depression at Christmastime and Dad always falling down drunk into the Christmas tree. Big laugh material. Honestly, I barely remember the real details, but suffice it to say it thumped at my chest like a ball-peen hammer, sending me back to my childhood, back to the most dreaded time of year when my mother was more depressed than ever and my father was allotted enough leisure time to take note of her excessive drinking and conjure his own foul mood over the sorry state of our family's mental health.

First there was Mom, carping about how nobody appreciated all she did. The Hope Diamond was not a big enough gift to show my mother the gratitude owed her at Christmastime. Her righteous indignation gave her license to wallow in the wassail, nod off into the eggnog, and suck down every last drop of the best that Bailey or Harvey or Jack Daniel had to offer in a fake-foil holiday gift bag tied off with fat red yarn. If I seem bitter about Mom, well, I guess that's because *I am*, dammit.

Then there was Sis, a trollop from the age of twelve when she began shopping on her own at the mall and returning with tissue-wrapped bundles of clothes and cosmetics. If I ever had any boyhood curiosity about the anatomy of a woman's breasts it was solved by the sheer reveal of Gia's outfits, the bursting cleavage, the clearly outlined nipples. Ma accused her of dressing like a whore, though it came out in the Queens two-syllable cadence: "Who-wah!" During the holiday season Gia brought flaming Santa red into her wardrobe . . . lots of red, the tighter and brighter the better. Put Gia in a tight cashmere sweater at Christmas and her boobs could have lighted the way for jets parking on the tarmac at JFK. Much to my parents' dismay, the mattress princess dressed more like one of Santa's harem girls.

Compared to Gia, Fat Frankie was low maintenance, though I think it bothered my parents that their first namesake was content to live his life in the kitchen downing cookies, crumb cakes, spumoni and holiday figgy pudding. When our father yelled at him to get the hell out of the kitchen, Frank took a can of peanut brittle to his room or a box of donuts to the family room, where Ma had dubbed Frank's favorite TV-viewing spot on the sofa the "Piggy Corner."

Once Frankie and Mom went at it over a batch of rum balls that one of the Mattress Queen employees had given them. "They're loaded with alcohol!" she said, with the gusto appropriate of a thirsty alcoholic. She yanked the Tupperware container away from him, but he held on tight. "It all cooks down," Frank spat back, and I mean spat, an explosion of powdered sugar and brown specks flying. I'm not sure who won in the end, but Frank ended up switching to Ho Hos and Ma went down to the corner liquor store for a bottle of vodka.

Me? I was always looking for the slightest excuse to escape. Usually that meant hanging out at Tommy McGee's house, where huge bowls of stew or spaghetti or potted pork chops made it onto the table each night at the regular dinner hour and the prevailing law of the land was "Fight your own battles!" The McGees were a big Irish Catholic family with eight or nine kids—who was counting?—and a rambling old three-story house with a walk-up attic and a laundry chute that never ceased to amuse us when we could afford water balloons or a carton of eggs from the corner deli. Secretly I thought Tommy was dull as a stick of butter, but it was easy to tuck into the McGee family, no problem grabbing some grapes from the fridge or copping a bowl of stew for dinner, crawling into a sleeping bag to stay the night, or two or three.

So I'd had more experience with defection than a Russian spy, a fact that probably angered my father. Or did he even notice that his youngest son was missing that Christmas morning when I was twelve and I'd opted to stay over at the McGees's house, where the mom served the kids hot mugs of cinnamon cider and the dad read them "'Twas the Night Before Christmas" before bed on Christmas Eve, where nearly a dozen kids dove into their wrapped packages under the tree the next morning without an onerous, dutiful mother yelling at them to "all take turns." That Christmas, before sticky buns winking with brown pecans were served, I scored a cool rechargeable car, courtesy of Santa McGee.

And so I sobbed over the dysfunctional family Christmas album on *Saturday Night Live,* realizing that it wasn't really so much funny as it was pathetic. My pathetic family, set to music and high comedy. It'd be funny to people like Tommy McGee's family, even to Ruby's family, a flock of decent people who actually enjoy each other's company. When Ruby and I got married, I was happy to take on the Dixons as my own. For all my ambivalence about marriage and kids, I wasn't at all reluctant to join her family. It was like pledging the best fraternity on campus, without the hazing or the asshole clown who steals your bio notes and aces the exam while you tank.

At the opposite end of the spectrum, Ruby was so well adjusted, with her head screwed on just right over a healthy dose of self-esteem, that she didn't understand the depth of my family's dysfunctions. She thought I was being generous when I agreed to spend the holidays with her clan. She thought I was playing hyperbole when I told her that my mother dropped miniatures of whiskey into all the stockings and Dad so hated fitting the tree into its stand that he once tossed it out the front door and kicked it out to the trash pile at the edge of the street. Ruby is so deeply ensconced in her cocoon of positive thoughts that she simply could not comprehend that family life is dangerous for some of us.

Ruby didn't get it . . . until she experienced the degradation herself. Now, after a decade of being the dysfunctional family's daughter-in-law, I think she's on to them. It's dawned on her that the Salernos aren't posturing or joking or having a bad day; they are crazy as a jar of Jiff, nuttier than a fifth of Frangelico, which Ma always tells Ruby to bring as a Christmas hostess gift. Ruby's starting to get the big picture, but I still can't tell her how totally done I am with my family, that this is going to be the last Christmas we spend with them, hopefully the last time we see them for a few years. Ten minutes with them sets me back twenty years, back to the days before Ma was a full-blown alcoholic, when she at least tried to emulate June Cleaver.

When I was a kid I used to think we were a happy family, Dad off at work and Ma driving the three of us around in a Caddy, taking us to the movies or Micky D's. We used to get together with Ma's sister, Aunt Angela, who was like my mother's best friend. Probably her only friend, when you get down to it. The only time we left Queens was when we were going somewhere with Aunt Angie. Every summer we spent a month in the Catskills, where Ma and Aunt Angie would hold court by the pool, the mahjong tables, the dance lounge—somewhere on the premises. I don't know what they did there that made them so damned happy, but I was so busy horseback riding, swimming and competing in shuffleboard and egg-toss tournaments that I sort of forgot I'd come with a family. (I also don't know what the old man was doing during all our trips, though I assume he was working his forty hours at the Mattress Queen offices and eating take-out, bringing home the bacon the way fathers did back in those days.)

Angie was my mother's younger sister, and people always used to ask if they were twins, which Ma loved. That was probably because they would go and get their hair done together, and when they emerged from the salon with the same helmet heads—"updos" Ma called them—they did look like two Fords that had rolled off an assembly line in red and yellow, red hair and blonde.

Aunt Angie was always over at our house, hanging with Ma. They'd visit the Mattress Queen offices for meetings, trade off magazines, watch soap operas together, drag us all out grocery shopping or stick us with Mrs. Maloney, who made an awesome PBJ and let us binge on Ma's secret supply of soda pop while they went out shopping in department stores. Or at least, that's where I think they went.

Sometimes we went over to Aunt Angie's apartment, where the curtains changed with every season, from sheers to those draped things with lace edges and she always had some candy handy to shut us up. Aunt Angie was always calling us "buttercup" or "snickerdoodle." She never yelled at us, and didn't worry that we might break something. She treated us like cuddly little lambs who occasionally needed shepherding. I guess I could have been jealous that she got all Ma's attention, but the thing was, she kept my mother happy. While Angie was around the old lady cared enough to get her hair done and spend time shopping and, most of all, Ma didn't need to drink.

One day when I came in from playing ball, Aunt Angie and Ma were sitting at the kitchen table all red-eyed like they'd been crying.

Being cautious, I didn't even ask, but the next day Gia managed to chisel out the information that Aunt Angie was sick. With what, I never knew, since nobody talked about breast cancer back then, especially to kids. Christ, my mother can't even bring herself to say the "B" word now; she'll still say something like "female cancer" or "a lady's disease."

A year later, Aunt Angie died in the hospital, and my mother was destroyed.

I think Ma started drinking at the wake, those long days between the person dying and the funeral, when friends and neighbors come to your house with casseroles and long faces. My father invited everyone in and Ma held court in the dining room, propped up in a corner chair beside the buffet table, where she could prop her glass. A jelly jar with the Flintstones on it. My prim and proper mother, who'd worked so hard to complete her Waterford Crystal collection was suddenly drinking vodka out of a jelly jar. It was a sign of her devastation, though I wonder what ever happened to that glass? It'd fetch a fortune on eBay.

I felt bad for Aunt Angie, dying so young. I felt especially bad that Ma had lost her best friend and would now be breathing down our necks. And I worried that if somehow Aunt Angie's body wasn't properly taken care of, that she'd come back to haunt us, falling out of the closet door when I opened it, or propped up at the kitchen table, pretending to read a magazine. In a way I guess she did haunt us, because Ma never got over her. If I had a nickel for every time I heard Ma say "I just wish my sister were here to see this," well, I'd be rubbing elbows with the likes of Bill Gates and Sumner Redstone.

After the initial soreness passed, Ma tried to corral us kids around town, but her heart wasn't in it. We tried to be good, brave soldiers. I think Gia was the first to snap, but then she's older and was probably suffering adolescence along with the consequences of bad parenting. One day Ma drove the three of us to this TV studio, where we had to wait around all day while Ma shot a commercial for Mattress Queen. Frank and I were cool for the first hour or so because they had a big plate of cookies and all the Hawaiian Punch we could drink. Golden. But our sister wasn't quite so happy, since Ma wanted her in the commercial and she was cranking that she didn't want to wear the dress the ad people bought her.

"Ruffles? What, are you kidding me?"

Gia had a tiny zit on her nose she didn't want anyone to see. Gia had plans to go to the movies with her friends. Gia gave the ad executive a lot of lip, finally telling him to f off.

"Is it that time of the month?" Ma asked with a pained expression, and I was so naive I wondered if a holiday was coming up, or maybe there was some kind of adult thing that happened on a monthly basis. Bottom line, Gia did not want to be in the commercial, and she stomped and shrieked and cried fat crocodile tears until she won. Sort of. She made them change the script so that she barely appeared on camera. While Ma was talking about the great deals at Mattress Queen, Princess Gia was now snuggled up under a thick purple comforter, half of her pink face the only thing peaking out, zit side down. Almost unrecognizable.

When the cameras stopped rolling, Frank and I ran onto the "set" and started jumping on the bed. "Get off, you morons!" Gia whined, squirming out from under the purple blanket.

Of course, Frank and I ignored her, happily jumping and bouncing down, ignited by processed sugars and pent-up energy.

That was when our mother came alive like a thundering dragon. With eyes popping and veins in her neck bulging, she roared: "GET OFF THE BED!"

As I bounced onto the mattress with a final thud, I felt the air knocked out of me. This mattress wasn't so soft or springy. It was like landing on a cement sidewalk.

That was when it hit me—that the whole Mattress Queen thing was a load of crap. With a sinking disappointment, I realized we weren't royalty at all.

When I finally pull onto our block in Bayside, a behemoth of an SUV is parked in front of our house. Of course. Three sleeping children in the back and we couldn't be so lucky as to score a parking spot. I open the back door and slide my arms under Scout's legs. "I'm so tired," she moans as I lift her little body and carry her up the porch stairs. She stirs in my arms, awake before I can make it through the front door. "Can I get a snack?" she asks.

I ease her to her feet. "Sure, but you'll have to brush your teeth."

I return to the car, double-parked with lights blinking and Ruby standing guard against kidnappers and carjackers. When I go over to take Becca, Ruby waves me off. "She's too big for that. I'll wake her up." I go to the other door and scoop Dylan from his car seat. His bottom is like a sack of wet rags. Wet diaper, as usual. But he drapes over my shoulder like a crash-test dummy, deep in sleep, undisturbed by the cold night air or the fumbling transfer to bed. There is something reassuring about having a baby on my shoulder, a tiny, trusting creature. When they're asleep like that I feel strong and capable of taking care of things. It's when they wake up and start to complain that I have problems. I lower him into his crib and strip off the wet diaper. He rolls away into the fetal position before I have a chance to get the new one on, and I have to improvise slightly, not sure if I've got the Velcro tight enough, but what the hell.

From the hall I see Becca brushing her teeth. Scout calls from downstairs. "Can someone make me a hot pretzel?"

Ruby calls down for her to go to bed, but I go down and pop it in the microwave, not wanting her to go to bed hungry. By the time I return from parking the car, Ruby is upstairs trying to settle Becca back to bed.

"But now I'm awake! I'll never fall back asleep. Can't I have a TV in my room?"

Scout stands in her pajamas at the threshold of their room, clearly annoyed at her sister's histrionics. "Let her go to sleep in *your* bed," Scout says, diving into her own bed. "Because I can't take the whining."

Scout is her father's daughter.

Becca seems on the verge of tears as Ruby walks her out the door. I sit on the edge of Scout's bed and kiss her forehead. I try to end with "good night" and "Merry Christmas" but Scout has questions about the day. Why didn't Santa bring her the hover disk she asked for? How come Mimi always picks out better toys than Grandma Mira? Why is Grandpa Conny so grumpy?

"We'll talk about it all tomorrow." I hug her tight, wanting to give her a little something. Reassurance? Peace of mind? Love?

When Ruby and I were dating I always pressed to keep things status quo. Why would we want to get married, get *institutionalized* and ruin the good thing we had? She used to laugh that off. She called me Jack Soo, the guy who sang that song "Don't Marry Me." One weekend she even rented *Flower Drum Song* from Blockbuster and tried to make me watch it. I had her forward to the song, which is pretty damned funny. You gotta love Jack Soo.

I love my kids, but sometimes I get wind of this other life Ruby and I could have had—the alternate universe of quiet mornings with the *Times,* blue smoke and a nightcap at the bar, and great sex without worrying about waking up the kids or being woken up at six in the morning. I get a strong hit of the old freedom we had as a couple and, God help me, I miss it. Which makes me feel guilty about wishing my kids away. Christ, what kind of a father am I?

That's when it all comes crashing down on me, the pressure to succeed, the desire to be a decent father and not a prick like my old man. Sometimes between the "yadah-yadah-yadah" at work and the "Shut up! No, you shut up! I had it first!" at home, I can barely hold my head up. I'd like to share this with Ruby, but she's spread herself thin in a dozen places. She's at her computer when I go to bed at night, and in the morning when I wake up she's already unavailable, feeding the kids or writing or packing lunches. The quiet, safe little space that Rubes and I once carved out for ourselves has blown up into this noisy, three-ring circus tent—not a place I ever wanted to be. I have always hated the noise, the drama, the gaudy tomfoolery of circuses.

God help me, some days I just want to go back into the little cocoon Ruby and I spun together. And I call Ruby crazy. I'm the one who wants the impossible. Like Mom wishing Aunt Angie back to life, I wish for something that ended long, long, ago.

9

Flying with Children

Two days after Christmas we went public with our news.

Jack called a family meeting—which basically meant turning off *SpongeBob* and standing in front of the television—and told the girls that Mom and Dad had some exciting news.

"Are you having another baby?" Becca asked, her tone surprisingly jaded. When Scout was born, two-year-old Becca, just beginning to talk, had placed herself in front of Jack every time we tried to change Scout's diaper. "No baby!" she'd told us sternly. Jack had felt guilty and sorry for her, but I kept reminding him that it was more important for Becca to have a sibling than to be the queen of the house.

"Nope, no baby." Jack shot me a cross-eyed look of relief. "But it's good news. Daddy's company wants him to work in another city, and we can probably get a bigger house there, with a yard and a garage. So we've decided to move to a new place, to Portland, Oregon."

"Is it close by?" Scout asked.

"Actually, it's very far away," I said, "on the other side of the U.S. The West Coast."

"North of California, right?" Becca asked, as if participating in a Geography Bee. "Does that mean we can get a dog? You always said if we had more room, and a bigger yard. Can we?"

Jack turned to me, deferring. "What do you think?"

"I guess." I'd forgotten about the dog thing, but if it was bait for Becca, then I could go for it. "Sure."

"Where will we sleep?" Scout asked.

Jack smiled. "We'll bring our beds."

"Can we bring our toys?" Scout asked.

I nodded. "You'll have to help me pack."

"And what about our clothes?"

"Clothes, too," I said.

Scout rolled over to the coffee table. "Will we bring this table? This book?"

"Yes, Scout," Jack said, "we're going to pack up the house and take it all."

"What about Dylan?" she asked, leaning down to touch his shoulder. "Are we bringing Dylan?"

I picked him up, sat him on my hip and kissed his rosy cheek. "Yes, yes, yes," I said between kisses. "Silly Scout! We wouldn't leave anyone in our family behind."

Jack pressed a palm to my shoulder, reassuring as we both listened for the resistance, the tears, the complaints about leaving friends behind and moving off to the great unknown.

But the girls seemed happy.

"Can I start packing now?" Becca asked. "I can't wait to tell everybody at school. And what kind of dog are we getting?"

Again, no clue on the dog thing. "Why don't you research it and we'll talk about your picks?" I said.

While Becca ran upstairs to pack, Scout asked, "Will we have to go to school there?"

"Of course," Jack said, hoisting her to one shoulder.

"Oh, no! I thought we were getting away from school!" she protested. "What if I get a mean teacher? School's out for me, Dad. I'll move, but I'm not going to school again." She climbed the stairs, calling to Becca. "Did you know we have to go to school there?"

"Scout, don't be an idiot," Becca replied. The word "idiot" had crept into her vocabulary when we laid down the law about calling anyone stupid. "Of course we're going to school there."

Jack twirled Dylan's pacifier on one finger. "Well, that went well, don't you think?"

"Why do you have to go all the way out to Oregon?" my sister Amber asked. "That's too far. How about Philadelphia or Boston? Philly is like an hour and a half in the car, and I've always loved Boston. I always get such a strong historic vibe when I'm there, like I was a colonist in a former life and—"

"Hello?" I interrupted her. "This is about Jack making a career move, not choosing a dream city."

"Oh, but I want you to be closer. Wouldn't it be fun to choose randomly? Like 'Where in the World is Matt Lauer?'"

"I've been researching Portland. You know, it makes it in lots of top-ten cities surveys."

"You're kidding me, right? Doesn't it rain all the time there?"

"Not as much as the state of Washington," I said, oddly defensive. "The streets are cleaner than New York."

"Well, sure, with all that rain washing them down."

"It's called Rose City. Lots of roses, in every color. Apparently there are bushes everywhere," I said, running out of ammunition.

"Mmm. That would mean lots of thorns. Anyway, how real is this? Are you sure you can't switch to Boston?"

I assured her that it was very real, that the girls and I were headed out for the last few days of the holiday break to look around and possibly begin house hunting.

The calls about the move started pouring in, and it seemed to consume all my time fielding them. Fortunately, I had finished and polished the manuscript for *Chocolate in the Morning*, and though I was supposed to be working on the last romance in my contract with Hearts and Flowers, it wasn't due until the middle of March, which gave me some leeway. So I faced the curious neighbors who wanted to know what price we were listing the house for. Jack's friends, the guys he'd grown up with, were beside themselves, charging him with everything from desertion to insanity.

One Saturday evening his buddy Ed left us a tearful message about how he couldn't believe it. "That's all just bull-sheet," he intoned, making me glad for the kids' sake that we'd switched from an answering machine to voice mail. I cajoled the moms of Becca's friends, who expressed lament that we were leaving and couldn't imagine how we'd manage in Utah or Seattle, Montana or Washington. For some reason no one could get our destination quite right; perhaps it was true about Americans failing geography. I had a long talk with Morgan, who seemed truly happy for me, and two shorter, crisper conversations with Harrison and Gracie, who seemed to think I'd gone bonkers.

Maybe I had, but that week I was boarding a plane with two small children and I actually was looking forward to the trip, my first jaunt on an airplane in five years. Call me crazy, but sometimes I get a thrill when life gets shaken up a bit.

"No machine guns. No knives." Scout was reading aloud from the electronic message board at the security checkpoint and people in line stared at her suspiciously. The line was backed up, typical for overcrowded LaGuardia International Airport. It gave Scout plenty of time to read the messages, over and over again.

"Honey, keep it down, please," I said as I struggled to remove my laptop from its case and place it in a plastic bin for X-raying.

"No bombs," Scout read vehemently. "No scissors."

"No children," a gruff voice snapped. I shot a look at the man in front of us, who grinned naughtily. Apparently, he thought that was funny.

"No ice picks. No saws," Scout went on.

"She just learned to read," I said to the woman behind us, her face pinched in a stern expression. "Gotta sound things out."

"She's not reading, Mom," Becca corrected me. "She's looking at the stupid pictures."

"No fireplaces," Scout said, frowning. "Well, that's just dumb. Who could bring a fireplace on a plane?"

"It's supposed to be a barbecue grill," Becca said scornfully. "Come on, Scout. Don't you know anything?"

"It's not a grill," Scout argued. "Is it, Mom? Nobody brings grills on a plane."

"I think it's just fire, or maybe fireworks," I said, trying to shove my driver's license and boarding pass into a safe pocket as I ushered the girls through the metal detector.

"Keep your boarding pass out!" a security agent said curtly, and I fumbled in my pocket, wondering how I was supposed to juggle three boarding passes, carry-on luggage and two kids.

"Aw . . ." Scout turned back after she went under the arch. "I can't read it anymore."

"We'll find you something to read at the gift shop," I promised, grabbing bags and hurrying the girls along down the corridor, where the air smelled of diesel fuel, stale coffee and wieners. We passed a duty-free shop and a bar, and rounded a corner. A gift shop and newsstand loomed at the far end of the corridor. "There we go," I said, pointing ahead.

"Uh, Mom?" Becca asked quietly.

"Yes, honey?"

"Can we go back to the security people?"

"Why? Do you like that? We'll go through again next flight."

"No, I need to go back there, now. I forgot my shoes."

I paused, glancing down to where her pink- and purple-flowered socks slid over the slippery tiles. "Oh, Becca . . ."

"Sorry." She stared down, on the verge of tears.

"It's okay."

Becca was so hard on everyone, including herself, that I rarely needed to punish her. I hitched the computer strap higher on my shoulder and turned back. "Let's hope your shoes aren't already in a sealed container, along with all the nail scissors and sewing kits they've confiscated."

"What's confra-skated?" Scout asked, making a skating motion with her Moon Boots along the smooth tile floor.

"Never mind," Becca and I said at the same time.

Although the seats seem to be shrinking down to kid size, commercial airlines are not designed for passengers under the age of fourteen. Traveling with two little girls, I felt like an alien with my underwear showing. As we walked down the narrow aisle people stared, scowled and moved away in discreet panic with the hope that they would not be seated near us on the plane.

Becca was afraid to say "excuse me" to strangers and the safety regulations frightened her. Scout questioned everything, touched everything and tried to climb anything that looked challenging. I ordered her off the carts at the airport, down from the escalator rail, and, no, she could not ride in the overhead luggage bin of the plane.

"But I can fit in there!" she protested.

I didn't answer, but shoved the squishy travel bag of stuffed animals into the overhead bin and quickly took my seat.

"Can we buy something?" Rebecca asked, perusing the menu a flight attendant had passed out. "This one looks so good. It comes with cheese and yogurt."

"Those meals cost extra, and we have cheese and snacks." Cheese sticks, Fruit Roll-Ups, baby carrots, crackers . . . I'd made an extra trip to the grocery store to stock up on portable snacks.

"Can I have a snack? Did you pack Doritos?" Scout smiled. "Please, oh, please?"

"Let's wait until we take off," I said, resting my head back against the seat and taking a deep breath. It hadn't been easy setting everything in place for Kristen to care for Dylan while we were away and Jack to take over at night. Not that Dylan was difficult, but there was so much ground to cover, from diet to bath times to doctors' numbers and insurance cards. Then there were all the travel arrangements, overseeing packing for the girls and keeping a lid on Scout, who at the moment seemed possessed by jumping beans. Hopefully, the seat belt would prevent her from escaping from the exit doors and performing wing stunts.

We lifted off into a stagnant gray sky with a bit of engine muscle and rose above the gloom, pulling away from my once-beloved New York City.

"Whoa . . ." Awed, Scout pressed closer to the window as buildings and ball parks turned into patches of gray, green and orange.

On my left Becca closed her eyes against the back of the seat, her fingers clutching the armrest. I patted her right hand and leaned over Scout. "It makes New York look so tiny and well organized, doesn't it?"

"And a lot cleaner," she agreed as the plane banked slightly over some multiplex theaters that I suspected were in Westchester. We gained altitude, climbing into a clear blue sky decorated with cottony clouds that seemed to be floating on a pressure system.

Delighted, Scout giggled. "It's like the clouds are sitting on a shelf!"

"Shh!" Becca snarled. "Everyone can hear you, Scout."

Eight hours and one stopover later we landed at PDX, where I scuttled with the girls up the Jetway, struck by the smell of the air. It seemed so clean, not like an airport at all. The deep emerald green carpet hinted at rolling fields and dense forests, and Scout enjoyed following the branches embedded in the rug, playing airport hop-scotch. Down at Baggage Claim our luggage came quickly. The agent at the rental car counter kept saying "You bet!" whenever I asked a question, and I began to think I'd shipped off to some lost fifties' civilization in which people were polite and actually looked you in the eye when you spoke to them.

The van driver for our rental car company made a fuss over the kids and insisted on lugging our bags on and off the van. As I drove along Airport Way in the cute mini-SUV and followed the signs to Interstate 5, which was clearly marked, I felt bold and capable, empowered to make this move and bring my family to a more appropriate place. "I can do this," I muttered to myself, smiling despite the slap-fight going on in the backseat. Can do!

Following directions I'd ordered on MapQuest back home, I drove us to the Lakeview Inn, a quaint little hotel right on Lake Green that had been recommended by Shane Hill, the human resources manager of the Portland station. Jack had met Shane a few times and declared him a "good guy," which was a good thing since he would be coordinating our move to Portland. We were scheduled to have dinner with Shane's family tomorrow night, but in the meantime he'd e-mailed me a list of hotels, restaurants and realtors to investigate.

The Lakeview was a square old wooden structure that reminded me of an old Catskills resort. Each room of the contemporary wedding cake of a building had a balcony overlooking the lake, and there was a lakefront pool below that would have been fun in summertime. We checked in and once in the room I jokingly suggested naps, but the girls protested loudly, claiming they wanted to explore and go house hunting. I called the realtor at the top of Shane's list, a Ms.

Linda Sue Mellun, who gushed over the distance we'd traveled and picked us up at the hotel.

Linda Sue Mellun turned out to be older than I'd expected, though the body work she'd had done, along with a blonde bob fit for a teenager made it difficult to pinpoint her age. Her eyes opened wide with enthusiasm when she spotted me at the threshold of her office. That look froze stiffly when she spotted the two children behind me. Had I neglected to mention that I'd brought the girls with me?

"These are my daughters, Scout and Becca."

"Aren't you the cutest! I love children." She leaned down over the girls with condescending sweetness, a move that put her party-balloon breasts right at eye level. Becca smiled and looked away awkwardly, but Scout was staring curiously, her brows knit together as the two mounds stretched buoyantly under an orange-and-white-print tank—one of the expensive fabric blends that never wrinkles or loses its shape. I sensed that Scout was just seconds away from giving Ms. Linda Sue Mellun's melons a squeeze to see just how ripe they were . . .

Quickly I stepped forward and looped an arm around Scout's shoulders, yanking her back. "She's a cutey, all right. Didn't you say you had a few houses to show us today?"

"Of course." Linda Sue straightened, her perfect rack never faltering. "Let's take my car and I'll give you the grand tour of the southwest pocket."

Driving around Lake Green, I felt very much like a visitor at a woodsy resort. Everywhere I looked was green, from the manicured lawns to the dense laurel hedges to the tall Douglas firs, some towering a hundred feet overhead. Was I actually going to live here? Would I miss the concrete, the security of having my neighbor within earshot, the iron and glass spread of Manhattan on the horizon as my train rounded the last curve on its way into the city? I didn't think so. First, the skyline of Portland, which we'd driven through along the Willamette River on the way from the airport, was majestic in its own right. The city was within reach, in case I needed a fix. And these suburbs southwest of Portland were unlike any bedroom community I'd seen in the great megalopolis that stretched along the East Coast from Boston to Richmond. Surrounded by tall fir trees and picturesque hills, the lake was lovely. Diamonds of sunlight danced on its rippled surface and someone sped by in a motor boat, reminding me of an old Disney film I saw as a kid. With boathouses, bridges, islands and floating docks, Lake Green seemed to have spawned a waterfront community of its own.

"Here's a handy-man's special," Linda Sue said, pulling into a dark driveway covered by dense fir trees. "Most people consider any old structure on the lake a teardown. You're better off clearing the lot and building your own, but I wanted you to see the view."

"What's it listed for?" I asked as we opened the doors of Linda Sue's Lexus.

"A million eight. A pretty good deal."

"Almost two million dollars?" I stood in front of Becca and pointed her back toward the car. "Back inside. We can't stay."

"I just wanted to give you an idea of the range," the realtor insisted, her pouty lower lip suddenly prominent. "Is everyone this pushy in New York?"

"We don't have time for a widespread search," I said through gritted teeth. "We need a place to live. My husband starts his job March first."

"Got it! Okay, New York, we'll save this place for another day," Linda Sue said cheerfully as she took her place behind the steering wheel.

"As I said, it doesn't have to be in Lake Saranac, and certainly not on the lake." Becca and Scout had taken swim lessons, but when Dylan came along I hadn't had time for the Mommy and Me swim classes. "We're also interested in West Green and Gantry. Do you have a few things in our price range?" I asked once we were back in the car, safe from the multimillion-dollar properties.

She faced me, as if the car was on autopilot. "You bet!"

But after three hours with Linda Sue Mellun, all bets were off. Linda Sue kept showing us places we couldn't afford. Giant tract homes in posh developments, each house with its own wine cellar, hot tub and four-car garage. I was all over the kids, reminding them to keep their shoes outside and stop sock-sliding on the granite floors. One house perched on the edge of a cliff side made me feel as if I was falling—extreme vertigo. When I mentioned it, she said: "But isn't it a spectacular view?" Another listing was actually a compound, with a tennis court, pool and maid's house in the back. Of course, the girls fell in love with it and fought over who would claim the maid's house as a bedroom. When I asked Linda Sue about the price range yet again, she cocked her head coyly and admitted that she knew my husband worked for a national TV network. Meaning, we must be loaded.

"He works for the network," I told her, "he doesn't own it."

"But, Ruby, we all need to stretch a little when we're buying property. You'll thank me later."

I suspected I'd be thanking her sooner, right after I said good-bye.

She didn't know much about the local schools, except to say that "they're all great!"

To further exacerbate things, Linda Sue didn't really like children. Not that she was mean or rude. On the contrary, she was all smiles and giggles whenever Scout or Becca asked a question. But the answers she gave them were so lame. Like: "It's so cute that you'd think of that!" or "Why don't you let your mommy worry about that?" But Linda Sue would stare in horror as Scout pressed her palms against walls, draped her arms over banisters and swung her feet along the pristine white molding, peeked into cookie jars and bathroom cupboards.

While we investigated a small ranch with moss insinuating itself under roof tiles, Scout had occupied herself out in the flat mulch garden. I emerged from the moldy house to find that my daughter had made a game of kicking up mulch from the garden, covering the tail end of Linda Sue's car with a coat of gray dust. All this was much to Linda Sue's horror, though she swallowed a gasp of pain and moved around the front of her car, away from the dust cloud. "So creative," she said, facing away from us, as if summoning patience from the wooded area. "I love children."

Liar, I thought, taking Scout by the hand and steering her into the vehicle as Becca started in with her "That was a dumb thing to do" speech for Scout.

Not that Becca didn't have her own virtues for offending Linda

Sue. In one retro hippie haven, Linda Sue was on her cell phone downstairs when my two daughters ran into a room decorated with bead curtains and lava lamps, where they leaped right onto the twin beds covered with SpongeBob comforters.

"This is my room!" Scout claimed.

"No, it's mine! I called dibs," Rebecca corrected her, spreading her arms wide in a half-hurkey as she catapulted over the bed.

"Are you out of your minds? Get down!" I roared.

The girls quickly flopped onto the beds and slid down to the floor. "Now fix the comforters and don't ever do that again." Noticing Linda Sue blinking from the doorway, I shrugged. "Sorry."

In the awkward pause, I prayed she wouldn't tell me one more time about how she loved children. "Did you see the master bath?" she asked, changing the subject, though she probably was making a mental note to nominate me for the "Most Failed Mom" Award.

"Where's the monster bath?" Scout asked, cutting ahead of us in the hall. "I want to see it!"

It was a relief when Linda Sue told us she had a dinner date and headed her lux-mobile back to her office. She dropped us at the hotel, and we went across the street for Chinese food—rice, dumplings and ribs for the girls, chicken and broccoli for me. The temperature dropped with the darkness, and we giggled as we left the restaurant, jogging to keep warm. We changed into our pajamas and the girls tuned into Nickelodeon while I pulled on my jacket and went out to the balcony, cell and newspaper in hand. While I checked in with Jack I scanned the paper, looking for real estate ads. I didn't bother getting into the foibles of Linda Sue, but I did tell him we'd lucked into a green haven. "We're going to find a the perfect house nestled in among some of these amazing trees," I told him. "You'll see."

"We've got trees in New York," he said. "What's the big deal?"

"Trust me. You're going to love it here."

"As long as I can still get the *New York Times*," he teased me.

We were still talking when the door slid open and Becca emerged onto the balcony. "Scout's asleep." That was no surprise, as it was after seven—ten o'clock in New York.

"Do you want to say hi to Daddy?" I asked, and she took the phone and talked with Jack. Afterward she crawled onto my lap and I hugged her in my arms, enclosing her shoulders in my open jacket.

"I think I'm going to like it here," she said confidently. "Everything smells better."

I snuggled her closer. "I think we're all going to like it here."

"I just feel sorry for my friends in New York. I mean, I want to tell everyone about how excited I am to be moving, but I don't want to make them feel bad, like I'm rubbing it in. I'll miss them and everything, but I still want to move here."

"That's a very adult observation." Our Becca, the social conscience of the third grade, the worrier of the world. In the past few months, during a few of our shopping trips and visits to the park, I'd noticed her watching the odd stragglers, vagrants bumming quarters or sipping a beer in a bag as they watched the world go by. They frightened her, and rightly so, as she was wise enough to be aware of the dangerous possibilities, but also morally conscious enough to worry about the welfare of these people. "You're right not to rub it in," I told her, "but it's okay to feel happy about the move. Enjoy those good feelings, honey." I kissed her cheek, and she pointed to the lake.

"What's that light in the lake?" she asked.

"The reflection of the moon. Do you see it, that slice of moon pie up in the sky?" We tilted our heads back and soaked up the silver wedge that lit the inky dark sky. "That's the same moon that's shining over Daddy and Dylan right now."

She let her head rest against my chin. "Same moon, but cleaner here."

We giggled together, our voices skittering over the surface of the night lake, the lake that I felt sure would hear many of our conversations over the next few years.

10

Into a Rockwell Painting

The dawn brought gray skies with diffused light on the moss green lake. An overcast day, and yet there was a certain quiet beauty and dignity to it. Peering out over the smooth surface of the water, I realized how different the ambient noise was here. Absent were the shriek of truck brakes, the roar of emergency vehicles, the hum of traffic from the expressway seven blocks from our house in Bayside.

As we ate breakfast in a cheerful diner called Tillamook Ice Creamery, I called a realtor I'd found in the local paper last night. The opening line of Debbie Tory's ad was "We help families find their homes!" I figured it would be a lot more pleasant all around if we could look for houses with a realtor who could deal with kids.

Debbie called me back before I'd finished my first cup of coffee. "Wow, all the way from New York!" she said cheerfully. "That's quite a move."

"And we're looking to make it fairly soon. I know it's the New York way to push, but do you think you could help us now?" I told her our timeframe, down payment and the price range we were looking for.

"Let me put the information in and do a search of the listings," Debbie said. "I can print out anything that seems like a good fit. Do you want to stop into the office, or should I pick you up at the hotel?"

We made a date to meet at her office later in the morning . . . and we were off.

From the beginning, Debbie got the kid thing. With a daughter in fourth grade and two kids in high school, she'd been there, done that. She was attentive but not condescending. She put forth very clear parameters on what they could and could not do: Yes, they could play on the swing set out back; no, they could not play with the toys inside the house. Whenever we found a house that was a possibility, Debbie would take us past the local elementary school so the kids could get a sense of how it would feel to live in that neighborhood.

And somehow Debbie was able to produce affordable houses, many of which were strong candidates, all of which were better than our small Queens row house where we were popping at the seams. As we peeked in through doorways and walked through strangers' bedrooms and bathrooms, Debbie gave me a few local tips on the Oregon DMV, kids' intramural sports, local taxes and Douglas firs. "These trees are beautiful, but you really don't want to be under them," she said, gazing up at some towering evergreens. "They drop needles and sap, cones and branches. It gunks up your roof and makes for a lot of cleanup. It's hard to stay on top of it. Not what the tree-huggers want to hear, but there you have it."

I nodded, soaking it all in.

"What's that smell?" Scout asked in one house.

I was glad the owner wasn't around, but there was no disguising the smell of mold.

"It appears they've had some water damage," Debbie said, pivoting in the main entryway, then turning back to the listings in her hand. "With that in mind, I'm not sure you want to take the time to go through this house."

"Let's keep moving," I said as Scout pinched her nose and crowed: "P.U.!"

By the end of the day, we'd narrowed our search down to three houses, one that happened to be down the street from Debbie in

West Green. I took some photos with my digital camera and Debbie e-mailed them along with the listing information to Jack with the plan to look it all over before we kibitzed.

That night I tried to keep Jack focused on our house search, wanting to tell him about the beautiful French doors on the house in West Green, the gurgling natural stone fountain in one front yard . . . but he kept changing the subject to Corstar, clearly unnerved by the hotbed of malice the New York office had become.

"Numero Uno keeps whining that she can't live without me, that they'll never survive April Sweeps, that I need to give her at least six months' notice."

"Six months? That's ridiculous. Our closing date on the house here is six weeks away; we can't put the brakes on now."

"That was yesterday. Today she's saying she's going to call Dallas and put the kibosh on the whole thing."

"What? She doesn't have the power to do that!" I gasped as my new fresh-air world fizzled before my eyes. "Does she?"

"She's even talking about calling Bob directly."

"Oh, no!" Though unconfirmed, Numero Uno Laguno's relationship with Bob was the stuff of corporate legend. Although Bob Filbert is the "happily married father of two law students," it seems evident that some hanky-panky had gone on between Bob and Numero Uno over the years. One employee claims to have heard her unmistakable shriek of "Oh, Bawb! Oh, Bawb!" emitting from his office during late-evening conferences.

"They're screwing," Jack argues when I assert that perhaps she's waxing orgasmic over his proposal of a raise and stock option package.

Britta Swenson confided in Jack and Judith that she saw Numero Uno in the ladies' room washing out her diaphragm more than once. "The things we women have to put up with," Numero Uno lamented. "I wish I was a man. Wouldn't you love to pork around with abandon and have people think you're that much better for it?" All this while rinsing the latex disk, dabbing it with a paper towel and popping it back in its case. Britta swears that the diaphragm appears only when Bob is visiting the New York office.

When faced with the rumors, Numero Uno says repeatedly, smugly, that "Bawb and I have a very special relationship." Jack is sure that entails sex. Looking at Numero Uno, with her spindly long arms and wavy dark hair, I sometimes wonder what Bob might even see in her. But Jack reminds me that sex equals power for some men. "And who knows," he always says, "maybe she knows some kind of sex trick with hot wax and ice cream." At that point in our discussion of the Numero Uno/Bob legend we both laugh and try to stop thinking of Phoebe Laguno and Bob Filbert naked. Not a pretty image.

"Look," Jack said with a sigh, "we both know that Numero Uno isn't really number one. She doesn't run Corstar and she probably can't get in the way of my move. But for now she's going to pretend she can stop me. She'll throw her tantrum, make my life a living hell because it's what she does best."

"I'm sorry," I said sincerely.

"I know. I wish I was there right now."

"I do, too. Why don't you come? Forget about finishing up there. The company mover will close up the house. You can fly out and we'll live in the hotel until we can close on the house." I knew it wouldn't work, but the fantasy was sweet.

"Nice try, but no. Portland doesn't want me till March, and I think the girls need a chance to say good-bye to their friends, to the grand-parents. You've got friends, too. And then there's the matter of clos-ing the gas and electric accounts, returning the cable boxes . . . all that crap."

The crap of living . . . I knew it well. "But we're going ahead with the house here, right? Did you see the extra photos I sent? There's a house that gives the feeling of a bed and breakfast, with etched glass windows and—"

"I'll look at it all in the morning, Rubes. Right now, I need to close my eyes and try to block out the sound of Numero Uno's shrill voice."

"Sleep tight," I said, with visions of hot tubs, etched glass, hard-wood floors and gurgling fountains dancing in my head.

* * *

The next day we took a family vote. Oddly, we all chose the same house, the newest construction down the street from Debbie. It also didn't hurt that the house was already vacant, the sellers anxious to make the sale, having been transferred to Seattle.

"Welcome to the neighborhood!" she said that afternoon as I stopped into the office to sign the contract. She beamed, looking like a cross between a Keebler elf and a cheerleader. "You'll have to come over for a glass of wine sometime. And it's an easy walk to school for the kids. There's a path that cuts through the neighborhood so they don't have to walk on the roads."

I nodded and signed away, thinking that it would be nice to know someone in the neighborhood, and feeling fortunate that the someone was Debbie Tory and not the likes of Linda Sue Mellun.

"Oh, and when the weather gets nice we'll take you out on our boat, tubing," Debbie added. "And if you're here for the Fourth of July there's a fun parade down Main Street. All the kids decorate their bikes in red, white and blue streamers and flags, and there's usually an Uncle Sam on stilts who throws candy into the crowd. And, of course, you won't want to miss the fireworks on the lake at night."

"You know, you're selling me after the fact," I teased her.

"Oh, I just wasn't sure what you knew about the community. I know you did your online research, but I don't want you to miss anything."

"Consider me a blank slate. I'll need to learn everything."

"Good! That's the right attitude. Just think of it as Mayberry without the goofy deputy. You're moving into a Norman Rockwell painting."

I thanked Debbie for everything including the invitation to join her family for pizza that night. Becca and Scout were eager to meet other kids their age and they'd be attending the same school as Marin Tory.

That night, while the kids were playing air hockey in the Torys's basement, Debbie, Scott and I took a walk down the street to show him our house from the outside.

"Nice big yard," Scott said pleasantly, sweeping a hand back over his short brush of blond hair. "You've got room for a waterfall or a pond. Definitely a hot tub if you're the tubbing type."

"If I know my husband, he'll want some kind of waterfall or fountain, with lots of shrubs and flowers." I thought of Jack and his troubles with Numero Uno Laguno. If her resistance was giving him second thoughts about moving, he hadn't brought it up either last night or this morning. Granted, she was a pain in the ass right now, but once he got past these next few weeks, he'd be able to get a taste of suburban bliss in this, our new home. "Jack fancies himself some sort of gourmet gardener," I went on. "He loves coming up with schematics for planting flowers and shrubs, but in our one-tree yard in New York, he was a bit limited."

"Oh, then he'll like it here," Scott said. "He may even get involved in those garden competitions. Garden tours. People breed their own roses here for the Rose Festival in June. It's a planter's paradise."

As I circled the house and pictured the girls running through the yard, my husband in muddy jeans and sneakers lugging a balled seedling, Dylan learning to catch a ball with a baseball mitt, a giddy feeling bubbled up inside me, making me smile in the darkness. I'd been smiling so much in the past few days that my jaw was beginning to ache, but if that was the worst of my problems, I could deal.

Snow chips bounced along the tinted plane window. The temperature in the cabin seemed to drop twenty degrees, and as the pilot announced our final descent, a horrible smell penetrated the cabin, even as the flight attendant came down the aisle spraying a deodorizer. The smell persisted, and I could only venture a guess that, sadly, we were transporting dead bodies in the cargo area of the plane. Beside me Scout was moaning about one ear that wouldn't pop, and Becca clamped her nose against the stench, shouting at Scout to "put a cork in it!"

When we landed at LaGuardia Airport just a few yards short of Flushing Bay, I turned on my cell phone and saw two messages from Morgan. Since it was after seven, I called her at home as our jet taxied in.

"I have good news and bad news," she said. "Which first?"

I rolled my neck from side to side, not ready to leave the cocoon of bliss that had encompassed me in Oregon.

My cocoon was splitting.

"I'll take the good," I said.

"We've got a juicy offer for *Chocolate*. Six figures."

My heart raced a little, like a revving engine. "That's great! Wonderful!"

"What?" Becca asked me, shoving Scout's hand off the armrest they shared. "What? Tell me!"

"It's business," I said quietly. "Mommy sold a book."

She frowned, finding the news lacking since I'd been cranking out romance novels her entire life.

"Morgan, thank you!"

"Thank yourself! You pushed so hard to get the entire book finished, and look—we got three solid offers. It'll be published in hardcover first, Condor Books, and I'm confident we'll sell the film rights, too."

That now-familiar swell of joy bubbled up. I'd sold my breakout book. I've been given a voice, a chance to write something different from now on.

"The editors at Condor loved, loved, loved your manuscript. They're rushing it through to make it their big summer release. *This* summer. Ruby Dixon will be on the *Times* list before you know it."

"You're not supposed to say things like that to your clients," I said.

"So I'm a bad agent. *Bad* agent! But probably not wrong. Anyway, soon as you're over your jet lag you need to get a photo done for the inside cover."

A photo . . . the romances I'd written didn't include author photos, as they were packaged like bars of soap, according to marketing geniuses like Oscar Stollen.

As I hustled the girls down the aisle of the plane and into the diesel smell of LaGuardia Airport, I felt a flash of anxiety. Was I ready for a high profile? Should I have taken a pseudonym years ago to hide behind?

Then I remembered. "What was the bad news?"

"Oh. Lindsay called." Her voice dropped two octaves. "Hearts and Flowers needs the last book of your contract. Pronto."

"But Lindsay said it wasn't a huge rush."

"Apparently Oscar has intervened. Probably hoping to make us squirm. Anyway, they're sticking to the original deadline."

"But that's February first!" I said so loudly that two passengers who'd risen and piled into the aisle in front of me actually turned back to stare. Tomorrow was New Year's Eve. That gave me one month to write, while juggling kids, trying to keep the house presentable to show potential buyers and packing up a household of five. "That's crazy."

"They're sticking to the contract," Morgan said. "Just do your best. It'll be good to get this book behind us, fulfill your contract. Then we can step back and take an objective look at where you want to go from here."

My "Can Do!" quality was wounded as I envisioned my month of reflective, efficient packing crunched into a slap-dash mess. "I don't know. I'll try."

"That's all anyone can ask. Listen, we know Oscar is trying to bust chops for you publishing elsewhere, but he got a shot at *Chocolate* and he passed. It's his funeral."

"His funeral, my death," I said with a tired sigh.

"I feel for you, sweetie. I do feel for you. I remember when my kids were young, all those sleepless nights. I don't think I got a wink of sleep between 1983 and 1986."

"I can do this." My confidence returned as I passed one of the small airport bookshops and imagined *Chocolate in the Morning* by Ruby Dixon stacked in an endcap at the front of the store. "I've written the outline. It's just a matter of banging it out, right?"

"Attagirl!"

"What's the worst that could happen? I mean, no one ever died from writing a romance, did they?"

Words I would live to regret.

11

Life Inventory

On New Year's Day I crawled out of bed, glad that I'd limited myself to one glass of champagne. While Dylan worked on Cheerios and *Sesame Street,* I sat at the dining room table with a calendar. Four and a half weeks; thirty-one full days to write 270 pages. Hmm. Without distractions I could write ten pages a day. Toward the end of some books when I was on a roll, I'd occasionally had a day when I'd churned out more than thirty pages, but that was at a time when I didn't have children. I'd read articles about romance writers who checked themselves into luxury hotels for weeks to finish off a manuscript. I wish. I'd have to shoot for ten pages a day during the week, five a day on weekends, and pray my muses didn't desert me.

I nuked a bowl of oatmeal, woke Jack and told him he was on kid duty. Wedging myself among the dirty clothes strewn over the chair in our room, I feasted on apple-and-cinnamon oats while my laptop warmed up.

"Just think, our new house has an extra room that can be my office, so I can work without bugging you," I said to the lump in the bed. "People out there call them bonus rooms. Bonus! Don't you love that?"

Slightly hungover, Jack moaned in acknowledgment.

"Compared to what we can afford out here, that whole house is a bonus." I licked the spoon as the lump in the bed stirred.

"What time is it?"

"Nine-fifteen."

"Too early."

"I know, but you'd better check on Dylan. He's been unsupervised for about five minutes now and we don't want him to burn down the house before we sell it. Becca's still in bed and Scout was in the kitchen trying to program her robot to pour cereal."

As if on cue, a crash came from the kitchen downstairs, followed by Dylan's "Uh-oh!" and Scout hissing: "Don't tell Mommy!"

I pushed the computer off my lap, starting to get up.

"Don't . . . I'll get it." Jack's growl resembled an aged bear as he slapped back the covers and rolled to his feet. "Happy New Year," he said sardonically as he shuffled out the door in his boxers and T-shirt.

Three pages later when I darted downstairs and prodded Jack to shower and get the kids out of the house, he kept agreeing half-heartedly as he hid behind his *New York Times*. For an intelligent, business-savvy man, Jack struggled to comprehend my career issues. He could not understand why I had to step up my schedule now, during the holidays. "If you sold the big book to Condor, and you're going to make all that money, why do you even have to write this book?"

I told him I'd signed a contract, that I'd made a commitment and that I didn't want to piss off the biggest romance publisher on Planet Earth. In turn, he asked me if the Bronx Zoo was really going to be open on New Year's Day. I insisted it was . . . not what he wanted to hear.

An hour later I sent the girls out the door behind him with kisses and Fruit by the Foot. "Take your time!" I muttered through my big smile at the door. Were the situation reversed, would he stay home from Dallas because I didn't understand why corporate needed him? Highly unlikely, but I didn't have the energy to waste stewing over the stubborn male psyche.

Must write book . . .

"Is this the dress you were talking about?" Harrison adjusted his glasses, his face long as he circled me. "Oh. My. God."

The man who'd come into the photographer's studio with him put down his toolbox and propped one foot on top of it to examine me. "Oooh."

Were they good exclamations, or signs of my fashion failure?

"Too flashy?" I ran my hands over my hips, now covered in a rainbow explosion of sequins. I'd purchased the dress years ago for a wedding, sort of an impulse buy when I went with one of the bridesmaids to a wedding boutique. It was a Bill Blass, a simple, shimmering shift with a scooped neck. It hugged my curves and, by the grace of God, it still fit.

His hands in prayer position, Harrison pressed them to his lips. "Did you just step out of *Project Runway*? This is an amazing creation. This is the real Ruby Dixon!"

"You don't think it's a problem that it's seven years old?" I'd bought the dress after I had Becca, before I was pregnant with Scout.

"Oh, no, no, no!" said the thin man with mocha skin and eyes that seemed too big for his body. "It works for you. If only I could say the same about your hair, lovey."

"Ruby Dixon, meet your stylist and makeup artist, Ari Otani." Harrison put a loving hand on Ari's shoulder. "Ari is a miracle worker."

"And in the nick of time," Ari said, reaching out to tweak my hair. "What are we doing here? Blonde? Brunette faded to red? Or are we going for tutti-frutti?"

I forced myself to smile. I'd done the golden highlights to cover some gray, but then it all got mixed up over time. "You're the expert," I said. "Do with me what you will."

Ari came up with ringlets—yes, the Shirley Temple look is alive and well—which he spray-painted gold and pinned back from my eyes. After Ari had done his magic, I stood before a mirror and honestly didn't recognize myself. "Who are you?" I asked my reflection.

Behind me, Harrison and Ari laughed.

"Why, that woman is the new Ruby Dixon!" Harrison said as the photographer, a woman with tumbled red hair named Apple walked in. "Soon to be a best-selling novelist!"

"So you're a writer?" she asked.

Harrison had booked her for me, letting me know that she was only able to squeeze me in because she had cleared her schedule for

Christmas vacation. "She's the photographer to everyone who matters," Harrison had told me.

"Ruby's new book, *Chocolate in the Morning,* is coming out in a matter of months!" Harrison said. "It's so good, it's being rushed to press."

Apple reached down to adjust her light meter. "You'll have to get me a copy when it comes out. I read all my clients' books." She pointed to a wall behind all the equipment, its floor-to-ceiling bookcase lined with books.

"I'd be honored," I said, striking a chick pose.

I often felt as if I had, indeed, died and given my body over to ghostly spirits who forced me to stumble through the house, which was, as I packed, becoming more and more of a skeleton of a former home. There was the mommy spirit, wrenching me out of bed in the middle of the night to answer Dylan's cry or take out the trash before the four A.M. garbage run. Gently reminding Scout to finish her vocabulary words and dozing off in Becca's bed as she read a chapter of *Charlotte's Web* for Scout and me. The writer wraith would jerk me awake from my slumped position at the computer monitor and remind me to erase that page of j's I'd made when my index finger pressed into the keyboard as I dozed off. The wifely ghost was not a very good wife, I fear, but she did possess my body for the weekly coupling, probably motivated by the chance to warm her icy feet for the first time that day.

"Good morning! David Chong here," sang the realtor we'd listed with.

"Hi, David. How's it going?" Yesterday had been the first day our house was listed, and though the realtors would have preferred to have me out of the house I had remained in my room, typing away and trying to look thoughtful as flocks of potential buyers passed through, eyeing me and my bedroom with either embarrassment or glowing smiles.

"Your home, it is quite beautiful," one elderly Asian woman had told me with a bow. I'd returned the bow gratefully, glad that the kids had let me toss out broken toys and ship their favorites out to

Mimi's in New Jersey so there would be walking space in their rooms.

Only one day on the market and already this real estate business was taking a toll on me. Not yet engaged with the characters in my manuscript I was easily distracted, and each visitation ruined my focus for ten or twenty minutes. Someone had insisted on coming through at nine o'clock last night—a sleek couple who worked late, two doctors looking to leave Manhattan—and I'd let them peek in quietly and check out Dylan's room by the glow of his Jimmy Neutron nightlight, his gentle breathing the only sound in the room. As the female doctor had cooed over how cute he was, I'd hoped that the odd exposure wouldn't drive Dylan into therapy in later years, complaining of a subconscious memory of strangers watching him sleep.

Most of all, keeping the house neat for buyers was sort of like holding one's breath—indefinitely. Feeling weary and oxygen-deprived, I dared to ask David about the early feedback on the house.

"Very good news for you. We have two offers at full price."

The shock sent milk sloshing onto the counter. "Two? Full price?"

"Your house show very well. Very nice," he gushed.

I mopped up the spill as sweet adrenaline surged. Jack and I had argued with David, who didn't want us to make the listing price twenty grand higher than the last town house sale in our area. But we'd replaced the downstairs carpeting and refinished the wood floors in the hall just last year, and I knew our place was in better shape than most of the neighbors' houses, which hadn't seen a facelift since the days of Ward and June Cleaver.

"You were right to make that high price," David said, as if reading my silence. "I come over tonight and present you the offers. In the meantime, we still keep showing the house, in case something fall through."

"I'd rather not. Listen, I'll take my chances and recover my peace of mind and privacy. If both offers fall through, we'll list it again."

"Ah, but maybe you miss some very good buyers," David pointed out.

Listen, palsy, all we need is one, I wanted to say. Instead, I told him no more visitors, and called Jack with the good news.

"Unbelievable!" he said. "We should have listed it even higher!"

"I know, but David says they might have trouble getting a bank loan if we go too much higher."

"Who knew? Who knew we were sitting on a gold mine all these years. Holy crap!"

"I knew you'd be happy," I said, settling back down at the laptop.

"Happy?" He lowered his voice so that everyone at the station wouldn't hear. "I've got a woody to beat the band." The money-equals-power thing has always been good for Jack's virility. "I wish I could do you now."

I laughed, thinking that I'd have to wake up the wifely ghost this evening. "Hold that thought until you get home, and I might even whip out my little red nighty and play naughty schoolteacher with you." Jack loved it when I wore sexy lingerie with my eyeglasses.

"You're killing me."

"Now get back to work," I said, "or the naughty schoolteacher will have to punish you tonight," I said, picturing the sparkle of passion in his steely-gray eyes.

"Why work, when you make misbehaving so much fun?"

The house sale was one of the few smooth transitions. Becca began to have misgivings about the move when some of the girls in her core group of friends turned on her, excluding her from playdates and sleepovers because she was going to be leaving. Whether they felt betrayed or simply wanted to cut her loose before they'd invested any more emotion in friendship, I wasn't sure, but I felt sorry she'd had to learn this life lesson at such a young age. Scout was late with two school assignments, having decided that she was finished at P.S. 188, so what was the point of doing all that work? Jack felt that everyone at the station was now taking shots at him behind his back, calling him a "flipper" and "Benedict Salerno."

Only Dylan seemed unaffected, probably because he was unaware of the changes to come. "You're going to love your new home in Oregon," I told him one night as I chased him around with a towel, trying to dry his hair. It was a game we seemed to play after every bath, and I loved plucking at his downy curls with the fluffy towel, loved the way he cackled with glee whenever I caught him in my

arms, loved the sweet, baby-powder smell of his skin, especially the
rosy spot where I kissed him on the cheek. "You're going to have
your own room with a real bed. A big-boy bed."

That gave him pause, and he went over to his crib and slung an
arm up onto the lowered side gate. He'd been climbing in and out
for awhile so we just left it down for safety, but it was time to retire
the crib and move Dylan to a real bed. "No bed," he said, though it
came out sounding like "no bet." My son the gambler.

"A snuggly, soft big-boy bed," I said reassuringly, wrapping the
towel around him and scooping him in my arms. "You'll love it."

"Mommy, no." He flattened his chubby palms against my cheeks
and turned my face to meet his. "No bed."

"You're going to sleep so well in Oregon. Your bedroom is bigger,
more space for your toys. And there's a nice yard for running and
playing." His dewy brown eyes were fixed on mine, trusting yet
slightly concerned that I was speaking of foreign, incomprehensible
matters. "It's gonna be great!" I roared, reaching for a Pull-Up.

"Gonna be great!" he repeated, putting his hands up in the goal
sign his father had taught him. "No bed!"

"Oh, stop being a nagging bitch and just kiss the man," I said
aloud at the computer monitor, annoyed at the behavior of Faith,
my current heroine. Whenever I sat down to work in the pressure
tank of January my characters seemed hackneyed and shrill, and I
found myself fantasizing about writing inappropriate scenes that
would wake up my reader. What if the stressed-out heroine kicked
off her shoes and lit up a joint? What if she caught the hero parad-
ing in front of the mirror in her panties? What if they stopped playing the romance game, declared their love on page fifty and lived
happily ever after? Skimming through old favorite romance novels,
as I was frequently doing these days to stay on track, it was becoming
increasingly apparent that romance characters were patently proud,
egotistical and severely lacking in communication skills. If someone
in these books—anyone!—just took a moment to say what they were
really thinking, the story obstacles would have been solved immediately.

Still, I was producing my daily quota, sometimes working till two

AM to finish. I had moved my PC down to the dining room where a wall of boxes was forming like overgrown LEGOs. Whenever I felt blocked I grabbed one of the boxes the movers had delivered and stuffed it with old blankets, Halloween decorations or rarely used items like the Crock-Pot or the silver tea service my mother had given me as a wedding gift. Between writing and packing I had no time for anything else. My bangs had grown into my eyes. I owed Gracie two phone calls and cancelled a celebration lunch with Morgan. Harrison was threatening to disown me, but I warned him that I was not very pleasant to be around when I needed a haircut and a shower. After a pause, he'd conceded, though this reminded me that we had to get together before I left. Before I left? Sometimes, when I was scraping snow off the car windows in the morning or circling the school for a parking spot at dismissal, it seemed my departure was just a frothy dream.

And yet, the boxes added up quickly, and I was amazed at the junk four people and a baby could accumulate, much of which did not deserve to make the trip across the country. Broken plastic toys and old LPs that no charitable organization would accept cluttered our trash cans. It seemed silly to wrap a plastic air pellet gun the size of a small alligator in a plastic bag, but the New York City Department of Sanitation wanted everything bagged and I'd found that they tended to be prima donnas, leaving behind anything that wasn't encased in neatly tied-off plastic. In the corner of the living room I'd piled bags of clothes that could go in the charity bin at the supermarket. I called parents of the girls' friends and tried to pass off sleds and kiddy furniture and the basketball hoop and the backyard grill, but there were no takers. "We don't have the room to store a sled," said one mom, and everyone with a backyard already had a grill.

The carpool moms were not happy with me. From their looks of disbelief and questions about the level of civilization in Oregon— "Do they have cable?" and "How far will you need to drive to buy milk?"—I sensed their feelings of horror and betrayal. I had deigned to leave New York City, and although they couldn't fathom leaving themselves, there was a tinge of worry that my choice to leave was a statement that New York was yesterday's Apple Martini.

Becca's friends threw her a tearful farewell party, imparting her with a morose collage of photos framed in black with black doily matting. Funereal was the word that came to mind when she showed it to me.

"Why did they make everything black, Mom?" she asked, pressing her head to my rib cage and snaking her arms around my waist.

"Did they, maybe, think it was your favorite color?" I asked, and then told her we would reframe them once we arrived cross-country.

Usually I kept packing until I hit an impasse that made my writer's block seem easier by comparison. There were so many decisions to be made in the inventory/packing process. Jack had three racks of dress shirts, "Half of them crap," he said. But despite my nagging he couldn't find time to put aside the shirts he wanted to give away. Should I keep the bag of fabric scraps that I used for the kids' school projects and costumes? What about the gingerbread kit we'd never opened? Toss it or try to donate it to a food bank? Should we transport iron skillets and canned peaches across the country? What about the dirt weasel, a menacing, medieval device on a stick that Jack had bought from a TV commercial when he fancied himself a farmer?

And then there were the boxes and folders and bags of kiddy artwork and photographs of all our lives—an insurmountable mountain of memories and overexposed, shoddy camera work that slowed me down every time I approached with a pragmatic drive to weed through and straighten it all out. Do you toss out an overexposed photo that captures your son's delighted, gummy smile as he pulled himself up in his crib for the first time? The photo of a blue-gowned Becca crumpled on the steps of the stage, crying because the halo of her angel costume hurt her head? Or Scout shirtless in the fountains at the park, her pale skin slick as a mischievous grin lit her face?

One box contained photos of Jack and me taken before we had children, some before we were even married. Gracie and me with party hats at Times Square. Gracie, Harrison and me with the late actor Jerry Orbach inside Joe Allen's, where we'd noticed Jerry and his wife having dinner after a show. (Harrison had insisted, and Jerry didn't seem to mind.)

The Bayside Boys, back in the day when they had passable hairlines and waistlines.

There was a photo I'd taken in Antigua of Jack standing in front of a sailboat, the startling turquoise of the sail and sea bringing out the light in his eyes, so pale against his suntanned face.

During a group trip of twentysomething couples to Block Island, someone snapped a shot of Jack and me on a bluff, our hair blowing back, our peaked smiles revealing that we'd had too much to drink the night before but were able to sleep in.

That was the weekend Becca had been conceived, when I'd forgotten to pack my diaphragm and Jack had gotten a little too buzzed to worry about a condom. At twenty-seven, I'd felt well bonded to Jack, who'd been living with me in Manhattan for two years. I'd felt ready to move on to the next phase of my life: marriage, children, a house in the suburbs. Jack, on the other hand, was, at twenty-nine, very content with the status quo and worried about creating his own nest of torture, repeating the sins of his parents.

"But I'm not an alcoholic, and you're not your father," I'd said repeatedly, trying to calm his fears. "We're going to do things differently."

At the time, I checked out library books for him on risk-taking and self-help for the children of alcoholics. I pressed him to come along with me to the obstetrician, and he did, crying when he saw the little peanut moving inside me on the ultrasound. "We're having a baby," he'd said, taking my hand.

As if the marriage fairy had swooped down and hit him with the commitment stick, Jack decided then and there that we would get married at Queens City Hall that weekend. Operating under "total secrecy," as Jack put it, we met at City Hall. I'd brought Gracie to be my witness and maid of honor, Jack was supposed to choose a friend but ended up bringing his parents, which really curled my toes.

"So much for total secrecy," I'd said as I linked my arm through his and headed in the door.

When the ceremony was over, Gracie managed to get at least one photo of Jack and me sans les parents.

My eyes fell on a photo of Jack's mother at the cooking island in

their grandiose house, biting her lower lip in annoyance that someone would take her picture before she had a chance to primp—as if
she'd just snapped: "Cut that out!" or "Out of my kitchen!" or "I told
you not to take that!"

Studying the photo with a sigh, I realized that that was Mira's expression whenever she slipped and had "a little something to drink,"
which usually entailed a twenty-ounce tumbler half-full of whatever
alcoholic beverage she could get her hands on—white wine, vodka,
beer or whiskey. When it came to getting blotto, Mira wasn't choosey.

I flipped to a photo of Jack and his mother in her waterfront yard,
both of them looking strained and inconvenienced. There was no
explanation for Jack's desire to please his mother after the way she'd
mistreated him, creating an environment of fear and rage, blame
and distrust in their home. Ironically Jack still craved her approval,
and Mira still snapped at him and put him down whenever she got
the opportunity. Not that Jack's behavior was unusual. I'd read that
children tend to gravitate toward the parent who abuses them, always hoping to gain love and approval. I closed the box of photos
and dropped it into a cardboard box, where it fell with a dull thud.
Let the movers take it; there'd be time to sort through it on the
other side, buffered by time and distance.

Thank God Jack was able to let go now, able to move clear across
the country and leave his family and their web of torturous guilt behind. For that, I was proud of him. Now . . . If I could just get him to
sort through his dress shirts . . .

12

The Secret Society of Mommyhood

When Jack was called to Dallas during moving week, I thought my head would explode. "Aren't we moving to Portland so you don't get yanked to Dallas all the time?" I sputtered as I sorted through drugs in the medicine cabinet, tossing out kids' Tylenol that was too gunked up and eye drops for pink eye that had expired. Jack's usual response—a silent sulk as he loaded up his garment bag—sent me off on a rant that fueled my packing, getting me through the kitchen drawers and the deep, dark cabinet over the fridge.

I was fuming the next day when Morgan called to check in. I gave her an earful of anti-Jack propaganda. "He hasn't made a decision about any of the moving issues, the cars, the furniture. I can't even get him to sort through his goddamn dress shirts."

"Have you taken a good set of scissors to his goddamn shirts yet?" she asked slyly. "Perhaps he'll come alive when he finds his clothes sliced into swatches."

"I would, but my sewing shears are sealed into an unlabeled carton, somewhere around here."

"What's Jack's response to all this?"

"He says he's a simple guy with simple needs, not very good at sweating the details. Unless, of course, it means sweating on the phone with one of his Corstar bosses."

"I admit, simplicity can be a talent. It's nice to be free of attach-ments, not to give a rat's ass."

"I used to think the passive-aggressive thing worked for us. Low-maintenance Jack was quite attractive back in my twenties, but some-where along the way I decided I wanted a partner who cared about . . . things. Someone who appreciated the difference between a frothy, no-fat latte and coffee with skim milk, who thought it was worth driv-ing three extra miles to get a decent tuna salad sandwich."

"So you're thinking, underneath those jaded eyes he really does care; he's just playing a power game by not admitting it."

"He says that he trusts me to make the right choices."

"Passive-aggressive bullshit."

"Thank you for the validation."

"The upside is, he's not a complainer," Morgan said. "The down-side? They trick you into doing all the work."

When Morgan had to take another call, I reminded myself that this all would pass. Moving was an anomaly, a stress pot. Wasn't it up there on the top-ten list of major life stresses?

Left to my own devices for the worst of it, I reminded myself that Jack was a good husband, a fun friend and confidante, an under-standing, loving father. The whole Dallas thing was just about Jack trying to shine at his job, trying to appease the big guys. I also held on to the fact that we were getting the hell out of here despite his strong Queens connection, and maybe that alone was enough of a contribution to the move for Jack right now.

I made it through with the help of my family. I pulled the girls out of school and plunked them over at Amber's house for a few days of cousin bonding. The moving van had come and gone today, and after the crew left I'd walked around the near-empty house, past tufts of dust attached to walls that had once borne the dining room hutch or a chest of drawers, over pristine spots of carpeting that had been covered by beds or sofas. It seemed odd that these were the only remnants of the life scenes that had taken place here, the daily routines, the poignant moments. I sat on the old paisley chintz chair in our bedroom, one of the things we were leaving behind, and sunk into memories of Jack and me, snuggling together to watch *Jeopardy!* on this, our first joint purchase. Curling up, hugging my knees, I recalled those early years with Jack, the polite steps into a relationship, the newness of having a warm, breathing person in the same bed, the tentative dance of shared meals and newspapers, night walks and nightcaps that became routine. He'd sat on the arm of this chair and massaged my swollen feet when I was pregnant—all three times. In turn, the babies had nursed on this chair, spit up into the cracks of its seams, rammed their toys into the base of the upholstery. I laid my cheek against the arm of the chair, drained. "All that abuse. You served us well."

But the old chair, faded and smelling of Lysol, was to be left behind. I planned to put the last few items of furniture and chachkies out at the curb tomorrow—with some appealing signs taped to them, stating: TAKE ME! or THIS IS FREE!, so that passing motorists might make use of Dylan's crib, that hideous planter Mira had given us for Christmas or Becca's old desk—before Sanitation came along to throw them in the junk heap. Morgan, good friend and great agent, was coming in the morning to help me move a few last things out and take me to the airport. After I grieved the loss of the old chair, I ran the vacuum borrowed from my sister, then showered and hopped a train to Manhattan, knowing that this truly was my last chance to say good-bye to my best friends in the world.

"Here's to Ruby and the big move," Harrison said, lifting his martini glass. "Enjoy those greener pastures, those gargantuan trees you keep raving about, the proliferation of drive-up cafés and microbrews." His eyes matched the green of his shirt and the hue of the shiny skewered olives in his glass. Leave it to Harrison to order a drink because of its complimentary colors. "Here's to you, kid! Westward Ho!"

"Are you calling me a ho?" I quipped before clinking glasses with him and Gracie and sipping my margarita.

Gracie nibbled at her virgin margarita—she'd groused that she had a migraine when she ordered it—then set it aside, clearly not in a party mood. Her curly orange hair, usually the color of a copper penny, was wound into a coil pierced by chopsticks atop her head. Beneath the mound of twisted curls her gray roots were in evidence. Gracie going gray . . . It was the first time I had ever noticed, the first time she'd ever let her hair go this long, apparently, and I took the roots and the migraine to mean that things were not going well with Fernando. Fernando was her on-again, off-again steady, the guy who seemed most compatible with Grace but for the fact that he didn't want to commit.

Should I ask the dreaded Fernando question, or just hope that her bad mood would evaporate? I was hours away from departure, the kids tucked away at my mother's house in Jersey till our flight out of Newark tomorrow.

"So you found a house?" Harrison asked without a trace of awkwardness. It was as if he was asking if I'd downloaded the soundtrack from *The Boy From Oz* onto my iPod yet. "A lovely suburban home for your two point five children and dog?"

I nodded. "I think we will have to get the dog to appease Becca, but she's had a puppy on her wish list for years and, well, I guess I can potty train Dylan and the dog together."

"Okay, there's too much information." Harrison sipped his martini carefully. "And really, Ruby, usually you're good about filtering out the inane child-rearing tedium. I've got to say, the mommy thing didn't warp your personality, thank God. I lost three friends when they had children. Jill and Stephanie seem to have suffered a brain lapse and now their only topic of conversation is their children. And then there's Willow, who won't leave New Jersey now. She actually asked me to come out for a soccer game last year. And a birthday party with laser tag. Has she lost her mind?"

"Willow never had much use for the urban scene. She was an urban poser," Gracie pointed out. "And she was always trying to sell me on something: vitamins, then Amway, then knockoff handbags. I was glad when she dried up in the Garden State."

"Haven't you heard? She's selling Tupperware now," Harrison teased. "And she wants to have a party at *your* apartment." On the emphasized "your" he pointed a finger at her dramatically.

Ignoring him, Gracie reached across the table and pressed her fingers onto the back of my hand. She manacled my wrist and gave it a shake. "But you . . . I never thought you'd leave New York. I mean, you married the King of Queens. Jack breaks a sweat when he leaves the outer boroughs. What are you guys thinking, moving so far away?" Her amber eyes glistened with unshed tears.

"We just want a break from the frenzied level of pressure that drives our every move here," I said, thinking that they might understand that aspect of our choice. "And then there's the career boost for Jack, more space for the kids, a slower pace, a lower cost of living. And of course, those magnificent trees," I finished with a sanguine shot at Harrison.

But Harrison curled back into himself in horror, arms crossed over his olive-lime sweater as he observed Gracie's emotional meltdown.

"I can't believe you're leaving me now . . ." Gracie sobbed, "now, when I really need you."

Harrison squirmed, uncomfortable with raw emotion, and I felt myself wanting to do the same but Gracie held my arm so tightly I didn't want to move and make her think I was flicking her off. Gracie and I had been friends for years, good friends. When we'd been newbies at the insurance firm, we'd been inseparable, sharing lipsticks, handing off wrong-match guys and bailing each other out of bad dates and heartbreaks. Our jobs, revising and filing forms with state insurance commissions, were so tedious and undemanding that we poured ourselves into our social lives, throwing impromptu parties and diverting each other for inspired shopping trips. However, after I left the insurance biz we drifted apart, reconnecting only every month or so. At times we'd gone for weeks, even months without seeing each other, which made it that much more surprising that Gracie was having trouble letting me go now.

"Oh, Gracie, I'll miss you, too," I said. "But I'll be back for visits. And you can come out and stay with us."

"Really, Grace," Harrison chastised her. "With Ruby living on the West Coast you'll probably see even more of her now. That's how random the universe is."

"But I need you here now," Gracie whined. Although her thick mascara remained intact, her eyes and nose were turning red. "You guys can be the first to know, I guess. I mean, when else would I tell you if you're outta here? I'm having a baby, and right now I'm feeling pretty lost about the whole thing."

"You're pregnant?" I felt my eyes bulge. Apparently I'd missed quite a bit by cancelling our last few dates, but now it all made sense—the virgin margarita, the moodiness, the gray roots. "Gracie . . ."

"Hence the hormonal tears," Harrison deduced. "Face it, nobody's going to miss Ruby enough to merit tears."

Although I appreciated his levity in the heat of Gracie's crisis, I couldn't resist the opportunity to flick him across the table.

He turned to Gracie. "Well, this is unexpected . . . that you're expecting. Although I was going to get on you for looking like death warmed over, but now I'll be kind."

She shot him a barbed look and a mocking laugh came out between sobs.

I reached toward Gracie, my voice full of concern. "Does Fernando know?"

"It's not Fernando's baby." She released my arms and gently pressed her hands to her flat belly. "I broke it off with him a few months ago, for good, I hope. Freakin' mama's boy."

"Then who, pray tell, is the lucky daddy?" Harrison asked, scooping salsa with a chip.

Gracie pressed her napkin to her mouth and muttered. "I think it's this college kid."

"Again . . . in conventional English?" Harrison prodded.

"It's probably this NYU student I was sleeping with, and I don't want to ruin his life over this because, really, we have nothing in common, zero relationship. It was all about the sex."

"You don't feel morally obliged to tell him?" Harrison asked.

"Not at all. I figure his karma will thank mine, someday, when he's got his own neat little life free of guilt and child-support payments."

"And you don't need the money," Harrison said. "Thank God for that." Gracie had studied like mad and taken the battery of tests to become a full-fledged actuary. Although petite, red-haired Gracie was not the conservative naysayer one pictured when thinking of the number crunchers who jacked up insurance rates, the job paid her six figures back when the rest of us were lucky to top fifty grand a year. She owned a Manhattan condo, a house in Westchester near the corporate office, and a beach house in Surf City, down on the Jersey shore. Financially, Gracie was golden. Her baby would be

born with a silver spoon . . . and excellent mental and dental cover-
age.

"Aren't we skipping ahead here?" I asked, trying not to react emotionally to Gracie's news yet. "I mean, it sounds like you're having
the baby. Is that what you've decided?"

"Well, yeah." Gracie dipped a chip in guacamole. "I've always
wanted a baby."

In my mind nothing was further from the truth. At my baby
shower, Gracie had remained aloof, hovering near the door, making
jokes about how she'd better avoid the water lest my condition be
contagious, and about how much the Diaper Genie resembled a
bread maker.

"And I'm turning thirty-five and there's no prospect in sight. If
not now, when? When would it happen for me?"

It was clear that Gracie had thought this through without my help
or input. It made me feel a little guilty but proved Harrison's point
about distance being relative. In the past few months I'd been less
than ten miles from her apartment and we hadn't been able to connect at all.

"If that's what you want, honey, then I'll do everything I can to
help you." I put my hand on her back and gave her a gentle massage
between the shoulder blades. "Actually, have I got a deal for you. A
charming sleigh-style crib in bleached oak. And tons of baby clothes
for a boy."

"Dylan's crib? Oh, Ruby, that would mean so much to me."

"Not that you'll need it for awhile, but I've got to get rid of it, like,
now."

"November," she said. "I'm not due till November, but I'll put it in
storage."

"And I'm not going anywhere, though you might wish otherwise,"
Harrison said. "I can't offer much beyond the loan of my significant
other, but you know I'll be here for you when it's time to take the kid
to see *Nutcracker* or *Peter Pan* on Broadway." This last bit surprised
me, as Harrison had met Gracie through me. Sure, we'd all partied
together plenty of times, however, I didn't think they'd ever spoken
to each other on the phone aside from planning my baby shower.

Corny though it seemed, I was glad they'd found each other before I left town.

"Thanks, you guys." Gracie stretched her arms out to our shoulders and pulled us close, in a huddle over the table. "I'm really going to need you with this single-parent business. Harrison, you may have to be the surrogate daddy."

"Oh? Well . . . Let's not get too crazy with this. I was born without the paternity gene."

Gracie and I laughed. "Don't worry. I'm not asking you to be my childbirth coach."

"Now that's a relief," he said. "Of course, Goldberg will be thrilled. He's got lots of nieces and nephews. Totally in tune with runny noses and screaming monsters. You two will have to get together and debate the merits of breast milk over formula."

Hearing them plan, I felt a sliver of sadness that I wouldn't be around as Gracie made the move into the mommy world. Of course, I'd never expected to see Gracie have a baby at all, but now that it was happening I wanted to be involved. "Maybe I can fly back for the birth!" I said. "Or at least for the first week, after you come home from the hospital. That can be the hardest time. I'll be your doula."

"Would you? That would be so perfect." Gracie hugged me again as Harrison sat back and reached for the nachos.

"I don't know what a doula is," he said, scooping sliced olives, "but judging from the way it sounds, feel free to keep it a secret in the society of mommyhood."

Part Two

If I'm a Domestic Goddess, Where's the God?

13

Ms. Bliss

Fast-forward to domestic bliss.

It was April, almost two months since we'd landed in Oregon, three weeks since our furniture arrived and we'd been able to move into our house. I'd triaged the unpacking, purchased a new chair for the master bedroom, and realized that nesting was a process that unwound over time, not the procedure of emptying a box and leaving its contents scattered in the family room, as Jack kept trying to do.

Life was good. Well, at least it was better.

The Portland office seemed to be low maintenance for Jack. Now his only stress was the barrage of phone calls from the Dallas office, from Tiger and Hank and Desiree and even Big Bob, the grand *fromage* of the corporation. Now that we'd left New York, it was as if they'd suddenly discovered his cell phone number.

My new job title was chief assimilator. Now that beds, towels, linens, and pots and pans were in place, I kept the extras in boxes and allowed myself two shopping trips a week to browse for accents that fit this house—chachkies for the wide kitchen windowsills, hanging plants for the trellis out back, a dinosaur border for the walls of Dylan's room. With our sofa and loveseat filling the family room, our new living room sat empty, a dance studio and gymnastics arena for the kids. I wasn't sure how I wanted to decorate this spacious room and I told Jack I was allowing myself the luxury of time to shop and mull it over.

"Take your time," he kept telling me. "Just don't be shocked when the people from the station start talking about us."

The station . . . I'd forgotten that, in Jack's new position, we'd be expected to entertain colleagues and clients, throw a few humble but elegant dinners designed to reinforce just how much fun it is to do business with Jack.

"Can we stave them off?" I stood at the kitchen counter leafing through a flyer from a local furniture company while I waited for the coffee to drip. One after another, assortments of room furniture made me frown. Leather sofas resembling beached whales, burgundy or olive velveteen with tons of throw cushions that would be in permanent disarray in my household. Who bought this stuff, and where did people find their nice furnishings? It was as if there was a supersecret sofa source that kept eluding me. "Why don't you drop some hints about entertaining in the fall? I'll have this place whipped into shape by September, October at the latest."

"Fat chance." Jack pulled the carafe out to pour a cup, and although it was designed to interrupt brewing, a few drops always sizzled on the burner. "We gotta get 'em here sooner, Rubes."

"August? July? Don't these people take family vacations?"

"That's why I was thinking June," Jack said. "Before the kids get out of school. In fact, Connor already hinted around that his schedule's open in June."

Connor Gibbs was a lean, mean general manager machine, an avid runner with shaved head, pushing sixty we suspected. Calm and polite, Connor delivered ideas, strategies and anecdotes in the dulcet tones of a country preacher. In the few times I'd met him I'd felt compelled to press my palms together in prayer position and listen with rapt attention, lest I be called upon to fall to my knees and repent.

I didn't fancy having Connor Gibbs in my new home, not this soon. "That's not fair," I protested. "Don't they realize we just moved here?" I didn't like being rushed, especially since no one in Oregon was doing the hustle. People at the grocery checkout would hold up a long line so they could chat with the eternally cordial cashier about the weather, their kids, or the taste of a new energy drink. Sometimes I wanted to wave from the back and yell: "Yelllo? There's a bunch of us waiting here!"

"Don't freak." Jack palmed the KJZM station mug with one hand. "We'll bring the lawn furniture in, if we need it."

"No, we won't," I said. We had purchased the patio furniture from the previous owners, and while the voluminous Grand Bahamian wicker with floral print cushions made me want to kick off my shoes and sip a cool mint mojito, it would not pass muster indoors unless we were trying to replicate the set of the *Golden Girls*. I scrunched up the furniture flyer. "This stuff is crap. I finally have the money and space to have a real living room and I hate everything."

He finished his coffee and placed the dirty mug on the counter. "You're so emotional, Ruby. Don't take it too seriously. It's just a room."

"A room to you. A manifestation of my creative expression and homemaking abilities to me."

Jack pinched the bridge of his nose, a sign of tension that I couldn't recall seeing since we'd moved here.

"What's the matter? I'm not complaining about decorating, sweetie. I mean, this is all good. You just go to work and kick some lazy Oregonian butt, honey." Since Jack had joined KJZM Portland, his biggest problem had been getting people to move. Perhaps lazy was the wrong word. His staff worked at their jobs, but their pace was so slow Jack felt as if he'd stepped into a time warp. When he tried to light a few fires under his staff, people nodded and answered: "You bet!" or "I'm on it!" And then they got back to their jobs at their usual slow-as-molasses pace.

He pulled me close, cupping my bottom with one hand. "That part's easy. It's explaining the lazy Oregonian butts to Dallas that's the problem."

I looked behind me at his hand. "That's no lazy butt you're holding there."

He gave a squeeze. "All New York Prime. That's why I like you so much."

Hugging him, I decided not to remind him that I'd actually grown up in New Jersey. Jack was scheduled to fly down to Dallas on

Monday, his first time away since we'd moved here, and it seemed to signal the end of an era, the end of our adjustment to our new lives. The moving honeymoon would be over.

"It's all good," I said, my lips against his neck, and though he didn't speak, I sensed his usual answer, the dubious "I hope so," of a former lost boy.

Our embrace ended with the ring of his cell phone. He left for work with it pressed to his ear, telling Tiger he would look into—something I couldn't hear—for her.

I woke the girls, who came downstairs with bedraggled hair and glassy eyes.

"Waffles, please!" Scout chorused as she tucked her feet under a sofa cushion and clicked on the television.

Becca put her well-worn, folded section of newspaper on the kitchen island and sat on a stool. "Good morning, Mom. Do you think you'll have time to maybe call some of these breeders today?" she asked so politely my heart squeezed.

I thought of my to-do list—the outline I was writing for Padama Kahil, my new editor, checking in with Morgan, the living room furniture I needed to order pronto, and the matter of chasing a bare-bottomed Dylan around in an attempt at potty training. More than my fill of chores, but Becca had been mulling over the classified ads for American Kennel Club puppies for the past month, patiently waiting for either Jack or me to have time to call and inquire about some of her picks. In the past two weeks a Pug she'd been interested in and two Cavaliers had dropped out of the ads, presumably snatched up by eager pet buyers, and Becca had lamented the possibility of missing out on the perfect pet. Having done her doggy research, she'd narrowed her desires down to three breeds that fit our requirement for a dog that wouldn't grow to be bigger than Dylan: a Chinese Pug, a Welsh Corgi and a Cavalier King Charles Spaniel. Back in New York Becca had fallen in love with a Cavalier in a pet store, a fluffy little puppy with cinnamon and white patches. But its eyes seemed swollen with something like pinkeye and it yapped incessantly, reminding me of the warnings from friends to avoid buying from pet stores. Every time she visited that dog, she'd found it hard to say good-bye.

"I will make time to call some breeders today," I told Becca, rubbing the back of her T-shirt as we both looked down at the ads she'd highlighted in yellow and pink. "Why don't you take one last look and number the ads, with one being your top choice?"

"Okay." She hopped down from the stool and went to the drawer for a pen, her freckled face so smooth it reminded me of an old TV ad for cornflower powder. Gone were the purple half moons under her eyes and the gray pallor that had given her that haunted look when we lived in New York. Soon after we'd moved here Becca had begun to fall asleep at night, sometimes conking out so quickly that I didn't have time to start reading a book to her.

Our Becca had found a place in the world where she felt safe.

After breakfast the girls grabbed their lunches and headed off to school.

"Bye, Mom!" they called as their bikes rolled down the driveway.

"Scout, strap your helmet, please," I said as I ventured down the driveway in my sweatshirt and flannel pajama pants with pink flying pigs, hoping no one would pass as I bent down to pick up the familiar blue bag that contained the *New York Times*. It was the same telltale blue bag that our *Times* had been delivered in back in Bayside. Apparently, the blue bag was nationwide. My friend Hal, from insurance firm days, moved to the suburbs of Jersey after living twenty years in Manhattan. He admitted that he'd spent one Sunday morning driving around the neighborhood, counting the number of blue bags on lawns in the five-block radius surrounding his new home. Hal had been encouraged when he discovered more than twenty of his neighbors subscribed to the newspaper that he felt sure would keep their minds open, stimulated and reasonable. I thought Hal's survey was a good way to gauge the neighborhood and possibly build a list for Christmas parties, but so far I hadn't noticed any other blue bags on lawns in our development.

As luck would have it, our neighbor Eric Lundquist chose that time to back down his driveway. A discreet person would have been satisfied with a quiet wave, but not Eric. He rolled down the window and leaned out. "Hey, neighbor," he said, reminding me of a character in a Chevy Chase movie. He nodded at my newspaper. "*New York Times*, eh? You guys just can't let go, can you?"

I held the blue bag behind my back, as if it was dirty underwear. "But we're equal-opportunity readers. We get the *Oregonian,* too," I said, pointing to the clear plastic bundle in the middle of the driveway as he chuckled. That was Eric's schtick; he was always chuckling with forced amusement at something Jack or I did. Oh, those wacky New Yorkers!

"You and Jack are so funny," he said, backing out without looking away from me. An orange and black Beavers flag flapped from his car—the Oregon State Beavers. Eric's got lots of Beavers paraphernalia and flags, which I always found ironic since he's got a stubby, flattop haircut and a pronounced overbite. Go Beavers!

I turned and motioned for Becca to stay clear of his driveway; Eric drove in the manner of someone not accustomed to avoiding kids and animals.

"Come on, Scout. Don't make us late," Becca called from the end of the driveway.

"I'm trying!" Scout was struggling with a knot, trying to adjust the strap of her helmet.

"Let me help." I took the helmet and found the strap tangled like sticky spaghetti.

"I don't believe you, Scout." With cool impatience, Becca rolled her bike back toward us, scooped up the *Oregonian,* and found her section. I heard a gasp, then she was back to her angelic voice. "Oh, Mom, there's a Cavalier. A female Blenheim! You have to call. Adams Family Farms. That's my new first choice."

I nodded, my eyes and fingertips on the knots. "Great, honey." Once I'd fixed the strap, Scout quickly pulled on her helmet and rolled away before my hand could pat the back of her T-shirt.

I waved good-bye and, seeing Scout wobble slightly on the bicycle that was probably too large for her short legs, ran back into the kitchen to write myself a note about a story element.

I wrote:

She grew up in Manhattan. Can't ride bike. He plans bike ride upstate/Central Park. Comedic antics ensue.

Hmm . . . a tad goofy, but at this point nothing could be ruled out. I was in the throes of outlining my next women's mainstream novel, which Morgan and Padama Kahil kept asking for. Being thousands of miles from Manhattan, I was finding it hard to muster enthusiasm and cull memories of the Big Apple, finding it hard to get excited about a handful of women who survived by the strength of their manicure, Grapefruit Martinis and palsy female camaraderie. Even in my last years in New York City, there'd been few opportunities to dine in restaurants sans booster seats and Crayolas on the table, and gone were the days when I could stay out late because I'd met an interesting man or spend the evening in an impromptu pub crawl with Gracie and the bevy of neurotic single women who liked to travel through Manhattan nights in packs.

The truth: after just one novel, I had lost touch with my muse. The quietly desperate, jaded girl in my head had stopped slinging sardonic wit into my psyche.

And why? I was just finding it plain hard to shed my bliss at nesting in this fabulous new place and slither back into my writer's shell, and, oddly enough, I didn't worry much about it. Instead, I wallowed in the surge of fresh air as I walked with Dylan down that lane that led to his Montessori school, both of us dwarfed by enormous fir trees taller than the spires of Gothic cathedrals. I spent half an hour each evening reading my son a story in bed. I went about my errands, giddy with the ease of finding a parking spot, of having the clerk look me in the eye and smile, of receiving help with my groceries (and no tip expected) and having a latte card at the local café.

No doubt about it; I was living the American dream.

"Aren't you bored?" Morgan asked one spring morning when we checked in via phone. "I'm still having trouble imagining you in suburbia. Don't you ever drive down the road, past one strip mall after another or phoney Tudors or Mission-style MacMansions in a development and get that trashy suburban ennui? That's how I feel when I wander out to Jersey or Long Island. It's scary."

"But it's so beautiful, like a secret garden that happens to have lots of Starbucks. Baskets dripping with flowers hang from every lamppost. The street dividers are bursting with tulips, red and yellow and pink. There's this busy intersection up the hill, surrounded by stores and shops, and when I get stuck there in my car waiting for the light, I sit back and gape at these amazingly tall fir trees rising over the Shell Station. I ran into a city engineer last week who told me some of the trees in West Green are over two hundred years old."

"Every day is Arbor Day in West Green," Morgan muttered, not falling for my newfound love of all things green. "Tell me, Nature Girl, is there anything about New York that you miss?"

"I miss my friends," I admitted. "You, and Harrison and Gracie. She's in her second trimester now and it's killing me not to be there for her."

"Well, I'm glad you haven't lost all reason, though I'm sure you'll make new friends there in the Garden of Eden. No agents there, of course, but plenty of friends."

"I'm not so sure about that," I said as I pulled open the plantation blinds in my office, the gray, watery light of an overcast sky filling the room. "People are friendly up front, but it's hard to peel down to the next layer of the onion. And God forbid you cut right to the heart—"

"—the way a New Yorker would," Morgan put in.

"Exactly. Push, even a little, and people either back away or clench their teeth like you've pinned them to a mat. I'm just not used to the dance . . . the slow approach, circling, bowing. Do-si-do."

"Give it time," Morgan said. "Your New York friendships didn't happen overnight. You and I knew each other for a year before we really started talking on a regular basis."

I knew Morgan was right; solid friendships evolved. And, really, what did I expect from the people I'd met here? It wasn't as if I'd invited the school moms over for coffee, or Eric over for a family barbecue. But in my New York way I wanted the deluxe girlfriend package, *now.* "Even a casual friend would do. My hair is a nightmare—so long I can barely see anymore, but I can't just walk in somewhere and ask for a haircut. I called one salon that looked okay, but then when they asked who I wanted, I couldn't bear to fall into just anyone's chair."

"A salon slut?"

"Exactly, but there's no one I can ask for a referral except my realtor, and since she gave me my doctor, dentist and cleaning lady, I just hate bugging her for one more thing."

"What about the school moms?" Morgan asked.

"I rarely see them since the girls love riding their bikes to school."

"You'll just have to come back to New York six times a year so you can visit Vita at Melange Salon."

"That would be one expensive haircut."

"You're talking to a woman who's commuted from New York to Boston for a martini."

Morgan had hooked up with a man in Boston last year at Christmastime, a teacher at Harvard named Ronald Goldsmith whom I'd taken to calling the Professor. Her children disapproved, unwilling to share their mother after having her to themselves all these years. Personally, I thought they needed to move on, but then I didn't lose my dad to a Harley.

"How is the Professor?" I asked.

"A dream. He's coming for Memorial Day weekend. Staying in a hotel, of course."

"Is this the first time for the kids?" I asked. TJ and Clare were in college, but I realized they'd be out of school this time of year.

"Yep. I don't know what to expect when they meet him—a scene from *Desperate Housewives* or *Survivor.*"

"Afraid they'll vote him off the island?"

"If they don't string him up and roast him over a pit."

Not having older kids with parenting issues, I was in unfamiliar territory here. "Relax. If you're crazy about him, they're bound to like him. They'll see his good qualities."

"Somehow, I don't think the fact that he's good in bed will impress them." As Morgan deliberated whether to sneak off for an overnight with the Professor at his hotel or invite him to stay over at her place, I logged onto MapQuest and typed in the addresses of the breeders I'd spoken to. Kathy Adams, the Cavalier owner, already had one interested party. That made my competitive New York instinct kick in. We now had an appointment for us to meet the pup.

"Don't think I don't hear you clicking away," Morgan said. "Are you writing while I'm spilling my guts to you?"

I explained about the puppy quest.

"Becca's been doing so well since we got here," I told Morgan. "We've all benefitted from the move. But Jack leaves for Dallas Monday—his first trip away from us since we moved—and I worry that Becca's fear of crashing airplanes will rear its ugly head again. Not to mention my state of mind, which tends to deteriorate quickly without adult company."

"Mmm . . ." Morgan understood. "I remember how long the weekends seemed when he who shall remain unnamed left. The kids would go to Grandma's for a weekend, which should have been a good thing, but I felt so alone and abandoned. I'd walk down to the deli to get a sandwich and strike up a conversation with the deli man, all the while nervous that I was talking too much or too little, that the people in line were getting irate because I was so chatty. I felt sure they could tell I didn't get out enough. I felt like a moron. I was losing my powers of speech by not using them."

"Well," I said, pulling the map to the breeder out of the printer, "if worse comes to worst, I can talk to the puppy."

"Who will probably be a better listener than any husband," Morgan said. "Definitely get the dog. If you want someone to come home to, it better be four-legged and furry."

14

Afternoon Shmooze

After a spring of gray skies and brief but frequent showers, we awoke Memorial Day weekend to vaulting blue skies with the promise of temperatures soaring near eighty degrees.

We started the day with coffee "on the veranda," barefoot and in our boxers, something we never could have done back in Queens, where our neighbors' homes peered into our backyard. While Jack fielded a business call on his cell, I played a game Dylan had created, in which he came to the table for a handful of Cheerios, crowed: "Sank you, Mommy!" then ran off and ate them at strategic points in the garden, by the pink flowering rhododendrons, on the flagstone path, near the azalea bushes that had shed their bright red petals onto the bark dust. Occasionally I suffered a lack of control and snatched up my son for a hug, nuzzling his chubby cheek that smelled of baby powder–scented soap. He giggled, then demanded freedom to fulfill his Cheerio mission, and I reluctantly released him.

Although Jack had finished his call, he seemed oblivious to this game, distant and unattached, like a passerby who'd stopped in for coffee. His mind was elsewhere, probably wrapped up in the details of his itinerary of next week's trip to Dallas. "Dylan never could have played this game in New York," I mused, trying to draw Jack in. "Not in that mud pit of a yard we had."

"Nope. This is spectacular!" Jack tossed his newspaper onto

the table and leaned back into the sunshine, his arms stretched wide in an expansive yawn. "It's like California."

"Without the traffic," I said, resting my mug on the arm of the wicker chair. Overhead wispy threads of clouds traveled slowly through the cerulean sky, reminding me that I was on a beautiful spot on this spinning planet. All around me birds chirped, insects darted into the cool shade of shrubs, and young blooms strained toward the sunshine. "I love this," I said wistfully. "Does that mean I'm getting old? I mean, I never was a garden sitter before."

Jack rubbed his jaw, not liking my comment for some reason. "Yeah, it's nice. Right, Dylan?" He turned and spotted Dylan in the corner of the garden, beside a bed of yellow and purple tulips. "Hey! Don't do that there!" Jack yelled, jumping to his feet. "He's copping a squat!"

I glanced over and confirmed. Yes, Dylan was in poop position.

"When's he going to learn to stop shitting in his pants?" Jack asked indignantly. "He's two now and doesn't have a clue. The girls weren't like this."

"He's a boy," I said defensively, ruffled by Jack's anger. "I've read that boys are harder to potty train, and if you remember clearly, the girls weren't completely trained when they were two." I wanted to add: "And you never show him how," but I knew that would turn Dylan's transgression into a full-fledged argument, since we'd been over this territory countless times before. Jack had been so patient when it was time to potty train the girls. He'd sat with them in the bathroom, reading storybooks. He'd instituted the Gummy Bear reward system for each time they made it to the bathroom. When he went out with the girls and they needed to go, he'd thrown himself at the mercy of New York shop owners, guiding them into the back of bagel shops and ice-cream parlors. He'd understood that toilet training was a process, not a quick, one-time lesson.

Unfortunately, Dylan didn't receive the same attention from Jack, not just in potty training, but all around—at mealtime or bedtime. Not that Jack would turn Dylan away if he crawled onto his lap, but Jack rarely swooped down and spontaneously pulled our toddler into his arms. One night when I noticed that he didn't kiss Dylan good night, Jack claimed he didn't want to wake him, but I smelled a lie. He'd always kissed the girls, even Becca at her most colicky was afforded a whisper of a kiss if she ever fell asleep. I'd called Jack on this behavior a few times, and he sloughed it off as being the mellowness of dealing with the third child. "You know how that goes. How you take a bazillion pictures of the first baby, dozens of pictures of the second, and one roll of film for the third? It happens to everyone when the novelty of the baby thing wears off."

Well, novelty or not, I didn't care to miss our son's childhood.

Jack strode toward Dylan, a man on a mission. "I don't know. Maybe we should have him checked," Jack said.

As if there's something wrong with him? I felt hurt as Jack took him by the hand and marched him toward the French doors. "Here, go with Mommy," he said sternly, leaving the cleanup to me. I was tempted to tell Jack, the potty training expert, to change the goddamn Pull-Up himself, but worried that he'd say some awful things to Dylan. Instead, I took Dylan's pudgy hand in mine and led him inside, feeling a new protective patience toward my son . . . our son, despite the fact that Jack always told people Dylan was "an oops baby." That always made me cringe, and I worried that someday Dylan would hear it.

That morning, I was so annoyed with Jack that I relished his departure Monday morning. I realized that his position here in Portland carried more pressure, more hurdles, not to mention the fact that he was a stranger to West Coast culture. But still . . . to take it all out on a two-year-old? *Go to Dallas,* I thought. *Go, score points with Mr. Hazelnut, advance your career, bring home the bacon and leave the rest of us here to enjoy life.*

I hoped that Jack's former self, the engaging, charming Jack, would return with him next week. Surprisingly, I didn't have to wait that long.

As the afternoon air began to bake with that dry, arid heat of a desert, we decided to take Debbie Tory's advice and head to the swim park, a small park on Lake Green that had its season opener this weekend. Having only walked past the tall fence at the park's perimeters, we weren't sure what to expect, so we packed up towels and sunscreen and Floaties and headed down the road.

We passed through the gates and down a swirl of stone steps to the magnificent grassy slope of lawn shaded by a stand of Douglas firs. A teenager at the old snack shack near the park entrance waved us over, checked our ID and issued us a park pass for the season. A tall boy with sculpted cheekbones and a blond fro that reminded me of Richard Simmons, pointed to the array of snacks behind him— everything from hot dogs to popcorn to candy bars I hadn't seen since childhood—and gave us a rundown on all the sports equipment available. Ping-pong, basketball, badminton, shuffleboard.

Jack shot me a sidebar as we walked down the gentle slope toward the water. "Are we in the Adirondacks? The Catskills? Who the hell plays shuffleboard?"

I nodded toward the empty shuffleboard court on the right. "Apparently, no one."

The kids skipped ahead, smiling back at us when they spotted some classmates from school.

"Hey, Scout," one boy called as he waved, eager for her attention.

"Hey." She casually slung her beach towel over one shoulder.

"You wanna play badminton?" he asked, spinning a racket in one hand.

"Who is this guy?" Jack muttered to me. "Biff from Princeton?"

"I don't know how," Scout answered.

"Come on, I'll show you," the freckle-faced Biff said, and they went running off.

Becca hooked up with Madison, her best friend from school, and Dylan found his way to the short cyclone fence of the kiddy pool. "Dylan splishy-splash in pool? Dylan's boats?"

"You can swim in the pool, honey, but they're not your boats." As I guided him in through the gate, a mom I recognized from the Montessori school called a warm greeting. "Look, Zack, Dylan is here to play with you. Can you share your boats with him?" Zack floated a boat toward Dylan, then turned away to launch it underwater. "We have lots of extras," Zack's mom said, handing a boat to Dylan.

"Thanks. Can you say thank you, Dyl?" I stepped into the water of the wading pool. "I'm Ruby. I've seen you at the school pickup and drop-off."

"Hilary Parker," she said, sitting back on the edge of the pool. Hilary was a heavyset blonde with a sunny smile and a precision haircut that did the most to minimize the volume of her face and chins. Dressed in a discreet black tankini with shorts, she could have been a plus model for a sportswear catalog. From her meticulous appearance and gift of gab, she could have been a talk show host. She introduced me to two other parents of toddlers, a shy dad named Ken, and Barb, another Montessori mom who seemed happy to be on the receiving end of Hilary's running commentary.

"Is that your husband over there?" Hilary asked, shielding her eyes from the sun.

"And my two daughters," I said. "It's our first time here."

"Oh, well you just go and join the family," Hilary said. "I'll watch the little guys. Zack is happy to have another playmate, right Zack?"

With his boat coursing through the water, Zack didn't seem to care less, but I accepted Hilary's offer and headed out of the fenced-off kiddie area.

Being off Mommy Alert, I had my first chance to really take in the swim park, this shady parcel of land punctuated by Oregon's trademark towering fir trees. Picnic tables were scattered here and there among the trees, and Jack had paused by one occupied table, engaged in conversation. I spotted Scout playing badminton on one of the side lawns, but kept moving down the slope toward the sparkling main attraction, the lake.

A network of wooden docks stretched out from the shoreline, like an abbreviated crossword puzzle. Cement stairs had been built into the water's edge, but most of the swimming seemed to be taking place in the deep water, where Becca was now doing cannonballs and backward jumps with her friends. Floating buoys marked off the swimming section from boaters, who passed by, towing inflated riding tubes, wakeboards or kneeboards. People waved and hooted from their boats, and the dock thrummed with laughter and spontaneous dares. Party central.

I paused at the end of the dock without making the turn toward the swimmers, not wanting to cramp Becca's style with her new friends or get splashed by the jovial activity out there. From here, the lake seemed so accessible—a cool, watery home, and all mine. I sat cross-legged in the sun and studied the small, uninhabited island that sported two tall trees, one with a large bird nest. Beyond the small island, the houses of the far shore resembled miniatures in a toy-train village but for the thick foliage that created an unending line of green punctuated by triangles of evergreens that hinted of eternal Christmas. Here and there flowering bushes provided splashes of white, ruby-red or lilac. Along the water's edge the open bays of boathouses beckoned, dark caves of upside-down smiles in the stark sunlight.

It was heaven.

From this corner of the lake I was reminded of resort spas in Upstate New York, places in the Finger Lake region where the wealthy would go to recover after plastic surgery or retreat from society.

A boat of teens pulled up to the slip, and the bare-chested boys and sleek lines of the boat seemed to broadcast sexuality with the rap song playing on their CD player. Boat and boys were rather buff. Skis and wakeboards were strapped onto overhead bars. Two girls in bikini tops jumped onto the shoreline and walked right beside me, their hips swaying in their low-slung shorts with OREGON STATE printed across the butt. One girl had a gem in her navel, and both had those sexy dimples on their lower back—the matched pair over the butt. Those dimples used to drive Jack wild. I rubbed my lower back, wondering if mine had vanished in the folds of mommyhood.

Three boys who looked to be eight or nine darted around me, their swim trunks dripping on the dock. One of them held an enormous water gun, and he was after my daughter and her friend.

"Becca? Here's what you get for splashing me!" He hurried along the dock and launched an attack on the two girls, who squealed and shrieked.

"Cut it out, Ethan!" Becca shouted, though I suspected she was secretly happy for the attention.

I shifted into the sunshine. Did I look odd here, a middle-aged woman sitting alone in the middle of the dock, soaking in nature like a guru?

I moved off the water and joined Jack, who was in full swing back at the picnic table occupied by other grown-ups. One woman held an infant in a snuggly. She had long, blonde hair, naturally big hair, which sat atop her head like a giant cheeseburger deluxe. She smiled up at me with that copacetic grin of a woman in love with her child. "You must be Ruby," she said. I nodded and sat down beside her, immediately complimenting her sweet infant.

She introduced herself as Daphne Sweet. The baby's name was Luke. "We have an older son, same age as your Scout, but he's with a friend today. And that's my husband, Rick, bending Jack's ear," Daphne added.

"Oh, Jack likes to get bent," I teased, though the comment fell flat as Daphne pursed her lips together and turned to ask someone behind us the time. Maybe it was time for Luke to eat again?

I turned to the person who answered, a slender woman in a pink polo shirt with matching pink plaid skort. Did I smell Calvin Klein? The woman was blonde, of course, but fine-boned and imperious, like a descendant of royalty. Not only did she tell Daphne the time, but she also gave her breast-feeding advice along with a tip on how to make your newborn sleep through the night.

"Are you a nurse?" I asked, turning to the yellow-haired queen.

"Just a mother of four, all in elementary," she answered, a little coldly. "That's my Ethan over there with the water gun."

When Daphne introduced her as Suzie Snyder, I recognized the name from some of the flyers I'd received from school. This was the president of our PTA, the author of those very forceful mandates to serve and donate that came home in the children's homework folders.

I nodded, not wanting to identify myself as a school parent and potential victim of prey. Jack was still talking with the men, apparently having found common ground talking about their beloved first cars, Dodges and Fords and old Caddies they'd dropped new engines into and banged around town in.

A woman came down the slope with her daughter and waved at us. With their blue-black hair and brown eyes, they were positively Gothic in West Green.

"That's Ariel," Daphne cued Suzie under her breath.

"Hi, Ariel. How are you?" Suzie's voice made it clear she was not really interested in the answer.

"I'm great! Isn't this beautiful?" Ariel stopped beside our table and shooed her daughter toward the water. "Go! Get wet!" She operated with a frankness atypical of West Green moms.

"Ariel is from New York, too," Daphne said, as if it had just occurred to her. "Do you guys know each other?"

I extended my hand. "I'm Ruby, and that's my husband, Jack. An unpleasant historic way to remember our names is Jack Ruby."

"Ha!" Ariel shrieked, shaking my hand briskly. "I love that! Don't you love it?" she asked. Daphne seemed repelled, Suzie unaffected, and for a moment I wondered if she got it at all.

"Where in New York are you from?" I asked Ariel.

"Brooklyn."

I pointed to myself. "Queens."

"No way! Oh! My! Gawd!" She pretended to fan her face with one hand. "What are you doing here?"

"Job move."

"The same!"

"How long have you guys been here?" I asked.

"Since February."

"March!"

"Oh. My. Gawd." Ariel reached out and grabbed my wrists. "I'm shpitzing!"

"Me, too!"

"Come walk with me, talk with me," she said, tugging me toward the lake. "I just have to check on my daughter, but we can talk."

And we did, down by the waterside for nearly an hour in that nononsense New York shorthand that cuts through crap and pretension. Ariel Cohen of Westchester, New York, had moved here in February when her husband, an account executive with a Madison Avenue agency, had been hired to work one in-house advertising campaign for a giant Oregon-based sportswear company. She loved the green space and freedom for her daughter Michelle, though she still felt like a bit of an outsider. Michelle had been attending another school while they were transitioning in an apartment, but now that they were in their house in West Green, she'd be at West Green Elementary, in the same grade as Scout.

"We are leading parallel lives," I told her. "Except that I'm Catholic and I've got a few years and pounds on you."

"Small difference," she said, shooting a subtle glance over her shoulder. "Do you think the other ladies are offended that we didn't include them in our bonding?"

"I think they're happy to have me out of their hair. Conversation was strained, and you noticed that no one else got the Jack Ruby thing."

"They have a different frame of reference out here," Ariel said. "Exactly what that is, I couldn't tell you, but . . . whatever."

"Well, we'd better watch ourselves with Suzie Snyder," I said, lowering my voice. "If we don't play it right, we'll get kicked out of the PTA."

"We should be so lucky. No, she'd just make us run the charity auction." Ariel squeezed my arms. "Do you know what they say when you've been stung by Suzie Snyder? It's the kiss of the Snyderwoman!"

I let out a raucous laugh, then covered my mouth. "Stop! If they think we're having too much fun, they'll come down here and join us. So . . . Tell me where you got that great haircut and where I can find a decent bagel."

"Please! You can't get a decent bagel west of the Rockies. My husband has them FedExed to the office from Essa Bagels. But hair I can help you with. I go to this fabulous person in Portland. I'll get you her info."

We talked quickly, as if running out of time on a pay phone. "Can I tell you, I miss this so much," she said. "The rapid-fire conversation. The dark humor, a good bagel, a decent newspaper." Ariel told me she loved the green of West Green, but failed as a domestic goddess. Lately she'd begun doing volunteer work for Planned Parenthood. When her daughter was born she'd given up her job as an editor of a science journal but used her knowledge of anatomy to get certified as a personal trainer. I told her I worked at home, writing women's fiction, and her eyes widened with a flicker of knowledge. "That's so wonderful. My father is a writer, too."

When she mentioned his name, I dropped to my knees and bowed. "All hail, Simon Lowenstein!" He was a member of the Beat Generation, a contemporary of Alan Ginsberg and of Jack Kerouac, one of the few writers who survived the drinking and LSD and wild road trips.

Ariel pulled me to my feet and leaned close. "Do you know, you are the only person I've met in Oregon who recognized my father's name. What's that about? Is the curriculum that different here? I mean, I checked and they have his books in the West Green Library."

I shook my head. "I don't know. Maybe we're hanging in the wrong mommy circles."

"Wouldn't that be great?" she enthused. "To pick the mommy category you'd like to be in? I'll take an egg roll, sweet and sour pork and the intellectual mommy circle."

"Give me the multicultural pupu platter with a touch of liberalism."

We both laughed again, perhaps a little too loudly, considering the way sound travels over water. Of course, the kids and the teenaged lifeguards didn't care, but I noticed some of the parent groups looking toward us curiously.

I turned back toward the water, rubbing the back of my neck. "God knows, I never wanted to be defined by the mommy thing, anyway. I love my kids, but I can't make it all about them."

She nodded and said wisely, "Kiss of the Snyderwoman."

I was reluctant to say good-bye when Ariel and Michelle had to leave, but we exchanged phone numbers and I walked her up to the gate, our words still rattling out like machine-gun fire. Afterward, I felt charged up and giddy. I stripped off my shorts and T-shirt and took a dive into the deep end of the lake, and swam over to the rafts where Becca and her friend Madison Woodcock were now floating around, locked onto each other's raft. The water smelled like damp earth, but it was crisp and cold and billowed around me like a natural spa. After threatening to tip a squealing Becca over, I swam two laps along the bobbing rope, then climbed onto the dock and sat in the late-afternoon sun, hoping to drip-dry before I had to return to the deadbeat adults at the picnic table.

While I was basking in the sun, a shadow came over me. I opened my eyes to find Becca and Madison.

"Hi, Mrs. Salerno," Madison said in a sweet tone that brought to mind Eddie cajoling Mrs. Cleaver.

"Hello, Madison. Long time no see."

Madison giggled.

She had white-blonde hair, a tiny little face and a beaklike smile, reminding me of a delicate baby chick. "We were wondering if Becca could sleep over at my house tonight?"

"Oh, I don't know." I sat up straight, looking at Becca, who nodded vigorously. She hadn't stayed overnight with anyone for the past year or so since there'd been a pattern of aborted sleepovers, tying into Becca's insomnia. "That would be okay with me if your parents agree. But first we should check with Becca's dad." That would give Becca a way to bow out gracefully if she began to have second thoughts about the plan.

Madison clapped her hands together. "I'll go ask my mom."

Once she was out of sight, Becca dropped down on the dock beside me.

"Hey, honey," I said. "Are you sure you're up for this?"

"I definitely want to do the sleepover," she said. "But I'm worried about tomorrow . . . that appointment for the puppy. You won't go without me, will you?"

I shook my head. "Definitely not. This is going to be your puppy."

"Will you come get me? What time is the appointment?" she asked. When I answered, she outlined tomorrow's schedule with the efficiency of a seasoned office manager.

"Works for me," I said, slinging an arm over my oldest daughter's shoulder. In the warmth of the sun I allowed myself a moment of pride at how far she'd come in the last three months, moving to a brand-new place, a new culture, making friends and finding a sense of calm in herself. Together, we headed in from the dock and cleared the plans with Madison's mother, Lexie. I checked on Dylan, whom Hilary insisted was playing so nicely with Zack, then returned to the dreaded adult table, where I was relieved to see Scout's legs dangling from the table as she ate a hotdog. Suzie and Daphne were discussing something, but they spoke slowly in scattered words, as if on a decibel level I couldn't decipher.

"Mom, guess what?" Scout asked, swinging her legs from the bench. "The hot dog was only a buck. Isn't that a good deal?"

"A *buck?*" I mimicked, leaning over her. "You sound like you were raised at OTB. How about a dollar?"

She swallowed. "What's OTB? Oh, wait. Is that the breathing disease?"

"No. Don't worry." I pulled a beach towel over my shoulders just as I caught Suzie's husband eyeballing my bustline.

"Hey, how's the water?" he asked, his gaze sliding up to meet mine.

"Refreshing." I sidled onto the bench beside my daughter, wondering why these people seemed so attracted to my husband. Granted, Jack was on, charm bubbling like a Central Park fountain, but I didn't expect Oregonians to fall for East Coast charisma.

"Mom, can I have money for candy?" the kid with the water gun begged, the gun dripping at his side.

"Ethan, I said no," Suzie snapped, a little harshly, I thought. When you treated a kid like a pest, he tended to rise to the role.

"But, Mom, you said—"

"Here, take this." His father handed Ethan a bill. "Now get lost."

The kid escaped without a word of thank you. "I'm Mike," the man said, extending a hand. "Mike Snyder."

That would be the husband of Suzie. "Nice to meet you, Mike. You've got kids at West Green Elementary?" I asked, playing dumb.

"Four," he answered, clearly not wearing the badge of parenthood as proudly as his wife. "And you're Ruby, right? Do you work at KJZM, too?"

"No." But that explained part of Jack's charisma of the moment. When people heard that he worked at a television station, they thought he was some sort of network star. "I'm a writer," I said.

"A writer?" Suzie's brows rose as she nodded around the group. The message: I'm impressed. Shouldn't we all be?

The hair on the back of my neck tickled; I knew Suzie would be disappointed when she found out the dirt. I wasn't a Lost Generation coffeehouse writer or a warm and fuzzy picture book Mother Goose.

Scout's brows creased as she eyed Suzie suspiciously. *Good instincts, honey.*

"Have you written anything I might have read?" Mike asked.

I felt my lips frost over with a stiff smile. What were the chances that Mike Snyder had read any of my books? Somehow I couldn't imagine him stretched out on the family sectional couch with a copy of any of my top sellers: *Logan's Woman, Logan's World, Logan's Life* or *Logan's Wife*. In the years since I'd been writing I'd gotten past the stigma of romance, the fact that my mother's book club would never choose one of my books and that men like Mike Snyder would look down his nose at me. The romance genre used to be the shunned stepchild of the publishing industry, but the little girl was growing up, with romance novels now generating nearly a billion dollars in sales each year. Booksellers loved romance writers; it was the general public who perceived romance writers as pink Cadillacs.

"You probably haven't picked up one of my books," I said carefully. "I write for women. I've done lots of category romance." Blank stares, as if I'd lapsed into the language of the ancient sea scrolls. God help me, I knew I shouldn't expand, knew I shouldn't talk about something that really mattered to me, but I'd poured a piece of myself into writing *Chocolate in the Morning*, and maybe these people would be able to understand where I was going with it. Perhaps, I told myself, this was a novel-savvy crowd, real book people. "I've got a new book coming out that I'm sort of excited about. It's a novel about a woman who—"

"Romance?" Mike grinned mischievously, and I thought how his face resembled the mask of comedy, a giddy grin at the ready. "Now we're talking. You know, I think I could write that." He assumed a queer posture, his prayerful hands drawn up to the side of his head as he recited: "His face pressed close to her heaving bosom . . ."

Scout's mouth puckered distastefully, recognizing Mike's lunacy.

"He swept her into his arms, and they walked off into the sunset. Two lovers, alone . . . walking off . . . into the sunset."

Everyone laughed, and I thought what a fool I'd been to think that this crowd might be book people, to think that there were, in fact, any book people left in this age of e-mail, iPods, Blackberries and TV screens in cars, airports and grocery stores.

"Talent abounds," I said graciously.

"That was inappropriate and random," Scout said.

"Sorry, kid," Mike said, though his eyes twinkled with satisfaction. "I know all about those books. My secretary devours them."

I forced a smile, thinking how I hadn't heard the politically incorrect "secretary" in years since most people in New York now said "assistant." "Yes," I said, trying to reduce it all to a business, "they reach a wide market. Did you know that half of all paperback fiction sales are romances?"

"I'm working on a picture book for children," Daphne said. "I have so many ideas."

I smiled. "That's a difficult market, from what I hear," I said. "But you never know. Follow your dream." I didn't want to be a naysayer, but I also didn't want Daphne to think that I could help her get her picture book published. I couldn't.

"It's the story of a little boy who finds a monster under his bed," Daphne began, and with a deep breath, I realized I was in for the long haul, the whole story. I shot a desperate look at Jack, beseeching him to turn up the volume and pull us into his conversation, which was bound to be more interesting, even if it was about fishing and hunting wild game. Scout left the table when the little boy helped the monster scrape his scales off. Smart girl.

For the first time this year, I prayed for sundown.

Later, as I was stir-frying chicken for dinner, I took a sip of Jack's beer and asked: "How did you manage that? You were trapped in conversation with those people for hours."

"I enjoyed it," he said, turning down the burner under the rice. "People are people, and if you can have a few laughs together, what's not to like?"

This afternoon's shmooze was more like the old Jack I know and love, but somehow it bothered me. Not that it was a competition, but he seemed to be melding with the locals better than I was. "If that's true, how come it's so difficult to light a fire under the staff at work? You're the one who keeps telling me how different Oregonians are from New Yorkers."

"Don't be obtuse. I'm talking social ethics, not work ethics."

I hated being put down; it was Jack's way of ending an argument before it even started. But I let it go at that. Sometimes, I did not like my husband, and I figured that was okay. As long as the feeling eventually passed . . . and I didn't kill him in the meantime.

15

Jack: The Guilts

It's a cool May night—Portland cool, with a dry chill greeting me as I bail out of my car in the long-term airport parking. The Oregon air smells crisp and clean, like a clear, sweet liquid. So unlike the air in Dallas or New York. Oregon definitely wins in the fresh air category.

Which doesn't quite make up for its deficits in the workforce.

At first I told myself it was just my office, that some inept HR person had assembled the laziest workforce in the history of Western civilization. But then I noticed how it surrounded me— that pervasive lackadaisical quality. "Take your time," the security guard at the front desk tells me each morning. The woman in front of me at the sandwich line definitely takes her time, and mine, too, as she wavers from ham and cheddar on rye to a meatball hero, then back to ham and cheese. I have to grit my teeth to keep from nudging her aside, telling her: "Make up your mind before you get to the front of the line, lady! Can't you see there are people waiting behind you?" The baristas at the coffee shop are so fucking chatty and mellow. "How are you today? What can I get you? Shall I leave room for milk? Any pastries?" I appear at the same damned coffee shop five mornings a week, and none of them can get that I want a cup of black coffee, no room for milk, no chat, and no tip for wasting my time with idle chatter about the weather or their new caramel mocha frappe.

If I sound like a prick, it's because I've been driven into that role, wedged between a mediocre sales team and an icy-calm general manager who moves with such stealth that I've had nightmares about him silently creeping up behind me in his three-hundred-dollar running shoes and slicing through my back with a stiletto.

The other night Gibbs was behind me, whispering something about failure in my ear, his icy breath sending chills down my spine, when Ruby reached out in bed and touched my shoulder.

"Jack? Honey, are you okay?"

I realized I was moaning like a geriatric patient. She put her hand on my chest, but I turned away.

"You were having a nightmare. What were you dreaming about?"

Failure. But I couldn't tell her that. Fear of failure is a form of failure itself. "I don't remember." I wish I could have told her, because she's usually so good at getting that sort of stuff: tyrannical bosses, office politics. Back in New York, Ruby gave me the best advice on how to play Numero Uno. But I can't really figure out the problem so I can't describe it. If Ruby could live one day in my shoes, go into the office and deal with the grazing herd, maybe she'd get it.

First, there are George and Ali to contend with, but you have to wait around till, like, nine thirtyish because they missed the memo telling them that office hours are from eight to four so that we can be more in synch with our East Coast affiliates. George is the office curmudgeon, a hundred years old, with brows that spider into his eyes, a gravelly voice and a paunch that looks like he's about five months' pregnant. George comes loaded with experience, but he'll never let anyone forget that and he's more than a little resistant to change. Suffice it to say, George will die in the saddle; he'll probably be bullshitting at the water cooler or doing a sales call from his desk—sometime *after* nine thirty AM.

Ali is a cordial, thirty-two-year-old salesman who, I suspect, is playing the minority card for job security. He claims to be an Afghan Hindu, but his real name is Alan Dubinski—I looked it up in his HR files—and, really, what practicing Hindu comes to work in Italian leather shoes and stylin' eyewear a different color every day? Don't Hindus think cows are creatures to be revered, not worn to keep the feet dry? I mentioned this to Ruby and she pointed out that he might be Afghan on his mother's side, and, really, what right did I have to judge the way the man practiced his religion? I told her that employees can't be making up holy days whenever the wind shifts, but she just finds it refreshing that Ali, who calls himself "Ollie" and spent five years selling cars before this, can be a stylin' guy amid Portland's conformity.

George and Ali are the best and the worst: the best because they're my top sellers, the worst because they're totally resistant to any changes, incentive programs or motivational modifications I've tried to facilitate. The other people on the sales team, well, they could all be sloshed in together in a big pot of flavorless oatmeal. White, mushy, boring. Percy Miller has three kids from three different marriages and now fancies himself a weekend farmer in Canby. Taylor Grimble is an itinerant horndog who lives with mommy. Amanda Anderson has a husband and two kids in college and a desk decorated with green ducks, which I've learned is the mascot for the University of Oregon. The highlight of her year seems to be the Civil War—not the historical one, but the made-up war when U of O plays Oregon State in football. Now that's excitement.

Our sales team is incredibly pleasant. Whenever I challenge them to approach new clients or sell in a new program they answer cheerfully. "You bet!" or "Will do." Then they proceed to ignore everything I've suggested and return to their status quo—phone calls and lunches with clients. They don't answer my e-mails but instead "pop in" to my office to waste my time in long-winded answers. When I send them documents to download they claim computer illiteracy and impose themselves on one of the office assistants to print and distribute everything. Half of them refuse to learn how to work the Corstar voice mail system, the other half waste office hours playing games on their cell phones and acting out family soap operas over the office phone.

And this, according to the GM Connor Gibbs, is one of Portland's leading sales teams. "A crack staff," he says. More like they're on crack, or just cracked, or wacked, though I do not say this to Connor Gibbs because I sense he doesn't like me. He doesn't approve of my forthright approach, my tendency to push ahead and ask permission later. I suspect that, were it up to Connor Gibbs, I would not have been hired for this position, but he was overruled by the corporate guys in Dallas.

I am not one bit sorry to be leaving the Portland office behind for awhile, and though it gives me the guilts I'm happy to be getting away from the family, too. "Separation makes the heart grow fonder," my former boss, Numero Uno, used to say. Of course, she meant that as an excuse for her track record of three bad marriages.

My marriage is okay. But right now I just feel like all these pressures, Connor, my staff in Portland and Ruby's shit, with all those deadlines—it's all squeezing the whole family scene down to a scant few seconds of each day until it becomes just a matter of meals and diaper changes and carpooling the kids around and having very perfunctory sex in bed late at night. Nobody's fault, just a reality.

Well, maybe my fault a little. The guilts. I made a mistake in Dallas that Ruby doesn't know about, but it was a one-time thing and I figure the guilt eating away at me is punishment enough.

I climb down the steps of the van from the parking lot and tip the guy who hands me my bags. Walking into the airport under the high atrium that allows sunlight into the draping vines, I feel taller, as if I can stretch my spine and pull my shoulders back for the first time in weeks. Dallas will be good for me, even if it does mean seeing *her* again.

It really was an accident, a fluke. At least, on my part. I think Dez has always had a crush on me. From the first time I traveled to the Dallas office, she made me feel very welcome, like a visiting dignitary from a foreign land. Dez let me know early on that she believed in me. She was always dropping hints about Filbert, his likes and dislikes, the way to get him on your side. And although she's a junior vice president, I've always seen her as a little-sister type, sort of like the supportive office assistant. No sexual attraction, but then she's not my type, with the bleached blonde hair and all that spray and makeup. Helmet heads, Ruby and I used to joke when we'd encounter someone with that much hairspray at the kids' school or the DMV. "Enough lacquer to save your life in a car crash," I used to say.

In my defense, I thought the whole thing was an obligatory business engagement, one of those office things that spills over to a weekend, and she made a big deal of pointing out that it was for me, to fill my weekend—"since it must be so lonely being away from your family all this time." Dez said it was a few people for dinner. I got there with a six-pack wearing an open shirt and jeans and found people dressed in, like, Academy Award attire sipping champagne on her little balcony that overlooked a manmade pond. Dez was wearing this black and gold dress that rippled over her shoulders and left a bare back down to her butt. It was one kick-ass dress, and I have always had a weakness for the small of a woman's back, that flat part just above the butt where those two dimples glimmer. I apologized, told Dez I didn't dress right, but she just laughed it off, telling me there's no way to dress wrong.

Truth was, no one else from the office had showed, which made me feel like a bit of a dick till I got to talking with some of Dez's friends who had formed a start-up company that just bought a small hotel chain. They were hungry for some of my information on different markets, and we talked through a few bottles of champagne, which I normally don't drink, and a plate of salad and some chicken dish that everybody kept raving about. Another guy at the party owned a car dealership, and we talked about making local TV advertising work for him. I didn't even work in this market, but I know this stuff. It's what I do.

By the time the guests were saying good-bye, I realized that my peripheral vision was shot and it was really hard to get out of that chair on the balcony. Too much champagne, which I was still pouring from a bottle basking in an ice bucket by my feet. Dez came back from letting everyone out and sat down. She brought a cat, a mangy thing that she called Twiggy. She told me she adopted Twiggy from a shelter, "saved her from execution," as she called it. Twiggy had been hiding in the bedroom, not one to brave crowds. I put my hand out for the cat to sniff like a dog, but Twiggy just let out a shrill meow.

"That is one loud cat," I said.

"I think she likes you."

"Sure she does. All women like me; it's the men who're the problem. Men like Bob Hazelnut."

"You always say that but I know it's not you. Mr. Filbert always wants you around." She cuddled the skinny cat on her lap. It looked feral, like a rat with a healthy coat. "Aren't you going to ask if you can touch my pussy?" she asked.

My jaw dropped. I didn't know what to say.

"It was a joke! Didn't you ever see that old clip with Johnny Carson? Geez. You can stay if you want," she said. "Or else, I'll call you a cab."

I nodded over my champagne glass, looking out into the dry darkness. "I shouldn't drive."

"You're not driving." She kicked off her gold sandals and stretched out her feet. "Do you mind?" she asked, lifting them onto my lap. "These shoes are a killer. I don't know why I do that to myself."

Balancing my glass on the railing, I placed my hands over her feet. Small and sharp, with boney curved toes. "I'm an expert at this," I said, beginning a foot massage.

"That feels great." She sighed.

We sat like that for awhile, me massaging, Dez claiming I had therapeutic hands. Then we decided I would stay on the couch. Dez went inside to get me sheets. I don't remember collapsing on the couch, but my face was pressed into a cotton pillowcase when I heard water running. I had to go. I made my way toward the light, relieving myself in the bowl as it became clear that someone was in the shower in the inner bathroom. Still semi-inebriated, I was beginning to remember where I was when the door opened and Dez walked out, wrapped in a towel. Her blonde hair was damp but toweled off so that it stood out wildly in all directions, like a newly hatched duck.

I had to touch that sweet, downy fur, needed to smell the scent of her without hairspray and perfume and God knows what else. I put my arms around her and she hugged me hard as I took in the scent of apple shampoo, the softness of her hair. My lips went to the beads of water on her neck, my mouth consumed her earlobe. She was so light, I easily carried her into the bedroom, where I fell into her without looking back.

Hours later, at dawn, I dressed quickly and got the hell out of there.

We've never mentioned it since that night, but I think Dez would say yes if the opportunity arose again. Not that I'd ever do it, but I think she's got this irrational crush on me. Like I'm some media hero. Which, I admit, I don't mind. Sometimes it's nice to be appreciated.

16

Puppy Love

Having grown up with a guinea pig and a cat who was so egocentric that we couldn't bring another creature close without a hissing fit and flying fur, I was not schooled in the way of puppy care. Sure, I'd skimmed some of the book Becca had checked out from the library, even made myself read *Dog Care for Dummies*. I was prepared as any scholar could be without having done any field research.

With Jack gone to Dallas, I was the fearless leader of the pack, driving the kids up to Adams Family Farms, which Kathy Adams had told me was "just north of Vancouver." I wasn't sure how big the farm was or what they grew, but I'd always reached Kathy at a law office, Biddle and Crenshaw, that reminded me of New York—busy, fast-paced and "Can you hold?"—I figured that any woman who could juggle a busy law office and farm life was the breeder for me.

After forty miles and nearly as many minutes of woodsy roads and small towns, I was learning that "just north of Vancouver" was code for "shoot through Vancouver, then drive your ass off." The last landmark we'd passed on this twisting country road was a general store. The kids had stopped asking "When are we going to get there?" and now gaped out the window wide-eyed as we passed a lot brimming with brown boulders, where a toothless man with a beard down to his belly sat holding a sign that said FREE ROCKS. Farther down the road we came to a roaring open fire, flames enveloping massive tree trunks and unplugged roots, tended by overweight men in lawn chairs.

"Are you sure we're going the right way?" Becca asked as strains of the banjo music from *Deliverance* plucked in my mind. What the hell was Kathy Adams of Biddle and Crenshaw doing out in this god-forsaken land? And how could this no-man's-land be just on the northern outskirts of the Portland Metro area? I mean, Portland was a fair-sized city. Who knew you could drive for less than an hour and find yourself in a hillbilly moment?

But I sucked in my wariness, telling the kids we were on track as the Volvo wagon began a steep climb up a good-sized hill that, in Queens, would have been dubbed a mountain. Much to my relief, we came over a rise to a flat, groomed area of grass and the gray stone wall Kathy had mentioned, bearing a hand-carved sign that read: ADAMS FAMILY FARMS.

"We're here!" I said brightly, relieved that we'd made it past the root-burners and twisting roads that made Scout whine with car sickness.

The little house on the flat hilltop appeared tidy and quaint, and I suspected it was one of those prefabricated structures that had been dropped here amid the free rocks and blazing root fires. The doorbell was answered by Kathy, a middle-aged redhead with enough lip gloss to pose for a Clairol commercial. Her husband, Todd, a personable man in khakis and an oxford shirt, welcomed us in and I felt relieved that they seemed to be exceedingly normal people. Stepping inside, we were immediately greeted by the puppy's parents, two Cavaliers with American Kennel Club papers. Honey, a Blenheim with patches of orange-red fur on white, came forward to sniff us out while her mate, Charlie, circled excitedly.

My kids fell to their knees and extended their hands. Even Dylan seemed to understand the protocol of meeting a canine . . . until he let out a shriek of delight that may have injured the hearing of every dog in the southwest corner of Washington State.

Todd Adams gave us some background on Cavaliers, the choice pet of the British, raised by the royals to be lapdogs. He explained that Cavaliers came with four colorings: the brown and white spotted Blenheim, the Black and Tan, the Tricolor and the Ruby, like Charlie, who were ruddy-red. He told us that they'd adopted Charlie when they lived in Los Angeles, and then, just last year, "Santa" had delivered Honey to the children on Christmas morning.

"They're very sweet," I said, extending a hand and hoping that no one licked me, which both dogs did. The dogs *were* precious, but I'm not a fan of being licked, even by my husband.

"And here are the puppies." Kathy led the way to an old-fashioned washtub placed in the nook at the foot of the stairs.

"Aw . . ." my girls said in unison.

"Puppies!" Dylan exclaimed. "Puppies. See the puppies, Mommy?"

I stepped forward to see two miniatures of Charlie and Honey scrambling around in the newspaper-lined tub, their small, fluffy tails wagging vigorously. A male Ruby and a female Blenheim. "Aw . . ." I cooed, unable to help myself.

"Can we hold them?" Becca asked the Adamses.

"Of course." One by one, Kathy lifted out the puppies and showed the girls how to hold them. Ten minutes of puppy love, chasing and petting ensued. The breeders watched, calm and slightly amused, not at all disturbed by Dylan's shrieks or the girls' frolicking. They probably realized they had a sale, which they did.

"Can't we buy both of them?" Becca asked as I corralled the puppies back into the tub so that we could talk deal with Kathy and Todd. "They're both so cute, Mom. And that way, we'd never have to fight about who gets to hold it."

"Absolutely not," I said firmly. I had read that females were more docile, less aggressive, and I was sticking by it. Besides, with my luck if I adopted a male we'd probably end up with the alpha male of the pack, who'd spend all his time chewing up shoes and carpeting and postal workers, when he wasn't stealing Jack's favorite spot on the sofa. "One puppy is perfect for novices like us, and, remember, we agreed that we need a female."

Kathy flashed me a knowing smile. "The Blenheim?"

"Can we, Mom?" Scout asked. "Can we take her home tonight?"

"She's almost seven weeks old," Todd said, his hands tucked casually in his pockets. A born salesman. "And all the puppies have had their first round of shots."

Looking down at the expectant faces of my children, I dug into my bag for my checkbook and said: "We'll take her." I knew it was the right choice. Besides, I didn't want to have to venture out to hill country again.

As we were driving back on I-5 through Portland, my cell phone beeped with a message from Morgan, and I realized I'd probably had no service in the outlands. I called her back and started in with the puppy news, but she overrode me.

"*Publishers Weekly* reviewed *Chocolate in the Morning* and loved it. Listen to this . . ." And she began reading the glowing review in its entirety.

"Oh. My. Gawd." I mouthed as Morgan barreled on with words like "clever," "delicious," and "insightful."

"Mom, what's wrong?" Becca asked, concerned in the backseat, where the puppy was cradled in her arms.

"It's okay," I whispered. "Good news, honey."

" '. . . the rare novel that entertains even as its characters experience epiphanies . . .' Are you getting this?"

"Barely," I admitted. "I'm driving and, well, I'm sort of blown away by it."

"I'll e-mail you the full text," Morgan promised. "But wait. There's more."

"Another review?"

"Even better. I talked to Padama, and she said the buzz is so positive that the chains increased their orders." We'd met briefly before I'd left New York, and I admittedly spent most of the lunch marveling at her hint of a British accent—Liverpool, she said—and her sparkling nose stud, and the many rings on her fingers and ears. I couldn't help but wonder if she had pierced body parts I couldn't see and if this was part of her native culture, as she seemed to be Indian or Malaysian. However, she spent so much time enthusing over my manuscript and Condor's promotion plans that I found it difficult to segue to a discussion of body piercings and ethnicity.

"Long story short, Condor Books is going back to print already," Morgan went on. "Tripling their print run, Ruby. Print run times three. They're putting out numbers that could put *you* on some best-seller lists, my dear."

"Whoa." I braked, allowing a little more space between me and the SUV that I was following. Any more news like that and I was liable to accelerate out of control. "This is all sounding incredibly good. Like a dream come true."

"It's got all the right ingredients," Morgan said. "And God knows, I could use the lift."

Morgan's e-mails had summarized her Memorial Day weekend, which "sucked." Professor Goldsmith had canceled, her son had announced that he was spending the summer working at a children's camp in the Catskills, and her daughter Clare had gone off to spend the weekend with girlfriends on the Jersey shore "living out of a car," Morgan wrote. Overall, Morgan was feeling that she had no personal life, no family, no "irons in the fire" beyond her work. I felt for her, and honestly wished I could loan her some of my own "irons"; with trying to write and exploring this new territory and juggling children and husband and now puppy, I had too much going on.

"Well, you can take credit for all this, Morgan," I said. "You were the one who thought we should go with Condor."

"Agenting is what I do," she said. "At the moment, it seems to be all I can do, but let's not go there."

"So what's next? What do we do now?"

Morgan let out a laugh, a delicious, gutsy sound that revealed her enjoyment. "Honey, from here we cross our fingers, say a little prayer, sit back and enjoy the ride."

17

Fiction and Literature

Over the next two weeks, Ariel Cohen and I made the most of the schooltime hours while the kids were occupied. At first I was reluctant to leave Taffy, our sweet puppy, alone, but she seemed comfortable in her crate and I didn't want to get her in the habit of having my attention 24/7.

So Ariel and I stole into Portland to explore the Pearl District, Twenty-third Street, the Pittock Mansion—which was a home built by the pioneering entrepreneur who came West and bought the *Oregonian* newspaper—Chinatown and the Portland Art Museum. We took in an exhibit at a gallery in the Pearl: a new interpretation of playing cards, by fifty-two different artists. On Twenty-third we found a funky mirror for my bathroom and an umbrella stand with monkeys crawling up the side for Ariel's entryway. In another store that sold only clogs, we decided to join our Northwest sisters and switch to clogs. I bought a pair with emerald green leather uppers that made me feel like Elphaba hiding out in Holland. Ariel and I shared dim sum at a small restaurant in Chinatown and burned it off with a walk through the rose-strewn hilltop garden. Another day we visited the Impressionist exhibit, then went across the street for salads and microbrews at South Park Grill. All of these forays were accompanied by nonstop chatter on a variety of subjects ranging from infant allergies to proper preparation of potato latkes to deconstructionist theory.

Being with Ariel had unleashed the adventurer inside me. After weeks of nesting, I was through with decorator magazines and paint swatches. I wanted to live again, and Ariel seemed to share my craving for grabbing Portland by the balls.

By Friday all gray had burned off from the sky and we parked ourselves at an outdoor bistro on Twenty-third next to a table of Goths, with an assortment of blackened eyelids, waxed mohawks, tattoos, piercings and black laced leather.

"Just like home," Ariel sighed happily as she scooped a spoonful of whipped cream from her mocha. Leaning forward, she twirled a dark curl around one finger. "I almost went with a mohawk this morning, but that hot wax is such a bitch to get out."

I stifled a laugh and flipped open the menu. Everywhere we went, it seemed we were the only ones laughing. I wasn't sure whether we simply laughed louder than West Coasters—when she got going, Ariel let out a basso profundo bellow—or maybe we just laughed a lot more than our fellow Oregonians. "You and I are going to need a lot of work if we're ever going to get this slacker thing down," I said.

"Hello? We're in our thirties," she said. "That's the age when you go from slacker to just plain old and lazy."

"Well, I'm thirty-six, and I'm here to say that I think I can still slack." I shifted back in my chair. "I can definitely slouch."

"That you can." She perused the lunch menu. "Truffle tart. Not really in the mood for that. Not sure I've *ever* been in the mood for it, actually." Ariel's secret dream was to become a food critic, and she loved to critique menus and sample as much fare as she could without running up too huge a bill. She adored the perversity of a science-and-health editor turning to the dark side and exploring culinary cuisine without a lick of worry about fats and carbs. It was something she hoped to pursue down the road, when Michelle was in high school, but for now she was content to taste, take a few notes and concoct witty opening lines of a restaurant review. "Shrimp Ratatouille. I just love to say that word, ratatouille. It sounds vile, and so often it is. And don't you think it's just what you want on this sunny spring day—a bowl of warm, stewed tomato concoction?"

I grinned. "Next?"

She was working her way down the menu when my cell phone rang—Morgan. "It's my agent," I said, looking at the caller ID.

"How exciting is that? Go on, answer it!" Ariel insisted.

"Hold on to your hat," Morgan said, "and say hello to record-breaking initial sales for *Chocolate.*"

My stomach felt queasy, as if the plane I was flying on had suddenly lifted off. "You're kidding."

"I kid you not," Morgan gushed. "And Condor is shipping out more copies of *Chocolate* with floor displays. They're buying space for you on endcaps and summer reading tables. Looks like you're going to be creeping onto the best-seller list, my dear!"

"I can't believe it!" I gasped.

"Whatsamatter?" Ariel asked. "Should I nix the goat cheese salad and order a Caesar?"

When I told Ariel the news, she closed her menu. "That's fantastic! I didn't even know your book was out. Let's go to a bookstore and see." She waved down our server.

"Condor is through the roof about this, of course," Morgan went on. "There's talk of sending you on a tour, and their publicity department is making a few calls, shaking down contacts and pulling in some favors. They're setting up phone interviews for radio and print, and they want to book you on some local morning shows—an impossible feat with you being a virtual newbie, I know, but I give them lots of credit for trying."

"Are you talking about television?" I squirmed. "I can't do TV."

"What do you mean? You can talk, can't you?"

"If I went out as me, everyone would find out I'm actually a middle-aged mother of three, instead of that glam bombshell on the book jacket."

"TV is awesome publicity," Ariel assured me. "And I gotta see this book."

"Your friend knows what she's talking about," Morgan said. "Listen, honey, if it happens there probably won't be much notice, so get your sitters in place or call Nanny 911 or something. TV would be an opportunity you can't turn down."

As I said good-bye to Morgan, I noticed that Ariel had taken care of the bill and was already sipping the last of her mocha. "Hurry up and finish your latte," she said. "We're going on a bookstore junket."

Using the navigational system that Ariel had named "Kit," we found every bookstore in Portland—nearly a dozen of them—and Ariel punched in a route linking one to the other.

"Do you think we can do them all before the three o'clock bell?" Ariel asked as we cruised down Burnside with the windows open. The school had a great aftercare program that our kids could attend at a moment's notice, but I knew that Friday was a special time for Ariel's family, when they shared a relaxing Sabbath meal at home. Watching Ariel and her husband, Micah, practice this family ritual, I felt a twinge of longing for some tradition that might bind our family together, beyond sharing microwave popcorn over a rented Disney movie. My jealousy was made worse by Jack's phone call earlier that day to let me know that he wouldn't be home that night. He'd been in a breakfast meeting, but I'd heard female laughter in the background. Just the Dallas gals—Tiger and CJ, Elsa and Desiree, he'd explained. Oh, and Hank, of course. It was as if he'd joined a club in a foreign country.

"Let's make a bet," Ariel went on, bringing me back to downtown Portland. "How many stores do you think we can hit?"

"That depends on what you're planning to do when we get there," I said.

"Just shop. I mean, think of the novelty. This is a moment! How often does anyone get to see her friend's hardcover book in a real bookstore. Like . . . never!"

I savored her appreciation. When I told Jack that I found *Chocolate* at our local book shop in West Green, he moaned that the writing of that book had been painful for the entire family. Okay, maybe he was right, but I thought I'd done a good job juggling writing, Christmas and moving.

"At intersection in 30 feet, turn right," Kit ordered, with the firm professionalism of a trusty robotic voice.

"Right turn it is!" Ariel said.

"We love Kit." I patted the edge of the little monitor on the dashboard as our destination appeared, a bull's-eye on the screen.

Inside the bookstore, Ariel followed my lead to the fiction and literature section. "All my other books were in the romance section," I told her. "But this is exciting . . . filed in FICTION AND LITERATURE with the greats."

"Your mom must be proud." Ariel paused, squinting up at me. "What's your last name again?"

"Dixon," I said with a laugh. We walked casually down the row of D authors, scanning the rainbow of spines.

And there I was, two copies, on a lower shelf under Charles Dickens and Emily Dickinson.

I felt a rush of pride to be in these hallowed aisles. Then I reminded myself not to swell too much. I'd written a women's fiction novel, for God's sake. A sexy, hip little romp, I hoped, but no matter what the sales, *Chocolate in the Morning* was not going to become required reading for college lit classes in the next decade.

"And here it is!" Ariel slid the book out and held it back for our inspection. "Love the cover. Yummy!"

The artwork of a chocolate bar melting into a coffee cup balanced on a cartoon woman's sleepy head had been much debated by the editorial staff at Condor Books. Padama had found it demeaning to women and had argued fiercely against it, but in the end the publisher, Trip Caldwell, and his art director, Kyra Olgati, had prevailed. Personally, I found it sassy and suggestive and a hell of a lot better than those embracing, weary-looking couples found on the covers of my romance novels. My former editor, Lindsay, had always reminded me that I was witnessing dewy-eyed passion, but every time I got a new romance cover in the mail, I'd wished someone had pinched the artist in the ass when he was painting the faces of the enthralled couple.

Ariel flipped open the cover. "And here's Ruby Dixon in her Hollywood press photo. That is an amazing dress. Is it covered in jewels?"

"Sequins," I said. "And it didn't make the move. Some loyal Goodwill shopper is now wowing the guys at the trailer park in that dress."

"And she's looking good. So, author-girl, what do you think?"

Ariel swiveled my book as if we needed to purvey it from every angle. "Pretty exciting, huh?"

I realized I'd been standing there grinning like a fool. "I've seen my books in stores before, but this . . ." I looked around and lowered my voice. I suspected that years later I would recall the crisp bookstore smells of newly cut paper and coffee from the café, the slanting light shining on slick coated covers, the subdued hush of the carpeted floor and deep leather armchairs embracing readers. "A hardcover? Under Charles Dickens? It's beyond my wildest dreams."

"I'm buying this one," Ariel said, marching toward the checkout counter. "This is so exciting!" She waved *Chocolate* at a woman lingering at a mystery table. "She wrote this! Did you know we had a published author in the store?"

The woman nodded warily, as if she expected us to try to sell her a set of Ginsu knives.

With Ariel at the wheel and Kit navigating, we hit five other bookstores that afternoon. Most stores had two copies of *Chocolate in the Morning*, with no signs of an endcap or floor display. In Portland, my new book wasn't even a blip in a bookseller's day—at least not yet. After Morgan's big setup, I felt slightly deflated and worried that maybe Condor Books was holding on to false hope. *Chocolate* had hit bookstores with barely a whimper.

"You've just got to take it all in stride," I said as Ariel's SUV zipped down I-5 to West Green, directly to the elementary school. "The book's not really on anyone's radar yet, but I guess that could change. Morgan thinks it's going to change."

"I'm sure it will," Ariel said. "And as soon as I get home, I'm going to e-mail every woman I've ever met and tell her to hurry up and buy your book."

Thanks to Ariel's need for speed we arrived at the school with five minutes to spare, and joined the flock of parents gathered at the quaint red schoolhouse doors.

Scanning the pack of moms, I was hit by the sameness of their hair color. Stepford Mom blonde. Platinum. Goldilocks yellow. Or brown with gold highlights so extensive they'd crossed the line into the land of blonde.

Ariel was the only standout, with her black hair coiled into a twist behind her head.

I tucked a clump of hair behind one ear, feeling every inch the blonde clone. The look that had worked so well for me in ethnic Queens made me just another slice of white Wonder Bread here in suburban Portland.

Well, that would have to change.

"I drink mine without the sesame seeds," one mom was saying. "Those seeds are disgusting, floating around like little bugs."

"You've got to include the seeds!" a swanlike mommy insisted, twisting her long neck into a condescending stance. "It's not a Happy Life Cocktail without the seeds."

"Did someone say *cocktail?*" I wriggled my eyebrows suggestively.

Ariel clamped onto my elbow and pulled me away, closer to the school. "They're not talking about our kind of cocktail. It's this Happy Life Diet they're all on. Trying to lose weight. Can you believe it?"

I shot a glance over my shoulder. A superhero's X-ray vision would reveal that these women inhabited the bodies of goddesses. "They're already so trim."

"Tell me about it. If Jessica Marshall loses five more pounds she'll be able to pass through the eye of a needle." Ariel leaned one arm against the brick building. "I'd like to be that thin. I could be that thin if I didn't like food so much."

"I hear ya. When it's a toss-up between being a runway model and eating a dark chocolate raspberry truffle, the chocolate wins."

With visions of truffles, we stared into a row of windows, watching as the students loaded up backpacks and leaned into their cubbies.

"Oh, look there's Michelle's prison cell—I mean, classroom," Ariel said under her breath. "Looks like the inmates are getting ready for parole."

We both laughed.

"You two sound like you're having fun." A female voice, crisp and cool, insinuated itself into our joke. Suzie Snyder stepped in between us with her toddler son turning circles around her, occasionally falling into her legs. This would be one of the four children she'd mentioned at the swim park, though it was hard to believe this woman in hip-hugging jeans and short tee was a mother of four. "Has anyone talked to you gals about the school auction yet?" Suzie asked. Her West Green signature blonde bob looked freshly highlighted.

Ariel and I exchanged a dumb look. "Well . . . no."

"It doesn't happen until September but we're looking for donations. All the money goes to our school, of course. I'm the person to talk to if you've got something to donate—a week at your beach house, a gift card from your husband's place of employment. Some people offer a boat ride on the lake, and two years ago we had one family who donated their ski chalet in Snowbird."

"Wow! That's pretty impressive, right?" Ariel asked, nudging me.

I was too busy picking up my lower jaw to answer. I don't think any of the parents from our school in Queens owned their own summer home. Certainly not ski chalets, though on occasion I wondered if some of the shadier types had thousand-dollar bills sewn into their mattresses or buried in coffee cans in the backyard.

"So think about anything you can donate," Suzie went on. "If your husband has an extra set of golf clubs, or if you got two cappuccino machines for Christmas." She cocked an eyebrow and faced me as her son flung himself against her, wiping his nose on her jeans. "Maybe your husband wants to donate a tour of the television station? I'm sure a lot of folks would find that exciting."

I wanted to remind her that Jack sold air time. Boring sales. She made it sound like he was an on-air personality. A regular Matt Lauer. "I'll run that by him," I said, mostly out of fear of Suzie. "But they don't really give tours at KJZM."

"Which makes a tour that much more valuable," Suzie returned.

"Forget about the station," Ariel said. "We've got a best-selling author in our midst! Suzie, did you know that Ruby's new book just came out?"

"Mmm." Suzie cooed and shot me a look of alarm—as if I'd thrown a party and forgotten to invite her. "Of course. I've heard of your book. What's it called?"

"*Chocolate in the Morning,*" Ariel supplied. "And I don't think I'm out of turn saying that Ruby will donate a copy for the auction, right Ruby?"

I shrugged. "Sure. I can get you copies of my romances, too."

"We could organize a book party." Ariel's splayed hands reached up, as if she was trying to block out the glare of the sun. "It could be a buy-in party, where the author speaks about her book, with free coffee and a discussion group afterward. We could do it at my house, a dessert party."

I winced. Nobody had said anything about public speaking. Nothing could reduce me to a limp noodle faster than facing a room full of hungry listeners.

"Fantastic!" Suzie clapped her hands together midpoint of her champagne-glass breasts. Four kids and they were still perky; I had to be doing something wrong. "I'll run it by the other girls on the board, but it sounds like a winner."

"Wouldn't that be great?" Ariel turned to me. "And it's good promotion for your book, too. Right?"

I nodded, still a little hung up on the prospect of public speaking. Maybe I could spin it into a coffee party, no speaking involved . . .

"But the TV station tour would also be a winner," Suzie said. "Can you work on that for me?"

"I'll talk to Jack," I promised as the bell rang and the red doors popped open.

"Gotta go," Suzie said. "I've got four kids and they're just impossible to corral."

Ariel and I nodded our condolences as she dragged her toddler through the stream of kids spilling out of the school.

Ariel smacked her forehead. "I've got one kid and I can barely make it through the day," she said dramatically.

"Bad girl!" I scolded her with a dark laugh.

She walked off toward Michelle, calling, "Ah, but bad is such good fun! And don't worry. We're going to have a blast at your book party. Trust me."

I did trust her. I had found a friend in Ariel, even if that friend was another transplant like me.

18

Karmic Boomerang

Although I held no cachet in Portland, Ruby Dixon's star seemed to be on the rise in other major metropolitan areas.

On Saturday Jack called from Dallas to let me know that my book was the first thing he saw when he walked into the mall bookstore there.

"Great," I said, bending down to spray Nature's Wonder on a spot on the carpet that the puppy had mistaken for grass. Becca was great about house-training the dog, but when Becca wasn't around, things got a little dicey. "What are you doing in a mall?" Every time I talked to him he was either in a meeting or on his way into one—not a schedule that lent itself to much mall dwelling.

"My hotel is attached to it. Down here, everything's either in a mall or a shopping center. They've got doctors' offices next door to Best Buy. I swear, the local elementary school is in the back of a Wal-Mart."

I asked him if it was a special dump or the bookstore's own display, but in the middle of my question someone started talking to him and, of course, he had to go. "Dinner with the grand *fromages*. All the big cheeses are here. Numero Uno's being a royal pain in the ass. Keeps saying: 'I still don't forgive you for schtupping me!'"

"Just be glad you're rid of her in your everyday life," I said.

"You never get rid of people like Numero Uno," Jack said. "They keep boomeranging back, yanking your chain."

"Maybe it's your karma," I teased. "Something you need to work out before you two can move on and separate for good."

"Now that's a depressing thought." Jack promised to call the kids at bedtime and was gone.

Monday morning I was making oatmeal for the kids when Gracie called me from the OB's office. "You should be here," she beseeched me. "I'm collecting all these ultrasound pictures, and, really, no one in the office can stand to look at them. It's sort of primeval, this little blob with a big head and bulbous limbs. Only a mother could love it, and you're the only mother I know, besides my own."

"I miss you, too. I've found one friend here, at least, but I wish I could be there for you. Do you know if the baby is a boy or girl?"

"Not till the amnio, and I'm not sure I want to know. I mean, if you don't leave something to surprise, then what's the pain of child-birth worth? So the doctor can say, look, you've got a baby! Like I didn't know that."

"We always waited to find out," I said. "Jack insisted. And it worked out, mostly. Of course, poor Dylan had to travel home from the hos-pital in a sleeper with little pink bunnies on it because Jack couldn't find the bag of nongender infant clothes I'd set aside."

"Typical guy," Gracie said. "Now, if Dylan picked out a shirt with pink bunnies, you know Jack would go through the roof. But it's okay if Dad screws up."

I smiled at the bittersweet memory. Jack had struggled during those first few days with Dylan, from the moment the anesthesiolo-gist held up the baby and announced: "It's a boy!" the disappoint-ment and betrayal on Jack's face silenced the delivery room. I didn't understand what Jack was going through, but I knew I would love and protect this scrappy little boy. My baby. Our baby . . . even if Dad was in a funk.

Shaking off the blast from the past, I turned off the burner, picked up the pot and let the oatmeal slop into three bowls. Gracie's experience would be different, without a mate to contend with. In some ways I envied her independence, though I would never have had the nerve to go it alone.

"Oh, Gracie!" I laughed. "I've just had a psychic flash. You're having a boy!"

"What?"

"Wouldn't that be just the thing to balance your karma? It might be the first time you really connect with a member of the opposite sex."

"Very funny . . . What?" she asked someone in the room. "Look, I gotta go inside. But before I forget, I want you to know I'm already on the third chapter of *Chocolate*, and it's going everywhere with me right now. I can barely put it down."

"Thanks, honey! It's great to get the nod from the harshest critic in New York."

"Oh, fey! I'm easy," Gracie said. "But I'll talk to you later, gotta go, bye!"

I hung up the phone, nearly dropping it into a soaking pot as I lifted my ear from my neck.

"Can I have honey on my oatmeal?" Scout asked.

"I hate oatmeal," Becca said, sounding betrayed. "You know that, Mom."

"How about cinnamon toast? Cheerios? Scrambled eggs?"

She peered into the lower cupboard. "Do we have any Pop-Tarts?"

"Dessert for breakfast? I don't think so."

"But Mom, it's the only thing I like in the morning, and look at her!" She pointed to Scout, who was slathering rivulets of honey atop her oatmeal. "Look at all that honey! That's like dessert, isn't it?"

"Scout, that's enough," I said, tucking carrot sticks into all three lunches. "Becca, you can put Pop-Tarts on the shopping list, but you'll need to find something else for breakfast today. Preferably something healthy."

Dylan gurgled happily as a fat spoonful of oatmeal went into his mouth. "More, please!" The puppy lingered under his chair, sniffing curiously at a glob of oatmeal that had landed on the floor.

With a groan, Becca started pouring cereal into a bowl. I tried not to watch, not wanting to encourage her dramatic performance, but just before I turned away she rolled her eyes, reminding me of my own preadolescent snits. Not even nine and already a teen prima donna. And Jack had wanted three girls?

"Who's the most handsome, cunning, clever publicist on Manhattan Island?" the voice on the phone asked.

"Harrison!"

"Yes, thank you, although I realize you have caller ID. I'm calling with a delicious scoop. How would you like to appear on the *Allie Davis Show?*"

"Gasp! I'm trembling in my clogs." Allie Davis was a talk-show host in Detroit who'd begun her career as a teacher in dangerous, downtrodden city schools. She'd started writing a crime-beat column for the *Detroit Free Press* that quickly found success in syndication, making her name a household legend. Talk show host was the next likely career move, but Allie Davis had succeeded in rising from the pack by pushing her weekly "book club," which aired live from the various high schools in Michigan. Although people criticized her for a stomach-stapling procedure and for appearing in designer wardrobe among kids who were selling their sneakers to score crack, Allie had made her mark as book critic extraordinaire.

"Here's what happened," Harrison went on, his voice animated and giddy. "I just had lunch with my friend Tab Assante, who's now a producer for Allie's show. Tab was in New York drumming up celebrity bookings, and I happened to mention that I knew a rising star in the book world—a real find for Allie."

"You didn't!" I was awed by his nerve and overwhelmed at the prospect of actually appearing on a live television show.

"I did. Of course, he's never heard of you. But that might be all for the better since Allie loves to take credit for discovering unknowns. Anyway, I talked you up and after lunch we went to Barnes & Noble to pick up a copy of your book, which you owe me for, muffin. When did hardcovers get to be so expensive?"

"I'll write you a check. So he took the book?"

"Took it with him and he just called me from the W, where he's sitting in the lounge reading it. He love, love, loves it. Can't put it down. He's cursing me for ruining his concentration for his New York meetings."

"That's great! Maybe Allie will like it."

"Allie will like what her staff tells her to like," Harrison snorted. "You don't think Allie Davis actually reads all those books, do you? Anyway, I'm sure it's good for a plug on the show. They might even have you on. Live."

"Which would be profoundly better than dead," I joked.

Harrison didn't even snicker, he was so caught up in the pitch he'd made for me. I sensed that a booking on the *Allie Davis Show* was far more exciting than booking an ad in a medical journal or arranging games for the sales force at a convention. "Can you get your little fanny to Detroit? Have you lined up a nanny to pacify the droolers?"

"My children don't drool," I said. "And I've got some childcare going, but what kind of time commitment are we talking about?" Besides other kids' parents and aftercare, I'd recently found a sitter named Ashley Sparks, a college student at Portland Community College, who was willing to watch the kids overnight sometimes. But I'd been saving that for a weekend with Jack, and I hated leaving the kids without a parent right now, with the move being still fresh. "It's just an interview, right?"

"Details, details. I don't know, but if I were you I'd be ready to jump on a plane when Allie's people call."

I thanked him profusely and hung up to call Morgan and Padama, but I dialed Jack first, eager to share the news. His voice mail kicked on immediately. I was about to leave an excited message but stopped myself when I heard his voice in my head, talking me down, telling me that nothing had actually happened yet. There was no interview, so why was I creating such a commotion, jumping the gun again?

I thought back to my recent career victories, during which Jack seemed more focused on getting the books done and getting the check from the publisher than on the thrill of accomplishment, recognition or building a readership. What was that about? Could it be that my wonderful, charming husband was jealous of my success? After we had traveled three thousand miles to advance his career?

Nah . . . not Jack. He may be self-absorbed at the moment, but he wasn't the type to compete for success. I would have to make a point to involve him more. It would probably help if he read one of my books—a point of contention for us, as he'd always shrugged out of it. Jack was a nonfiction reader, not one to indulge in the fiction of a novel or a Broadway musical. "What's with those people bursting into song in the middle of a scene?" he once snarked after I dragged him to *Fiddler on the Roof* on Broadway for our anniversary. "I mean, how self-indulgent is that? It's just so far removed from what real life is about. I'm afraid it's all wasted on me, Rubes."

A brilliant performance by Harvey Fierstein, as well as a one-hundred-and-fifty-dollar ticket . . . wasted.

Okay, so maybe Jack and I weren't compatible on every level, but *vive la différence.* For now, I knew someone who would flip over the ripe potential of my news. I called Morgan.

19

Adapt or Die

Morgan was equally thrilled by the possibility of a promotion on the *Allie Davis Show*. We talked for awhile about how to market Ruby Dixon, the women's fiction writer. We decided that Ruby would not mention her husband and children but would appear as an up-to-the-minute urban woman with witty observations of life, love, fashion and relationships.

"And who are we going to hire to play me?" I asked. "Susan Sarandon? Julia Roberts? Sandra Bullock? What will they say when I don't match the woman in the bio photo with the ringlets and sequined dress?" And why had I thought it would be a good thing to paint myself as a swingin' single socialite?

"I believe in you, Ruby," Morgan said. "You did, after all, write the book. Stay true to your voice and things will fall in line."

I groaned. All this talk about public appearances caused a queasy feeling in my stomach, as if the creature from the movie *Alien* were squirming around inside. I decided to change the subject. "How's the home front?"

"We've called a cease-fire for now. Ron was so apologetic about cancelling, but I totally understood. His daughter was in a car accident and he flew out to Pittsburgh to stay with the kids. Ava, his daughter, is okay, but they kept her in the hospital for a day or two. Anyway, he must have called me from every kiddy location in suburban Pittsburgh. Playgrounds, McDonald's playlands, farmers' markets, the mall merry-go-round. He's the one who suggested that Clare and I see a therapist, and that's what I've been working on."

"Did you find someone?" I asked.

Morgan related well to one woman but was waiting for Clare's approval. "Not that I'm expecting a rave. She's so negative about everything I suggest. Right now she hates me so much, and, honestly, with the way she's acting, the feeling is beginning to be mutual."

"I'll bet a lot of this is misplaced anger toward her father. It can't be easy to have a parent bail on you."

"Transference. That would make sense, since I found out she tracked him down in Podunk. They've talked a few times and she's got this fantasy about going off to live with him."

I squeezed my eyes shut, feeling for Morgan. "And how does he feel about having a daughter again?"

"I haven't gotten that far yet."

Just then another call beeped in, and I asked Morgan to hold while I answered.

"I'm calling for Ruby Dixon?" a polite male voice asked.

"Speaking."

"Hello, Ruby. My name is Tab Assante, and I'm a producer for the *Allie Davis Show* in Detroit." He spoke slowly, in a hushed tone, as if telling a bedtime story to a child.

"Hey, Tab. How are you?" I bellowed, instantly realizing how inane I sounded.

"I'm just fine, thank you. I met with your friend Harrison today and wanted to call you and explore the possibility of an appearance on our show. Do you have a publicist or manager I can speak with?"

This was all happening so quickly, I felt as if I was coasting on a bicycle with no brakes. "Tab, I'm sorry, can you hold on one second?"

"No problem."

I clicked back to Morgan and quickly explained. "And he wants to know if I have a publicist."

"You don't need one. He can get promo materials or your bio from the publicity department at Condor Books. Tell him that. And call me when you're done!"

Back with Tab, I let him talk while I wrote down pertinent details, doing a little dance on the kitchen floor when he mentioned how he'd set everything in motion since Harrison had tipped him off that I was fielding a few other public appearances. "Thank you, Harrison!" I mouthed silently. Reminding me that everything was tentative, he said that Allie would like to broadcast her show in two weeks from FIDO, the Fashion Institute of Detroit in Oakland, tying in with all the insider fashion information in *Chocolate*.

Not the fashion thing! Did he know he was talking to a woman wearing green clogs and cut-off denim jeans? And two weeks from now, the kids would be out of school. What would I do with them? How was I going to steal away to Detroit and perpetuate the "independent woman" image of Ruby Dixon?

"The format sounds great. But in two weeks . . ." I went on, thinking aloud. "Well, I'm not sure about squeezing in a trip to Detroit. It's all timing."

"We can patch you in via satellite," Tab offered. "Of course, the broadcast would still be live, but you could do your part in a studio in Portland."

"That would be easy enough," I said, trying not to pant with excitement and nerves as I thought of the many books that had soared on the *New York Times* bestseller list once Allie Davis had featured them on her show. In the literary world she was as close as you could come to a star-maker.

After Tab hung up, I lunged across the kitchen and belted out an operatic: "Laaaa!" Things were happening for me. After a decade of plugging away at it, I might actually become known as a writer. I spun around and then bent over in front of the toaster to inspect my appearance. The warp of the image didn't do anything to thin my face, but it did reveal the gray sprouts in the part of my hair, the slightly shagged eyebrows and pores that brought to mind Oregon's natural wonder, Crater Lake.

I needed to call Ariel and get the name of her hair stylist, pronto. I needed to call Morgan back. Then Jack to make sure he really would be coming home next week.

It was showtime.

* * *

Over the next week as Tab called with more information on how my appearance on the show was gelling, my physical appearance began to come together, too, much to my relief. Ariel's stylist, Sondra, was an artist with scissors, a genius with coloring. I enjoyed watching her fiddle with bowls and tubes of color, mixing up a palette of reds and browns that Titian would have envied. When she was finished, I had a sophisticated A-line cut that flipped in to my chin with a sheen of bronze, eggplant and crimson hues that danced in the light. I splurged on a visit to Ariel's facialist, Leslie, who insisted on an oxygen treatment that didn't smell as yummy as her masques and toners but did succeed in bringing down the pink in my skin and "relaxing the pores," as Leslie cooed.

With the show's emphasis on fashion, I felt lost. I knew that my standard black pants were out, but I didn't have the body or the budget to compete with the college students who would be on camera, wearing designer originals as well as their own designs.

"Tie it into your book," Ariel suggested. "Isn't there a character in the book, one or two scenes, in which someone is wearing something you could pull off? It doesn't have to be the same design, but you could use it as a plug and say, like, "I chose this classic black Halston dress because it reminded me of the Calvin Klein that Sofia wears in chapter five. Something like that."

I was nodding my head, yes, yes! "I can do something like that, but I'll have to comb through *Chocolate* with a new eye. And then, of course, it will require a trip to Saks or Nordstrom."

"Another shopping trip in Portland." Ariel pressed a hand to her chest, as if feeling faint. "I guess we could suffer through."

By Friday evening, when we'd planned a casual dinner to celebrate the end of school with the Cohens, my makeover had come together. Ariel was bringing over a few pairs of shoes to test with my black Halston suit, since she refused to let me wear "last year's Manolos" despite the fact that I'd managed to remove all traces of Scout's pine cones and glue.

Jack seemed a bit surprised when he came in through the garage door with his garment bag in hand and found me layering noodles, red sauce and a cheese mixture into the lasagna pan.

"Rubes?" His brows came together.

"What, are you surprised to see me cooking? Welcome home. The kids need to be picked up in twenty minutes, and they'd love to see you turn up at school. Would you mind? I'd like to get this in the oven and start putting together a salad so that I can enjoy myself when Ariel and Mick get here."

Jack watched me carefully while I spoke. "You cut your hair."

"Like it?" I flipped a few bouncy strands away from my face.

"It's nice," he said carefully. "Just took me by surprise."

"Oh, don't be a stick in the mud." I began to sing an old Beach Boys' song we'd once lamented over: "Where did your long hair go? Where is the girl I used to know?"

One corner of his mouth lifted in a wry grin as he bent over to untie his dress shoes. "Are you trying to say I'm an old poop because I liked your hair long?"

I shrugged. "Gotta go with the change, man," I said, feeling a little stung that he hadn't come over and kissed me after two weeks away. "Adapt or die."

He grunted.

"How Neanderthal of you. You know, they're extinct now," I teased as another layer of red sauce went onto the lasagna. "They didn't adapt." The "adapt or die" principle had been touted by Professor Kaczorowski, my anthropology teacher in college, and Jack and I often reminded each other of it when we resisted change or got cranky about a new bureaucratic procedure.

"I'm still trying to adapt to living in the land of nuts and berries"— he frowned down at my feet as he lifted his shoes—"and clogs. Let me go change if I'm going to pick up the kids."

"They're very comfortable," I called after him. As I sprinkled grated mozzarella into the pan the squeaky noise of Taffy's paws against the glass of the French doors signaled that she wanted to come in. I opened the door, let her lick a piece of cheese from my hand, then pointed her toward the stairs. "Sic 'em, girl."

She sniffed at the stairs, caught onto Jack's scent, then pranced up, her fluffy tail bobbing behind her. Good dog.

I fully expected Jack to bellow down the stairs a minute later, but instead I heard laughter. I crept quietly up the stairs, my head rising above the second story to find Jack sprawled on the floor of the master bedroom in his boxers and T-shirt, the puppy leaping over his chest and circling, homing in to nibble his ears. "Hey, you," he chuckled, gently batting Taffy away and rolling back. "Where did you come from?"

I was reminded of the years when the girls were babies, how playfully Jack got down on the floor, face-to-face with them, how he'd spend hours napping with Scout on his belly or walking Becca around in that special position so that she could see the world.

I was relieved to see that playfulness still existed inside him. Gaining access to that vulnerability for myself was the challenge.

"I understand we're dining with a celebrity tonight." Mick Cohen held on to my hand, giving it an endearing squeeze. "Ariel tells me you're going on television next week. Tell us all about it."

"Yeah, how's that going to play out?" Jack asked as he handed out glasses of crisp, cool Pinot Gris. I placed a cheese platter on the coffee table and plopped down beside Ariel, tucking my feet under me. Since I still hadn't yet dealt with the purchase of living room furniture we were hanging out on our old stuff in the family room, which had taken on some vibrant color from the Cézanne and Monet prints I'd hung on the wall over the couch and fireplace. Dylan was toddling around in his pj's, getting some last-minute truck action in before bed, and the girls were in the backyard making the most of the evening sun.

"I'm all set to appear on next week's show," I said, lifting a bowl of nuts away from Dylan. "Which is going to be broadcast from Detroit's Fashion Institute, to tie in with the characters' fashion sense in the book."

"That sounds like a superb marketing plan," Jack said, his eyes narrowed as if taking it in. I'd explained it all to him before on the phone, but there he sat, his silver eyes thoughtful, his fingers on his chin like a student of marketing. I had to wonder how much he was listening during our frequent long-distance phone calls.

"It's a great hook, Ruby," Mick said, and Ariel nodded her head as if to say: *"See? I told you!"* "You couldn't pay for a better advertising spot. What are we talking, twenty solid minutes of air time?" He whistled through his teeth. "You hit the gold mine."

"You're giving me goose bumps," I said to Mick, who knew his advertising. "It's happening so fast. Now that Allie Davis is having me on, it's helped my publisher stir up interest in the book on some other local shows. They're talking about sending me out to the Midwest to do some quick appearances."

"That's the beauty of something like this," Ariel said, "the domino effect."

"Absolutely," Mick agreed. "This will probably snowball for you, maybe even impact the other books you've written."

"The romances?" I hadn't thought of that. "Most of them are out of print."

Mick shrugged. "They can reissue, right?"

"Wouldn't that be great?" Jack raised his wineglass. "Here's to the snowballing success of all Ruby's books. I'm proud of you, honey."

Honey? Jack never called me honey. What was going on with him? Part of me wanted to call him on it, but I restrained myself, smiled and clinked glasses.

"And who's going to be watching the kids while you woo the nation's readers on television?" Jack asked. "Or have you planned a segment for them, too? Fashion for the playground."

"You got 'em, Mr. Mom," I said. "Though it'll be easy. The girls will be in camp, and Dylan can go to the Montessori school until the end of June." In a panic over the end of school, Ariel and I had found a nearby craft camp that seemed suitable for our three girls. They had a drop-in policy that made summer scheduling very flexible.

"I should have guessed I'd get stuck with them," Jack said, and I wanted to smack him. The martyr-dad act wasn't going to fly with me. Who had been taking care of our kids for the past few weeks? "Nothing like kids to kill your publicity buzz."

"I don't think Brad and Angelina would agree. Or Ben and Jen," Ariel said before I could jump in. "All the celebrities seem to be having babies these days. Babies are hot!"

"She swatted a butterfly!" Scout shouted, pointing at Ariel's daughter Michelle. "We were playing badminton and this butterfly flew by."

"I thought it was the birdie!" Michelle chirped, and the three girls doubled over laughing.

I sent them off to wash their hands for dinner. Although Michelle was a lot more of a girly girl than my daughters were, the three of them got on well, and Michelle actually defused the competition between Becca and Scout.

While the girls shared a kids' table out on the patio, with strict orders not to feed Taffy people food, the adults dined by candlelight, much to my delight. I couldn't remember the last civilized meal I'd shared with adults, and Ariel and Mick made good company with their easy banter and energetic segues to countless topics. Jack and Mick got along like long-lost golfing buddies and seemed to find plenty to talk about, from the best pastrami sandwich in New York City to the richness of Oregon Pinots.

We were lingering over last sips of wine when the girls brought their dishes in from outside, where the sun had set behind pink and purple clouds. I ushered them into the family room and popped *Finding Nemo* into the CD player. The three girls snuggled on the couch with Becca in the middle, holding the puppy, while Scout and Michelle scratched under her chin and stroked her silky ears. For all of the commotion Taffy had brought into our household, moments like these made it all worthwhile. To see my daughters nurturing the puppy and taking some responsibility for something beyond themselves warmed my heart.

As we cleared the dishes, Mick commandeered the sink. "Leave this stuff to us. I'm no stranger to a sink."

Jack was tossing leftover spinach salad into a Ziploc bag. "When we're done, I'll crack open a double-bock I've been saving. It's like having an out-of-body experience."

"Aah!" Mick groaned with delight, holding the glass into the light. "Honey? How much wine have you had?"

"Just a glass. Go on, enjoy. I'll be the designated driver." Ariel grabbed the shopping bag she'd deposited by the door and headed up the stairs. "Let's go figure out how to dress you for the big event. I brought—" She silenced herself, pointing at Dylan's door but I shook my head.

"He's a heavy sleeper," I said. "He has to be, living in the same house with Scout and Becca."

Up in the master bedroom, we quickly decided on her sling-back Jimmy Choos, which I placed in the corner of my closet beneath my interview wardrobe.

"Love your master bedroom," Ariel said, dropping back onto the small rolled arm couch I'd found for the window niche. "And thank you for having us over, with Jack barely in the door. Really, with him being out of town so much, it's so generous of you to share him with us."

I stepped into her Dolce & Gabbana high heels and tried to walk elegantly across to the standing mirror. "I wanted him to meet Mick, and I can't thank you enough for helping me pull everything together for this interview."

"My pleasure. We had fun, didn't we?"

"A blast," I said, looking down at my feet. "Thank God we wear the same shoe size."

"Look at this. You've got a couch in your bedroom that could sleep a family of four. Did you ever dream of this kind of space when you lived in a hovel in New York?" Ariel asked, stretching out on the loveseat. "Jack must be glad to be home."

"Do you think? He's acting like a shit tonight, and I don't know why."

"He's been traveling. He's still adjusting to this new place. We all are. I'd cut him some slack."

"I always do." I stepped out of the heels and sat on the edge of the sofa. "I think the problem is, I don't speak husband."

She laughed. "None of us do. That's why we occasionally have the urge to kill them."

"And I thought it was only me."

"Oh, no. Mick is lucky to be alive, believe me. Though I love him dearly. Marriage is a process," Ariel said. "You give and take, you argue and make up, you love him and hate him. It's all part of growing up together."

I nodded. "I just hate loose ends. It's the romance writer in me, wanting to tie everything up in a neat, happy ending."

"Lucky for you, you have your fiction," Ariel said. "The rest of us poor schmucks have to rent a movie."

* * *

That night in bed, I edged over to Jack, who was facing away, and slipped my arm around his waist. "Hey, stranger."

"Hey." He cupped my hand and laced his fingers through mine.

"I'm worried about you."

"What? Did the doctor call with bad lab results?"

"Save your sarcasm for Corstar meetings," I said. "It's just . . . You seem so disconnected. So far away from us, even though you're back." I wasn't so naive as to believe that two people in a relationship could expect a constant feeling of closeness; I was aware of the peaks and valleys. But that didn't mean I was willing to wait around while Jack wandered, navel-gazing in the valley.

"Ruby, I came through the door eight hours ago. Can you give me a break?"

"I can, but I'm still worried. Did we know this job was going to be so stressful for you? I mean, didn't we come here to notch it down a peg?"

"Isn't Becca's insomnia gone? Has Scout learned to pop wheelies on her bike? I think we're succeeding."

"With the kids, sure. But at what cost? Are you happy, Jack?"

"Have I ever been?" His voice was tense and brittle, as if he resented me asking him such a personal question. "I've never been the type to dance around the house."

True, and it was no surprise, considering the house he'd grown up in. As I pulled my hands back and started massaging Jack's shoulders, images of Mira's drunken pout, of Conny's stern disapproval, of brother Frank's puffed, vindictive smile flashed through the dark. I didn't want to be counted among the "people who love but torment" in Jack's life. I didn't want to be part of the problem.

"I'm sorry, but I worry," I whispered.

He turned around in bed, pressed his body against me and nuzzled his mouth into my neck.

"I know, but I'm fine," he whispered, and I could feel his quiet pain and his hardness as if in one descending cloud of sensation. Although I knew it wasn't something I could fix completely, I did possess the ability to make things better—a small burst of healing passion.

20

Open-toed Shoes at a Funeral?

Thank God I borrowed Ariel's Jimmy Choos, I thought as the studio camera pulled back and panned down to my feet, which were gracefully crossed at the ankles. Somehow I'd imagined myself sitting behind a desk like a news reporter, but instead the unit producer had sat me in this swiveling leather chair on a carpeted platform in front of a blank screen.

Of course, the studio camera was a robotic one, operated by some unseen person in the production booth, and the shot was just to check camera angles and lights, as the show wasn't airing just yet.

I turned slightly in the posh leather chair, checking the dark screen behind me. "Is that supposed to be blank?" I asked Thorne, the producer who'd greeted me with a prickly attitude to match her name. "Shouldn't it have, like, the Allie Davis logo?"

"The production team at Allie Davis's studios will fill in the screen behind you, probably with an image of Mount Hood," Thorne answered. She made me feel as if I was inconveniencing her, adding work to her already busy day, though I couldn't imagine what in Portland could be as important as doing a live feed to the *Allie Davis Show.*

"You need to stop twisting around like that," Thorne told me. "You're creating static on your microphone."

Reflexively I touched the mike pack that I'd tucked into the back of my skirt. "Oh, sorry. I didn't know it was on."

"Don't touch the pack—you'll screw up the levels," Thorne groused. "Just try to sit tight, okay? Three minutes till air."

And she thought I was squirmy? I should have brought my kids along. Lucky for me, they'd all been fast asleep when I ducked out of the house at six AM.

"And when the show opens, don't talk," Thorne instructed. "Just let Allie do the intro. She'll introduce you and cue you in, okay?"

"Got it." I nodded.

"And don't move your head. It throws off the lighting. Two minutes."

"Okay, then." I tried to smile without moving my jaw and felt a sudden tick in one eye. Having spent the morning sitting for Candy, the makeup-and-hair stylist, and getting prepped by the prickly Thorne, I hadn't really had time to be nervous . . .

Until now.

"One minute," Thorne announced, and the monitor went on, showing a Macy's commercial that lulled me into feeling I was at home, watching in my pj's. Next was an ad for a sitcom about nuns, which looked just awful; I suddenly wondered if Jack had seen it, since it was part of his job to watch a little bit of every network's offerings. It had been so long since we'd had a chance to talk about anything beyond essential items.

"And we're on," Thorne said, backing away until she stood well behind the robotic camera.

As the credits for the *Allie Davis Show* rolled, I felt a flash of panic, a silent white bomb exploding in my head, obliterating my name, my memory of my book and a few million words from my vocabulary. I was an imposter—a poser, as Becca would say.

Then the monitor was filled by Allie Davis's face, her brown rosebud of a head with perfectly round coiffed fringe of auburn hair, big brown eyes and dazzling smile. "Hi! I'm Allie Davis, and have I got something for you to read today!" she enthused in her trademark opening line.

And suddenly I was back, Ruby Dixon, a dark-eyed, almost exotic bundle of writer in designer suit, precision bob and borrowed Jimmy Choos. I was me, and Allie liked me . . . I could feel it through the satellite feed.

"Now, you all know the importance I place on reading," Allie Davis said, her arm sweeping wide toward the audience of students gathered at her feet on the steps of the Institute's most prominent building. "And being a former educator, I like nothing more than to bring a good book home to students. So when I read *Chocolate in the Morning*, a fast-moving novel that had me both laughing and crying, I knew it wouldn't fly in junior high. This book gets down and dirty in the morning, and at night, too, if you know what I mean."

Laughter rose in response to Allie's witty remark, and I felt relieved to have passed one hurdle. At least she wasn't going to tar and feather me for waxing erotic in my writing.

"*Chocolate in the Morning* takes on some issues we're all familiar with, like how far should loyalty to a friend go when that friend is killing himself? Should we look the other way when a friend breaks the law? Is sex with a stranger foolish or adventurous?"

She got those issues out of *my* book?

"And, most important, is it ever okay to wear open-toed shoes to a funeral?"

The audience chuckled, clearly relieved that this was going to be a fun one. I would have laughed, too, except that Thorne had ordered me not to move my head.

"And joining us today," Allie said, looking directly at the camera, "live from our studio in Portland, Oregon, is the author of this wondrous chocolatey adventure, Ms. Ruby Dixon!"

More applause as I smiled and nodded. Oops.

"Hello, Allie!" I said sprightly. "I'm so happy to be with you today."

"Ruby, I'm just grateful to you for writing a fabulous book for me to share with friends and students." Allie cocked her head slightly, peering at me coyly under her fringe of bang. "But I have to say, you are not at all what I expected."

"How so?"

"After everything I read in your book, I expected you'd be wild

and wearing something wild, something, oh, I don't know . . . a sequined halter top and plaid tights? Or maybe one of those diaphanous, daring gowns we see draped on celebs walking the red
carpet."

"Did you really?" I asked merrily, as if we were sharing a joke.
"Sorry, but I don't do diaphanous."

"Amen to that!" Allie chimed. "You and me both, honey. But people, look at Ms. Ruby Dixon there. Oregon isn't known to be a fashion mecca, and yet she's looking sharp in what I'm sure is a designer
suit—the little black suit, a wardrobe essential, right? That's in the
book. Isn't that what Barb wears whenever she's meeting with potential investors?"

"How astute of you to pick up a detail like that."

"I read the book, all right. Every delicious word. Which leads me
to the hot-hot-hot love scenes. Page ninety-three is the first really
juicy one."

"I hope you'll excuse me if I can't do a recitation," I joked. "I
haven't committed the entire book to memory yet."

This time the audience laughed at my joke, and Allie's smile went
wide, loving it. "Actually, one of our staff prepared an abridged version that our censors approved. Standards and Practices can really
take a bite out of these things, but let's see how this goes."

I expected to wince and writhe in my seat as she read the excerpt
of the first sex scene, a scene in which my Maggie character makes
love in the storeroom of the restaurant with a waiter she just met. It
was a quick, juicy bang—a scene more likely to be in a porn movie
than in even the wildest era of my personal life. I worried that it
would sound insipid and gruesome when read aloud, but with so
many things cut it came out comically, like a Three Stooges sketch. I
laughed, tossing my head a bit for dramatic effect. (Thorne would
have to deal with it.) The curved tip of my new hairstyle swung
against my chin, making me feel *très* chic. I hoped it looked that way
on TV.

Fortunately, the audience was laughing along with me.

Allie finished the passage and looked up at me with a wry smile.
"Now, I realize it's a little different in the book."

"Just a little, but I guess readers will have to explore that on their own. Wouldn't want to break any FCC rules."

"You are so right!" Allie said with a wry smile. "But, people, I want you to know that Ruby Dixon is a good sport, because the passage I just read doesn't do justice to her book, which is a fine send-up of urban relationships in this age of entitlement. It's set in New York City, which is almost another character in the book. The other non-human character would be the clothes that these women wear . . . delicious designs, elegant shoes, hats and bags. Ralph Lauren jackets, Dolce & Gabbana heels, DKNY jeans . . . These characters got it goin' on. Which led me to pick this fine learning establishment that we're broadcasting from . . ."

At that point the camera panned back to show the hundreds of students sitting below Allie on the stairs and on chairs that had been set up on the plaza. ". . . the Fashion Institute of Detroit in Oakland, or FIDO, as it's affectionately called here. This is a school that cares about fashion as much as the women in Ruby Dixon's book. And the ladies on my staff tell me you have all your details just right, Ruby. How do you do it?"

"Research?" I asked coyly. "I'd love to say that I have an inside track to Seventh Avenue, but the truth is that I have every issue of *Vogue* and *In Style* published in the last three years, and I comb the pages in search of fashions that might fit my characters."

"Tough research, isn't it folks?" Allie asked the crowd. "Now, Ruby, we have a little pop quiz for you." She stood up and twirled around, making her dark print halter dress billow slightly. "A little test of your fashion IQ. I'm wearing attire—shoes and dress—from two top designers. Take a look, because when we come back from the commercial break, we're going to see if Ruby Dixon can name those designers. Stay put! We're back in a few!"

The audience applauded as the camera pulled back again to show the huge crowd gathered at Allie's feet. I squinted, trying to focus on the dress Allie was wearing, a purple, green and yellow print that featured circles reminding me of the rose windows in Gothic cathedrals. The bodice was a V-cut, adorned with gold sequins—or at least, that's how it looked from fifteen hundred miles away, here in Portland.

Damn! How was I supposed to know who designed the dress, let alone the shoes, which I'd barely noticed?

I needed help . . . a lifeline.

I pushed out of my chair and scuttled off the carpeted platform.

"Where are you going?" Thorne pouted. "I told you, you can't move."

"My legs are falling asleep," I said, scooping my cell phone out of my purse. "Don't worry, I'll be back in place by the time we're on air again." As I spoke I extracted my cell phone and speed-dialed Harrison's number. He had to be watching. The man worked in PR, for God's sake.

Thorne wasn't happy with me, but I turned away as Harrison picked up with a cheery: "Helloooo!"

"Harrison, I need your help."

"Isn't that juicy?" He giggled. "That Allie can be a stinker."

"Are you watching? Tell me you're watching."

"Of course I am, and that hairstyle does work for you . . ."

"Tell me you know who designed her fucking sundress."

"Her sundress is actually a boho dress. Trendy, but I think it works for her. I'd say it's a LaROK. And you must recognize the shoes?"

"Recognize what? I didn't even see them!"

"They're Manolos, cream puff."

"I love you! I owe you," I gasped into the phone as I climbed back into my pedestal seat.

"Kiss, kiss!" he said, and I ended the call and tossed the cell phone out of camera range in the general direction of my purse, hoping it wouldn't break, but what the hell . . .

"And we're back at FIDO, Detroit's Fashion Institute, with Ruby Dixon, author of *Chocolate in the Morning*. Ruby's going to guess at who designed my dress and shoes, which I'll model once more," Allie said as she walked along the top of the marble steps, flirting with some of the male students who sat up close to her chair. "What do you think, Ruby? Can you venture a guess?"

"The dress is a tough one, Allie," I said. "It's a fabulous boho dress, and you wear it well. I don't know, it looks like it might be LaROK?"

Allie turned like a model at the end of a runway and laughed. "I could get used to this modeling thing. LaROK, you say?" She nodded. "Very good, Ruby. Our wardrobe stylist here thought it was way too tough, but you nailed it. Any idea on the shoes?"

"One of my favorite designers," I said. "Manolo Blahnik."

"Yes, again!" Allie said brightly. "She's two for two, ladies and gents!"

Thank you, Harrison! I smiled, feeling lucky to have such a good friend . . . a friend with keen fashion sense.

On the way home I thought about how I might even allow myself the guilty pleasure of checking my book on Amazon.com to see if the appearance on Allie's show had impacted the sales of *Chocolate*. A writer named Doreen something or other had tipped me off to the Amazon fix at a romance writers' conference in Atlanta. After she'd pointed out that the website listed the sales rank of a book along with the other publishing information, I'd gone home and looked up all my old Hearts and Flowers titles, some of them years old, and found dismal results such as "no sales rank," or that my book was somewhere in the millions. Meaning that more than a million other books had sold more copies than my book did on Amazon that day.

It was devastating. I imagined a million books lined up in front of mine, like a queue for bread in a Russian gulag.

"Amazon doesn't matter for you," my editor Lindsay told me, since I wrote series romances, most of which sold through book clubs. A guaranteed sale.

Jack pointed out that the sales rank was based only on Amazon's sales figures, and that anyway, some people didn't buy their books online, preferring the tactile thrill of picking them out at bookstores. "What are you worried about? Some people don't even own computers," he'd told me.

Then I had a new book released, *Logan's World,* and when I

checked Amazon it had hit 72,450. That may sound like a high number, but remember that it's being ranked among all the books on sale through Amazon. It was my best number yet!

I started to check *Logan's World* on Amazon daily, and noticed the numbers fluctuating every hour. I imagined some weary librarian type, bun and all, sitting at the computer with bloodless knuckles as she waited to post the new sales figures each hour. I wanted to call her and plead my case, beg her to slide my book into the top one hundred, hell, the top twenty!

Still, I stared at the figures.

When it came time to send out copies of my book to enter a contest, I ordered them from Amazon—all eight of them. My number went up to 59,022! I ordered ten more copies to give away as Christmas gifts (although I had a case in the attic.) I made it to 23,691!

This pattern might have gone on were it not for Jack waking up in bed, back in our New York house, to find me staring guilt-red at the laptop screen. "Go to bed, Rubes!" he grumbled, jolting me back to reality.

After that I'd tried to stay away . . . until today. Today, I'd appeared on the *Allie Davis Show!* I had good reason to indulge.

Hyped up on publicity adrenaline, I pulled the Volvo wagon into the garage, planning to chat some more with Morgan and check my many congratulatory e-mails. I stepped in the door to a vault of ear-splitting noise: blaring television, shouting children, barking husband. Taffy dashed to greet me, dancing around my feet with the clear message that drama was in the air.

"Don't be a dodo-head," Becca called from the couch.

"I'm not a doody-head, you are," Scout retorted from the kitchen island, where she and Dylan were elbow deep in paint. Jack paced the kitchen, cell phone to ear, his shirt sleeves rolled up to his elbows. He refused to make eye contact, knowing that I'd motion him to cut off the phone call.

"Jack?" I paused in the middle of the kitchen. "What's everyone doing here? Did something happen?" Then I noticed the paint dribbled down the side of the kitchen island. Blue dots splattered on the wood floor, slightly smeared by paw prints.

"You're making a huge mess, Scout. Why are you painting here in the kitchen?"

"You told me I could finger paint today!" Scout protested.

"I meant at camp. You were supposed to go to camp."

"She didn't want to go," Jack said, holding his arms out as if the gesture would help me grasp this difficult concept. His cell phone was closed, call ended.

"I didn't want to go, either," Becca said. "Why did you sign me up for a stinky art camp, Mom? That's for geeks."

"You thought it sounded like fun when I read the brochure. You get to make a birdhouse. And ceramic bowls. Stained glass art."

"We hate that stuff," Scout said.

The little traitor. "Well, you seem to like painting, at the moment. And what about Dylan? He was supposed to go to the Montessori school."

"I didn't think it would be fair, with the girls taking a day off," Jack said, folding his arms.

"Jack, it's not a punishment. He likes it there. And the girls will probably like camp"—I glared at Becca, who had her sneakers on the couch—"once they get there. Shoes off the couch."

Becca shifted her feet, sitting up.

"So I let them stay home," Jack said. "I didn't know what to do. They didn't want to go, and I wasn't going to force them."

Just leave that to me, I thought bitterly. I had already slid out of Ariel's shoes and my jacket and was rubbing the paint-splattered floor with a paper towel. With every swipe, the puppy skittered on the floor, chasing the paper towel in my hand. "So you decided to take the day off?" I asked Jack.

"Just till you got home. I moved my morning meeting to this afternoon."

"Fine," I said, and unfortunately my tone was laced with all the venom I felt. "You might as well go to work. I'll handle this." I spoke into the floor, not wanting to make eye contact with Jack. If I looked at him, I was afraid I might pucker up and glare like an angry dragon, and confrontation was not a dynamic of our relationship. Suck it up, tuck it in and move on.

"Okay." I heard him gather his suit jacket and briefcase, and kiss the kids good-bye. When his car purred out of the garage, I told the girls to get their shoes and lunches together. "You're going to camp." Five minutes later, as I drove the kids off to their respective stops, I wondered when it had become my job to keep the children in line. Didn't Jack see that they were manipulating him? That they were making him miserable? That they were getting paint all over our beautiful hardwood floors?

And when did I get into this all alone?

21

Crank Up the Muses

"The public has a voracious appetite for Ruby Dixon," Padama told me over the phone a few days after the Allie Davis interview, "and Condor Books wants to make sure that hunger is satisfied. We'll rush your next book through production in three months, and I'm talking about a super-duper rush. So, say you delivered it August first, we could have it in stores sometime in November. Got to get ahead of the holidays. How soon can you get us the manuscript?"

The manuscript? Since I had submitted the first five chapters I'd been shopping and playing in Portland with Ariel. Of course, I didn't want to admit that to Padama Kahil. "I didn't know the proposal was approved." I sounded lame, I knew. "I mean . . . Did you like it?"

"It's the story about the girls who love to shop, right?" With her slight British accent, she made girls sound like *gulls,* right like *roit.*

"Retail Therapy," I said.

"I love the title. I absolutely adore it. When did you say it would be complete?"

I waffled, telling her I had to check my calendar. Yep, I needed time to check my calendar and my sanity, because I'd have to be crazy to tell Jack I needed to drop everything and put the household on hold once again so that I could write a book.

"Doesn't the contract say October first?" I asked. "I mean, technically, that's when the book is due."

"Yes, but this is a big hurry-up! We need that book, Ruby, and we'll make it worth your while. I've already outlined a bonus plan with Morgan, allotting two thousand dollars extra for each week ahead of the scheduled delivery date."

"Really?" My throat went dry as I greedily tried to calculate. Four weeks early, eight weeks early . . .

"I do hate to put your schedule in an uproar," Padama said, pronouncing it *shed-duelle,* "but this is a deadline emergency. Rush, rush! We need another Ruby Dixon, pronto!"

"What about the TV appearances?" I asked. Condor's publicity department had booked me on two morning talk shows in the Midwest, and I couldn't write while I was touring.

"Oh, right, isn't that fabulous? It will mean even more publicity for *Chocolate* and a nice big boost for your second novel, *Retail Telepathy,* was it?"

"*Retail Therapy,*" I corrected, disappointed that she was missing the point.

"*Roit.* Let me jot that down so I can bring our publicity department into the loop on book two."

"Padama, I can't write and tour at the same time."

"Of course you can't. So we'll stick with the two TV dates and stave off publicity till the book is in. You'll let me know when you've got a firm delivery date for the manuscript?"

I promised her that I would, then called Morgan, who put me on hold while she finished talking to a lawyer. When she finally got on, I had to ask. "Is this a lawyer you're dating?"

"Ach! I wish it were so copacetic. He's defending my daughter."

"Clare?" I'd just talked to Morgan yesterday. "What happened?"

"DWI. Driving while intoxicated. A beach outing with her friends. Too many cold beers, and somebody brought lemonade mixed with vodka. Zigzagging in traffic on the Garden State Parkway. Showing off."

"But she's not drinking age yet, is she?"

Morgan groaned. "Which is another charge. I'm fit to be tied. The only silver lining is that no one was hurt in the accident."

"Accident? Oh, no."

"Totaled my car. And I realized how sexist I am. When the phone rang in the middle of the night and it was a New Jersey State Trooper, I was sure it involved my son. Isn't that wrong, to assume the boy would be in trouble? But no, TJ is safely tucked away upstate at camp. It's Clare who's decided to ruin her life. And mine."

"Leave it to you to be introspective in a time of crisis. Morgan, what are you going to do?"

"What *can* I do? Besides ground my daughter for the next ten years and pay this attorney."

"Oh, Morgan. It must be so hard for you."

"I'm totally schizoid. There's a part of me that wants to kill her, and another part that . . . I just want to take her in my arms and hold her, keep her safe there until . . ." Her voice cracked with emotion. "Until she grows out of this idiotic stage."

And I thought I had problems. At least my children were on the right side of the law . . . so far. "I feel for you."

"And then she has the nerve to tell me she wants to go live with her father in fucking South Dakota. Can you imagine?"

"She's hurting, probably embarrassed about her own actions, too."

"I must have been a terrible mother."

"Join the club," I said. "I'm about to pawn off my children on any sitter, friend or camp counselor who'll take them for the summer so that I can write another book."

"You talked with Padama," she said in a singsongy voice. "She told you to rush, rush, rush. I see it went well."

"She told me to jump, and I asked how high. The thing is, I was going to ask you to get me out of it, buy me three or four more months, but I don't want to add to your bad day."

"Roit," she said, imitating Padama. "But don't let pity for me push you into compromising your life for your art. Unless, of course, that works."

"It might. I have to talk to Jack."

"And of course, he'll support you in this, being the good guy that he is."

"I think he might be tapped out on supportiveness. And then

there are the kids. After Mommy nearly cancelled Christmas, they're not going to be loving the cancellation of summer."

"That's thankless kids for you," Morgan said. "They want Christmas, summer vacation and life with Daddy in South Dakota."

Putting an end to summer vacation is not the sort of plan you want to spring on your husband. Instead, you'd like to ease into it when he's in a good mood, maybe over a glass of wine or after a leisurely dinner.

Unfortunately, I didn't have that luxury since our dinner hour was full of crumbs and spills, the hectic preparation, with a puppy underfoot, of three different meals for picky eaters, meat-cutting and the careful separation of food items so that corn didn't run into mashed potatoes. In our house, mealtime was stress time.

Besides, there was no time to wait around for an opportune moment. Padama had called me back to turn up the heat, letting me know that August first was a do-or-die date. "If you deliver after that, we'll need to delay the publication of the book until after Christmas, since December is sort of gifty, novelty-book month in stores. Too many books wither on the racks in December, and we can't let that happen to you!"

August first gave me most of June and all of July, around fifty days. And the proposal was almost a hundred pages. If I wrote six pages a day, polished and perfect by end of day, I'd have four hundred pages by August. Seven pages a day would make four hundred fifty. That sort of pace had been easy before I had my children, when I could write all night and sleep the next day. Now . . . ?

Could I turn my muses on for six or seven pages a day? I'd learned years ago that if a writer waits for inspiration to strike, nothing gets written. Once I nailed down a plot in outline form, I usually had no trouble expanding it into a story. I could do this, but I needed Jack's support.

So after the dinner rush, when the dishes were tucked away in the dishwasher and the counters cleaned, I joined Jack on the sofa, where he had gone to read the paper.

"We need to talk," I said, pressing onto the sofa beside him.

"What?" He lowered the paper and I realized he'd been about to doze off. "Don't you know those are loaded words?"

"Sorry, but this can't wait. The thing is, with *Chocolate* doing so well, Condor wants me to write the next book really fast."

"How fast?"

When I told him about the August first deadline, he rolled his eyes. "Didn't we just go through this a month ago?"

"Yes, with fantastic results!"

He shook his head. "You're a pushover, Rubes. You forget that they're making pots of money on your book, too. And they come to you with an insane demand, and you say yes, right? 'Can do!' Because you don't know how to say no."

"I know how," I said. "I choose not to. Jack, this is a huge breakthrough in my writing career—a giant step—and I don't want to sit back and watch it go by because it will cut down on the time I spend with my family this summer."

"Okay, all right," he said crossly. "So you're going to do it anyway. Make your family sacrifice and make up your mind before you talk to me. Fine. What I was trying to say is, you should demand that the publisher give you some incentive for finishing the book early."

"They've already offered a bonus. Two grand for every week it's delivered ahead of schedule."

"Two grand?" He let out a gust of air. "That's not bad."

"Eighteen thousand dollars if I get it in by August first."

"Really?" His tone changed, his dark brows softened. "We could swing a new car with that."

I nodded.

"So what do you want from me?"

"It would be great if you could occupy the kids for a few hours on weekends. I'm planning to write every day, so I'll need time on Saturday and Sunday. Maybe a few trips to the zoo or the International Rose Test Garden."

His gray eyes glazed over with a tepid disappointment. "So you want me to be busy on weekends, too. The seven-day plan."

"Just for two months," I said. "Look, I know it makes this tight, but—"

"Why did we move here?" he asked bitterly. "Why did we pack up our lives and uproot our kids and cut off our friends? For what? A seven-day workweek?"

"We came here for a plethora of reasons," I said, "which we don't have the time to go into right now." I folded my arms. "Why so cranky, Jack?"

"I don't know." He rubbed his eyes with the butt of his hands. "I'm not happy here, I guess. It's just not home for me, and I wish I never went along with the move."

Something slithered under my skin, a lizard of betrayal. We had initiated this move for Jack's promotion; it was all about him. And telling me he wasn't happy, he was just reminding me of my own personal failure. I was not making my husband happy anymore. I had to be doing something wrong.

But what? I was writing, cooking, cleaning, dancing, mommying . . . doing it all as fast as I could.

"I'll do what I can." Jack unfolded the newspaper and used it as a shield. "Go. Start writing your new bestseller. I'll go look for a car."

I squeezed his arm, trying to connect on some level. "Very funny. And thanks."

Without taking down the paper, he muttered: "I wasn't joking."

22

Life with Daddy

The second week in June I set to work writing full time, which somehow seemed like a much easier task this time. I felt encouraged by the positive reaction *Chocolate* had received, and it was easier to work in a less stressful environment, in my own office, which looked out onto a stand of towering fir trees that my neighbor Eric told me were some two hundred years old. Somehow, it brought me peace to know that those trees were there before my birth, that they would most likely still be standing after my death, after the pages I was writing today were bound into a book, and long after those pages turned gray and dry at the top of someone's bookshelf.

Dylan attended Montessori's summer program, while the girls went off to an assortment of camps covering lacrosse, soccer, basketball, ceramics, outdoor survival skills and acting. Becca signed up for a two-week country camp that Madison was attending—a guaranteed carpool—and Scout decided to attend a volcanology camp at the base of Mount St. Helens, sponsored by a Portland science museum. The kids seemed to like Ashley Sparks, our new sitter, and Debbie Tory had given me the name of another college student as backup.

The first week was a breeze, with cloudy skies motivating me while the kids were off in their programs. Then came Saturday, when Jack hauled the kids off to the zoo, returning two hours later with a red face and a very smelly but sleeping Dylan.

"Back so soon?" I asked.

"Dylan pooped, and he smelled worse than the elephants!" Scout complained.

"Why didn't you change him?" I asked Jack.

"I forgot a diaper," he said with so much self-loathing that I couldn't join in with "you idiot!" He carried our son in and left him, a sleeping bundle, on the kitchen floor. Guess who would get to change him? Taffy galloped over and danced around his bottom, sniffing madly.

"I hate the zoo," Becca said, her arms crossed.

"Great," Jack muttered, "I just bought a membership."

"It smells bad. And you have to walk everywhere."

"I asked if you wanted to ride the train," Jack said.

"The train is for babies. Can I call Madison?"

"Ask your dad," I said, picking up Dylan and heading up the stairs to change him. "He's in charge for the next two hours."

For Sunday Jack had purchased tickets to watch the Portland Beavers, the city's minor league baseball team, play in PGE Park. My crew seemed grumpy as they left, loaded up with sunscreen, hats, water bottles and, yes, extra Pull-Ups for Dylan. I felt a slight sting of guilt as I watched them go, knowing I could turn things around and make it a fun outing if I was going along. But why didn't Jack get that? He was amiable and charming at work—a hospitable cruise director for the station. Why didn't he shower our children with that positive energy?

I had to put my annoyance and guilt aside and dive into work. When they returned nearly four hours later with smiles and happy exhaustion, I felt charged up with new hope. Fetching a beer for Jack and juice for the kids, I began to think my plan would work out just fine. In fact, maybe it was good to push Jack into the caretaker role.

Unfortunately, subsequent outings weren't nearly so successful. Jack couldn't seem to get the kids out before Dylan's nap time, which made the toddler cranky all afternoon. Their trip to the car dealership to look at Hummers—"They are awesome monsters, Mom!" Scout beamed—went awry when Dylan fell on the sidewalk. I hoped Jack wasn't thinking of buying one, but I held my tongue and went back to work while the TV went on in the family room. When Dylan wandered off and went missing at a local amusement park while Jack was in the restroom, Jack told me to hire a sitter for him the following weekend while he took the girls out to Mount Hood.

Fine! Just palm him off on someone else, I thought as I dialed Ashley Sparks and outlined the dates we needed her. But as I talked with Ashley, I realized the activities that interested the girls—bungee jumping and water slides at Mount Hood—were not appropriate for Dylan. Why should I make Jack feel guilty about that?

At the moment, the tension was so thick between us that Jack and I didn't discuss his parenting participation. I was a little bent out of shape that he begrudged the kids his weekends, but I was also beginning to see his lack of parenting skills, his lack of patience, his indifference to the subtle symptoms of a child growing cranky because of hunger or exhaustion. Was it any wonder, considering his own childhood, playing the scapegoat of Mira and Conny? Not everyone possessed the ability to relate well to children, but that didn't mean Jack couldn't be a good father once our children matured somewhat. Certainly Jack would feel more comfortable once Dylan got out of diapers and was able to communicate clearly instead of whining or curling on the floor in a tantrum.

I also worried that I was blaming Jack to escape my own share of guilt. Much as I enjoyed writing, escaping into my characters and their antics, their glamourous and gritty worlds of broken hearts and loyal friends, it did seem wrong for a mother to spend her summer avoiding involvement with her children. At least, it felt wrong for me, Ruby Dixon, the mom who could make dental exams and grocery shopping as fun as a round of Chutes and Ladders.

Occasionally I beat myself up with guilt, but then I had to remind myself of the long-term goal here. Adding money to the kids' college funds. Trading in our old wagon for a minivan with enough space to tote our three kids and their friends. If working moms in the twenty-first century suffered a good share of guilt, I reminded myself, we also had an array of retail choices that could make our lives—and our children's lives—more comfortable. The bottom line was I had to stop trying to blame myself or Jack just because the kids were cranky about their current schedule. For now, the Salerno kids were going to have to buck up.

The Mount Hood weekend went well, the girls returning in slightly sunburned euphoria over the fun activities, towering slides and trampolines. We decided to keep the sitter in place for Dylan the following weekend, especially since I would be leaving Sunday to fly to Chicago for an appearance on the *Wake up, Midwest!* show.

"It's ridiculous that they expect you to make these appearances *and* write a book in two months," Morgan told me. "Absolutely ridiculous. I can't believe we agreed to this." I was in the limo on my way to the *Wake Up, Midwest!* studios and she was in her office, longing for a bagel but fighting off the urge since she'd made it to the second week of the South Beach Diet. "You're a working mother with three children. They can't expect you to do two jobs."

"I brought my laptop with me. Got a few pages done in the hotel last night. Besides, the publicist told me they've got a ton of appearances for me to make after I finish writing *Retail Therapy*. They're lining up a Ruby Dixon tour—ten days, TV and major book markets." At this stage, it was actually painful to be wrenched away from my book, like being diverted from the unfolding plot of a spy thriller by a whining child who refuses to go to sleep. It helped to live, breathe and dream a story, and the distractions of life were, well, annoying distractions. And while Morgan could wax indignant at the demands of my publisher, I couldn't deny the high from being in this position, playing the coveted author. People were waiting for my next book; there was an insatiable appetite out there for Ruby Dixon's writing. Despite the pressure and lack of sleep, my heart danced with glee. People liked me. I was on the verge of celebrity.

I yawned, feeling the odd prickles of nervousness despite the early-morning hour. It was seven AM here in Chicago, eight in New York, but five for my body clock. "And although Padama knows I have three kids, the rest of the world thinks Ruby Dixon is a middle-aged gigolo."

"Please—a chicklet. Call yourself a chicklet. You know, that brand of gum is coming back? I just saw a few packs on the newsstand downstairs. Anyway, you've been a great sport about all this. It would have looked bad to cancel after these were all set up, and the commitment was made before you knew you'd be in crazy-writing mode."

"It's just two appearances." I would return home today, then fly to Phoenix for another morning TV show next week. I yawned again. "I'm sorry. I've got to get these yawns out before I get on camera, and I'm getting nervous. Not that anyone's counting, but this is only my second time on TV. Tell me what's going on with you."

"Sorry, sweetie, but I've got no high drama to distract you with this morning. Clare and I have been plugging away with the therapist, separately and together. Ron has been great about everything. He's willing to stay away for awhile if the therapist thought that would be best for Clare. That's all still being decided, though I've been seeing him, of course. He was here this weekend to see an exhibit at the Museum of Natural History. He did the museum Saturday, then did me all day yesterday."

I laughed. "Well, I'm glad somebody's getting regular sex."

"*You* are a married lady. You have constant access."

"Well, just because the ATM is working doesn't mean you can make a withdrawal."

Morgan laughed as my limo pulled up in front of a building of green glass connected by silver grids.

"Gotta go. We just arrived at the studio."

She told me to call her afterward, and I was ushered into the building by a young production assistant who seemed to be barely out of high school. Unlike the *Allie Davis Show,* where everything seemed to revolve around Allie, *Wake Up, Midwest!* was a more formatted morning magazine—a well-oiled machine that churned through weather and news twice an hour with a few features on cooking, books and movies in between. Hosts Shannon Fry and Reggie Wilson made a point of greeting every guest waiting in the green room, but they didn't fawn or gush. Watching them interview a police profiler, a chef from one of Chicago's hottest restaurants and a comedian who had a small part in the new Ben Stiller movie, I decided I liked Shannon and Reggie. If I lived in the Midwest, I'd be happy to spend my mornings with them in my family room.

I settled into the green room chair, my energy lagging, a soothing nap looming dangerously close. It pulled my eyes shut, my mouth open. Fly-catching position, yes, but so darned comfortable I couldn't help myself.

"Ruby Dixon?" the production assistant called. She ushered me onto the set, and suddenly I was on, facing Shannon on the creamy microfiber sofa. Adrenaline shot! Energy up! Smile on! After being grilled by Allie Davis for a good twenty-five minutes, I told myself it would be a breeze to stay animated for a ten-minute interview with Shannon. I was right. Shannon focused on living the life of a "chick" in an urban city. I was able to dredge up a few anecdotes from my single days in Manhattan—or were those scenes from *Retail Therapy?* Not sure, I winged it. Who would know?

"It sounds like a blast!" Shannon said. "Though, pushing thirty myself, I do have to ask the question, Ruby: What about . . . well, 'settling down' sounds so old-fashioned, but I think most women feel that tug of maternal instinct, the desire to start a family. Do you ever think about children?"

I felt my skin shimmer with a slight green pallor as I answered: "I love kids. But, at the moment, I have to say they're not foremost on my mind. You know—there's a time and a season for everything."

May the good fairy of desperate housewives everywhere have mercy on my soul.

Shannon quickly moved on to another topic, but I felt a little sick inside, Benedict Mommy. Okay, at the moment, here and now in the studio, the kids were safe at home, not foremost on my mind. It was the truth in a very literal sense, but it felt like a betrayal of my family. Good thing *Wake Up, Midwest!* did not air in the Northwest.

After the show I turned down Shannon's offer of ten AM tea—apparently, an invitation extended to all the guests—and had the limo take me straight to the airport. Although the set and crew of *Wake Up, Midwest!* was hospitable and warm, I couldn't get home fast enough, back to my real life as a wife and mom, back to my book.

Unfortunately, Chicago to Portland is more than four hours in the air, which didn't put me in my own driveway until nearly five PM. I hoped that the comment about family life would die in the Midwest, but when I heard the shrill, sad whimper that penetrated the garage as I climbed out of the car, I wondered if I had brought a curse upon myself. It was Dylan, I could tell, and there was an odd quality to his cry that reminded me of a wounded animal.

Inside, I found my baby crumpled in a heap on the family room carpeting.

Jack stood facing out the kitchen window as he talked on his cell phone, clearly ignoring Dylan. It wasn't clear if Dylan had been chastised or put on time out for something or was just throwing a tantrum, but he seemed so pathetic, balled up on the rug.

I slipped out of my shoes and kneeled beside my baby boy. "What's the matter, honey?"

"Daddy, no! Daddy says no . . ." he whined, sobbing again.

I ran my hand through his curls, wet with tears. Or was that sweat? I pressed against his forehead, the smooth skin giving off an alarming ray of heat.

"Jack?" I sat up. "He's burning up with fever."

Jack nodded, phone to his chin. "Yeah. Okay, look, I'll have to call you back." He closed the phone. "Don't be so emotional, Ruby. He was throwing a tantrum, maybe he worked himself into a sweat."

"Can you get him some juice? How long has he been like that?" I asked as I went to the tall kitchen cabinet, the one with kids' vitamins, Tylenol, Motrin.

"Crying?" Jack raked his hair back with one hand, his dark hair standing in clumps, reminding me of the Nutty Professor. "Since birth," he said sarcastically, opening the fridge. "He's been cranky all day. Didn't eat much, but I thought he was just pining for you."

Kneeling, I pumped a dropper full of pain reliever into Dylan's mouth and pressed a kiss to his hot forehead. "You should start feeling better soon. Where does it hurt, honey?"

His sobs had ceased, but his face was damp with congestion and tears. "Daddy, no . . ."

Jack reached down, lowering a sippy cup, which Dylan snatched and began drinking from, like a desert traveler at an oasis.

"You're welcome," Jack said.

I wiped Dylan's face with a bunch of tissues, then reached for him. He climbed into my arms and clung like a chimp, a cozy position, though I was finding it increasingly difficult to get on my feet bearing the weight of a growing two-year-old.

"Poor kid," I said, swaying slightly.

"What about me? I'm the one who had to listen to that screaming all day."

"It wasn't all day, was it? There was a sitter here," I pointed out, but Jack picked up the newspaper and made a show of opening it to block us out. "Don't do that . . . Don't play aloof."

"How do you want me to play, Ruby? I'm here, aren't I? What more do you want from me? A pint of blood? You already got my firstborn."

"What does that mean?"

"It means this is not fun anymore."

"Well, I'm sorry to cut in on your fun, but while you were hanging on the phone our son was burning up with fever. Do you think that was fun for him? And while we're on the topic, I haven't been wallowing in too much fun myself."

"Oh, no? Your own hotel room? Meals without interruptions? You're always after me about my luxurious hotel living."

"One night, Jack?"

"Not to mention the big TV appearances. Sorry if the rest of us just don't fit right into your bookings."

"Jack, do you hear yourself? I think you're jealous."

"That's ridiculous. I don't want what you have. I just want . . ."

"What?" I demanded. "Spit it out, so we can all make sure you get exactly what you want, your perfect life. What do you want, Jack?"

"I don't know. I don't know, but it's certainly not this." He sat down at the kitchen island and rested his face in his hands. "I hate my life. There, I said it."

I was speechless, as if the viciousness of his words had pierced my lungs and deflated my breath. How dare he? Who did he think he was to hate his life, when all he was doing was glossing over the parenting thing so that he could get back to his cronies at work and play big business? Who the hell did he think he was?

Struggling under the weight of Dylan in my arms, I moved to the French doors and faced out, unable to stop the tears sliding down from my eyes. "That's awfully sad, Jack," I said, glad that my voice didn't betray me with childish quavering. "Can I ask you why you hate being here so much?"

"I don't know." His voice was heavy with regret. "Things just haven't seemed right lately."

"Is it the move?"

"The move, the job. Me, you, the kids. This wasn't what I signed up for. Nothing seems right anymore."

I bit my lower lip to hold back the angry lashing he deserved. How could he do this to me now . . . now, when I was in the middle of the book, when I needed his support. He picked a hell of a time for a breakdown.

"You need to make it right, Jack. We need to fix this." And fast, I thought, thinking of all the other things I had to do, the book, the heavy child in my arms, sick with fever.

"Do you think I haven't tried?" he snapped.

"What can we do to make you happy, or at least to make you feel better? What can *I* do?"

"I don't know," he said.

"I hope that's not going to be your new mantra," I couldn't resist joking.

"The days are so long when I have to entertain him," Jack went on. I turned and saw him looking at our son with regret. "I know I'm lousy at it. I'm just not cut out to be a father. I never—"

"That's not true," I interrupted. "Look at your relationship with the girls. You can do it, Jack."

"Scout's different, and Becca, once she grew out of that baby thing . . . She sort of went from infant to adolescent overnight."

"You're not a bad father, Jack. Don't be so hard on yourself." Let me do that for you, I thought, realizing I was the one who'd pushed him to this precipice. If I hadn't thrust him into caretaker mode, he wouldn't be feeling so inadequate right now. "Look, you're feeling the pressure of having the kids all weekend, and rightly so. But this will pass. We'll get the sitter for Saturday and Sunday. I'll be finished with the book in a couple of weeks." I went to the granite cooking island and stood beside him, swaying Dylan in my arms. "This too shall pass."

"One way or another," he agreed, folding his arms across his chest, "it's my last weekend on Dad duty. They want me in Dallas by Wednesday, planning for September sweeps."

"Oh, no! That's not fair," I protested, though it gave me a sense of relief to think that Jack would be tucked away, taking his angst and his anger out of the house for a week or so. He seemed to have forgotten that I was scheduled to appear on that Phoenix talk show Thursday morning, but it wasn't worth reminding him now, making him feel even more guilt-ridden, more a failure as a father and husband.

Jack turned to me, his steely eyes narrowed, assessing. I thought he was going to try to lift the tone a bit, maybe tell me that he still loved me despite everything. Instead, he patted Dylan's head awkwardly and said, "You'd better get him up to bed."

My arms ached as I carried our toddler up the stairs. Aching arms, swollen heart.

23

Eleventh Floor—Ladies' Lingerie

That night, we didn't talk about Jack's unhappiness, though it was a cloud over our heads, like a giant billboard that shrieked of failure. I hated to leave things unsettled but Jack seemed wounded and vulnerable, and I sensed that any attempt on my part to straighten things out would be construed as pushing. So we talked about what to have for dinner—a roasted chicken from the grocery store—and whether we should spring for custom upholstered furniture to complement the plum walls of our living room or buy premade and have the purple walls painted. Jack usually had no interest in this sort of discussion but he rallied his enthusiasm as he toured the empty living room, his fingertips grazing the rich royal color.

"I wouldn't think twice about it if we lived in a colonial or a Tudor," I said.

"Or a palace," he added, and I was glad to see the old Jack back.

"Plum is just not a very Northwest color. You see a lot more greens and corals, yellows and brick reds out here. I'll bet they barely sell blue paint in the state of Oregon."

He took a swig of his porter. "Are you saying Oregon's a red state?"

I would have laughed if my spirits weren't weighed down by a feeling of impending doom. What do you do when your partner isn't happy and he doesn't want to talk about it?

*   *   *

The next morning, with Jack at work and the kids at camp and
school, I let my fingers do the walking in the Yellow Pages. The only
listing under SHRINK was for shrink-wrap. Only five listings under
THERAPIST–BEHAVIORAL, and I had to ask myself, what kind of therapist needs to advertise in the phone book? Then I went online to our
insurance company's website. Sure enough, there was a long list of
therapists, all of whom accepted our medical plan. The first one I
called, Cory Savoy, turned out to be a man. His voice on the answering machine was deep and thoughtful, sort of like a disc jockey high
on granola and Jesus. I hung up at the beep, realizing this could take
forever. Was I crazy? I didn't have time to screen a therapist!

I scanned the list for the perfect name, a woman, of course.
Preferably one with children, someone who was open and yet organized, nurturing but firm. Eve Griffin. I put my finger on her number
and punched it in.

"This is Dr. Griffin," the voice answered, and I gasped in panic. A
person.

"Oh, hi!" I clambered awkwardly. "I'm calling about becoming a
client, getting some therapy."

"You'd like an interview?" she asked.

"Yes, I guess. Well, my husband's the one who really needs it, but I
can't see him coming in." Silence. Did that sound paranoid? Socio-
pathic?

"Would he come with you?" she asked. "I do couples counseling,
too."

My heart lifted. Maybe Jack would come along if I could be the
buffer. When Dr. Griffin and I tried to come up with a date that
worked for the three of us, it turned out we couldn't get in until September. "That's probably all for the best," I said, telling her about my
book deadline and the kids being out of school for the summer.

"You're a writer? I'll bet that's an interesting job," she said, "and
you don't have to deal with insurance companies."

Although the phone is not an accurate gauge, I liked Dr. Griffin.
Just knowing she was out there, eventually prepared to talk with Jack
and me, made me feel better.

With a therapist in place, I decided not to confront Jack right now

when he was feeling tender and I was looking down the cannon of a deadline. Besides, he seemed better, occasionally smiling at Scout, playing spud with the girls in the backyard. It was light until nine thirty at night, and he started taking the kids for walks to the ice-cream shop after dinner. One night he even drove the children and Taffy to a dog park on the other side of West Green, where Taffy could frolic and run off leash. That night, when I came down to find Jack and Dylan belly down on the family room carpet, Taffy scampering around their heads as the girls giggled, I wanted to ask Jack if he was feeling better. *Aren't you happy now?* I wondered, reassured that he seemed to be giddy and content.

Jack flew to Dallas early Wednesday morning. The next day, with Ashley installed as the fun-time summer sitter, I took off for Phoenix, where I was surprised by the number of cowboy hats and people who called me "ma'am." It reminded me of Morgan's long-lost lawyer husband.

As I headed down to Baggage Claim, my cell phone rang. "I was just thinking of you," I told Morgan.

"Pretty thoughts, I hope. Listen, there's been an addendum to the plans. Can you keep your sitter one more day?" She explained that Condor's publicist had booked me on a morning show in Dallas. "They'll pretape the interview and run it sometime next week, but you need to shoot over there tomorrow afternoon. Can you do it?"

I told her I'd have to check with Ashley, but since our college sitter had been making noises about needing more cash, I figured she'd go for it.

From that moment on, I was all about my surprise visit to Dallas. I could hook up with Jack, spend some time alone with him, the way it was ten years ago. It would be only one night, but one night could make all the difference. With Ruby Dixon–style fantasies of sitting through dinner with no panties on or greeting him at the hotel in a bath with floating rose petals, I grabbed my luggage and headed to the limo.

Admittedly, I was on autopilot during the Phoenix interview the next morning, but I found that I could repeat a few of the anecdotes that had gone over well in the previous interviews, and the cohosts, Trixie and Kyle, seemed entertained.

After that I moved through the Phoenix airport like a seasoned traveler, stopping for chewing gum and a Starbucks latte before getting on the plane toward the end of the boarding process. Why wait for all those other people to be herded in and settled when you can breeze onboard at the last minute?

In Dallas I checked into the hotel, freshened up, then headed to the studio for the "canned" interview, as the production assistant called it. This interview thing was becoming methodical, like one of those paint-by-number sets. A little dab of paint went a long way, and I never mixed my colors. Of course, I realized that if I ever really toured I would need to flesh out a fuller bio of the mythological Ruby Dixon, the fast-track glamour-puss. But for now, my Dallas host, Kendra Skyler, enjoyed my well-rehearsed stories of living single in Manhattan.

I had been calling Jack's cell all morning, hoping to get a better sense of his schedule, but every time I called it kicked over to voice mail. Frustrated, I went straight to the Corstar offices from the studio, hoping to track down Jack without him seeing me. Maybe I could get CJ or Desiree in on my plan so they could steer Jack back to his hotel room, where I would be waiting seductively in the hall. On the second floor, I was stopped dead by a receptionist who didn't know me.

"I'm looking for Jack Salerno," I told her. "Do you know him?"

She shook her head. "No, but what's his extension?"

"The problem is, he doesn't have one. How about CJ?"

"CJ what?"

Another problem: I couldn't remember her last name. "Desiree Rose," I said, "try her."

She did, but there was no answer. "Do you want to leave a message on her voice mail?" the receptionist asked. She shifted behind the desk and I noticed that she was wearing jeans—white jeans with sparkly beads down the side, but jeans nonetheless. The workplace certainly had changed since I was a grunt.

"No . . ." I hated to do it, but it was time to let the tiger out of her cage. "How about Terry Anne Muldavian?"

Her eyes went wide in awe—or was it terror?—at the suggestion. "All right," she said with resignation.

Success! Tiger picked up and told the receptionist she would be right out.

"Ms. Ruby Dixon?" Tiger strode out into the lobby, looking monstrously tall in spiked heels. "It is you." She reached out and shook my hand, briskly. "What in glory's thunder are you doing here today?" Her wide, thick lips, which Jack had once described as predatory, were expertly glossed in cardinal red with a hint of orange that complemented her creamy mocha skin.

"I had some business to do in Dallas—a last-minute thing. I thought I'd surprise Jack, but he's not answering his cell. I dropped by, hoping to catch him coming out of a meeting."

She nodded as I spoke—the head-moving thing Jack complained about. "Well, let's see if we can track him down, shall we? Come along to my office. I know he was in a morning meeting with Bob, but I haven't seen him since then." She led me into an office with art deco furniture and cobalt blue walls—not your typical office, but I could imagine Tiger writing a decorating budget into her contract.

"I'm sorry to bother you," I said, sitting in a smart visitor's chair covered in mauve leather. "It just seemed that, since I was in town, I thought I'd surprise Jack."

"Well, of course. How could you not?" She pressed the intercom button and told someone named Nadine to see if she could find Jack Salerno. "He's staying at the Fairmont, right?" She tapped out a number with a pencil and asked for Jack Salerno.

"I could have called the room," I said apologetically. "I knew about the Fairmont, but just assumed he'd be here, working."

"No answer in his room," Tiger said. "But you do know he's in eleven-seventeen?"

"Oh, sure," I said, not positive where I'd filed that information away. I'd never expected to be in Dallas, tracking down my husband. "Maybe I should head over there . . ."

"In a few minutes," she said, taking a sleek glass tray from the credenza. "First, have a glass of sherry with me and tell me all about why you're in town." She poured a glass and handed it to me, studying me through her long dark lashes. "Jack doesn't give us nearly enough information about you. Let's dish a little, darlin'."

An hour later I was outside Jack's room at the hotel, armed with information from my new best friend, Tiger. Well, maybe not best friends, but we'd bonded over sherry and the copy of *Chocolate in the Morning* that I'd pulled from my tote bag and signed for her sister Nicole, who, she said, "loved that sort of book."

Tiger had walked me through the empty cubicles at the back of the office and the conference room Jack liked to turn into his command center with his laptop and phone. "No Jack," she'd pronounced, then suggested I check his room. Maybe his cell phone was turned off or "all screwy." On my way out she'd told me that a bunch of people from the office were meeting Jack at his hotel at six. "Just drinks and office scuttlebutt," she said. "You'll have to join us," she said in that imperious voice that had once put me off.

So I'd landed at Jack's hotel, which, from the posh lobby and gold-masked elevator, appeared much grander than the dinkster motel Condor had booked for me. Since he wasn't answering his phone, I suspected he wasn't there, but I knocked on the door of room eleven-seventeen. Hard. A few times.

I thought I heard a muffled noise behind the door.

"Jack?" I knocked again. "Are you in there?"

At last the door opened a crack and Jack's familiar face appeared, looking a little pale and sick. "Rubes. What are you doing here?"

"Well, let me in and I'll tell you all about it," I said magnanimously. I pressed the door, but he held it, braced himself against it.

"Actually, I was just on my way out."

"Well come back in and let's talk," I said, pushing past him into the suite with a desk, loveseat and conference table at one end, and a king-sized bed opposite a marble bathroom. "Nice digs. So this is roughing it on the road?" I walked past the bed, surprised to find the duvet covers tossed to one side.

When Jack didn't answer, I went on, as if to fill the space for both of us. "Although the maid service is slacking off, if they haven't made your bed by now."

"It . . . I was taking a nap."

I paused at the foot of the bed. "You feeling okay?"

"Tired." He raked one hand back and massaged his neck—the stress spot.

"Here . . . let me," I said, recognizing the perfect segue to a session of frenzied lovemaking. But as I crossed the plush carpeting a wad of balled up cloth caught my eye. I paused, nudging it with my toe, alarmed when it caught on the beaded satin of my Manolo as I lifted my foot in the air.

Jack and I stared at the scrap of lingerie dangling from my shoe. Black panties. Texas tea. "What's this?"

"It's . . ." He covered his eyes with one hand.

"I know what it is, Jack," I said with a nervous laugh. "What the hell? Have you taken to sampling women's lingerie while I'm not around?"

"I let one of the guys from work use my room last night. A single guy, lives with his parents."

"Parents? Really? I didn't know you were hanging with minors." I blinked. "And where did you sleep?"

He shrugged, as if that was a crazy question. "Here. He only needed the room for an hour."

"An hour." I frowned down at my foot, which I was getting tired of holding up. "Your story is amusing, but a little rank. Aren't you a little old for the old frat-boy-necktie-on-the-doorknob trick?"

"I guess." Using his thumb and index finger as pincers, he nabbed the panties from my shoe and dropped them into the trash.

"You might want to wash your hands," I said, nodding toward the marbled bathroom. When he frowned at the suggestion, I amended, "Or not. But you're not touching me with those cooties."

"You always overreact."

"Do I?" I knew he wasn't having an affair—not Jack. Men like Jack threw themselves into their work, which didn't allow time for the extra baggage of arm candy. Jack had seen affairs take some good men down in the past, leaving them to be passed over for promotion by holier-than-thou bosses who held their employees morally accountable.

Still, the high sleaze factor iced over my libido; Jack gave up that bed so that someone else could do the nasty in it? All visions of throwing myself into Jack's arms and soaking with him in a bath strewn with rose petals dissipated, I sat on the desk chair, feeling like an intruder in exclusively male territory, a visitor in a fraternity house.

His cell phone rang, indicating a text message. "We really can't stay here," Jack said, checking his cell. "I'm meeting some people from the office for drinks, and I can't keep them waiting."

"I know, in the bar downstairs," I said.

His dark brows shot up. "What?"

"Tiger told me. She's expecting to see me there, and I don't think she'll mind if you're late."

"You talked to Tiger?"

"When you didn't answer your cell, I went to the Corstar office. I wasn't going to spend the night in Dallas and not connect with you, dummy." I stood up and went over to him, loving the way he looked in his dark blue suit. Formal, smooth, incorruptible. If he hadn't been so tense, I'd have slid a hand inside his jacket and explored. "Aren't you forgetting something, Jack?" I asked in a teasing voice.

His eyes narrowed, suspicious. Did he think he'd forgotten my birthday?

"You didn't even ask me what I'm doing here in Dallas." I moved close to him, almost touching. Almost . . .

"You can tell me downstairs." He made a careful cut around me and pulled open the door. "Tiger has a hissy fit when someone's late."

We spent the rest of the night in the hotel bar with Tiger, Desiree and Hank, who had grown a goatee that filled in his chin nicely. Here, in his own element, he seemed less hyper, and for a moment I thought that maybe he wasn't gay . . . until he ordered a Wild Turkey and Coke and excused himself to call "Bruce" and let him know he'd be out late. Tiger talked about redecorating the condo she'd recently bought, and I began to see a new side of her, the tough Southern lady who would cajole, kick or hoodwink to get what she wanted. Desiree was surprisingly quiet, but she seemed a little uncomfortable, as if it wasn't cool to have drinks with the boss.

When the party broke up, I followed Jack up to his room and tried to convince him to spend the night with me at my hotel, since all my

clothes and cosmetics were there. "Why would I want to stay there?" he asked, pausing to unlock his door.

I pressed into him from behind. "To be with me."

"But you're here." He stepped inside, as if he didn't notice me.

"My luggage is at the other hotel." We were inside his room. From the embossed paper on the walls and the richly patterned carpeting, I could see this was a few stars above my little motel. "Come on, honey." I crept up behind him, massaged his shoulders, then wrapped my hands around his waist. "Come with me."

"I'll come with you," he said as my hands dipped lower, grazing the hard-on that pressed against his trousers. "Just not at that crappy motel."

We kissed, and I pressed myself against him seductively, loving the feel of his hard body against my softer curves. I wanted to win him over tonight, to feel close to him once again, but I hated being in this position, feeling as if I had something to prove. What happened to equal footing, the smooth balance in our relationship? I'd never realized how fragile that equality was.

We made love under the thick duvet covers, feeling and sensing for the familiar arousal points. It felt fine, but my role reminded me of the bob and weave I'd begun to do in interviews . . . by the numbers, a paint by number.

After we'd both shimmered to a halt, I snuggled against him, secure and tired. "I love you," I whispered.

"Mmm," he growled, squeezing me close with one arm. "What time is your flight?" he asked.

"Early. Seven."

"Why'd you book it so early? You know, you'd probably better go."

His words stole the air from my lungs. He wasn't coming with me? I'd assumed he'd been kidding before.

Stung, I sat up and reached for my underwear, flung at the foot of the bed. As I dressed, I reminded myself that I was tired, hence my emotional reaction. Overreaction. It was just a few hours, for God's sake, but it seemed like a betrayal.

"I'll walk you down to the lobby." Jack sat up on the edge of the bed and leaned over, rubbing the back of his neck. "Get you a cab."

"No, that's okay," I said, not wanting him to see my tears. *You're so emotional, Ruby.* I couldn't bear to hear it now.

"Have a good flight," he said.

"Okay." I pulled my jacket closed around me, feeling chilled. Then, without another word, I opened the door and stepped out alone.

Wiping my eyes in the elevator, I promised myself that we would get through this rough spot. As soon as my book was done we would start therapy together and sort through the issues that were making Jack withhold affection, making me trip all over myself to appease him.

Unable to trust my voice, I nodded when the bellman asked me if I wanted a cab. I must have looked like yesterday's lunch, my hair limp, my makeup worn off. A lonely middle-aged woman, unwanted and unloved.

But that would change. Jack and I would be in love again—really in love—just as soon as I finished this book.

24

Bad-Weather Moment

Physically and emotionally exhausted, I slept all the way from Dallas to Portland. By the time the plane landed at PDX, I had put the emotional turmoil behind me. Chalk it up to disappointment and exhaustion, I thought, as I accelerated onto the I-5, eager to get back to the kids in West Green. I had missed them acutely last night, alone in my motel room. I'd even thought of checking out at two AM and waiting for my flight at the airport, but then rationalized that it wouldn't get me home any faster.

I felt a rush of relief when I pulled into our driveway, stopping in front of the garage to pick up today's newspapers in their plastic bags. I turned off the engine and stepped out, taking in the smell of moist earth and enjoying the feel of sunlight on my bare arms. The pilot had said the temperature might hit ninety today. Summer . . . My mind raced back to the summers of my childhood . . . golden times of swimming pools, watermelon and bike trips around the neighborhood. I didn't want my kids to miss out because their mom was writing and their dad was out of town. Maybe I could do my work in the early morning and late at night?

"Rrrruby . . ." growled a voice from the bushes. I snatched the newspaper and bolted upright. Was that my conscience? Wow, I really did need more sleep.

A head popped over the hedge, the feral eyes and shiny teeth of a beaver. My neighbor Eric. "Thought that was you."

He sounded petulant, and I braced myself for a complaint about Dylan uprooting his flowers or Scout putting tire tracks in his lawn with her bike.

"How's it going, Eric?"

"It's going okay. Are you and Jack all right?"

Actually, we're not tracking anymore, I wanted to say. *One of those sad plateaus you reach in a marriage. Nothing you can do, but thanks for asking.* Instead, I answered, "We're fine. Jack's away on business, and I just returned from a commitment."

"Oh. I thought I didn't see you around." He reached around the hedge, handing me a stack of plastic-wrapped newspapers. "Just so you know, that sitter of yours doesn't pick up the newspapers," he said. "Here they are, and I want you to know, Jan and I didn't read them."

"You could," I said slowly. "We wouldn't mind if you want to take a look." I extended them back toward him, but he waved me off.

"Oh, no. I just pick them up because it looks terrible, and it transmits to potential burglars that you're not at home."

"Good point. I'll mention it to Ashley." I stepped away, but he remained at the hedge.

"How's the little guy doing?"

"Dylan? He's fine. Probably on a walk with the sitter and the dog."

"Jan and I hear him crying sometimes. Noise travels through the hedges."

I nodded. "I hope we don't disturb you?"

"Nothing we didn't hear while we were raising our own." As he waved it off and disappeared behind the bushes, I wondered if he'd meant the comment as a complaint or a friendly observation. At times like this I longed for New York where people told you exactly what they thought, whether you wanted to hear it or not.

Inside I found a note saying the children were at the swim park with Ashley. Nearly tripping over Taffy, I ran upstairs, changed out of my travel clothes and pulled on my swimsuit and flip-flops. Ashley was planning to spend the afternoon with the children so I could work, but I couldn't wait.

Moments later in the cool shade of mile-high fir trees, I held my children in an unwieldy group hug, kissing their pudgy cheeks, pressing my face to the silk of their hair and taking in their kid scent of wet grass and raspberry ice pops. *How does Jack stay away from this for days or weeks?* I wondered without animosity or resentment. How did he manage it?

Maybe he was right when he said that men and women are wired differently.

I became a slave driver to myself, up at six to work without interruption till breakfast. The sitter took the kids from nine till one, then I took them to the swim park for a few hours of my undivided attention. Scout still wanted to do basketball camp, and Becca was committed to a camp with her friend Madison, but otherwise our swim park routine ruled our days. The weather cooperated, giving us hot, dry days of sun that hit the nineties by day and dipped down into the low sixties at night.

My characters were cooperating, tossing off rejoinders that had me cracking a grin. If only the setting wasn't so slippery, that evolving Manhattan scene where grapefruit martinis were suddenly replaced by green apple cosmos. Dance clubs became private clubs, which turned into supper clubs. Safe sex became safer sex. Brazilian waxes gave way to laser hair removal. I had read that vaginal plastic surgery was now one of the field's fastest growing sectors.

And I hadn't even had my eyes done yet.

I was so out of touch. So many of the places Jack and I had gone when we were dating were closed now. I wasn't even sure people "dated" the same way. Did they go ice skating at Rockefeller Center? Did the city still sponsor free concerts in Central Park?

I went online, to a tourist site about Manhattan, to city restaurant reviews. I ordered travel guides from Amazon. Get creative, imagine yourself in that boxy restaurant with the funky orange drop-down lights. Pretend you're young and your most taxing worry is whether your lip gloss will last the night. Make it up . . . fake it up.

One evening, as we were walking Taffy in full sunlight at nine o'clock, I paused on the path to savor it all. Three happy children scampering on an expansive carpet of grass with a puppy, the sun setting into purple and pink clouds beyond the spires of green trees. So perfect, except for one thing . . .

How did Jack fit into this picture?

He'd been in Dallas for more than three weeks now. I had a lot of questions, but I wasn't ready to ask them yet. I had to keep my head on straight, keep my mind clear until I finished *Retail Therapy.* Just finish this book . . .

I was always saying that, like a junky promising: "Just one more fix," an alcoholic celebrating her last drink. I'd always thought myself clear-headed, full of solutions, but maybe I'd been wrong all along. Maybe *I* was part of the problem?

It was 1:37 PM and I sat in my pj boxers and old NYU T-shirt with one knee hiked up to my chin, slugging back cold decaf and staring at the title page of *Retail Therapy* on my computer monitor. The manuscript was printing, the printer spitting out page after page. Padama had told me I could just e-mail the manuscript in, but I needed to have a hard copy—that fat chunk of paper, tactile proof that I was done . . . done, finished, *finito, Mamasito!*

With a sigh of relief I stared down at my desk calendar and tried to figure out what day of the week it was. The kids were off with Ashley, so that would make it a weekday. Now, if Becca had a piano lesson two days ago and last week was when Taffy got her shots and I dragged the kids to church on Sunday, the day before last, that would make today . . . what?

When my eyes landed on the day outlined in orange marker, I leaped forward so fast I spilled my cold coffee. It was Tuesday, *the Tuesday.* Of course! This was the reason I'd stayed up working until three this morning . . . my own personal deadline. Jack's flight came in tonight, and I had an appointment for a haircut in . . . about twenty minutes. I mopped up the coffee with some old Starbucks napkins that seemed to have jelly on them, tossed the whole mess in the kitchen sink, then ran upstairs to throw on some clothes. I skipped makeup and plunked a baseball cap on my head, looking just like an Oregonian except that it was a Yankees cap.

I tried to contain my smug contentment at the hair salon, but it kept oozing out in little waves as Sondra worked her magic on my hair, painting in layers of highlights like frosting on a designer cake. Maybe it was the wine she so graciously served me, but I found myself admitting that, yes, in fact I had just finished writing a book this morning. My husband's been away, but he's coming home tonight. The children are blossoming; they really love it here.

Beneath the gown and the gooey hair gels I knew my life was far from perfect, but for once, I felt as if it was all coming together in one serendipitous day.

By the time I finished at the salon it was after four and I rushed to the health food store for a gourmet salad and some half-baked whole grain bread. Stopping in the wine section, I reached for a bottle of chilled champagne. A celebration was in order, and nothing washed away blood, sweat and tears like a bottle of bubbly.

I sped through a yellow light on the way home, wanting to get to the house and have a chance to straighten things up, change clothes and prep the kids. Taffy greeted me at the door, whimpering. I could smell that she'd had an accident—and there it was by the back door. No wonder, since she didn't get out this morning. Dog walks had been sparing since I dove into this book, but that would change now. As I was cleaning up the phone rang. I decided to let it go, wanting to wash up before I touched anything.

On my way up the stairs I grabbed the phone and dialed the voice mail—two new messages. From Jack, telling me that he wouldn't be coming home tonight. There was a bad-weather system over Texas—no flights out. Sorry.

Crumpling onto the top step, I felt my lower lip jut out as tears filled my eyes. Tonight, of all times. We were going to celebrate. It had seemed so right to share this victory with him, a bonding experience. Dammit, we were going to get a new car out of this book! Jack would have been ecstatic.

The rumble of the garage door opening made me hold my breath. The kids were home. I swiped at my tears, kicking myself for being such a baby. I could celebrate with Jack tomorrow.

"Mommy, Mommy?" Dylan called.

"We found a salamander in the woods and I caught him!" Scout spouted as I came down the stairs, forcing myself to smile. "I wanted to bring him home but Ashley said he wouldn't survive."

Thank God for Ashley. "She's right," I said, nodding at the sitter over Scout's head, "and I know you wouldn't want to hurt a living creature that way."

"I don't want to hurt him," Scout said, "but I'd like to keep him."

"It would never work." Becca was on the carpet, face-to-face with the puppy. "Taffy would chase that thing all over. Besides, it's too slimy."

"That's a great haircut, Ruby." Ashley tilted her head to the side, her spun-gold hair sliding over one shoulder. Model thin, with wise brown eyes and a broad smile, Ashley seemed like one of those girls who could wake up in the morning photo-perfect. Some people were simply born with beautiful genes, while people like me needed a great haircut.

"Thanks," I said, and proceeded to tell the kids that while Daddy couldn't make it home tonight, we were going to have our own personal party with champagne for me, sparkling cider in glass goblets for them, popcorn . . .

"And Nickelodeon?" Becca asked. "Will you watch TV with us?"

I put an arm around her shoulder. "Sure."

Dylan got to have popcorn before I tucked him in. Scout and Becca were given an extended bedtime so they could watch the end of a movie on television. By the time it ended, Scout and I were dozing on the couch, my head a little woozy from champagne for one, though I barely finished half the bottle.

"That was so good." Becca turned off the television and closed the armoire as if she was the mother. "I can't believe you guys fell asleep."

"I was up late last night working," I said, "but now I'm done. Hurray."

"Hurray," Scout echoed as she sat up, her eyelids drooping. "Can we go to bed now?"

I pointed her up the stairs and she brushed her teeth, on autopilot. After tucking the girls in a second wind hit me, and I went back and turned on the television, wanting the company. Switching to the local news, I realized how pathetic it was to be celebrating a personal victory with the Action 4 News Team.

A few kids had gotten hurt jumping from rocks into a local river. One of Portland's bridges was going to be closed for repairs. And Action 4 meteorologist Ace Morris had a sunny smile to match his forecast.

"The day brought clear skies across the nation, and we'll see more of the same tomorrow with the same pressure system bringing us sunny, dry days."

"Thanks, Ace." I smiled, then felt a jolt as the clear map of the United States flashed behind him. Did he just say clear skies across the nation? But Ace was already on to the local forecast. I switched to the Weather Channel and waited, squinting sternly at the screen. Maybe Ace was wrong—bedazzled by Portland's sunny summer weather.

And there it was—the weather in Texas and the South Central region—delivered by another cheerful meteorologist. "It's looking good across this region of the country . . ." he said.

I shivered, though it wasn't cold. What happened to the weather system that had shut down all flights out of Dallas this evening?

A sick feeling peeled the lining of my stomach as I dialed Jack's cell phone. He answered on the first ring,

"What are you doing?" I asked quickly.

"Ruby? Hey. You got my message?"

"Yes, and I called you back but you didn't pick up."

"Yeah, well, I should be able to get out of here tomorrow."

Should? "What's the problem, Jack?"

"I told you, a bad-weather front."

I was having a bad-weather moment. There was noise on the line, as if someone had coughed. Then a woman's voice.

"What's that noise?"

"The television," he said in a monotone voice. "Can you hold on a second?" I heard a muffled sound, a hand on the phone. My stomach roiled. "I'm back."

"Where are you, Jack?"

"My hotel," he said, sounding annoyed. "If you want to know, I was asleep. It's later here, remember?"

"You're sleeping with the television on?"

As he answered, some lame excuse, a cat meowed loud and clear. It could have been an ad for the clarity of digital phones.

"Since when do they provide cats in hotel rooms?" My voice quavered as a shiver consumed my body.

"Ruby, you—"

"Jack," I cut him off as the image of my husband reclining under the covers with a seminaked woman beside him bled into my psyche. "When were you going to tell me that you're having an affair?"

Part Three

After the Fall

25

Filling the Void

That horrible night, I cleaned my kitchen floor.

The minute I hung up on Jack I had a panic attack on the living room couch, my heart racing, beating painfully in my chest, my body quaking uncontrollably. I felt paralyzed, unable to lift my neck from the cushion as I contemplated my damaged life. My life was an eggshell cracked in two, and I could not escape the trauma at the scene of my own accident. I couldn't look away, was unable to shake off the sting of adrenaline.

Hugging myself, I rocked on the couch, trying to make my heart stop racing. Could the heart just pop if it got overtaxed? Calm yourself, I told myself, and for a moment I did. But then my mind greedily returned to the unfairness of it all and the deceit of my husband. At this very moment he was in the arms of another woman, flesh on flesh. Sharing intimacies and secrets. I wailed like a baby and stamped my feet on the floor.

It didn't help. I pulled myself aright on the couch and turned off the television. I had my life together. I knew what I wanted and worked hard toward that goal. How could Jack do this to me? How could he?

And how could *she?* What kind of woman had an affair with a married man who had three young children at home?

Giving up on sleep, I went to make myself a cup of tea and accidentally knocked a bag of coffee beans over. The bag opened up, beans skittering across the wood floor like dancing cockroaches.

"Oh, no!" I whimpered, staring at the mess.

Then I got the broom and started sweeping. I couldn't fix my life, but I could swipe these coffee beans up from under the table and counter.

When the beans were cleaned up, I decided to wet mop the floor and then set the wet mop in the corner. Three AM and I was cleaning my kitchen floor like a zombie mommy. Methodically, systematically, one portion at a time.

Who was this woman?

Obviously someone he worked with. Was it Tiger, who'd treated me with extra kindness when I'd stopped into the office? Desiree Rose, the hairspray blonde? Or maybe CJ. She had the spunk, the sense of humor Jack always went for. Well, that is, he'd gone for it when he'd hooked up with me.

I hated this woman, this invasive monster who'd wrapped her tentacles around my husband.

No, I didn't hate her. She could have Jack.

Because he was the one I hated.

He said he would be coming home tomorrow, though I wasn't sure what that meant. Was this still his home? Was he planning to stay here? Was he planning to stay married?

A spot in front of the French doors didn't come clean with the first swipe. I delighted in rubbing it repeatedly, working it hard, till it disappeared. Maybe I couldn't rub the blemishes from my life, but I was going to have the cleanest goddamn floor in the Pacific Northwest.

The next day when I heard the garage door open that announced Jack's return, the house was meticulous. For once, everything was in its place, the magazines casually fanned across the coffee table, the burnished chrome handles of the cabinetry shiny, the vanilla-white cabinets now free of stray grape jelly or juice stains. I would swear to it, since I'd hand-scrubbed each one.

Jack's footsteps grew closer, but I didn't look up from where I stood, swiping fingerprints from around the handle of the French doors.

"Where are the kids?" he asked.

"At the movies with Ashley." I looked up, faltering when I saw his face, a little ashen but well rested. Damn it, how did he manage to sleep in the middle of this? "I didn't want to discuss this in front of them."

"Dylan can sit through a movie now?" he asked in disbelief.

"Dylan can do a lot of things you're not aware of." Already, he had me on the defensive—not good, Ruby. Down, girl.

He slid off his suit jacket, tossed it onto the couch and loosened his tie as if this was an average day. As if he lived here. "Is he out of diapers yet?"

"Pretty close." It was one of those developments I was going to spring as a surprise when Jack got home; now, it seemed to have lost all its luster.

"I was hoping to see the kids. I really miss them, but you're right. Let's talk."

I noticed how he sat on the couch, instead of flopping back in his usual manner. He realized the parameters had changed. I also noticed that he was a handsome guy, those flashing silver eyes and that thick dark hair. That thoughtful glow, the hint of inner fire. I'd always thought that I could soothe his inner conflict, smooth the roiling waters. Maybe I had possessed that magic for him at one time, but now the conflict was beyond my reach, a storm on a distant sea.

"You're staring at me," he said.

"I thought that, when I saw you today, I'd hate you. That the mask of deception would make you look hideous to me."

"And . . . ?"

I shrugged. "You're aging well."

He grabbed a pillow and hugged it to his chest. "Can you sit down? This isn't easy for me."

Like it's a breeze for me! I wanted to rant, but I sat at the other end of the L of the two couches. I couldn't face him, and I didn't want to sit beside him. From this spot I was facing the framed photos of the kids I'd taken at a Long Island amusement park two years ago. Color photos with the clownish façade of a carousel in the background. Suddenly, the pictures looked garish, a carnival headed for doom.

"Look, I'm sorry about . . . about everything. I don't know what's happened to me." He was staring at a small red bench across the room, a footstool Scout had claimed as her own personal chair when she was a toddler.

"How did it happen, Jack? I mean, I know you weren't thrilled with things here in the last few months, but a little dissatisfaction is no reason to . . . to . . ." It sounded so trite to say the words: *have an affair*. As if it was an everyday occurrence. Have a burger. Have a manicure. Have an affair. "It's no reason to ruin our lives."

"I know, I know that. It started as a mistake, my mistake, and then, I don't know, it sort of developed into a bad habit. Like smoking, or overeating."

I shook my head as that cloying feeling churned through my belly again. "A bad habit." Harmful and annoying. Did this woman mean so little to him? "Is it about sex, then?"

"No . . . no! Of course not. It's more like I feel sorry for her. She's a good kid, under all that makeup and hairspray. And she believes in me."

He was seeing a kid? How old was this woman? I stared at him in horror.

He collapsed around the pillow. "I shouldn't be telling you this, should I? I mean, I don't want to hurt you any more than I already have, but the ironic part is, you're the only person I *can* talk to. You're my best friend in the world, Ruby. Don't think I ever stopped loving you, it's just that . . ."

"You made a mistake," I supplied.

He nodded.

"With someone at work?" I had to know. Details . . . I needed lots of details so I could niggle at each component in my mind, over and over again.

"It's always someone in the workplace, isn't it? I've always disapproved of guys who fished off the company pier, but now I fell for that one, too."

I couldn't help myself. "Who is it?" Spell it out, Jack!

"Dez. Do you remember Desiree Rose?"

How could I forget? Blonde, dressed with anal precision. Shellacked with makeup. I felt my face crinkle in distaste. "Now I know you're really over the edge. She's not your type at all."

"You'd think that, but underneath all the crap she pours on her face she's a really nice person. Smart, too. You'd like her if you got to know her, Rubes."

I didn't think so. I shook my head in disbelief, not wanting to hear one more word about her but unable to make him stop.

"She's really good at her job. She knows everything about the Dallas office, all the players there, the lay of the land. And she believes in me."

I believe in you, Jack. At least, I used to . . .

"She's got a tiny little condo, but it's quiet. Like a retreat." He closed his eyes. "I feel safe there, Rubes. I don't know why, because she's really close to the freeway, but I sleep really well there."

"You're veering off, Jack."

"Right. Sorry. I guess, the thing is . . ." He let out his breath in a heavy sigh. "I just don't know how to pull myself out of this thing."

"So you haven't ended it? The affair isn't over?" I couldn't believe this could be true, but again, he was shaking his head no.

"I just don't know what the right thing is for me. I mean, I miss you and the kids, but when I'm with her, I feel so . . . *alive. Liberated.* Like myself again."

A tiny cry escaped my throat at the thought of Jack finding his home somewhere else in the world.

"Rubes, I'm sorry. I didn't want to hurt you."

Tears pooled in my eyes, but I pressed at my eyelids to make them run down my cheeks. "So, what are you saying, Jack? That you're moving in with her?"

"No! That's not it. I mean, I don't want to move out, though I understand your anger."

"So you want to stay here and, what? Keep seeing your girlfriend when you visit corporate headquarters?"

"Look, I'm not saying I've got the answers, today."

"No shit! You know, Jack, a lesser woman would kill you now."

He held up his hands. "You said you wanted honesty."

"You are not going to keep a wife and three loving children in Portland while you go off and . . . and fuck around with your girl-friend in Dallas. It's not going to happen, Jack. If you want to save the marriage, give up the girlfriend."

"It's more complicated than that. My life isn't so simple anymore. Ruby, look, I love you and the kids, but I just don't see myself as a suburban father of three."

I shot up from the sofa. "Don't *see* yourself? Take a look in the mirror!"

"Okay." His hands lowered. "I'm an asshole, I know. But at least I'm trying to be true to myself. I'm trying to be a man about this."

"You've read too many self-indulgent articles in those glossy in-flight magazines on your plane rides to Dallas!" I leaned over him. "True to yourself? Oh, give me a break! You've got three little kids out there who haven't seen their father for weeks, because, why? He's busy being true to himself. Which is a euphemistic way of say-ing he's shacked up with a girlfriend."

"Ruby, the thing with Dez just happened, don't you see? There was this huge hole in my life and she just stepped into it. It was a matter of the right place and time."

I straightened, as if the shrieking velocity of his words threw me back.

A hole in his life.

And here I'd thought that *I* could fill that void.

I turned away and the tears started again, welling in my eyes. Salty face, salty sinuses. *This is how a marriage ends, how your life goes off track. It happens before you're even aware of it, spinning down a parallel road that you can't even see until suddenly, the damage takes a turn, crosses your path and strikes you down.*

"Ruby," he said behind me, "I'm sorry. I feel awful about this."

"Take my word for it, I feel worse."

"See, that's one of the things I love about you. Even in crisis, you're still cracking jokes."

Hardy, har, har. I guess comedic ability wasn't lure enough to hold on to my husband. "You'd better pack up your stuff. Whatever you want to take, for now."

"Should I go to a hotel? I mean, can't I stay here? You could have the bed."

"You need to get out," I said firmly. "To a hotel, Dallas, wherever."

"What about the kids? I was hoping to see them . . ."

"Get your stuff out and you can come back later. You can take them to dinner."

"Okay." His soft footsteps moved behind me to the stairs.

I cringed as he walked by, afraid he would touch me and make me shatter into a million pieces. Or at least, it would feel that way.

While Jack was out with the kids that evening I decided to test the waters for support. Although my feelings were still raw, I had to talk. But what should I say? That Jack and I were taking a break? In his defense, it seemed so trite to say that he was having an affair; reducing everything to those sordid terms diminished the value and complexity of our relationship. I dialed Harrison's number, winging it. Once I choked out "this woman at the office" the rest just leaped out.

"Dump him!" Harrison advised. "You're Ruby Dixon, best-selling author, and you can do much better than a man who wears off-the-rack suits."

"I think his suits are fine," I said, "it's the girlfriend that's cramping my style." It was easier to talk about it over the phone. I could toss off sardonic witticisms without having to account for my red eyes and quivering hands.

"Did you say the girlfriend has crabbing mai tais? Is that contagious?" Harrison shouted into the phone as the music behind him blared. "I'm sorry, lamb chop, but I'm in the middle of the premier party for *Evita* and it's getting wild."

I sighed, missing the insanity of it. "How goes it in Sodom and Gomorrah?"

"Sometime tomorrow?" He struggled to piece the conversation together. "You want to talk tomorrow?"

"I could use a party like that tonight."

"Well, you just get yourself back here and we'll do it all. I think New York has some kissing up to do to Ms. Ruby Dixon, best-selling author."

"And I will be there, in two weeks or so. My big media tour ends up in New York!"

"Losing you again . . . Something about a meat-eater landing in New York?" he asked.

"We'll talk tomorrow," I said.

"Yes, yes, and don't let the boy get you down. He's history!"

"Got it." I liked the way Harrison could move on.

Gracie was more coddling, her maternal instincts filtering through the phone. She wanted to mother me and my children. "Oh, Ruby, the kids! Have you told them yet?"

"Not yet, it's too new. I want to read up on the right thing to say. I'd also like to know what the real status is between Jack and me. I mean, are we now separated, or is this just a cooling-off period?"

"Would you take him back?" Gracie asked.

"With his tail between his legs and a commitment to meet with a couple's therapist."

"I can't believe him, leaving you and the kids, and out in the boonies of Oregon." Despite my tales of paradise found, Gracie refused to accept the belief that my family was better off in suburban Portland. "Men are so self-absorbed," she went on. "Honestly, I don't know how you put up with Jack this long. How many years has it been?"

I struggled with the calculation. "Ten? Twelve?" Jack and I weren't big on celebrating anniversaries or marking milestones in our lives. We often joked that, if sales relied on him, he'd put Hallmark out of business.

"Amazing. You know, I think all relationships are doomed from the start. If people were meant to mate for life God wouldn't have created plastic surgery. That's why I'm glad to be getting my family without the scourge of a man in the picture."

This was a slightly different tune from Gracie's old "Where the hell is Mr. Right and why isn't he calling?" song, but I decided not to press it since she was six months pregnant and staying up late to listen to my tale of woe. "How is the little peanut?"

"Sucking up my energy and kicking like a soccer star. Did I tell you the technician said it's a boy? I can't believe it. What am I going to do with a boy? I don't even understand them when they're grown up beyond the grips of testosterone."

"You'll have awhile to enjoy your baby," I said. "They're sort of genderless in the beginning."

"Dr. Levin says it's a textbook case. I'm his star patient."

"He said that?"

"Almost. Let me ask you, did you fantasize about your OB when you were expecting?"

"Dr. Kuliac?" I winced as I recalled the greased comb-over of dark hair over a shiny pate—my view of Dr. Kuliac from the stirrups as he was taking care of business. "Gracie, if you ever saw him, you wouldn't be asking me that now."

"I gotta tell you, my guy looks like a young Tom Hanks. The first time I was in the office he had sunglasses on top of his head, tucked in thick curls. I found myself a little miffed that he wanted to take a look down there without at least some heavy petting first. Of course, since the first visit it's been clothes on. Checking the baby's heartbeat. Ultrasound. Asking about my diet. He's so pleased when I tell him about all the skim milk I drink. He says he's proud of me."

"Sounds like a nice guy. It's important to have a good rapport with your doctor."

"Rapport—shmor. I'd like to see *him* naked."

And this from the woman who just told me that all relationships are doomed. "Is he married?"

"I'm trying to find out, but the receptionists are not forthcoming with dirt."

"Guarding his privacy, are they?"

"You'd think they were his mother." She giggled. "The baby just kicked. Oh, Ruby I wish you were here. I'm really showing now. Maternity clothes are so forgiving, but I'm afraid my belly button's going to pop out. Did that happen to you?"

"I honestly don't remember."

"And there's no one to rub my belly or feel the kicks, aside from Dr. Levin. I wonder how old he is . . ."

At the sigh in her voice I felt a quivery sense of homesickness. How perfect it would be to head over to Gracie's place right now, open a bottle of wine (for me) and spend the night watching repeats of *Friends* or *Frasier*. I dropped onto the couch, sinking back to my glum cocoon of crisis. Jack was leaving me . . .

Morgan was more of a level touchstone. "Oh, honey, I had no idea you were going through this."

"Apparently, I didn't either, until yesterday."

"You are a rock, Ruby. The way you've held everything together, your writing and those kids with Jack gone most of the time, anyway. You've been a single parent, whether you realize it or not."

A single parent. My lower lip crumpled. It seemed such a sad role, a place I'd never wanted to be.

"What are you going to do?"

"Right now I don't think there's anything to be done. Jack has to figure out his priorities in life."

"But you're not sitting by and waiting for him to make all the decisions? Ruby, you can't. You've got just as much say in this; you're half the partnership. And what if Jack decides to come back a few months down the road and you then realize you don't want him? Don't think things will ever be the same, that you can settle back into the old patterns. You need to evolve, both of you."

She seemed so passionate about it, but I wasn't ready to deal with any of the issues yet. "I hadn't really thought about myself."

"Well, get thinking about it, honey. And let me know if there's anything I can do. You're on tour like, next week, right? How are you going to handle that?"

"Jack promised to cut his hours short to take care of the kids. He'll have to fly back and . . . handle them."

The thought of Jack juggling to meet the needs of our three children now filled me with dark satisfaction. And he didn't see himself as the suburban father of three? Well, next week he'd have a chance to take a second look at himself.

"Let me temper bad news with good," Morgan went on. "Condor's publicity department has really been pushing you for this tour. They posted that dolled-up glitter-girl photo of you on their website, and the buzz is good. Apparently Lolly's people have been in touch. Lolly might have you on the show."

"*The Lolly! Show?*" Quite a few years ago Lolly Peters had just become "Lolly" when she moved from talk-show host to megamedia mogul. Lolly is huge. "I can't go on Lolly. She'll eat me alive. She'd be just the person to expose me for the mediocre mother and house frump that I truly am."

"Ruby . . ." Morgan's voice was stern, reproachful. "She's a fan."

"A fan of Ruby Dixon the madeup slick chick. I'm really not up for this, Morgan."

"If it happens it will be a phenomenal promotional opportunity and you will rise to the occasion as you always do," Morgan said. "You don't, by any chance, have that sequined dress hanging around?"

The Bill Blass of seven years ago. "I gave it to Goodwill when we left New York." Morgan groaned, and I added: "It seemed so impractical to keep. Who knew I'd actually *need* a sequined gown in my wardrobe?"

"Ain't that the truth. You just can't anticipate these things . . . *any* of these things."

The need for a glitter gown. The departure of a husband for nubile territory. Who knew?

26

Jack: Stepped On It

To be honest, I don't believe in therapy. How does rehashing all your unfixable problems make them better or make them seem fixable? Talk about deluded.

But I meet with a therapist. I do it for Ruby, whose trembling phone voice destroys me, and for the kids. Even if Ruby and I get divorced, I figure the kids are stuck with me as their father for life and I'd better figure out a way not to screw them up the way my parents did a number on me.

Dr. Gretchen Epstein is an excellent listener. When I hit on certain topics, like my mother's drinking or my reluctance to have kids, her brown eyes go wide, and I know I have her. Ruby picked her from a directory of Dallas shrinks in our insurance plan. I thought it was sort of ballsy of her to find a shrink for me in Dallas, but I guess it was a lucky pick in the end. In our first session when we laid down the ground rules I tell her no couch. I will sit on it, but don't feel comfortable lying down. She says that's okay, but later I find that facing her is sometimes a distraction, as I go off wondering if her hair has turned prematurely gray or if she bleached it out, if her husband is a decent guy (a rarity in my book) and exactly how old *is* she? What is the deal with those argyle socks peeking out from under her pants? And that accent . . . It's more Chicago than Texas.

Dr. Ep loves my family crap. She was always up for another

story about how Ma's drinking ruined a baseball tryout or a class trip. But I got tired of telling those stories pretty fast, and my mind went back to a time before she was hitting the booze, the first time I saw her cry.

"It was when President Nixon resigned," I said. "I was seven or eight, but I've never been that big on dates and history."

"It was 1974," she said, her eyes going wide.

If I looked away from Dr. Ep I could see the television screen clearly. "It scared me to see the president of the United States crying, sobbing, as he said good-bye to the White House staff. I mean, it seemed like suddenly no one was in charge and that was scary. But to see how much he was hurting . . ."

I remembered Nixon in his dark suit, with the staff, housekeepers and maids and gardeners lined up before him. How he gave them each a handshake or a hug, his shoulders shaking with sobs.

"The man was so wounded. Adrift. Like, he could never again feel at home in the country he'd once ruled. I remember thinking, his life is ruined. I'd never seen a man cry, except for in movies, and then . . . My mother burst into tears, sitting on the living room sofa. I remember asking her what was wrong, though I sort of knew, but she just ignored me and grabbed a dishtowel from the kitchen and sat back down, pressing it to her face while Nixon gave that painful speech."

"You must have been frightened," she said.

"Freaked out. The country was falling apart and so was Ma. I remember thinking that no one was in control, no one was really watching out for any of us, making sure things would be okay. Those guys had been dying in Vietnam, and when a bunch of bodies came home we just seemed to be replenishing the supply with another planeload of men. I was a kid, but I'd seen enough nightly news on TV to know something smelled. Nothing was going to change or get better. I remember thinking that I was just ten years away from it— the draft, Vietnam. I could see my mother sitting on that couch years later, crying when she heard that my body was coming home on a plane." I rubbed my temples. "That was the beginning of my jaded attitude, I think. Fatalism at, what? Age eight?"

"But things did change. The war ended."

"It hadn't even begun for the Salernos. Aunt Angie was still alive then. Ma had her best friend, she wasn't drinking yet." I covered my mouth with one hand, squeezed my lips together. "That changed. It all went downhill. But there was something about seeing my mother cry that day—cry with the president—I don't know, it just rocked me to the core."

"You realized there were certain things your mother could not fix."

"I realized that nothing could be fixed. We're just stuck on this spinning planet and it's all out of control."

Dr. Ep argued with me about control and order for awhile, but I came away feeling that my life was now the orb spinning out of control, and in the mad, wild frenzy my kids and my wife were being flung into deep space.

All these years later I now understand why Nixon burst into tears when he said good-bye to the White House staff, all those house-keepers in their aprons and caps, lined up along the staircase. I get it. He stepped on his own dick and now he had to pay. He fucked it all up for himself and his family, with no one else to blame.

I get it.

Because I stepped on mine, too.

My fault. And I have no idea how to fix it.

Corstar does not take kindly to philanderers. Though they cannot publish this in their HR manuals, everyone knows the corporate rap. So I do not entrust the developments in my personal life to anyone. No one has a clue, except, of course, Dez. I have to pull some strings to pretend I'm still needed in Dallas, which I've been doing for the past few months, anyway. In trying to make myself indispensable at headquarters, I get pulled onto an acquisitions team, and now I must give my full attention to a station in Dallas that will be the cherry on Corstar's sundae if we can swing the deal.

The timing stinks. Ruby's got her tour and I've promised to get myself back to Portland to watch the kids. Dez knows the shit has hit the fan with Ruby, and she thinks I'm pulling away from her, too, though I'm really just spending fourteen hours a day at the office and collapsing back at the hotel.

The kids are a problem for me. Every time I talk to Scout on the phone, it tears at my heart. When we were riding bikes together we found a path into a small stream and she acts like we discovered America. She calls it the grotto, which reminds me of the way the nuns used to talk about St. Bernadette back in Catholic school. "Can we go to the grotto again, Dad?" she keeps asking me on the phone. "I want to catch a lizard in the grotto." I've got to get back and be her dad, even if it's just for a week or so.

As I snake through Dallas traffic, I decide to tell Bob Filbert that the acquisition will have to wait. A temporary delay.

I'll tell Filbert today . . . just as soon as Heather, his assistant, can squeeze me in.

27

Road Runner and Bambi

In the days leading up to the tour I stretched mommyhood to the brink, loading up our schedule with crowd-pleasing activities aimed to delight the children and exhaust me so that I would have no time or energy to examine my marital crisis. The impatient, snippy, bad mommy who'd been chained to her computer had left the building and at last I was free to take the children on long hikes, with Taffy tethered to Dylan's stroller. Oregon gave us waterfalls to behold, fountains and pools we could splash through, play structures and fragrant flowers, all surrounded by Kodak color green. The state was scrounging for educational funds, but there was plenty of green for the park system. Becca had Madison over for a three-night marathon sleepover. I took a carload of kids to the zoo, to ice skate, bowl, play laser tag, and munch popcorn through G-rated movies.

I thought this level of activity would save me from the real world. I kept the television off news and adult dramas, and newspapers went from the driveway to the recycle bin as soon as I picked them up in the morning. But I had to check my e-mail, and as soon as I logged onto the Internet the home page splashed shocked and teary-eyed faces of women who'd been cheated on. Heartbreak was everywhere, its invasive fingers putting the squeeze on my heart when I read about poor Jennifer and bad Brad and evil Angelina. Was it too soon for Jennifer to let Vince into her heart? Would Jessica get over Nick? Was Nick still pining for Jessica?

I felt sorry for Jennifer and Jessica, really I did. It probably stunk to have your emotional life made so public. On the other hand, I suspected they were also surrounded by sympathy, coddled by supportive sycophants, and at the moment I would have loved one or two suck-ups here in my pocket telling me it wasn't my fault, that I'd do better without him, that he didn't deserve me, or that it probably just wasn't our destiny to be together. It would be so much easier to accept advice from a real person rather than the *You Can Survive Divorce* book checked out from the library and hidden under the mattress so the kids wouldn't get wind of their impending doom.

Because I didn't have the heart to tell them yet. Tell them what . . . beyond the fact that their father had shacked up with a bimbo from the office? According to the divorce book, this was not the vernacular one should use when speaking to children of a marital split. So I put off the talk. Denial was my blithe, peppy friend, my personal bimbo for the moment. I hadn't yet mustered the nerve to tell my family back East. My parents would be worried, and I knew my sister would come back at me with some pointed questions I couldn't answer right now, so what was the point? Why cause them pain when I could spare them for a week or so and tell them in person, when I headed east for the book tour? So I burrowed into bed with one of Jack's old sweatshirts on the pillow beside me, his scent reassuring, despite the fact that I hated his guts.

When my lunch date with Ariel came around, I was sorely tempted to cancel. No one in Oregon knew that Jack and I had split, and I wasn't sure this lunch, Ariel's first restaurant review, was the time to burden her with my problems. On the other hand, it would have been rotten to bug out on her and leave her to sample an entire menu alone. I decided to go and keep mum about my issues.

"Wild boar. Pheasant. Venison burgers. What? Ostrich!" Ariel's brown eyes crossed as she tugged on a curl over her forehead. "Okay, then. Now I know why they let me review this place. No one else on staff has the stomach for it."

"It is a little heavy for a lunch menu," I said. Even my voracious appetite accelerated by abandonment wasn't piqued by the prospect of ostrich medallions. "Quite an array of exotic meats. Lucky's should be called House of Meats."

"Or Meat Wagon. Or how about the Meateteria?"

"Welcome to Lucky's," the waitress said. "I'm Ivy, your server?" Ivy phrased it as a question. She seemed young, someone I'd hire to watch the kids. Her long hair cascaded over her shoulders in ringlets that probably required hours with a curling iron. I envied her that freedom, having enough time to spend the afternoon primping. "Have you dined with us before?"

"We're Lucky virgins," Ariel answered. "And we were just commenting on your menu. It's a carnivore lover's delight."

Ivy nodded eagerly. "People love our wild boar. We serve it two ways, roasted with fig, date and walnut stuffing, or as chops steeped in beer, served in a kraut casserole."

"We'll have to try that," Ariel said. "How about roasted with the stuffing? And venison . . . You've really got some hearty dishes on the menu for a beautiful summer afternoon." We'd opted to sit outside at a table shielded from the street by a potted tree, but the lemony August sunlight trickled through the leaves. More a gazpacho-and-salad day.

"We're out of the stir-fried venison, but Chef still has some venison stew?" Again, Ivy made it a question. Our own Oregon Valley Girl. I suspected she lived at home with her parents and a cat named Mittens.

"We'll have some of the stew, and the pheasant, too. We're going to share everything," Ariel said, pushing the single rose and salt and pepper to the side of the table to make room. "And could we have the ostrich medallions as an appetizer?"

"I'll ask Chef." Ivy wrote on her notepad, big swirly letters that I imagined had hearts for dots. "You ladies must be hungry."

Ariel grinned as she slapped her menu shut. "Ravenous."

We each ordered a mojito to drink, and Ivy did a prim little half-bow.

"Thank you!" Ariel called as Ivy skipped off toward the kitchen. "She's so cute! Too cute too be pushing wild boar. Just say no, Ivy!"

"It's gotta be a tough sell," I said. "Wild boar and ostrich."

"Beep! Beep!" Ariel head bobbed in a nod. "Yes, yes! Try our Road Runner!"

"And Bambi!" I said with a laugh. "Did you just order Bambi stew?"

"And that character from *The Lion King*. Wasn't he a boar?"

"Timon? I think he was a wildebeest," I said.

"Wildebeest, wild boar. Same difference." Laughing, she lifted her fork with glee. "Must sample Road Runner and Timon!"

I doubled over, laughing so hard that my eyes filled with tears. When I straightened, the tears remained, welling. My laughter had bubbled into hysteria. I pressed a napkin to my face, unable to stop crying.

"Yum! Yum!" Ariel went on, still caught up in the joke. A moment later, I heard a quieter, "Ruby? Are you okay?"

I lowered the napkin, nodding. "It's Jack. He moved out."

"You're kidding!" She pressed her palms to her chest, her mouth a huge *O* of concern. "No, you're not kidding. Oh, Ruby! I'm so sorry. Tell me everything."

I shook my head. "No, this is your day. Your first review!" My voice cracked with emotion. "That's so great, and I don't want to ruin it for you with . . . all this heavy crap."

Ariel reached across the table and squeezed my wrist. "Listen to me, you are about to eat Bambi and Road Runner for me. The least I can do is listen."

Choking back tears, I told her.

Ariel listened attentively, as if bracing for a final exam. Somewhere during my tale Ivy trounced over with our mojitos and a peppy, "Here we go!" When I stopped my sob story to thank her, she paused to look at me and, to her credit, seemed to sense that we wanted privacy. I got back to the salient points, that my marriage was broken. Fixable? Who knew?

Ariel sidestepped the usual conciliatory cooing and posed some questions. What attracted me to Jack in the first place? Did we still have shared interests beyond the kids? When did we lose track of each other?

I told her about our honeymoon period in Manhattan, not a true honeymoon because we weren't married yet, but a golden time in our relationship because Jack had left his family and Queens (all of eight miles away, but a break is a break!) to be with me.

"I got the big picture on his dysfunctional family fairly quickly when his parents invited us to Easter dinner. After the meal, while I was helping his mother serve dessert, she poured coffee over my wrist. Scalded me right here, but just went on serving a coconut cake shaped like a bunny. I remember the bottom of the layers were burnt, that blackened taste, but no one said anything. Later Jack told me it was a family tradition for his mom to bake an Easter cake, though it never seemed to turn out. Mira couldn't quite pull it together, but then, after three martinis, who can?"

"And your family was different?" Ariel asked.

"Less dysfunctional. Compared to the Salernos, we're disgustingly cheerful. But I knew that when I met Jack. Our upbringings were vastly different. I thought I could help Jack, that I could cure him of all that family misery. I wanted to show him that families could be healthy, that *our* little family would be healthy and happy. I even thought I could influence his family in a positive way. Each Christmas I would rack my brain to come up with creative gifts that spoke to their interests. Theater tickets, a fishing trip for his dad. Gourmet clubs for his brother Frank. I initiated weekend phone calls. I hosted holidays and remembered their birthdays with carefully chosen Hallmark cards. All to no avail. Jack didn't appreciate my attempts, and neither did his family. So I tried the opposite tack and encouraged Jack to take a break from them."

"And how did that work out?"

"Better, I think. He still feels guilty, but then all his family issues are mired in guilt."

Ariel plucked a sprig of mint from her mojito and tossed it onto the white linen tablecloth. "We all come to marriage with a huge cart of baggage. Sometimes I'm amazed that I'm still married."

I nodded. "Everyone has problems. I know that. But stepping outside the marriage . . . That's a major infraction in my book. It hurts."

She lifted a hand to her chest and closed her eyes. "I know, I know, I know. But have you considered that it might not be about you? Many a man has tripped on his own dick. And in the end, it's just sex for them—dumb instinct. A big sneeze. Like a bear scratching his back on a tree."

I took a sip of my mojito, the sweetness stinging my throat. "I wish it were that simple. For Jack, I think the sex is just a way to make the break more final. I think his mind was already gone."

She nodded. "I get it. I do. It'll take time for you guys to see your way through this."

Ariel treated the conflict with respect, as if it was a challenge, a difficult maze, which, once mastered, would build character. Personally, I just wanted to find the cheese at the end.

"I just want to let you know I've got your back if you need anything. I'm afraid this all has to play out over time. But I'm here for you. What can I do?"

I told her that she'd already done more than enough. It was good to have a friend that wasn't thousands of miles away. But Ariel persisted in constructing a support plan, a way to do something constructive in the face of destruction. "Shabbat," she said with a knowing nod. "You and the kids have to come join us before you go off on tour. I owe you a dinner, anyway."

"You don't have to do that."

"I don't, but it would be my pleasure. Besides, who else would come out and dine on a smorgasbord of wildebeests with me?" Ariel asked as a team of servers filed around the potted tree with steaming white platters of food.

"Be careful," I warned as Ariel poured juice for the children. I had brought Dylan's sippy cup, though he argued for a big-kid cup, and Ariel caved, as long as he sat down in the kitchen to drink. "You'll be fine, right, little man?" Ariel rubbed his curly head and Dylan smiled, staring up at her through starry lashes.

Closing my eyes against visions of Dylan walking into the living room and purple grape juice on her pristine white carpet, I set my sights on learning something about the Jewish faith, which I'd always lived on the fringes of but apparently hadn't absorbed. Dummy me, I'd thought the Sabbath was Sunday. But Ariel had informed me that it began on Friday. "That's my favorite time, a relaxing dinner, time to reflect, slow down. When we lived in New York, Shabbat saved my sanity. It was the only time we could relax as a family."

The kids giggled over their juice and crackers, Scout and Michelle sporting grape mustaches. Becca was setting up a Cranium Cadoo for Kids board, while Dylan sat attentively at the end of the table, nursing his big-kid cup as if it held the elixir of life.

Now I searched the kitchen counter for signs of matzoh balls or brisket. I wanted to help, but Ariel seemed to have everything under control. "What can I do?"

Ariel gestured to the living room, where two warm leather loveseats faced each other. "Sit, relax. Take off your shoes. Would you like a glass of wine? Looks like you brought a really nice Oregon Pinot Gris."

"Sure, but can I help you with dinner?"

"Dinner is simple." She opened the wine like the pro that she was. Ariel had tended bar during her college years at Florida State, and had gotten a taste of the high life back when *Cocktail* seemed to be a cool movie. "There's salad and corn in the fridge, and Mick is going to grill chicken when he gets home. What's to worry about?"

"Apparently not latkes and kugel." This was my limited frame of reference, a product of New York's kosher delis.

Ariel laughed and handed me a glass of wine. "Not tonight. I save the traditional foods for holidays." We moved past the kids to the leather sofas. "So, are you ready for the tour? Do you need to borrow my black shoes again?"

"Ugh." I sank down into the leather sofa. "I need the shoes. I need a glamour dress. I need to lose fifteen pounds and get a facelift."

"Tell me about it. Thirty is the point of no return. But, really, you look great, and no one is expecting a runway model, are they?"

The wine was smooth as butter on my lips as I thought of the glamour shot on the back cover of *Chocolate in the Morning*. "Oh, they're expecting a witty beauty with cheekbones and pizzazz. Unfortunately, they're getting me." I told her about the possibility of doing *The Lolly! Show*, which was still in the pitch stages. According to the e-mails I'd seen, every guest needed Lolly's personal approval and my name hadn't been presented to her staff yet.

"Oh. My. God." Ariel put her glass on the coffee table and leaped over the armrest to retrieve the bottle of wine. "That is fantastic."

"It's still just a possibility."

"It's going to happen, I can feel it." Ariel refilled my wineglass. "Your career is skyrocketing at warp speed."

I nodded, my mouth full of wine. "Apparently at the expense of my personal life."

"Oh, no. You can't go there." She leaned closer and squeezed my free hand. "None of that is your fault."

Maybe not, but sometimes it seemed that way. How could I not take some responsibility for my children losing their father for weeks on end?

As if reading my mind, Ariel added: "You can't make Jack's decisions for him. Some things are beyond our control."

I nodded, wanting to escape this conversation, wanting to run from my life. Glancing across the room, I noticed some sheet music on the piano stand with a Star of David on the cover. "Is there some special song you sing on Shabbat?" I asked. "Some prayers?"

"We're reformed. My favorite Shabbat song is James Taylor's 'Shower The People,' or sometimes 'Bridge Over Troubled Water.' "

"You're kidding me. James Taylor?"

"Don't you like JT?"

"Love him, but I was expecting maybe something in Hebrew."

"What a crackup. Michelle is going to have to start studying Hebrew for her bat mitzvah, but Mick and I are really bad at it. But you know what? We do light candles. Does that make you feel any better?"

It did, especially when the kids were gathered around the table in the waning light, a match flaring in Ariel's fingers as she raved about the fine chicken her husband had cooked and thanked me and my children for joining them for Shabbat dinner.

Although their household wasn't steeped in age-old Judaic traditions, the sense of family tradition was strong. This was a family that shared a bond, people who nurtured their love for each other.

As Ariel lit a second candle, I vowed to nurture my own family. Let Jack rediscover his single life in Dallas. I would make a family of four.

My explosion of frenetic mommyhood was coming to an end. I was packing suits and spangly tanks and stiletto heels for my upcoming role as women's fiction author when Jack called in a glum mood.

"What are you doing?" he asked.

"Packing for the tour," I said, trying to put that *Can't you see I'm busy?* tone in my voice. "Do you want to talk to the kids?"

"Nah, I'm between meetings."

Of course. Your time is soooo valuable. "What time are you getting here tomorrow?"

"I'm not," he said. "That's why I'm calling. Now that I'm onboard for this acquisitions project here, I'm sort of stuck here in Dallas. The grand *fromages* won't let me go."

I sank onto the bed atop a beaded blouse. "What? Oh, come on, Jack. They can't do that."

"They can, and they did." He sounded vindictive.

"Jack, I can't believe this. This tour has been scheduled for months. You promised."

"It's beyond my control."

"I don't think so." My voice rose, and I quickly pulled myself off the bed to close the bedroom door. "I think you can get the time off but you can't bear to part with your little blonde Pop-Tart."

"That's not true. This is not about her, Ruby."

"Oh, really? Then tell me, honestly. Did you sleep at the hotel last night, or at her place?" The question was out before I could stop myself.

He didn't answer, confirming my worst fears. I paced the bedroom, that familiar pain crushing my chest.

"Don't do this, Jack. I can't cancel this tour." The possibility of calling it off loomed before me like a slow-motion car wreck. My career, which had been going so well since *Chocolate,* suddenly slamming into a wall. "There are TV shows that have advertised my appearance. Bookstores have been advertising these signings, and if I cancel, they'll hate me."

"So go. Hire a sitter to watch the kids."

"For two weeks? They're too little for that, and they miss you. Becca had a nightmare about you the other night—that you were attacked by a shark in Lake Green. And Scout . . . She's been waiting to go to the grotto with you."

"Don't you think I miss them, too? This isn't my call."

"Because you're not taking responsibility!" I shrieked into the phone. "Tell them you have three children to take care of!"

"I gotta go." And the line went dead.

So typical of our relationship—whenever conflict between us reached a heated pitch, one of us disconnected. Instead of a fight, we'd have a dial tone.

I'd always been so proud of the fact that we didn't argue, but now I wondered. Maybe we should have gone for the fight. Better to have noise on the line than no connection at all.

28

My Posse Don't Do Paparazzi

"You're Ruby Dixon?" The driver sent to greet me at O'Hare Airport looked a bit miffed when Ruby Dixon the writer appeared not in spangled gown and stiletto heels but in jeans and a jacket stained with apple juice, toting three kids, four carry-ons, one gorgeous sitter and a booster seat. He had been holding up a sign that said: MS. DIXON and I had singled him out, with great relief to be off a plane that had been tossing through the air and making funny noises beneath our feet.

"Yes, I am," I said, forcing a smile. "Didn't recognize me without the sequins?"

"I was told there would be one person," he said, eyeing my passel of kids as the girls chased our luggage to an opening on the conveyor belt. "My car holds only four passengers."

"Oh." Someone was supposed to phone ahead and fix that. Padama had promised me. "That's a problem. We've got five, one in a booster seat," I said, stating what he'd obviously figured out on his own.

"Let me call it in and see if there's a van available."

As he phoned his dispatcher I pulled Dylan away from the luggage carousel and noticed his palms were already black from pressing them against the sliding belt.

"Tickles!" he said, delighted.

Across the loop, Scout and Becca were doing the same thing while Ashley watched for our luggage.

"Cut it out!" I yelled to them through the forest of passengers and the noise of moving machinery. "Becca, you should know better."

Frowning, she rubbed her palms together. "You always pick on me."

"Because you're the oldest," I shouted, saying one of the things I'd hated hearing as a child, one of the things I'd vowed never to say to my own kids. My poise and resolutions were systematically breaking down, and there was no end point in sight.

I turned toward Dylan, who had knocked over one of our suitcases and was climbing on top. He put his head down, as if it was his own personal bed.

The driver paced past me, telling his dispatcher, "Yeah, but she's got all these kids . . ."

Indeed, I did. After Jack had bailed on me I'd concocted an elaborate plan wherein each child would have their own personal childcare back in Oregon. Madison's mother, Lexie, was happy to take Becca for two weeks. Scout was going to share Michelle's room at Ariel's, and she'd had an offer to attend soccer camp with her friend Kevin. Ashley was going to move into our house and be Dylan's personal nanny when he wasn't attending Montessori's summer program.

It was ingenious, and I'd been extremely grateful to the moms who were more than willing to take on my kids.

Then I sprang it on the kids, and the tears began to fall.

"How can you leave us all alone like that?" Becca had asked. "Dad is never here anymore, and now you're going to leave?"

The Dad reference cut me to the quick; I'd hoped she wasn't really noticing, but I'd been wrong.

"I don't want you to go," Scout had insisted. "Please, Mommy! Please don't go!"

I'd collapsed onto the couch, feeling like the villain in an old Shirley Temple movie.

For his part, Dylan just climbed into my lap and curled onto me like a monkey in a tree. *I need to be attached to you,* he was saying. *What if I get sick or scared or lonely? That big girl Ashley is cool for a ride to the zoo, but* you're *the light of my life, Mommy. I need* you.

My face burned with guilt. My mommy ass was grass.

Then Morgan suggested the entourage. "If Condor wants you badly enough, they'll spring for the group. It'll mean spending more on airfare, but you'll still want just one hotel room."

"And the kids can stay with my parents or my sister when we get to New York," I'd added. They were still on summer break. It would mean a chance to see their family before school started.

Morgan made the calls and made it happen. I had to pay for the sitter's airfare, but that was no problem, and when I learned that Ashley had never traveled beyond Seattle, I realized she might reap some benefits of her own by the trip. Our neighbor Eric Lundquist surprised me by offering to take in Taffy while we were gone. "I heard the girls talking about your trip, and Jane and I would be happy to take care of the puppy," he said, leaning close to add. "You don't want her in a kennel. Bad news. It's traumatizing for a sweet little pup like Taffy."

The details had come together so neatly . . . until now.

"They can send a van," the driver said. "Only that's gonna take two hours or more to get here."

"Two hours?" I squinted.

"Or more. Which means you'll miss your first signing at the downtown Borders."

"Oh." That wouldn't be good. I'd seen the signing listed on the "day sheets" sent by the publicist, but somehow I'd thought I could get the kids settled into the hotel with Ashley before then.

"I didn't catch your name," I said.

"Alan." He flipped his phone shut and deposited quarters into the luggage cart machine. "We really need to get you to that signing. My boss is gonna be mad if you're late."

"Listen, Alan, why don't you take the luggage and the girls?" I suggested. "And I'll take a cab with Dylan."

He wheeled the cart over to our mound of luggage. "I'd feel better taking you."

"But I can't send my girls off alone in a cab," I countered. I held on to the booster seat but handed him my carry-on bags. "And if you could have the van meet us at the downtown store, we'll be able to travel together for the rest of the day."

Although Alan seemed less than pleased, I reminded myself that this would work for everyone. At least he wouldn't get in trouble with his boss.

The taxicab driver bobbed and wove to get us downtown, but there was no clear way through Chicago's I-94, which was moving at a slow crawl.

"Is it always this slow?" I asked him, trying to make conversation.

"This? This is good," he said in a thick accent I couldn't place. "At the least, we are moving."

I'd been spoiled by Portland, where traffic meant a few other cars on the interstate.

Getting into downtown Chicago was like driving into a city of LEGOs stacked high and glimmering black and gray. "Look, Dylan. There's water down there," I said as we crossed over one of the canals. I'd remembered seeing it in the opening credits of *The Bob Newhart Show,* which we Dixon kids had watched in late-night reruns when we were supposed to be in bed.

The community relations rep at the downtown store was not quite the savvy suit I expected but a thin, smiling woman who had that former hippy vibe with a puka shell necklace, knit poncho and corduroy slacks. Yolanda didn't seem fazed by the kids. Instead, she welcomed them all and added chairs at the signing table, where I would have been sitting alone in front of a pile of my books. Scout picked up a copy of *Chocolate in the Morning* and decided that she could do better at drawing a chocolate bar, which sent Ashley scurrying for paper and pencils.

"Well, hi! I'd buy your book, but I don't have any little ones at home."

Who ever heard of a kiddy book that was four hundred pages? I opened my mouth to tell her that this wasn't a children's book but from the way she fussed over Dylan's curls like a kindergarten teacher I sensed she wasn't my audience. A few people stopped by for signed books or just to chat, including one man who kept commenting that I didn't look at all like the woman in the photo on the back of the book.

"That's me," I kept telling him.

His eyes raked over me. "That's really hard to believe."

I bent my head over Dylan's and asked him what he was drawing, hoping the man would just leave. My New York defense system was on red alert. Was he a threat, or just a closet kook?

No such luck. When two young women stopped by the table, he insisted on showing them the photo and eliciting their opinion.

"He's not my agent," I told the women. "He just plays one on TV."

"Actually, I'm a photographer, and I could do a better shot for you," he said, standing tall.

Oh. I get it now. "Really? Why don't you give me your card? I never did like that glamour shot."

He produced cards for everyone. "Jonathan Thacker. Specialize in portraits."

"Do you do weddings?" one of the young women asked. She wore two T-shirts draped over her petite frame, though neither of them reached the waistband of her jeans. My sister's getting married next year."

"Please." Jonathan glared at her. "I paid my dues on wedding cake and loving embraces. Been there, done that."

I sighed with relief as they moved off to talk. Stalker averted.

The two hours went by quickly after I adjusted to the momentum of shmoozing with people and pretending that I didn't care whether they stopped by the table. Our van had arrived to whisk us off to the next bookstore, but not before Yolanda loaded us up with cookies and brownies from the café. "Take these with you," she said, handing Becca a bag. "You never know when you'll need something yummy."

Apparently we needed it right away, because Becca dug into the bag as soon as we got into the van, and I didn't object when the kids and Ashley passed it around, sampling the goodies. We crawled some more on the freeway, through another construction zone.

"You seem to have a lot of construction here," I told the van driver, a new one named Kurt.

"Chicago has two seasons," he told me, "winter and construction."

I laughed, breaking a large cookie in half for Dylan so that he wouldn't overdose on sugar.

Our next stop was a Barnes & Noble in Skokie, a huge store with a sparkling rep who had an East Coast wardrobe and energy. Sherry told me she was from Boston, but had moved here with her husband and raised three daughters in the area. She suggested that the kids peruse the children's section while I sign books, which was fortuitous, since Scout vomited within ten minutes of our arrival.

"Too much brownies," Scout said, staring at the floor. "I tried to make it to the bathroom, Mom."

"Not to worry, lovebug," Sherry said, patting Scout's shoulder. "We'll get this cleaned up in a flash. Do you need a quiet place to sit?"

Scout shook her head. "I feel better now."

"I'm so sorry," I told Sherry.

"Not a problem. I told you, I used to have three at home. But I think there are some people waiting at the table?"

Releasing Scout to Ashley's watch, I hurried back to the table to chat up the customers.

By the time we reached the next store, an independent bookseller, the kids' enthusiasm was drained and the crowd didn't seem so welcoming to Ruby Dixon's Traveling Minstrel Show. It didn't help when Becca stumbled on a display of books with "inappropriate covers," she claimed, pointing them out to me and the store manager as if someone had committed a crime on the end cap.

"That's just so wrong," Becca said, hands on her hips. "Little children are going to walk by and see S-E-X everywhere."

The manager, a tightly wound, I'm-too-busy-for-this man named Clive, folded his arms and pursed his lips in disdain. Clive was not amused.

"Boobies!" Scout laughed. "Mom, how come they show her boobies on the cover!"

"Would you shut up!" Becca glared at her.

"Look at that!" Scout pressed a finger to a cover while Dylan lifted a book titled *The Graceful Art of Tantric Sex* from the display. "You can see her boobies and his toosh!"

"No touching!" Becca tugged on the book, the edge of the cover crumpling. Dylan squealed, not willing to surrender.

Clive stepped toward the shelf. "Please don't touch the display."

"Oh, my gosh!" Scout covered her eyes and rolled back onto the floor at Ashley's feet, kicking her legs in the air. "Those people are naky."

Ashley lifted her up gently from her armpits. "Cool it, Scout."

Scout giggled. "But they're all naky noo-noo!"

Becca managed to wrench the book away from Dylan and handed it to Clive. "I told you, mister."

I tried to corral Dylan and Becca down the aisle. "The covers are a little racy," I told Clive.

"And this from the author of *Chocolate in the Morning.*" Clive's mouth pursed to one side, his fluffy mustache a caterpillar inching over his lips.

Guilt singed my cheeks. I wanted to protest that I didn't read my book aloud to my kids. I knew what was appropriate, damn it!

"Mommy?" Scout's chipmunk voice perked as we followed Clive to the table set up for the signing, "What is tan-rich sex?"

Clive's dark laughter incensed me as I sat Scout down at the table beside me and leaned close. "It's something we'll talk about later, when we're done here," I said quietly, not wanting to dismiss her the way Clive had.

A group of women were waiting at the table. Readers in smooth garb and stiletto ankle breakers. "Are you Ruby Dixon?" one asked, eyeing my kiddy entourage.

"In person," Clive said spitefully.

"Oh, I'm so disappointed," one of them admitted. She opened a copy of *Chocolate in the Morning* and flipped through the pages lovingly. "I so wanted you to be like the main character in your book. Footloose and fancy-free."

"Janna is a role model for us," her friend said. "Single and childless and proud of it."

I nodded and forced a smile. "I used to be single. A hundred years ago."

They laughed, warming slightly. Though I noticed that they stayed at the end of the table, away from the children. As if they worried that my real life might be contagious.

At the end of the day I was too strung out to face the hotel restaurant, so we ordered room service. The kids were delighted to eat from trays in bed while watching television.

"Mom! This is what rich people do!" Scout crowed.

Nibbling on a Reuben sandwich from the desk chair, I mumbled, "I hope not," but my words were lost in SpongeBob's barky laughter.

When Morgan called I took my cell phone down to the lobby so that I could speak away from little ears. "Houston, we have a problem." I summarized my chaotic day. The entourage wasn't playing so well with readers. "People aren't comfortable discussing adult fiction in front of cherubic children. I'm not sure that Ruby Dixon readers want to meet the SpongeBob generation," I said.

"Sounds like we need to switch to Plan B," Morgan said.

"Which is . . . ?"

"I haven't got a clue, but I'll let you know when I think of it."

Plan B was: Operation Kids Under Wraps. Whenever possible the children stayed in the hotel room with Ashley, checking out the swimming pools and riding the elevators. I booked the hotel an extra day so that the children could spend the afternoon there on the day we were flying out. Signings went more smoothly without munchkins in tow. A hot new romantic suspense novel had just been released, and every day as I passed its display at the front of each store, the cover depicting a dagger plunging into a woman's naked bosom, I said a prayer of thanks that my kids weren't with me to critique this one. Becca's voice pealed in my head: "Inappropriate!"

After three days in the Chicago area we flew to Indianapolis, where the kids enjoyed strolling in the central business district. "Mommy, it's just like a mini-New York!" Becca said.

From Indy we drove to Dayton, then Cincinnati, where colored lights flooded the crests of tall buildings as we drove into the city at night. On to Memphis. Mobile. Raleigh. Up to Detroit, then west to Minneapolis.

I lost track of how many socks and toothbrushes got left behind in the mad rush to pack everyone up at the end of each hotel stay. Becca was concerned that dirty clothes were touching clean. Dylan wasn't eating much but he slept like a stone at night. Scout was delighted to collect the sample shampoos and lotions from each hotel until one of them exploded in her suitcase. That was the night we sent a huge bundle of dirty, shampooy clothes to the hotel laundry.

Reliable and cheerful, Ashley was a huge help, and I knew I could trust her to watch the children. Three is a handful, but Becca was old enough and responsible enough to help.

Somewhere in the South I got word from Morgan that Lolly wanted me on her show. "She's squeezing you in between Brad Pitt and that schoolteacher who confessed to sleeping with a dozen of her students," Morgan told me in a voice thick with pride.

"I'm flattered, I guess."

"We're going to move some of the New York signings so that you can go back to Chicago and do Lolly's show next week. Chicago is a straight shot over from Minneapolis."

It may have looked that way on the map, but my time spent racking in the air miles had demonstrated that there were very few *straight shots.*

"Oh, and Lolly wants you to glam it up. When you get to Chicago, you'll have time, so shop for a special wardrobe. Another glitter gown."

"Does Lolly know I'm traveling with my kids?" Everyone knew that Lolly hated surprises. Rumor had it that Lolly fired her personal assistant for planning a surprise party on her fiftieth birthday. Lolly landed a karate kick to the solar plexus of a photographer who'd sprung out of the bushes one night. Lolly threw her drink in the face of a reporter when he revealed he was writing an unauthorized biography.

"I've got it covered. I talked with her production coordinator personally. A gal named Chiaki Owens. Charming. She says Lolly's people already knew you had a family. Of course, she still wants to stick with the glamour angle."

"Sure."

"I know it must be hard, honey, but it's a forty-five minute interview with incredible global exposure."

"Oh, I know," I said, trying to at least *sound* perky. "Even *I* can muster some glam for forty-five minutes. I think."

"I believe in you," Morgan said encouragingly. "I know you can do it."

I hoped she was right.

29

Lolly!

The king-sized, electric blue letters spelling LOLLY! in the building's lobby let us know we were in the right place. I told the security guard my name and he called upstairs, eyeing my brood sternly. "Are they with you?" he asked.

"My children . . ."

A brisk nod, and he turned to talk into the phone. Beyond the desk the kids played Don't Step On the Cracks over the granite tiles, all of them heading toward the backlit LOLLY! letters, as if approaching Oz. We were flying by the seat of our pants today, proceeding without Ashley. We'd left her back in the hotel room with two bottles of ginger ale and a bottle of Tylenol. "My head hurts," she'd said that morning when she'd awakened with bright red cheeks and glassy eyes. A fever. Her mother, on phone consult, thought she'd be okay with some rest and fever reducer. But better not take her out today.

Today, of all days.

By the time I'd showered, Ashley's temperature had come down, which made me feel a little better about leaving her alone in the hotel room. Becca had promised to be the nanny today, and I knew Dylan would listen to her. Scout was another story, but Becca relished the prospect of giving Scout orders. "I'm in charge!" Becca crowed, reminding me of Alexander Haig during a darker moment in our nation's history.

We would see about that.

I folded my arms over my wardrobe bag, trying to gain confidence by reminding myself that the cocoa-colored gown inside was stunning on me. Covered with copper sequins, the gown had a drop waist and handkerchief hem that flattered my marriage-in-crisis shape. Back in high school a magazine article about "boring browns" had turned me off the color, but yesterday when I slid this dress over my head, I knew it was time to change my palette. The coppery hues brought out my eyes and balanced so well with my newly darkened hair.

Unfortunately the lovely gown didn't keep me from wishing I could take a nap instead of having to deal with this day. *The Lolly! Show.* My stomach churned a very clear message. *You're not worthy! You're not worthy!*

Everyone knew Lolly's history. California child of German father and Japanese mother, Lolly was born in an internment camp in Minidoka, Idaho. Although she had to be over sixty she didn't look a day over forty. She'd been married twice, no children, fashionably thin (or ANOREXIC!—according to one tabloid, which Lolly had successfully sued). According to rumor, her staff consisted entirely of Japanese Americans; her way of getting back at those suspicious white-bread people who'd forced her family into a camp, causing the ruin of the family dry-cleaning business.

Okay, the security guard was African American. Rumor trashed.

"Are you Ruby Dixon?"

With the kids' shrieks I hadn't heard the elevator doors open behind me.

The thin young man who waited there had stubby eyebrows that were lifted high in interest and a black soul patch on his chin. "I'm Ikiro," he said, extending a hand. We shook and when he bowed a little I found myself bowing back to be polite.

"So nice to meet you. Those are my children over there. You did know they were coming, didn't you?"

"Uh . . . I didn't know, but that doesn't mean anything. I'm just a lowly PA," he said, waving to get the children's attention. "Kids! Over here! Time to go!"

"Aaah!" Their shrieks echoed through the hollow lobby chamber as they barreled toward us. So much for the speech I'd given them in the limo ride over, the one in which I extracted promises of exemplary behavior from each of them.

Ikiro slapped each kid a high-five as he learned their names, then led the way to the elevator.

"Do we get to meet Lolly?" Becca asked. She had watched bits of *The Lolly! Show* with me a few times, when I'd made a point of tuning in so I'd be hip to the format.

"I'm not so sure about that." Ikiro shot me a look I couldn't read, one side of his lips curving in a half-smile. "I don't even get to meet Lolly, and I work here."

"What?" Scout boosted herself up on the rails in the corner of the elevator, some trick she'd learned to suspend herself during suspension. "You have to see her if you work with her."

He shook his head. "I see her on the TV screen, just like you. Lolly doesn't have time to deal with everyone in the studio."

"Well, that's random." Scout leaped down to the floor as the elevator doors opened to more blue LOLLY! letters on the wall, this time fluorescent lights leading into the shadowed studio.

Reflexively, Dylan grabbed me by the thigh as we stepped into the cavernous space full of activity. The set, consisting of a plush chair and sofa, was only half-lit as two men on catwalks worked on the overhead lights. The dark audience seats were currently empty, but the rest of the space was full of foot traffic, people hurrying across the set talking into the wire mouthpieces of their headsets or clustered together, chatting. Three cameras the size of large kangaroos stood marooned at the front of the set, their operators off in chairs, talking with assistants. From my inexperienced eye, it looked like one big party.

"Whoa . . . cool!" Scout started to run ahead.

"Wait!" I lunged toward her, dragging Dylan along with me. I grabbed her by one hand. "Remember what we talked about?" I spoke in a stern undertone. "This is not a playground. No running, and keep your voice down."

Scout wrested her hand away. "You don't have to yell."

"She didn't yell," Becca pointed out.

"Okay, then." Ikiro eyed us with that cryptic smile. "Shall we take Mom to her dressing room so she can do wardrobe and makeup?"

"Is it boring?" Scout asked.

"Scout . . ." I had to restrain myself from grabbing her hand again. "Let's be polite, okay?"

Hands on her hips, Scout stomped forward.

I tried to follow Ikiro, but Dylan was an anchor on my leg. Slinging the garment bag over one arm—clothes inside be damned!—I hoisted Dylan up onto my hip. "Whatsamatter, honey?"

He didn't answer, but pressed the knuckles of one hand into his mouth, his brown eyes glassy with welling tears.

"Don't worry. After today we go to New York to see Mimi and Aunt Amber."

"Mimi Andamba," he said.

"I love makeup," Becca was telling Ikiro as they walked ahead of me. "My mom won't let me wear it to school, but she lets me and my friends try it on."

He said something I didn't hear as we went down a narrow hallway and turned into a room with a plaque that said: GUEST DRESSING ROOM. With a sigh of relief, I lowered Dylan to the couch.

He promptly slid off and wrapped his arms around my thigh again.

Meanwhile, Scout and Becca were already arguing over the stool at the vanity mirror lit by bulbs, tugging and pulling at each other with comments like: "Stop being so selfish," and "I know you are, but what am I?"

Trying to screen out the children, I focused on Ikiro. "What would you like me to do first?"

"Why don't you change into your wardrobe," he said, staring down at Dylan. Maybe wondering how I was going to get dressed with thirty-five pounds of toddler on one thigh. "I'll go get Terri, our makeup artist."

When he closed the door behind him I spun toward the girls, temper flaring in my eyeballs like a scorched cartoon character. "Stop it, right now! Separate!"

"She started it," Becca insisted.

"I. Don't. Care." I pressed my eyes closed and counted to three. Why did I think I could do this? "Becca, you're older and I'm counting on you to help me today."

"It's just that I like makeup and she doesn't, so I should have the chair."

"But *I* want the cool chair," Scout said.

"Let Scout sit there right now. Becca, you sit on the couch and hold Dylan."

"But, Mom . . ."

I couldn't bear that intolerable whine. "Do it now so I can change, okay?"

Becca slumped on the couch and held onto Dylan when I plopped him into her lap. "Just sit still, honey. Mommy isn't going anywhere right now."

He let out a whine of his own, a bad sign. I turned away and unzipped the garment bag, hoping that he would nap while I was taping the show.

By the time Terri appeared with her expanding cases of makeup, I had calmed down enough to survive the interview. I could do this. I had a good rapport with my children, and they possessed the discipline to remain contained for one hour.

Things were going to be fine.

Dylan had fallen asleep on one corner of the couch. Scout had taken an interest in the TV monitor with oversized remote, and Becca was happy to sit in Terri's portable chair beside me at the vanity.

"When the show comes on, you'll be able to watch your mom right on that TV screen," Terri told the girls. She had two at home, one in diapers, and had uttered a sympathetic: "What a nightmare!" when I told her about my sitter coming down with a fever.

"Why can't we watch her in person?" Scout asked. "I want to sit in the audience."

"They don't allow kids in Lolly's audience," Terri said as she spread the foundation down to my neck with a sponge she'd clipped off a large white block. "It's not really a family show."

"Well, that's just dumb," Scout said.

"Just because you're too young to understand it," Becca said, lifting her chin with an air of superiority.

"Girls . . . please."

Terri laughed. "I can see they don't outgrow the rivalry thing."

"Tell me about it."

Terri added concealer and eye shadow. She drew circles around my eyes and outlined my lips, then filled them in with rich, burnt-plum lip gloss. I hadn't worn this much makeup since the high school prom. It felt a little gushy and cool on my face, but when I turned to the mirror, an exotic beauty looked back. Cleopatra. A little creepy, but impersonation might work for me. Better to hide behind the image of Ruby Dixon—and five pounds of makeup.

"Mom!" Becca gasped. "You're beautiful!"

"Thanks for noticing." I took off the paper bib Terri had tucked into the neck of my sparkly cocoa gown and handed it to Becca. "Your turn." Terri had offered to make her up, too, and I had told Becca it was okay as long as she washed off the makeup before we left the building.

Becca pressed her lips together and tucked the paper bib into her T-shirt. Attention from a makeup artist was her life's dream.

"Your skin is flawless," Terri said as she shook two bottles. "I don't need to use concealer."

"But don't you want to cover the freckles?" Becca lifted her chin and closed her eyes.

"Honey, I know lots of actresses who would kill for freckles like yours." When Terri finished, she turned to Scout. "How about you? Want some makeup on?"

"Blech!" Scout's tongue came out.

" 'No, thanks' would be fine," I told her. Though I did see what she meant. With the thick makeup on, her brows drawn so dark, Becca did look a little clownish. Either that, or she might be mistaken for a preteen hooker.

"Do you like it, Mom?" Becca asked.

I dodged a total lie. "I've always known you were beautiful, honey."

"Yeah . . ." Becca angled her face as she inspected it in the mirror. "But makeup makes me look better."

With her supplies collected, Terri turned toward the door and paused to bend toward the couch, her head tilting toward Dylan. "Is he okay, Ruby?" She frowned. "His cheeks are so red. Looks like he's burning up."

I pressed a hand to Dylan's forehead. He was on fire. "He's got a fever." My stomach sank. "He must have caught whatever Ashley has. And what do you want to bet I don't have any medication with me?" I rifled through my purse.

Terri frowned. "I don't have anything here, but let me get Ikiro for you. The props cart is loaded with everything from chewing gum to Kaopectate."

Ikiro appeared a minute later. "You need something?" he asked with a half-bow.

"Children's Tylenol. My son has a fever."

"Oh." He pressed a hand to his mouth. "We don't have that. Sorry."

"Isn't there a pharmacy downstairs?" I opened the wardrobe to find my purse. "I'll go down and get him some Tylenol."

"Oh, you can't leave now." Ikiro folded his arms across his chest. "We're loading in the audience. We can't take the chance of losing you in traffic or something."

"It's right downstairs."

"We tape in fifteen minutes. I'll send a runner for it. What did you want?"

"Children's Tylenol." I was tempted to also ask for Excedrin, for the headache I felt coming on, but before I could get to it he was gone, off to tag a runner, whatever that meant.

While he was gone I began to pace. From down the hall I could hear applause and laughter. A male voice, some comedian? A warm-up guy to psych up the audience. With any luck, he could motivate them to applaud when I fell flat on my face. "Oh, right!" I'd tell them. "I meant to do that. Yes, I put my foot in my mouth all the time, and I can faint at will, too!"

I pulled out my notes from the publicity person at Condor Books. I looked at Lolly's list of questions for the bazillionth time. Morgan and I had gone over smart, positive answers for all of the questions. This was not an exposé, but a goodwill tour.

So why was I so nervous?

Maybe because I felt like a fraud. An expert on living wild and single, and here I was abandoned by my husband, jilted for another woman, trying to stave off my kids for an hour so I could climb the ladder of popularity, raise my Q rating, boost sales.

I turned to the mirror and eyed the sparkling, dewy version of myself. Squinting, I did my Jack Nicholson impersonation: "You can't handle the truth . . ."

"We're ready for you," Ikiro called from the doorway, making me jump.

"Aah, sorry." He bowed his head so that his soul patch landed in the palm of one hand. "Don't tell me you're nervous?"

"Very nervous. I'm not good at this publicity stuff."

"Aah, that's not true. I saw cuts of you on the *Allie Davis Show*. You seemed very relaxed."

I shrugged. "It was a feed from Portland. And I didn't have a sick kid that day."

Just then what looked like a kid, wearing jeans and a black T-shirt, came rushing down the corridor. "I got it!" she said, her dyed jet-black hair falling into her pale face. She handed me a brown paper bag. "Children's Tylenol, right? I didn't know what age, so I got both infant and kids."

"Thank you." I turned to the dressing room, where Becca had fallen asleep beside Dylan. She was faceup like a mummy, adorned and laid to rest with a layer of makeup thick enough to last a few dozen centuries. Scout had kicked off her shoes and was twisted in a half-somersault, watching the TV through her legs. "I hate to wake him for medicine now." Chances were he'd be upset, inconsolable, and I'd have to pry his little fingers off and extract myself to get onto the set. Bad mommy.

"Good, because there's no time." Ikiro put the bag on the end table and motioned me to follow him. "You're needed in the green room."

Showtime.

30

Stilettos Off

"When we return we'll have a Lolly moment with best-selling novelist Ruby Dixon. That's right after these messages." Lolly held her wry smile as the canned music swelled on the monitor and the warm-up guy waved his arms in a frenzy, motioning the audience to cheer and applaud.

From my vantage point I could see the stark white lights from the set spilling onto the tile floor of the studio, into the edge of the audience seats. I saw Lolly's face freeze on the monitor as Terri popped onto the set and brushed powder on her face.

"You'll go on after the commercial break," Ikiro whispered in my ear.

I nodded, unable to take my eyes off the monitor.

In a minute I'd be face-to-face with Lolly, who looked every inch the icon she was, today wearing a suede jacket with a mandarin collar in her signature electric blue. The blue that matched her eyes, a color unusual in Asian women. Her father's eyes.

I bit my lower lip, suddenly choking up at the mental image of Jack's silver eyes, the deep, round pools of compassion and pain I had to face every time I looked at Scout or Becca. Their father's eyes.

Don't go there, I told myself. *Repress. Pull yourself together, just for this next hour.*

With a quick burst of applause the commercial break ended

and Lolly was talking about me. People began to clap and cheer and Ikiro gestured grandly toward the set and I noticed that Lolly was now standing, waiting for me.

Oh, God.

I ran around the edge of the set as fast as my stiletto heels allowed and jumped onto the platform, nearly catching an edge on the carpeting. The applause grew louder as Lolly and I hugged.

In person, Lolly was even more beautiful, with high cheekbones and smooth white skin that reminded me of a figure sculpted of marble. Her glorious smile lit up her face, and her feathery dark hair was gently highlighted with subtle streaks of gold.

"I'm so thrilled to meet you," I blurted out as I sat down on the loveseat.

"I'm thrilled to meet you!" Lolly returned in a kind imitation of my mousey-sounding voice. "You know"—she held up a copy of *Chocolate in the Morning*—"I couldn't put this book down. But now that I'm seeing you in person, you remind me so much of your main character, Janna. Was she modeled after you?"

My voice evened out a bit as I launched into my standard spiel: A little bit of me, a little bit of imagination.

"Far be it for me to be the spokesperson for the many writers out there," I said, "but I'm glad that *Chocolate in the Morning* has opened the door for attention on women's fiction. Novels like mine offer a comedic take on women's experiences, usually with a motif of hope."

"Novels like yours *are* so positive," Lolly agreed, nodding.

"Sure, we've seen plenty of tales of jerky boyfriends and tyrannical bosses. But there are also many stories of a woman working her way through a crisis. Of friends bolstering each other. Coming-of-age stories."

Lolly switched tracks, to the success of *Chocolate,* and the effects of fame. "How has success changed your life?" she asked me.

"Living in the Northwest, I have to say, I'm still under the radar. My neighbors don't seem to make the connection between me and Ruby Dixon, best-selling author."

"I remember the first time I realized my image was bigger than me," Lolly said. She told a story about fans interrupting her at a restaurant while she was dining with her father. At the end of the meal, he asked her, "Who is this Lolly person they're so crazy about?"

Although I was familiar with the story, I laughed, genuinely moved to hear Lolly tell it herself. Lolly was still talking about the consequences of living in the public eye when I heard the first ghostly wail. "Mommy!"

My leg muscles clenched, ready to race off the set. This could not be happening. I was a good juggler, but no one could balance a screaming child with a voracious talk-show host.

When I didn't hear my name again, I tried to tune into what Lolly was saying. *False alarm. Don't lose track of the interview.*

But as Lolly spoke, I saw him from the corner of my eye. Dylan was doing a zombie walk into the pool of white light, his arms outstretched, a string of snot drooping from his button nose.

"Have you had any fans come up to you at airports, when—"

"Mommy! Mommy. Moooom!" he wailed.

"What's this?" Lolly shot up in her chair.

Scout burst onto the set, rounding a corner too fast and sliding on the tiles in her socks. "Whoa!" she bellowed. One of the cameramen followed as her feet flew out underneath her and she skidded to the carpeted step of the set. A dramatic stunt caught on tape.

"Ladies and gentlemen, don't try this at home," I said stonily.

"Dylan, no!" Becca bounded out of the shadows, still obviously groggy. The rouge on her face seemed clownish and gauche.

"Audience?" Lolly looked from one child to another, blinking. "Who are . . . Are they *yours?*" she asked me.

"They are, indeed. Come here, Dylan." I pulled him onto my lap, trying to cradle him in my arms, but he seemed insistent on facing out and bawling on camera.

"Aw!" Lolly made that wide *O* with her mouth, the look of someone who's just discovered a newborn puppy. She patted Becca's arm and motioned Scout to climb onto the set. "Aw! Aren't they precious?" She had to shout to be heard over Dylan's howls.

I jiggled him on my legs, trying to subdue him. A spot was forming on my gown. He must have wet his pants while he was sleeping.

"You saw it here first, folks. Let's go to a commercial break. We'll wipe this little one's nose and come back to learn about the real

Ruby Dixon. We're going to kick off our stilettos and get real, so don't go away!"

"And we're out!" someone called from the edge of the set. It was the signal for the people on the crew to come alive. They moved frenetically, the assistant director shouting orders that made no sense to me. But then, I was sinking like a stone in a sea of mortification.

Lolly leaned forward and confided, "Perfect entrance. And here I thought we were going to have a mediocre little tea chat."

"I . . ." My apology stuck in my throat as my mind raced to catch up with her.

Suddenly hands were reaching in with tissues, dabbing at Dylan's face. Terri was sponging off the most offending layer of Becca's makeup, asking if she should take the shine off Scout's face.

"No way!" Scout ducked behind the loveseat.

"Come out, little lamb!" Lolly cooed, reaching behind the couch. Scout emerged, dragged by the hand, her eyes wide like a deer in headlights. "I'll bet your friends at home don't know you're going to be on TV today," Lolly said.

It was the perfect bait. "They won't be able to see me," Scout said. "They have to go to school."

Lolly's blue eyes mesmerized us all. "We'll have to get you a tape to take home."

The assistant director waved at us frantically. "And we're back in five, four, three, two . . ."

And suddenly the crew cleared the set and the cameras rolled in around us. With a silent *POP!* Lolly was *on.*

"Lolly here! And we're back with Ruby Dixon, author of *Chocolate in the Morning.* Today Ruby has brought us a most enchanting surprise." She shot a secretive look over her shoulder, then turned back to the camera. "Apparently the Chick Lit writer has a few chicks of her own . . ."

31

Four Martinis and an Actor

"Can we rewind to my dramatic entrance?" Scout asked for the hundredth time. She was stretched out in a tent she'd built under the coffee table in our hotel suite. All I could see was one hand sticking out, remote pointed toward the television.

"Let's give Morgan a chance to watch the whole tape," I said, adjusting Dylan so that he wasn't pressing against the sequins of my cocoa gown, which had been dry cleaned and delivered to our armoire in the Waldorf-Astoria.

Dylan's fingers plucked gently at my hair while he watched himself on TV. It was a soothing gesture for both of us, and I was struck by the sweet potential of this child in my lap. So often he was pushed aside as the baby of the family, but he was coming into his own, hardly a toddler anymore, soon to be a little boy and then a man.

A person.

I pressed a kiss to his smooth cheek. My baby, but not for long.

Morgan had come up to our suite to watch what had turned into our family appearance on *The Lolly! Show*. After the viewing, Morgan was taking me out for some adult fun—the premier of a new Broadway musical, followed by a quiet dinner in a restaurant that did not feature dino nuggets and crayons on the table. I was relieved to be in New York, where my sister would pick up the kids tomorrow so that she and my mother could spoil them with hugs and ice cream and long days at the swim club pool.

"I can't believe I got sick that day." Ashley tossed her hair back. "Of all days."

"You could have been on the show with us," Becca said, her eyes riveted to the TV screen, where she and Scout were demonstrating a dance they'd learned from reruns of *Fresh Prince of Bel Air.*

"Now wait a minute," I said. "If Ashley had been there, none of you guys would have been on the show. There would have been no comedy of errors."

"Still . . ." Ashley sighed. "I could have met Lolly. That would've been cool."

Ashley was flying back to Oregon tomorrow, and I would miss her solidness, the way she could read my children's needs. Although she was nineteen, she possessed a very adult sense of responsibility mixed with a naivety of the world. The trip had been good for her, too.

Morgan was laughing and pointing at the screen, where Dylan slid off my lap and joined his sisters in the dance. "Too funny. You couldn't have rehearsed it better."

"We did okay, right Mom?" Becca asked.

I allowed myself a smile. "You were great."

"Lolly's people told me the show was beyond their wildest dreams, and I can see what they mean," Morgan said. "You shed the glitter author image and came through as a real person, a working mom with an adorable family. A thoughtful person." She squeezed my hand. "Kudos, sweetie! We couldn't ask for better publicity."

Harrison had said the same thing. He'd called me as soon as we finished the show, raving about how the surprise appearance of the kids was going to warm the hearts of mommies everywhere. "It's unfortunate that the boy had a runny nose, but I suppose it plays to that mothering instinct you gals have," he'd told me, speaking a mile a minute. He was frantically packing for Paris, where one of his clients was holed up in a publicity crisis. "I'm having my own fashion crisis. I know how to dress, but Paris. It's intimidating."

"Stick to black and denim," I'd told him. "They never go out."

"I'm hoping the airline loses my luggage so I can buy all new. Can you imagine me shopping on the Champs-Elysées? But how long are you here? Can I catch you on the tail end of your visit?"

"That depends on how long it takes for you to talk your client down from the Eiffel Tower."

He'd promised to call me as soon as he returned, adding: "I never thought I'd see *you* come out of the closet, Ruby, but congratulations. Isn't it liberating?"

Despite the calamitous moments on the show, I had been relieved to toss off the glitzy chick persona. I was a terrible liar, a worse actress. No more dodging questions about my family and pretending to be a party girl. Phew!

From now on, Ruby Dixon, the author, would be me.

"I've got to leave this on buzz," Morgan said as she silenced her cell phone in the theater. "It's been two days now, and I'm worried. I'm sure she's fine but . . ."

I shrugged. "You're a mom. We worry."

I wondered what Morgan's daughter was finding on her travels through the West. Having flown into Billings and rented a car, Clare was on a mission to find her father, the man who'd taken off on a hog when she was little and never returned.

"You know," I said, "it's great that she's doing this."

"I hope so." Worry lines formed above Morgan's mouth. "I know she can take care of herself. My greatest worry is that she'll be smitten with him and that she'll never come back to me."

I shuddered at the thought of letting go, sending my kids off to college or to live with Jack. Kids—You can't maintain sanity while they're under your roof, and yet you can't bear to let them go.

Billy was a revival of a British musical by John Barry that had lit London stages in the midseventies. After I relaxed into the initial thrill of having no one slap-fighting behind me or dragging from my thigh, I felt warmed by the show, the sweeping music, the popping action. Billy was played by Dashiell Gray, an adorable British comedian turned actor.

"Can you believe that Michael Crawford starred in the original?" Morgan asked as we filed out of the theater.

"I can't believe the show is more than thirty years old, and it was a thrill to see Dashiell Gray in person."

"Such a heartthrob. Too bad he's gay," Morgan said.

"That's just a rumor."

"It's why Sara Whirling broke up with him. I read it in *Star Ink.*"

"The definitive source for sexuality," I teased. The truth was, I'd felt such a strong connection for Billy, or, rather, Dash, during the show, that I didn't want the actor to be gay. Somehow, that would have made the connection false, and I wanted to hold on to that moment, an emotional salve to my broken heart.

I wanted to think that I wasn't dead to feeling. I couldn't bear the thought that Jack was the waning love of my life.

Jack the rat.

Now that we were on East Coast time, he always managed to call my cell after the kids were asleep at night. I was running out of energy to be angry with him, but it was replaced by a sense of loss, a sense of gloom for our children, who were drifting away from their father.

The premier party was across the street from the theater at a private club called Zanzibar. We passed by the minor stars doing photo opps in the lobby in front of a giant BILLY sign. Inside, we quickly saved a table and lined up for drinks and appetizers before the crowd rushed in.

"You haven't mentioned the Professor for a while," I said, choosing a mushroom cap from the small platter we'd assembled from the buffet table. "How's that going?"

"It's not. He still calls, but his weekends are taken up with the grandchildren and his kids' crap. I mean, building a fence for them? Moving his son? I've decided it's all a ruse to keep me at bay. He's smitten with the notion of having a girlfriend, but he doesn't want to do any of the real relationship work."

"I'm so sorry. He seemed like a kind man." I should have known there was a problem, since Morgan hadn't brought him up. "Why didn't you tell me?"

"It just sort of fizzled. And in light of your high drama and my wayward daughter, it just wasn't worth mentioning."

Morgan looked noticeably older. The gray streak in her hair was untouched and now feathered back over her forehead, and for the first time I noticed little lines at the edge of her eyes when she smiled. Older, but better, as if she'd grown into her own skin. She had a beautiful face, a face the Professor should have enjoyed growing old with.

"I've resigned myself to the life of a spinster," she said.

"A spinster with a double martini and a BMW convertible? Sounds good to me."

"Thanks to you, sweetie. That car was bought and paid for by *Chocolate.*"

But I was still mired in the Lost Boys quandary. "Why are men so damaged? I mean, have you ever met a man who's figured out his own issues and dealt with them successfully?"

"They all seem to be stuck, living under their mommy's rules or with their mommy, kowtowing to the ex-wife or sniffing out some arm candy."

"Why can't they pull themselves together?"

"Amen to that, honey, but you're preaching to the choir here." She lifted the skewered olives from her martini. "Oooh . . . stuffed with goat cheese. Yum." She popped them into her mouth and chewed thoughtfully. "Men. So tragically flawed, and yet, we yearn to fix them. We think we can do it. That's our tragic flaw."

"Just like the show tonight," I said. "You so wanted Billy to grow up. Be a mensch and take on the world."

"Another Peter Pan story," Morgan said, her eyes following a passing waitress. "Excuse me? Can we get two Tanqueray martinis, please?"

The waitress paused, pressing her tray to her crisp white apron. "You can get zem up at zbar, ma'am." Her dark hair was coiled in an elegant twist. I suspected she was an out-of-work Russian model.

That was the drawback of the big party. Although the multitiered club looked elegant, filled with small tables, covered with pristine white linen cloths, there was no service: the food and drinks could be obtained only by lining up at the far end of the room. By the time you got your appetizers and drinks, all the tables were taken. "It's

like the goddamn school cafeteria," Morgan had said when we first arrived.

Now Morgan extracted a twenty from her cute duck-shaped beaded bag. "We would love it if you could bring us four Tanqueray martinis when you have a chance."

Her eyes on the folded bill, the waitress nodded. "I sink I could do zat."

Morgan and I took turns spotting celebrities and exchanging that stream-of-consciousness dialogue we shared so well.

"Does Becca still suffer insomnia?" she asked.

"Not at all. She's out like that." I snapped my fingers. "Unlike her mother. Ha! I suffer major bed anxiety now. Sometimes I wonder if I'll ever sleep with a man again."

"But it's nice to have the bed to yourself sometimes, right?"

"To stretch diagonally across it?"

"Oh, and I added this feather mattress that would have made my husband overheat. It's heaven on Earth."

"Speaking of overheating," I said, relaxed by the powerful martini. It wasn't my drink of choice—too strong—but I'd wanted to feel sophisticated tonight, holding that elegant V-shaped glass. "I know it's crazy but I totally fell for Dash Gray tonight." I pressed my palms to my warm cheeks as the waitress returned and lined up our quartet of martinis.

Morgan thanked the waitress profusely and lifted a fresh drink. "Oh, honey. Dash Gray? He was great in the show, but he's so . . . so British."

"Confident. Quick-thinking. The man is like quicksilver. No ponderous silences there. Now there's a man who wouldn't leave you for a piece of ass in Dallas." I leaned forward, clinking my glass against Morgan's.

"Or South Dakota." Morgan grinned, those little lines making her eyes resemble stars. "Here's to the man of our dreams."

"To Dash Gray," I giggled.

"Even if he is gay," Morgan added.

I tossed back a swallow of burning liquid, shaking my head. "No, no! I won't believe it."

"Well, I for one, am relieved to hear it," said a male voice. A British voice.

A Dash Gray voice.

Morgan and I swung around to the aisle, where the actor himself stood with a group of men.

"I couldn't help but notice that you seem to have cocktails to spare on your table. Do you mind?" he asked.

His eyes were so blue. Turquoise ice. Contacts?

Who cared?

I wanted to answer but the adrenaline rush prohibited all logic.

"Please, join us," Morgan said. "I think those people behind you would be happy to lend you that spare chair."

In an instant, Dash dismissed his friends, swept a chair over to our table, and sat inches from my right hand. So close that the halo of his aura seemed to glisten on the amber stones of the tennis bracelet that my kids gave me last Christmas.

He tugged on one ear. "Damn burning ears. It always happens when someone bandies about my reputation."

"We're sorry," Morgan cooed. "Does it bother you when the media makes such a big issue out of it?"

"Nah. Those reporters are just doing their jobs. It's a certain ex-girlfriend who shall remain nameless. My issue is with her for starting the rumor. Vindictive little twit."

I giggled, an effervescent martini giggle.

"You like that, eh? Well, there's a fair amount of bitter rampage bottled up inside. Don't get me started."

"I'm Morgan O'Malley. A literary agent? And this is my star client, Ruby Dixon."

He nodded cordially, his eyes dancing over me. "I thought you looked familiar. You're the famous writer."

"Recently, famous," I said apologetically. "Commercial fiction, though. Not Pulitzer–Prize winning or anything."

Why was I babbling like a fool?

"Give yourself some credit there, Ruby. You're the flavor of the month." He cocked his head to one side, as if assessing my future. I wanted to reach out and press my palm to his face, cup his smooth cheeks, smooth his brow. I wanted to memorize him with my hands.

How often does a person like me come into the presence of a person who's bigger than life?

"If I were you," he went on, hunching over us, so close I could have touched the sandy brown hair that curled around his collar, "I'd bask in the limelight." He leaned across the table, as if nudging me aside. "In fact, would you mind sharing your limelight? I could use some decent reviews. The last two shows I opened in closed within a month."

Morgan and I laughed as I patted Dash's shoulder. "Hey, my limelight is your limelight."

Oh, how corny can you get? I wanted to slap a hand to my mouth and take back the words, but Dash seemed genuinely amused.

"True generosity." He glanced over his shoulder. "You won't find an actor in this room who'd make the same offer. That's why I've sworn off dating actresses. Especially conniving, two-faced vixens. Did I mention my ex-girlfriend? Am I boring you?"

We laughed.

Dash's friends had returned. "Time to go," one of them said.

He nodded. "Listen, the party is heading next door to a bar called Think Tank. Upstairs. Would you like to join us?"

Morgan's eyes went wide. I nodded.

Ten minutes later, we were seated at the Think Tank bar, talking with Dash and his friends. Some of them were actors, others worked backstage. He introduced one woman as his publicist, the other as his sister Emily, who was visiting from Great Britain.

Morgan and I talked with Emily for quite awhile, learning that she worked as a schoolteacher in a suburb of London. She had two children and a husband who worked as a bobby.

"Dash flew me over for the premier," Emily explained. "He hates doing the red carpet alone, and after everything with Sara, well . . ." She shrugged. "I decided to be his date for the event." She shared her brother's icy blue eyes and perky charm.

"I must admit, Mum and I are huge fans of yours," Emily told me. "You make us laugh. When is your next book coming out?"

After we talked about books for awhile, the group opened up and the conversation shifted to most embarrassing moments. As brandy was poured for everyone, Dash and his actor friends acted out their nightmare experiences, recreating funny scenes, some from their childhoods. I sensed that this was a cohesive group of friends, guys who had known each other for some time.

During one of the stories Morgan looked at her watch and slid off the barstool. "I gotta go. I've got a breakfast meeting in the morning."

As we hugged good-bye, she asked me if I was okay getting back to the hotel.

"I think I can make it to the Waldorf," I teased, swirling the dark brandy in my glass.

The anecdotes went on, each guy trying to top the previous story. When the bartender told us it was last call, I was sorry to see the night end.

"So, Ms. Ruby Dixon," Dash said, stepping right up to me. All sparkly blue eyes and perfect teeth. "I hope you don't find me too forward for asking, but I'd like to see you again."

"No." I shook my head as I pressed the brandy snifter to my mouth. The burn felt good, purging.

"No, you don't find me forward?"

"You don't want to see me again. I'm married, with children."

"Lovely little buggers. I saw them on *Lolly.* How's the little boy with the fever? Dylan, is it?"

"Much better. But really, I'm flattered, but . . ."

"No room on your dance card for a party animal like *moi?*"

"My dance card is empty, Dash. But I am married."

"Yes, so you say. Though I did hear the word *separation* rolling off people's lips."

"Whose lips?"

"Ruby, is every prospective social outing a full-scale negotiation for you?"

I laughed, which fueled his smile.

"I was thinking we'd start with lunch or a concert or a show. Marriage and happily ever after can wait a few years. Or, at least, till the second or third date."

Now I was laughing. "I guess we could meet for a concert or something. If you're sure you're not gay."

He shot a glimpse down to his lap, then looked up at me, his eyes turquoise ice. "My hetero manhood is well intact, despite your best efforts. I'd love to demonstrate for you, but I'm old-fashioned that way. I like to fall in love first."

He smelled of lavender, the sweet fragrance seeping into my subconscious. I felt a tug of desire in that dormant area I'd abandoned months ago. Dashiell Gray wanted me, but he was waiting for love. Was that not the sexiest thing a man had ever said to me?

"Let me take you home," he said.

"I'm staying at the Waldorf, with my kids."

He nodded. "The Waldorf it is."

If the cab driver recognized Dash, he didn't say anything. It was a different story at the Waldorf, where the doorman greeted him by name and made some friendly small talk. Dash pressed a bill into his palm and took my hand to lead me up the stairs.

Inside the hotel, I worried that someone would spot us, that a photographer would pop out of a paneled vestibule and snap a picture of us in a compromising position.

LATE NIGHT ASSIGNATION! DASH DASHES INTO HOTEL WITH WRITER!

Or did the Waldorf ward off journalism's bottom-feeders?

We made it upstairs without incident. As we walked down the long hallway—the posh print carpet suddenly making me want to skip from one red poppy to another—I wondered what I'd do if Dash tried to kiss me.

Did I even know how to kiss anymore?

It hadn't been so many months ago that I'd embraced Jack with passion, but that was Jack. Kissing someone else brought to mind the mechanics of such an action, and I wasn't sure that I was up for physical contact if I had to think about it. My mind went back to the stories passed among my roommates in college of boys who were fun companions but rookie kissers. I remembered the nicknames: Liver Lips, Quagmire and the Human Vacuum.

"You've become incredibly withdrawn," he said, squeezing my hand.

The heat of his touch made my legs feel weak. How could I be so adolescent?

"Tired?"

"That. And worried that this might be a mistake."

He laughed. "That self-censor again? You're really hard on yourself, aren't you?"

I recognized my room number and paused, gripping the plastic key in one hand. "I'm juggling a lot of plates right now."

He pushed back his sports jacket and rested his knuckles on his hips. Thin hips. Flat chest. Dash had a sprinter's body and had played an Olympic runner in one film. I felt a delicious flash at the memory of his nearly naked body in one scene. It had been a locker room shower scene—just an argument among the athletes in the film—but a few reviewers had noted how Dash, in his thirties at the time, was looking good. Singe.

"Listen. Ruby." He took my hands, separated them, then lifted my arms to rest on his shoulders. The space between our bodies seemed magnetized, supercharged. "You are spinning many plates, but you can't let that diminish your love of spinning." He leaned forward and pressed his cheek to mine, a chaste hug. "The joy is in the doing."

There was nothing chaste about the way our bodies pressed against each other, the way our lips brushed, then opened to a kiss. A hungry kiss.

My fingers combed his hair, sinking into the curls at his collar. Hard to believe I was touching this poster boy of comedic entertainment, pressed against a body I'd craved while watching his HBO special alone one night.

Our kiss meandered into a slow, leisurely good-bye, a smooth ending to the night.

A reassuring hug. Clinging to the last vestiges of passion.

I wanted more . . . much, much more of him. But that wasn't going to happen. We both knew this was just a short connection.

A very personal autograph to treasure and remember.

"Good night," I whispered as he stepped away, his fingers trailing down my arms.

He smiled, bent down to pick up the key card I'd dropped and pushed it into the door.

I was glad for that, not wanting him to see how my hands were trembling. Hell, my whole body was trembling, but I wanted to savor the sensation, let it rock me into a cloud of sleep.

"Good night." His blue eyes caught me one last time before I pressed my way into the dark suite. "Sweet dreams," he called after me.

Suddenly sweet had a whole new meaning.

32

Girl Talk

That night, I dreamed a gorgeous man was tickling my arm
with a daisy.

It wasn't Dashiell Gray, and it wasn't Jack. The dark-eyed,
golden-haired guy in the dream was definitely stranger territory,
but he was a nice guy. First he was trying to teach me how to play
tennis. Then he was fixing a flat for me on a road that cut
through a deserted field of flowers. I teased him about something and he chased me into the flowers, leaping like an ante-
lope over yellow Black-Eyed Susans and red poppies.

It seemed so innocent and right for us to fall down in the field
and begin tickling each other. Titillating. Gently leading.

When Dylan crawled into my bed and woke me, things were
just starting to get sexy. Dang it!

I wondered if my subconscious was trying to rationalize a relationship with Dash. I knew it wouldn't go anywhere, at least, not
right now. And yet, I couldn't help fantasizing. Couldn't help
creating pathetic scenarios in which he waited until Jack divorced me to declare his passionate love for me. We would be
the darlings of the tabloids. Dash and Ruby vacationing on their
own island. Dash and Ruby to fund a school for orphans in
Uzbekistan. Dash and Ruby leading the charge for world peace,
a decent health care system, and a tasty, fat-free French fry . . .

We had brunch with my sister Amber, who was trying to be especially supportive in light of the Jack situation. "You need time to yourself now," she'd told me on the phone. "You just let Mom and me fight about the kids. We'll keep them busy." She seemed so happy to see my kids that she almost didn't notice the bill. Almost.

"Oh. My. God." She went pale under her freckles. "Two hundred bucks for eggs and fruit? Do you know what it would cost to make this meal at home? Less than twenty dollars."

"We got toast, too," Becca said.

"And donuts," Scout added.

"I know," I told Amber as I tossed an American Express card onto the check. "It's decadent, but I'm going to fight world hunger in my next life." *When I'm Mrs. Dash Gray.*

"Not if you keep paying two hundred bucks for breakfast," Amber retorted, corralling the kids upstairs to get their luggage.

With the kids off to New Jersey and Ashley off to the airport, I went back up to the room to get ready for my New York book signings.

The light was blinking on the hotel phone.

It was Dash. My pulse raced, just knowing he'd called.

"Funniest thing. I woke up this morning dreaming that I'd met the famous author Ruby Dixon. Such a lovely dream. And when I called this hotel, well, there you were, registered. Fancy that."

I grinned. What a charmer. He left his cell phone number, which I quickly wrote down and programmed into my cell. Then I changed into gray linen trousers with a turquoise spangled boho blouse and went down to the lobby to meet my driver.

Gracie called while I was at the first signing. "When can we meet? I want you to say hello to your new godson."

"I'm free this afternoon," I said. "And do you have a copy of *What to Expect When You're Expecting?*"

"Please! I devoured that in my first trimester."

"Do you want to go shopping?" I asked. "I'd love to buy you something for the nursery."

"Sure. And I'll only let you buy things that match my Noah's Ark theme, being the control freak that I am."

I laughed, knowing that any semblance of control would be out the window once Gracie's little screaming bundle of joy was here. Nothing breaks in that lacy layette like a fat poopy diaper.

We met at one of those baby superstores, a building the size of three football fields that held merchandise to entertain and amuse parents through every phase of childhood development.

"You look fabulous!" I said as we hugged. In a pin-striped dress with empire waist and cap sleeves, Gracie could have modeled maternity wear for the professional woman.

"And you . . . brunette! When did that happen?"

"When I decided that I didn't want to be just like every other blonde mommy in West Green. Brunette is a rarity out there, so I went back to my roots."

"I like it."

I grabbed a shopping cart. With Dylan being just two, I was no stranger to baby stores, where bulk seemed to be the modus operandi of every item.

We perused aisles of infant toys, black-and-white mobiles, arched gyms that hung over matching blankets, brightly colored squishy blocks. I brought Gracie up-to-date, trying to minimize the ways Jack had hurt me, as she'd always been quick to find fault with him, even when his behavior was stellar.

"What are you going to do?" she asked. "I mean, not divorce or anything, but immediate plans."

"Therapy," I said. "Eventually I'll have to tell the kids that he's moved out."

"Ouch. I figured they didn't know yet, when you were so kind about him on *The Lolly! Show.*"

When Lolly had asked, I had said my husband worked at a job that required him to be out of town at times. "I wouldn't have dissed him on national television," I said. "And I don't want to rip into him in front of the kids. He'll always be their father."

She screwed up her face in disdain. "That sucks. You'll always have to be nice."

While we sorted through infant thermometers and monitors, I told her about meeting Dashiell Gray. "I'm seeing him again for lunch or something," I said. "And, I don't know, I feel a little guilty about it."

"Guilty about meeting a guy for lunch?" She shook her head. "Even when your marriage was good, you met men for lunch. Editors and friends. Harrison, for Christ sake."

"But I wasn't contemplating sleeping with Harrison."

"And it's a good thing, since you're not his type," she said, laughing.

Whatever happened to down-and-dirty girl talk, when you examined the pros and cons of sleeping with "him"? I let the subject drop, realizing Gracie was too distracted to give me the validation I was looking for.

"Now this is irresistible." I picked up a fuzzy yellow blanket and pressed it to my face. Although it was ninety degrees outside, I found solace in its downy folds. "Let me get you a few of these . . . one in every color." My voice was muffled by the blanket.

"I've already got a white one. How many could one infant need?"

"Are you kidding? One will get spit up on it and one will get poopy. They'll get caught in the door of the cab and they'll trail out of the stroller. You could go through five in one day, easy."

"Really?" Her voice seemed unsteady. "Five?"

I rested one cheek against the blanket. "You wash them in baby soap and fold them and refold them as you're waiting for the baby to be born."

"Five blankets? I had no idea." Gracie sniffed.

I dropped the blanket. She was crying.

"Oh, honey. It must be hard, being alone for all this. Do you think you should have told the baby's father?" I tried to make the question sound natural, tried to hide the fact that I couldn't recall the name of the young guy who'd fathered Gracie's baby.

"No . . . no! That would definitely make things worse. God! The last thing I need is some gawky boy asking questions and trying to pose as something he's not. That would be worse than just realizing that I'm a poser myself. I don't know anything. How am I going to learn all this . . . this *stuff*?"

Lowering the blanket from my body, I tried to ignore the white fuzz all over my black cotton tank. "You're doing all the right things, Gracie. You're supposed to learn from friends with babies. And books and classes."

"I just don't think . . ." She pressed a hand to her face as a sob broke. "Those breast pumps look positively primeval. And I can't imagine these breasts producing much more than a swallow."

"You'd be surprised," I said. "Although you've probably already gone up one bra size, right?"

"Two. And I can't decide on a name and I can't for the life of me figure out how to work that Diaper Genie thingy and I feel guilty about filling the planet with a thousand dirty diapers but you're talking to someone who dry cleans her lingerie and it's just too gross to have my baby wearing recycled butt linens."

"You've learned so much already." I touched her shoulder, which seemed small and soft under my hand. The shoulders of her maternity dress were padded, minimizing the belly. "Gracie, when I had Becca I had no practical experience with babies, and she seemed to defy just about everything I'd read in baby books. You'll learn from trial and error; we all do."

"I'm usually on top of things." She swiped at a tear with the back of one hand. "I've always got the numbers crunched, the research done, the colors picked out. But this baby thing—"

"Defies organization," I said, touching her tummy. "Who knew? Who could have imagined that by Christmas you'll already have a little baby? Your own little family."

Her sob turned into a laugh. "Sometimes I feel like my life is being cracked open like an egg."

"And the ducklings emerge." I thought of my children . . . sensitive Becca, sporting Scout, playful Dylan. How could Jack have any regrets about our path when he looked in their eyes? In the eyes of three unique little people?

"I am sorry." Gracie dug in her purse and pulled out a tissue. "You've got my problem times three. You should be crying on my shoulder."

"Believe me, the kids aren't the problem. I'm beginning to think you've made the right choice, doing it all without a man."

"Now you're talking." She tossed a bunch of fluffy blankets into our cart and waved me on. "Come on. I'll show you my layette pattern. Which just happens to be right next to the restrooms. Seems like I have to pee every ten minutes."

33

Jack: I Luv Dezi

I have got to be the most miserable bastard in the world.

It's dark and sticky and hot, another Texas night, and I'm sitting in my boxers out on Dez's balcony, amid the crickets and exhaust fumes and probably leagues of scorpions, while the rest of the world sleeps. Stretching and yawning and lazy, scratching their bellies. God, I envy the rest of the world, the ones who can sleep. I used to be that way.

But not anymore. Too many things playing through my head. Acquisitions and mergers, columns of figures and pages of text from prospectuses. The faces of my kids: Dylan's fat pink cheeks, Becca gripping a pencil, her lips pursed in deep concentration, and Scout, brutally honest Scout with those penetrating eyes, asking me when I'm going to take her to her secret grotto. It's been weeks since I've seen them and I'm sick with missing them and helpless to do anything about it.

I think about Ruby all the time. Dr. Ep says she sounds like a wonderful woman, and she is. Her sanity makes my insanity make sense. She's better for me than Dez; Rubes is a real friend. We could have grown old and died as friends if I didn't get sucked into this black hole.

I don't know how the hell I got here, but I'm sinking deeper by the minute.

Right now I'm all torn up inside over what just happened in the bedroom. After we did it—and I pulled out and saw that the condom broke.

The goddamn condom!

I cursed like a sailor and told Dez she'd better get up and take a shower or something. Not that it would make a difference scientifically, but it made me feel like we were trying to do the right thing.

But Dez just shifted her head up to the top of the bed, her blonde hair falling over the pillowcase, lazy with satisfaction. She wasn't worried. And the words that spilled from her rosebud lips before she fell asleep! "It's okay," she whispered. "It wouldn't be so bad if we made a baby."

Jesus H. Christ.

What the hell is she talking about? Does she really think I want to go down that road again? A repeat performance of all the pain and misery at the heart of every family?

Not for me. It's definitely not for me.

It's balmy out here, but I'm shivering at the prospect of what might have just happened. If Dez gets pregnant, my life is over.

A grown man, shivering with fear, stooped over on some chick's balcony off the interstate. Maybe my life is already over.

I rake my hands through my hair, wishing for sleep. When was the last time I really fell into a deep sleep? Now, whenever I let my guard down, that dream comes back. I'm in my old bedroom at home, the Superman curtains hanging open at the window, where something horrible keeps appearing. I'm hanging on to the bed, trying to think of a way to escape, when it happens. A growling burglar pops up in the window. Another night, it's my old man, only the skin is dripping from his face like a molten zombie. Sometimes, there's just a shimmering light in the mist outside, and I know it's a sign of unimaginable horrors. Terrible things to come . . .

But I never know exactly what, because I wake up in a sweat, my heart pumping like crazy. After that there's no getting back to sleep.

I want to down a few beers to dull the pain, only Dez doesn't keep any in the house. "I'm not a big drinker," she says. When you get down to it, she's not even a little drinker. I don't know how I fell in with someone so lackluster, so vanilla. Ruby was right about Dez not being my type, but then, Rubes usually is right. Her big mistake was hooking up with me.

Exhaustion weighs down my soul. Hunched over in my grundies, I twist around and try to prop my head against the chair. Up in the black sky, a full moon gleams. Moon of insanity. The man's face gloats at me. Scout used to say that the man on the moon is laughing. But it's a cynical smile. He knows a loser when he sees one.

34

A Cinderella Tale

In the light of day, I was afraid that Dash would feel all wrong, like a pair of shoes purchased in a moment of passion that kill your feet once you walk out the door of the store. A tingle of nervousness hit me as I pressed into the quaint red door of the Garment District restaurant and dropped Dash's name. The maitre d' nodded, but not without scooping a look at me, the latest dish of actor Dashiell Gray.

More nerves.

But then I saw Dash salute from a table by the window. Dressed in washed-out blue jeans and a black T-shirt, he seemed at ease here, at ease with himself. And, really, this wasn't so much a date as it was two friends meeting for dinner. Even if I wasn't still married, I was too old to date, too jaded and worn to spend time worrying about what to wear and say.

Okay, but what *would* I say to him?

"I took the liberty of ordering some fried oysters for us." Dash cocked his head, his eyes narrowed in glittering slits. "And aren't we sporty, the two of us in our jeans?"

I was glad he'd noticed. After much deliberation I had worn my jeans and a silky scarlet tank top covered by a sheer blouse embroidered with two simple flowers on the bodice. Just enough to cover my shoulders, which had lost their tennis court elasticity sometime around the second baby.

By the time I sat down, my nerves seemed to bubble into something else altogether . . . joy of the moment. Here was someone I could talk to, someone who would understand the sweetness of Gracie crying over fuzzy baby blankets and the humor of a bookstore owner sure that I was Ruby *Nixon,* granddaughter of the former president.

I launched into one of my tales of the week in New York City, and Dash followed with a story about how the airline bumped his sister up to first class when they'd seen her crying at the airport. The tears were actually an allergic reaction to a new contact lens solution, but she'd gladly accepted the upgrade.

As we talked, I realized my week of worries over this man had been overblown. The easy chemistry between us was like drugs in my veins, a muscle relaxant and a burst of adrenaline all at once.

Although we had talked on the phone a few times, I had put off meeting Dash until my last night in New York. A cop-out, I knew, but Monday night was also Dash's only real evening off unless I wanted to meet him for a late-night supper at eleven PM.

And I didn't. The easy way that our first meeting had flowed from premier party to after-party to four AM last call proved to me that the late-night hours had a mystical, ethereal quality ripe with dangerous possibilities.

As the waitress enumerated the specials, I pretended to read the menu, though my mind was giving me the proverbial kick in the pants. Tonight I would have to behave. No hotel corridor cuddles. No last call with the drinking buddies. My sister had dropped off the kids at the hotel, where a sitter from Nanny on the Run was with them right now. Tomorrow morning we'd be back on a flight home to Portland.

Home . . . It seemed strange to discover that New York City was no longer the center of my universe, that I had moved on. And I looked forward to getting back to Oregon, back to clean air, green space, a slower pace. Even if that world did come with bottle-blonde soccer moms who feasted on Happy Life Cocktails and drove hulking SUVs.

"Have I lost you, ducky?" Dash asked.

I looked up from my menu to find Dash and the waitress watching.

"Chardonnay or Sauvignon Blanc?" the waitress coached.

"Definitely the Chardonnay," I said with authority, as if I had a clue.

We sipped buttery Chardonnay with our crisp fried oysters, fat with pockets of meat that melted in our mouths. The red-and-white-painted wood inside the Red Cat brought to mind a quiet New England farm, unpretentious and comfortable.

Of course. Dash had enough personal flash; he didn't need to dine in a trendy venue thick with stale celebrities.

The chef split the Wild Striped Bass in White Wine Butter for us, and when the two small matching plates came, it seemed so intimate, the two of us partaking of one meal.

"You've got to try these fritters," Dash said.

Risotto Fritters with Blueberries. Savory steam spewed forth as I broke one in half. I blew on it and bit in, eager for the experience. "Delicious," I said, and Dash smiled.

"How I love to see a woman eat. It's so tedious to dine out and eat alone while a skinny hyena watches from across the table."

We both laughed, and I thought of a photo I'd seen of Sara, her clavicle clearly jutting forth above the V-neck of her dress.

"I've always envied those model-thin women," I said. "They must have great fortitude to stay so thin."

"They lead very dull lives. Bland lives of flax and unsweetened cranberry juice." He refilled my wineglass, twisting the bottle with a flourish. "That's not for you, Ruby. You have the courage to dig in and savor every bite."

Licking crumbs from my lips, I was suddenly conscious of a desire to dig into Dash and savor him.

No, no, no. It was not going to happen. Not tonight.

Still, in the fuzzy glow of wine and a cozy red New England barn, a girl could dream.

After dinner, Dash told me he wanted to take me to Manchester.

"I don't think my passport is current," I told him.

"In that case, we'll have to settle for Manchester, New York. It's a pub on the East Side, a haunt for homesick Brits, much like myself."

We took a cab to the pub, which was cool and dark, a welcome relief from the humid, hot air that had descended on the city this week, squeezing condensation out of every signpost and shop window. Dash seemed to know the players at the bar, and we sat with them and discussed the Yankees and the Mets over pints of nut-brown ale.

Moving around the city with Dash reminded me of the old days with Jack, the freedom and excitement of negotiating a tireless city with your best friend. High adventure and endless possibilities.

Was this the life that Jack missed when he said he didn't see himself as a suburban father of three?

"Dashiell Gray, the girls you bring by are just getting prettier and prettier," said one of the old-timers at the bar. He had black eyes and bushy gray brows that feathered back like a gull's wings.

"Well, thanks, I guess." I turned to Dash. "How many girls have you had in here this week?"

"None!" He jabbed the older man in the arm. "Don't go saying that, Chet."

"But it's true, lad!"

"That girl last week was my sister Emily."

"That's right!" Chet smacked his forehead. "Of course." He added, confidentially, "I'll have you know, none of us went for that Sara. All high and mighty. Colder than the queen, that one. But you're a right sweetheart." He squeezed my hand, and I squeezed back.

"You don't have to worry about me. The only royalty in my family is my dog, a Cavalier King Charles Spaniel."

The men gasped and launched into stories of the Cavalier pups they'd had as boys back in the old country.

When an inch of dark brew remained in my glass, I knew it was time to go, time to return to my kids. "I hate to say it," I said, checking my watch, "but I'm about to turn back into a pumpkin."

Dash frowned. "Don't go."

"My flight is in the morning."

"Stay here. Cancel the flight." He flung himself at me, pretending to sob on my shoulder. "Don't leave me."

The men chuckled as I patted his back. "There, there. You've got a show to do tomorrow, and I've got to get back to mommy land, kingdom of runny noses and PBJs."

"Blast it all!" Dash touched my cheek with one palm as he pulled away. He slid off his bar stool and tossed some bills on the bar. "Why does the drinking have to end, just when I'm getting really soused?" he joked.

As we stepped out of the pub a flash of light struck the shadows of the late-summer sunset, stinging my eyes.

A camera flash. Paparazzi.

"Oh," was my brilliant comment. I sounded like Betty Boop.

"Shadow?" Dash cocked an eyebrow at the photographer, but he didn't take his hand from my waist. "Glad to see you're keeping out of trouble by blinding me with your flash."

"Sorry, Dash. Do you want to pose for one? I think she might have had her eyes closed."

"Absolutely." Dash pulled me against him.

My hand slipped around his waist and I could feel his ribs. His T-shirt seemed slightly damp from the humidity, and he smelled sweet and lemony. Delicious.

Dash insisted on another photo, this one with his lips pressed against my cheek. I laughed, despite the awkwardness of it, the notion that we might actually appear together in a national tabloid, or, worse, on the home page of a website.

"This is the hot new novelist Ruby Dixon," Dash bragged. "She's in New York to do publicity for her book."

"Excellent." The photographer retracted his lens. "Thanks, Dash." And with that, he was heading down the street, gear slung over his shoulder.

"What newspaper does he work for?" I asked Dash, who shrugged.

"Freelance, I think. He'll sell the photo to the magazine or wire service that offers the best price."

I shook my head. "Isn't it a little demoralizing, having someone spring out at you like that and attack?" Suddenly I understood the logic of those cultures who believe that photographs steal or threaten the soul.

Dash seemed unfazed as he went to the curb to hail a cab. "It's a living."

During the cab ride, as Dash took my hand, he said, "You're upset about that photo. Listen, why don't we go back to my place? I don't want the night to end, and you probably don't fancy running into another photographer tonight."

I shook my head. "I don't think so. I have an early flight."

"Oh, come on! I won't get into your knickers if that worries you."

I laughed. "I'd like that, but no. Really. I need to call it a night."

And I'm still married. My kids don't even know about the separation. Some nights I sleep with my husband's old sweatshirt on the pillow beside me.

As the cab jerked crosstown, the air conditioner blowing stale air onto our feet, my mind went over the peril of people seeing that photograph of us.

People who knew me would understand. My sister. Ariel and Harrison and Morgan and Gracie.

But what about the neighbors back in West Green? Eric Lundquist. And—oh, God!—the PTA! Suzie Snyder. Daphne and Hillary . . .

I calmed myself with the reminder that women like Suzie Snyder did not read tabloids. They were too busy baking gingerbread cookies with organic flour, organizing raffles, antiquing abandoned end tables to auction at the school fundraiser.

Most of all, what about Jack? He would think the worst.

I didn't want to hurt him.

Or did I?

What if it did bother him, seeing me with another man? A famous man. It would stir up any last vestiges of feeling he had for me. Like stirring a pot of meatballs with a knife. Everything gets cut to ribbons.

Well, if he saw the photo, so what? Let him experience some pain. God knew, there was enough of it going around.

Dash insisted on seeing me up to my suite at the Waldorf. He knew the doorman by name—a different one this time. Fred, with the red hair and faltering gait. They chatted about Fred's daughter going off to college this month.

"How do you remember all the names of people you've met?" I asked Dash as we rode the elevator up. "It's as if you joined a fraternity in this town."

He smiled. "Manners. My mother always told me to be polite to the people who help you. And one never forgets a guy like Fred after he scrapes you up from the floor of the Bear and Bull and sends you safely home in a cab."

Dash's drinking exploits were the stuff of tabloid history. I was beginning to see why.

"I guess this is good-bye." I paused outside the door of our suite, frowning. "It's been really fun."

"Oh, Ruby, the fun is just beginning." Dash pulled me into his arms and pressed his lips to mine. The kiss made me feel vulnerable and sexy. I wanted to open myself to him, but there just wasn't time.

He brushed my hair back with one hand and nibbled my earlobe. I could have melted right there in his arms, lost in sensation.

But for a thump on the other side of the door.

"Get out of the way, you butthead!" one of the girls called.

"You're a poopy latte-head!" Dylan retorted. Just before he turned two he'd begun stringing together phrases and sentences. At the moment, I wasn't so thrilled with his verbal flexing. "Poopy latte head!"

Dash and I broke apart, a gush of laughter between us.

"I don't believe I've ever tasted a poopy latte," Dash said whimsically.

"They're great with pumpkin bread." I stepped back and smoothed down my blouse. My cheeks were probably red from the heat I felt there. Oh, well. Better to break it off before we got hot and heavy in the hallway.

"Thanks. For everything." I leaned forward and placed a chaste kiss on his cheek. "You're a great guy."

"I'm not dying, yet. And I'm not going anywhere."

"But I am."

He stepped back and lifted his fingers to his face in that *I'll call you* gesture. "Sweet dreams. And have a great trip."

"Stop it!" someone shrieked inside, and there was a bang against the door.

I waved to Dash, then knocked. A minute later, the Cinderella fantasy ended as the door opened to my real life.

I stepped inside without looking back.

35

Ask Salesperson for Mate

It didn't take long to get back into the swing of suburban living, with a few exceptions.

Our cranky neighbor Eric wasn't so cranky anymore. He and his wife, Jan, claimed that Taffy had been the light of their lives when she stayed with them, and now Eric was building a gate in the fence to his yard, hoping that the children and dog would spill over into his life every now and then.

"We're so happy to have you guys back," Eric told me. "Jan and I missed the little guy rattling around on his tricycle."

Seeing a lanky grown man roll in the grass with a two-year-old and a puppy, I kicked myself for pigeonholing Eric as a cold Oregonian. Okay, he was a scary driver, but the man had a heart of gold and I was going to have to learn to keep an open mind about people I met here. Go Beavers!

Then there was Scout's friend Kevin, who wanted her at his house every single day. "Kevin really missed Scout," Daphne told me. "It's been a different summer with the baby. Not as many trips to the zoo or the beach." One day, as I was dropping Scout off at the Sweets, Daphne started telling me about the adjustments Kevin had made in his life. "His first two years were pretty rocky," she told me as we watched them shooting hoops in the backyard. "Kevin's parents were abusive. He had some issues to work out when we first took him in."

"Kevin is adopted?" I asked.

She nodded. "He came to us as a foster child, and over the years the situation changed."

"That's such a wonderful story," I said, warmed by the thought of Daphne and Rick taking in this boy. "It's atypical of West Green."

"You'd be surprised." She picked up the baby's cup from the floor and handed him a cracker. "There are some cool people here. We're not all soccer moms."

"Time for me to head home and eat some crow," I said.

She laughed. "We all need a serving, now and then."

These neighborly gestures of support made me realize I'd been keeping people out, being a little unfair.

So as I was sitting by the kiddy pool at the swim park, I whispered to Hillary that my husband and I were separating. She squeezed my hand and told me to call her if I needed anything.

Over the phone I shared the same news with Madison's mother, Lexie Woodcock.

"What is wrong with men these days?" she quipped. "They think every minute has to be happy time. It sounds just like my first husband." Lexie then insisted on having Becca for a sleepover to get the girls out of my hair for awhile.

I appreciated their support in view of my recent loss. I rationalized that the breakup of a marriage was similar to losing your partner to death, only in my case no one was sending flowers or bringing over casseroles.

Sometimes I felt as if I'd had my teeth removed and I couldn't get over the gaping holes left behind, dark holes of embarrassment and pain visible to the entire world.

"It's not your fault," Dr. Griffin told me when I started therapy the week we returned. "You didn't do anything wrong."

"I was raised Catholic. I must be guilty of something," I joked, although she didn't laugh. Dr. Griffin didn't find me funny. I suspected that she was annoyed at the humor I used to dodge the pain.

In the throes of daily life, I realized that I missed Jack. I hated him. I couldn't stop loving him.

I fantasized that his plane would go down—preferably crashing into *her* house—on its approach to the Dallas airport. Though, admittedly, this was a dark-and-twisted longing, it would cut short Jack's torment, purge the world of one husband-stealing damsel, provide my children with a tidy life insurance settlement, and would allow me to save face before the world learned of my lying, cheating, cavorting husband. The Jack and Ruby mythology would be unsullied, and my children would be afforded a memory of their father as a kind man with a deep, underlying pain and a great sense of humor, rather than a sniveling weasel who'd left them for a piece of blonde ass.

Of course, if something like this really happened I'd be so consumed with guilt that my children would end up losing their mentally stable mother, too. But that didn't stop me from thinking about it.

I shared this fantasy with Dr. Griffin. I had hoped to shock her with my death wish for Jack, but she seemed to lap it up like a cat smacking its lips over a can of tuna fish.

Dr. Griffin, a painfully thin woman with curly red hair and Coke-bottle glasses, had children of her own, close in age to mine. I thought she'd relate to what I was going through, my concern about protecting them. I thought that somehow in our sessions she'd give me the pat on the back I deserved for holding together our little family, nurturing our children, keeping a positive attitude in a very negative situation.

Instead, our sessions made me feel like an even bigger failure, that I had lost my marriage and that I was not very good at this therapy thing, either. I kept trying to tell her how my ego had been damaged by the painful spankings my father had administered with a hairbrush when I was five, and she kept coming back at me with the importance of taking responsibility for my choices. Namely, the bad choice of marrying Jack.

Well, I was certainly feeling the consequence of that choice right now.

Dr. Griffin kept asking me questions about Jack, how we'd met, how I'd gotten him to marry and impregnate me, as if I'd roped him into paternity and happy suburban life. When I talked about Jack, she listened with relish, as if she was collecting details for a case study of wayward suburban dads. From her questions, I sensed she found Jack fascinating, from his dysfunctional family to his old Queens drinking buddies. If she had her druthers, Jack would be the patient she'd have on her couch. He was high drama—a TV movie on middle-aged male ennui—while I was just a thirty-second commercial for fabric softener.

Despite my lackluster psyche, one productive suggestion came out of our first few sessions. Dr. Griffin did push me toward one event I'd been avoiding: telling the kids.

"Don't make too much of it," she advised. "You don't want to call a formal family meeting that will cause the children anxiety."

I nodded. "But don't you think Jack should be there?"

"That would be nice, but how long can you wait? If he's going to keep up this passive-aggressive absence, you need to call it what it is. You can't have the children hearing it from someone else."

True. And the word was out.

"Don't give the girls more detail than they need," Dr. Griffin went on, her eyes enormous lobes behind the thick glasses. "But don't make excuses for him. Give them as much of the truth as you can."

I kept nodding, my stomach twisting in a knot. I didn't want to do this. I didn't want to look like the one who was taking their father away from them.

"You might want to talk to the girls individually. Approach it casually. And Dylan is really too young for the talk. If he asks about Daddy, you can deal with it then."

Dylan probably wouldn't ask. He hadn't bonded with Jack the way the girls had. But the girls . . . I dragged myself out of Dr. Griffin's office, dreading my future.

That evening, I saw my opportunity to talk with Scout. We were walking the dog at the school under a late-summer sky painted in brilliant pink, red and purple over the tall fir trees on the western horizon. Scout ran with Taffy, the dog's ears flying back as she galloped alongside my nimble daughter. Funny how everyone associated Oregon with rain; no one talked about the summers, the broad, green days of sunlight that range from 60 degrees in the morning to 80 by day. Summers were Oregon's best-kept secret.

Both Scout and Taffy were panting after their run. Taffy circled my ankles, as if trying to wrangle me in her leash, while Scout collapsed into the grass.

"Look at that sunset," I said. "Did you see the colors?"

"Uh-huh." Scout's red cheeks matched the hues in the sky. "Dad would love it." She rolled onto one side. "When's he coming back?"

"You know, I'm not exactly sure. Dad is going to be spending some time away from us for awhile."

Scout looked up at me, her steely eyes suspicious.

"What do you mean?"

"Dad is living in a separate place. He'll still be back to see you, but he's not going to live with us. Not right now."

"I thought he was just in Dallas for business."

So did I. "It started that way."

She scrunched up her face. "Is he going to live there?"

"I guess. We need to talk to him and find out what he's planning." I felt in the pocket of my shorts for my cell phone. "Do you want to call him? You can ask him about it."

"Nah." She sat up, her head hanging over the grass as if she was studying the clover. "Can I tell Kevin?"

"If you want to."

"I don't want him to move out."

"I don't, either, but it's something Dad wants to do right now."

"Well, that sucks."

I bit my lower lip. Normally I'd have Scout apologize for her language, but I knew it had come straight from the heart. "Yes," I agreed. "It really sucks. But we're going to be fine."

Scout shot me a look that said, *Well, duh!*

"We're going to be fine," I told Becca, summing up my ever-so-casual announcement to her. We were roaming the aisles at Payless Shoes, shopping for gym shoes for school, where the policy required students to keep a clean pair of sneakers on hand so that the gym wouldn't become caked with mud and twigs come the rainy season. Becca wanted pink sneakers, but didn't want any characters like Barbie or Bratz on them. "Too dorky," she said. The fashion code of the fourth grade.

"Do we have to go back to New York?" Becca asked. Her fingers worried the fluffy fringe of a pair of slippers, which I'd told her she could have. Not that she needed them, but in my state of extended crisis I was all about buying every vestige of possible happiness.

"No, honey. We're staying here." I hadn't considered the possibility of returning to New York. It would be nice to have the support of family in close proximity, but it would also be like a step backward, a regression into the jaws of a marauding shark that had to keep moving to stay alive.

She pressed the slippers to her chest, thinking ahead. "Can we stay in our house?"

"Yes, of course. It's our home, honey." I slipped an arm around her shoulders and gave her a tentative hug. "We're going to be fine, honey."

Becca took a deep breath, almost a sigh. "I know." She slipped out of my arms and stepped toward the shelves of shoes. "I might have to settle for white with a pink stripe."

"Maybe." I stood back, watching as she picked through the open boxes, back in shopping mode. Becca, our worrier, seemed unruffled. It was the best I could hope for.

From the rack behind her, a printed sign inside a shoe box caught my eye:

ASK SALESPERSON FOR MATE

My heart leaped. Could it be that easy, finding a mate? Was there a supply of eligible men lined up in the stockroom?

I pulled the sign out of the box. One line had been obscured behind the shoe:

THIS SHOE ON DISPLAY. ASK SALESPERSON FOR MATE.

"Too bad," I said aloud. That was shopping for you. The things you really needed were so hard to find.

36

Prodigal Dad

"Hey, hey!" Jack threw his arms wide in an unusually animated burst of emotion as he cleared the airport security area. The girls ran forward, landing against him for big hugs.

"Daddy! Daddy!" Dylan toddled behind them joyously.

I stood back, surprised Dylan remembered his father. How long had it been? Okay, not exactly months. But a few weeks was a prolonged period in the life of a two-year-old.

The girls watched curiously as Jack stepped forward and kissed me on the cheek. I felt tempted to rub it off, to turn to the kids and sputter: "Yuck! Ick!" Instead, I took Dylan by the hand and led him toward the escalator to the baggage claim area.

Stepping back as Jack goofed around with the kids, I noticed some silver shining in his hair. He seemed tired, and when he reached down to grab a suitcase from the belt, a circle of white shone at the crown of his head. Had that been there before?

He seemed older, wearier. On the other hand, his physical appearance didn't match the seething ogre I'd envisioned in my mind when we'd sniped at each other over the phone. Jack was still Jack, the important things still there. His steely-gray eyes still hinted at profound insight and painful secrets, and I suspected that he was juggling more pain and secrets now than ever before.

* * *

At home we shared a spaghetti-and-meatball dinner, and Jack pronounced the sauce delicious. "My mother's recipe is still the best,"
he said.

"Though I've modified it a bit," I said as I cleared away the salad
dressings. "It's hard to get ground veal here. Those were actually
chicken meatballs."

"*Really?* Chicken meatballs?" He cleared his plate and leaned
against the kitchen counter, arms folded.

Was he disappointed or impressed? I couldn't tell. I'd lost the
ability to read him.

While the kids played with Taffy in the neighbor's yard, Jack and I
went over the immediate game plan. "I got you a reservation at the
hotel down the road," I told him.

He blinked. "You're kidding me."

"Jack, you can't stay here. You can use the house all you want.
Hang out with the kids. Stay here until you put them in bed."

"I thought I could crash on the couch. Come on, Rubes, I'm
harmless."

I shook my head. "That wouldn't work. The hotel is close."

"And who's paying for it?"

"*You.* If you want, I'll deduct it from the mortgage money you owe
me."

He raked back his hair and let out a heavy sigh. "You're right.
We'll get the finances straightened out, okay? I . . . I just don't have a
minute to think about anything."

Oh, right. With all those demands on your time. "Is the dizzy blonde
that demanding?" I had to turn away to avoid glaring at him.

"Please don't pick on Dez. You know, she feels really bad about all
this. She really likes you."

"Well, she's got a strange way of showing it." I turned on the tap
water, letting the sauce pot soak. Maybe normal actions would offset
the bizarre tension of this conversation.

"We're both under a lot of pressure right now."

I turned to him, thinking that he was finally waxing sympathetic.

"I've never seen Dez so strung out."

"Dez?" My jaw dropped.

"I've got my nuts in a vice with Corstar Corporate, and Dez is all wound up about this thing with us. She's a planner. She wants to know what the future holds."

"Don't we all . . ."

"She wants me to commit. She wants a family."

It was as if I'd been mowed down by a truck. I turned off the water. The life sucked out of me, I slumped over the sink.

"What is it with women, that biological time clock thing?" Jack went on casually. "You girls need to have the babies. Men don't feel that urge."

"I can't believe this." I wrapped a dishtowel around one hand.

"I know it's crazy, but that's where Dez's head is."

"Did you mention to her that you don't see yourself as the suburban father of three . . . or, wait, make that *four?*" I wheeled toward Jack, wishing for violence. A sudden blow, a streak of lightning. Anything to wake him up. "Did you happen to remind her that you're still married?"

"Calm down." He held his hands up, his expression wary. "I know it's crazy. Didn't I say that?"

"But you're giving her play! You're letting her think it's going to happen with you!"

"Not really. I mean, I don't want to disappoint her, but . . ." He raked his hair back. "I don't know, Rubes. I don't know anything anymore."

"Just go. Get out of here." I slammed a wooden spoon into the sink, then tossed a plastic cup behind it. "Take the kids for ice cream or a movie."

"Okay." I worked at the sink, tears rolling down my cheeks as he gathered up the children and their clogs.

It wasn't until after the door closed behind them that I felt a warm tongue on my ankle. Taffy. She seemed to sense my raw pain. I collapsed onto the floor cross-legged and let the puppy lick my tears.

As the week went on, Jack revealed that he was negotiating a new job with Corstar. It was becoming clear that the Portland office was being largely neglected with Jack spending so much time in Dallas. Jack told me that he was here to interview his replacement for Portland. His new job title would have something to do with corporate acquisitions. Apparently, the CEO Bob Filbert had become quite attached. "Bob won't take a piss without me," Jack complained. "He wants me in on everything, every meeting, every golf game. It's nice to be wanted but Bob is putting a stranglehold on me. Well, I guess I fell into it myself."

He certainly had. Still, that didn't ease my perspective on the situation. Jack's plans with Corstar struck a blow to my heart. Maybe because it made the separation seem more real, or perhaps it was the sense of failure after we'd vested so much in this move to the Oregon office.

Bottom line? Jack was moving to Dallas, to *her.*

It really was over between us, and somehow I felt like the last to know.

37

Separations

"Look at the positive side," Morgan said. "At least you and Jack don't have to argue about money."

"True." I knew finances were a huge source of contention in most relationships, and I was grateful that I didn't need to lie in bed staring at the ceiling and wonder how I was going to pay my mortgage and VISA bill. "Things could always be worse."

A blue jay darted onto the back fence and shrieked at me. I pulled my legs up onto the patio chair and curled my hands around my coffee mug. Ever since I'd been on the West Coast I'd been waking up at six AM, so I'd started calling Morgan first thing in the morning, while the kids were still asleep.

"Jack will be there for them as they grow up," Morgan said. "I know he's emotionally unavailable now, but he'll work through that. He won't abandon the girls. He'll be Scout's best friend again."

"I'm not so sure. While he was here Scout did her best to win him over. She made a point of sitting next to him on the couch, choosing his favorite foods for dinner. She even made a FOR SALE sign for his car. Can you imagine? She knows how much he wants to dump that car. She sort of promised that he could buy a new car if he ever moved back home."

"Clever girl," Morgan said. "I'll bet that made him feel about two inches tall."

"I was too busy worrying about Becca and Dylan to notice. Becca was a little cold with him, as if she didn't want to betray me, and Dylan seems estranged. He would go along with Scout occasionally, but generally Jack was like some male sitter I'd hired to watch the kids."

Morgan groaned. "What a mess. But I have confidence in Jack as a father. He'll turn this thing around. He's no Jocko."

"My mind still reels when I think of what became of that man." After Clare's summer of searching she had found her long-lost father, living in a trailer on an Indian reservation with a woman who was missing her front teeth. Jacob O'Malley vehemently denied having fathered anyone, and Clare slammed the door on the twosome and their pyramid of empty whiskey bottles, and started for her rental car. As she started the engine, Daddy Dearest had emerged from the trailer and fessed up to fatherhood. He hadn't wanted to rile up the girlfriend with fond reminiscences, but in the privacy of the prairie he admitted that he missed his old life, and good ol' Morgan. Clare and her brother had been real cute as little kids, and he was real sorry he hadn't been around to watch them grow up. Took a lot of ingenuity for Clare to travel this far west to track him down, and, since she was here, could she spare some cash to buy the old man a drink?

"So how is Clare doing now?" I asked.

"She's back at work for the fashion designer. In terms of Jacob, she's gone from stunned to seething. One thing is for sure: the experience with her father certainly sharpened Clare's focus on the life she has. She appreciates me a lot more."

"Finally! A little appreciation for Mom! Is she helping around the house? Cooking you meals?"

"She hasn't gone that crazy, though she's stopped telling me to fuck off when I wake her up in the morning."

I laughed. "That's progress."

When the pain of betrayal and loss wasn't too overwhelming I worked on separating our lives. In my mind I began to divide the memories and cultural context of our two existences, assigning things as I saw fit. Fairly, I thought.

Jack got the Eagles and the Beach Boys, his favorites, and when I heard a song by one of his groups I was obliged to switch the car radio to another station or wince over the jingly bottled version of "Good Vibrations" in the grocery store. I cannot bear to hear Don Henley singing "Desperado," the song Jack used to embrace as his creed. I used to relish those lyrics "You'd better let somebody love you," thinking that I was the only one who'd gotten through his wall of bachelorhood, the only one who'd managed to overcome all the obstacles to intimacy.

Jack could have the boroughs of Queens and Brooklyn, and I would get Hoboken and Staten Island, where I went to college. Manhattan would have to be shared; can't be greedy. The Bronx, well, honestly, it had always been a corridor to other places for us—the Cross Bronx to Jersey, the Hutch to Westchester. The Bronx would be neutral territory.

Oregon would be mine, and Jack could have Dallas, no contest.

Which seemed appropriate. People always said everything was bigger in Texas, and I supposed that included affairs and deceptions. I would venture that everything was greener in Oregon—just like the green, trusting wife who didn't realize her husband had fallen out of love with her.

The sunshine and bold blue skies persisted, and the girls started school and Dylan scampered back into Montessori, jabbering in full paragraphs now. Although daytime temperatures soared up to eighty degrees at times, the swim park was closed, its primary staff gone back to school themselves.

Friday afternoon, we were invited to go tubing on the lake with the Woodcocks. While Dylan went for a playdate at the Parkers, the girls and I donned our swimsuits and shorts and walked over to the Woodcocks's tall, skinny house on a canal.

Because I had seen kids tubing on the lake, some bumping along at blinding speed, I thought it best to come along.

"Oh, great! I've got a spotter," Lexie said. She handed me a cooler to carry down to the dock. "Juice for the kids, beer for us, if you want."

The kids wrapped themselves in life vests and we cruised down the narrow canal in the Woodcocks's boat toward the main lake. "Don't mind my driving," Lexie told me while the kids kept switching seats in the back of the boat. "I'm really bad. Especially through these narrow tunnels. If it seems like I'm going to scrape the sides, well, I probably am."

With her short-cropped gray hair and stern eyes, Lexie wasn't a typical West Green mom. I liked her unapologetic style, which she told me came from twenty years of working in software companies.

Once we hit the main lake, Lexie gave me an orange flag to hold up while the girls pushed the float down to the water and climbed aboard. The four of them were all giggles as the tube floated back from us.

"Are you sure they're okay like that?" I asked, glancing back at Madison's younger sister. Haley was only four, her freckled nose wrinkled as she squinted into the sun.

"Haley's done it a hundred times," Lexie insisted. "Your job is to look back and do a head count every so often. Let me know if someone goes overboard."

I nodded tentatively. Beer onboard . . . children overboard. This didn't sound good at all.

Lexie hit the throttle and we sped off over the green water. Behind us, the slack in the rope ran out and the float jerked ahead. Four heads nodded as their raft took flight.

Four heads, I counted nervously.

Four huge smiles.

Their eyes went wide as the float popped the wake of another boat, airborne for a few minutes. With the churn of the engine and wind I couldn't hear them, but I could see that they were roaring with laughter.

"I've been thinking about you," Lexie shouted above the noise. "Your situation. I was there just six years ago, with Haley's dad." She turned to me, her eyes unreadable behind her sunglasses. "Do you think you'll get a divorce?"

"It's looking that way." I turned back to do a head count. Still four bobbing heads. "I'm really grateful that Becca has Madison. It's helpful for her to have a friend's support right now."

"Just let me know if you ever need me to take Becca for awhile," Lexie shouted. "She's a good kid, a good influence on Madison."

I thanked her as we cruised past the empty swim park, the picnic tables vanished, the maze of docks standing empty, yearning for the crowds of next summer.

I turned back toward the float, counted four heads, counted my blessings. We were in a beautiful place, cooling off on a hot, sunny day. Life after Jack could still be good.

When the girls were tired and soaked, Lexie told me to haul in the "water rats." We wrapped them in fat towels and headed back up the canal, passing cute little houses, some so tiny they could have existed in Hobbittown.

"Can we take the boat out again tomorrow?" Madison asked.

"We'll see," her mother answered as we approached their backyard dock. "Every summer we say that we're going to get more use out of this thing, and every summer we don't get it out of the boathouse till August."

"Mom! You're almost touching!" Haley called from the back of the boat.

"The hardest part about docking is"—Lexie lifted her sunglasses and squinted toward the wooden dock as the boat hit the pylon and bounced away—"not crashing. That's good enough."

Back inside the house, the girls orchestrated a plan for Madison to come to our house for a sleepover. I agreed, since it was the first weekend of the school year. Madison filled up a cute purple backpack with charms dangling from its zippers and we headed home.

"Can I call Kevin?" Scout asked. "Maybe he can come over and play."

"You can call him when we get"—as we turned onto our street, I spotted a sleek silver BMW parked in our driveway—"home."

"Whoa!" Scout cooed. "Did Dad get a new car?"

I pulled in beside the shiny car, which came with a woman. She was standing at our front door.

"Oh . . . Hi!" She clambered off the porch, the heels of her pumps clacking on the graveled pavement. She was petite and businesslike.

With her navy sleeveless sheath, her designer eyewear, her smooth complexion, she definitely belonged to the car.

"Can I help you?" I asked, my radar on alert. This was no solicitor.

"Well, I hope so. I'm looking for Jack Salerno."

I feared calamity as the girls spilled out of the car behind me, eyeing her curiously. Was this woman a process server? A disgruntled Corstar employee? A jilted lover?

Oh, Jack, what have you done now?

38

The Smart One

"Jack isn't here right now," I said, trying to be polite without sounding like a victim.

"Do you expect him back soon?" she asked, lifting her sunglasses to reveal smokey-gray eyes . . . weary eyes.

I didn't know how to answer. This woman didn't seem like a threat to me or my children, but then again, neither did Desiree when I'd met her at Christmastime.

Scout picked up a basketball from the side of the lawn and bounced it in front of the garage. "Do you know my dad?" she asked the woman.

"I used to know him when he was a kid." She pushed her sunglasses back in her shiny black hair and stole the ball from Scout's dribble. "I'm his sister, Gia. I guess that would make me your aunt."

Scout's mouth gaped open. "That's just random." She turned to me. "Is it true, Mom?"

"Gia?" The sister who'd split from the family and never returned. *"The smart one, because she got away,"* Jack used to say.

"I go by Gia Miller now." She tossed the basketball to Scout and I could see it now. Her mother's stance, her father's perfect teeth. The steely-gray eyes of a Salerno, brimming with pain and conflict.

"Have you spoken to Jack?" I asked. "How did you find us?"

"I was hoping to surprise my brother." She gestured to the three girls. "Bad idea, huh?"

"Bad timing."

"I found you through a friend of a friend who works at Corstar. Sort of a long story."

I nodded. The girls had moved over to the hoop, where Scout was being accused of hogging the ball. "By the way, I'm Ruby, Jack's wife. I guess." I glanced over to check that the girls were out of earshot. "Jack and I are separated right now."

"It's the dysfunctional family curse," Gia said, holding up her fingers. "Three times for me. My therapist says our parents didn't model a functional relationship for me. I haven't seen them for more than a decade and they're still ruining my life."

"I saw them last Christmas and I'm still getting over it," I said. "So I can understand lasting dysfunctions."

We both laughed, maybe because it was so sad it was funny. Then I asked her in and offered her a glass of iced tea. Carrying the pitcher and our glasses we went to the shade of the back patio, slipped our shoes off and talked.

I learned that Gia had moved from Silicon Valley to Seattle five years ago, following her most recent husband who was a developer in the Puget Sound area. When she left her parents, she headed west and put herself through college at U. C. Berkeley waiting tables. She'd gotten into pharmaceutical sales, and had made a tidy nest egg, only to "snort it all up my nose in the eighties," she said. She was surprised that Jack didn't have any obvious addictions, but then concluded that every guy has a different monkey on his back. When the sales thing fizzled, she got a nursing degree and worked in hospital emergency rooms. When that got too intense she went back to school and became a teacher. Recently Gia decided it was time to get licensed as a therapist, "Since I've read every self-help book published since Freud made Oedipus famous." She was still teaching but had begun taking psych classes at night.

A survivor of breast cancer, she vowed a few years ago to stop wasting time humoring the wrong men. That was when she left her third husband. She spoke frankly of things that disturbed or hurt her, though at times she scoffed memories off with a self-deprecating laugh that struck me as slightly manic, but who was perfect?

When I asked her why she'd come looking for Jack, she said she did not want to live the second part of her life without any family. Her parents were intolerable. A phone conversation with Frankie had confirmed that he was still an oaf. Jack was the last man standing, and she had fond memories of Jack trying to keep the peace at home, of Jack jumping on the beds at Mattress Queen with such joyful abandon. Gia was lonely, and she'd learned that standard romance was not going to satisfy that yearning.

As she talked, I fantasized that Gia had been sent through some divine intervention to make my family whole again—a Salerno angel, magically appearing to plug the hole in our lives left by her brother Jack. It might be possible, considering that Gia didn't have any family of her own left. There were no children, no ex-husbands she really liked. I wasn't completely sure why I wanted her in our lives, except that she had those familiar gray eyes, eyes laden with hurt and pain that I'd always been so sure I could heal.

Talking about her life came naturally to Gia, as if it was a honed talent. When it was my turn to talk, I wasn't sure what to say, where to begin.

"I guess I should tell you that we're not expecting Jack back anytime soon. He was here last week with the kids, but he's back in Dallas now."

"That's where the woman is?"

I nodded.

"Is it difficult, being married to my brother?"

"I didn't think so, until recently." I told Gia about our life in New York, our decision to move here to Oregon, Jack's subsequent exit from our family.

"And he probably would hate it if you called his turmoil a midlife crisis?" she asked.

I nodded and poured her more tea, surprised at how well she got it.

When Dylan was dropped off from his playdate, I called Jack and told him about our drop-in visitor. He seemed shocked, even a bit in awe. I put Gia on the phone and left her sitting on the patio while I went inside to fix dinner.

Scout followed me in and, leaning into the open fridge, asked, "Is that lady out there going to stay for dinner?"

"Take what you want and close the door, please. That lady is your aunt, and I hope she stays."

"What are we having, anyway?"

"Veggie lasagna."

"Yuck. She can have mine."

It was impossible to cook for my family. I tore into some lettuce. "You can have a peanut butter sandwich."

"Is she really my aunt?" Scout asked suddenly. When I told her yes, she jumped high, her fist in the air. "Yes! That means more presents for Christmas and birthdays. I gotta tell Becca."

Part Four

New and Improved Mommies

39

Retail Therapy and Green M&Ms

"How are the children?" asked a woman in a tartan plaid skirt that reminded me of Catholic school. She nudged her friend. "Did you see them on *Lolly!* last summer? Absolutely adorable."

"Remember the one who kept doing somersaults on the floor?" her friend joined in.

"That would be Scout." I looked down as I hurriedly signed my name on the title page. I'd have to tell the girls they'd acquired some fans of their own. They'd been a bit miffed that they weren't invited on the *Retail Therapy* launch tour, feigning shock that they would have to stay in school instead of traveling along with me to New York.

"But who will keep you company?" Becca had insisted. "You always said it's no fun sitting alone at the table."

"And who's going to eat the free cookies you get from the bookstore café?" Scout had asked.

"I'll bring one home for you," I'd promised her, relieved to be doing this tour on my own. Although my flight into New York had been delayed the night before, it had been a breeze killing time at the airport and taking a solo cab to the hotel. I'd forgotten the solitude of traveling alone, curling over a book or staring out the window at tufted cloud sculptures. And the quiet of a luxurious hotel room . . . sheer heaven.

My week was packed with book signings and author panels, though it wasn't going to be all work and no play. Morgan had freed up some time to hang. I had a date with Dash tonight, though it would have to begin later, after his show. And Harrison was organizing a bash to bring all of our old friends together. "It'll be my last night out without a sitter," Gracie had told me on the phone, since she was due at the end of the month. It was to be a week of grown-up fun, much to my daughters' dismay.

Although I didn't think my children would be thrilled at the prospect of hanging around in this discount store in the Westchester suburbs, tucked between women's lingerie and infant accessories, to celebrate the release date of *Retail Therapy*.

It was just the first of many signings Condor Books had arranged for me. This first gig set the day off to a rocky start when I learned that I was supposed to give a little speech for the sales force while they were eating lunch. There I stood, my mouth dry, my palms wet as I backed against the rumbling soda machine and tried to compose myself before two dozen people in red smocks, trying to be quiet as they popped open their Tupperware casserole containers and unzipped their Ziploc sandwich bags. Kind people. Polite people. People about to have their lunches ruined. I knew my public-speaking limitations. It was enough to make them all lose their appetites.

After my anesthetizing deliberation, I discovered my faux pas—my lack of a hostess gift.

"The last signing we had here, the author's publisher sent cheese-cake for the whole staff," one salesperson had told me longingly. "Little personal cheesecakes in tiny boxes that we could take home." She looked me over, hoping to find a forklift of minicheesecakes behind me.

"That is so sweet!" I said. "I'll never top that."

But I could try for a consolation prize. I promptly ventured over to the snack aisle, located three boxes of gourmet chocolate truffles and purchased them to set out on the signing table for staff and customers. "Inspired by my previous book, *Chocolate in the Morning*," I told people as they dipped into the crackling brown wrappers.

"So who's watching the children?" asked the woman in plaid.

"They're with their father," I said, feeling good about the way Jack had insisted on being with them for this week. I'd noticed a marked change in Jack during his past few visits with the kids. He seemed more at peace, better rested and able to have fun with them again. Last week he'd surprised us all by flying in for Halloween and taking the kids trick-or-treating dressed as a big green M&M.

"Aren't the green M&Ms the ones that make you horny?" I'd teased under my breath.

"Pure myth," Jack answered, though he didn't meet my eyes. For some reason he had trouble looking me in the eye. I didn't get it, since he seemed to open up during our recent phone conversations.

"Men find face-to-face discussions confrontational," Gia had explained in Seattle when I brought the kids to visit her for the weekend. We were standing on the observation deck of the Space Needle, looking into the gray rain shadowing Elliott Bay, moving in our direction. "Did you ever notice how men chat at sporting events? Side by side, staring off at the game or the TV. Standing at the bar. Their aggression is focused in front of them, leaving them free to reveal their subliminal thoughts."

"This explains why Jack and I had our most serious conversations while watching television," I said.

"And why we're into a deep discussion as we look out over the greater Seattle Metro area," Gia said, adjusting Dylan on her hip so that he could get a better view.

"You too short," he teased, pressing her nose with his fingers.

"So are you," she responded, "but you'll grow. I'm finished."

Auntie Gia had assimilated into our family with humor and grace, gaining the kids' trust and soothing her brother with an alacrity that surprised all of us—even Gia.

"At last, all that education is good for something!" she joked.

After talking with Gia, my new psychology expert, I'd fired Dr. Griffin and found a new shrink. Not that it required a grave act of courage; I called midmorning when I figured Dr. Griffin would be in a session and got her answering machine. "I just think we're a bad match, but I appreciate your time and interest," I told her voice mail, feeling supremely professional. To hear it, you'd think I was composed, that I knew what I was talking about. Ha!

From my conversations with Jack, I did get a strong sense that he'd gotten the better therapist of the two I'd picked so blindly from the list. Dr. Ep, as he called her, seemed to have her finger on the pulse of Jack's issues: his narcissistic mother, his controlling father, the drinking dysfunctions, the nightmares. In fact, last month when Jack had been very forthcoming in the progress he'd made in therapy, I'd been pleased that his issues didn't really involve me and a little jealous that my therapist gave me only disapproval and a hefty bill.

Dr. Jane Carson was different. When I voiced my complaints with my previous therapy right up front, she suggested we work together on cognitive therapy, coming up with ways to change my behavior now in order to better cope with the crisis. While I didn't have the satisfaction of blaming Jack or my parents for this dilemma, the sessions with Dr. Jane left me feeling positive and empowered. Finally, I could do something about my rotting marriage.

It was time to heal myself and become a better me.

The second signing was in a large Barnes & Noble near Columbus Circle, a corner building that had the energetic vibe of being placed at the center of two dividing avenues. The air was crisp, golden sunlight mixed with November's cool fingers of wind wrapping around city blocks. This staff didn't expect cheesecakes but seemed delighted with the giant box of Godiva chocolates I'd picked up on the way. You live, you learn.

"Is this book as good as your last one?" asked a customer, a sleek woman in a shimmering olive suit that brought out the peach tones of her skin. She had a matching olive bag in to-die-for leather. "What was it? *Chocolate for Breakfast?*"

"*Chocolate in the Morning,*" corrected a sales clerk who was scarfing up a handful of chocolates.

"Which is why I brought chocolates," I told the woman. "Would you care for some?"

"Oh, no, I don't do carbs."

Hence the spectacular figure in the spectacular suit. I passed her the signed book and smiled, trying to cover my wardrobe envy.

Toward the end of the hour, there was a lull, during which the bookstore began to empty. I stood up to stretch, then wandered over to the nearby self-help section to check out the books on surviving divorce. I was skimming a book called *Crazy Time* when Morgan and Padama arrived.

"Ruby! So good to see you!" Padama's hug was all flowing veils and cool skin punctuated by rings and the scent of musky herbs. I was never sure whether she was an aspiring Buddhist or simply a girl into diaphanous gowns and jewelry that sounded like wind chimes. "How're you holding up?"

"I'm fine, but the chocolates are running out."

"We're all very excited," Morgan said in her business voice. She slid an arm over my shoulders and whispered: "Outstanding advance sales. Numbers you wouldn't believe."

"Based on the way I seemed to empty out this bookstore, I would have trouble believing in big sales."

"It's our slow time of day," the store manager said with a wry smile, "don't worry. We have lots of Ruby Dixon fans in the neighborhood. These books will fly off the shelves."

"Fabulous!" Padama tilted her head, rings jangling. "Morgan and I just had a little meeting about a new contract. We'd love to keep you at Condor Books."

"I'm not sure they can afford you, Ruby." Morgan popped a chocolate in her mouth. "But we can discuss it over dinner."

"You've got a tough negotiator here, Ruby," Padama said, bowing to Morgan deferentially.

"It's all good," Morgan said.

My cell phone began to chime, and I excused myself and answered.

Surprisingly, it was Becca's voice. "Mom . . ." she sobbed. "Mom, I'm really sorry."

"Becca?" My blood ran cold as I ducked into the mystery aisle for privacy. "Honey, what is it?" I checked my watch. Barely four thirty, one thirty on the West Coast. "What's up, honey? Aren't you in school?"

"I got in trouble on the playground."

Becca? My model citizen? "Honey, are you okay?"

"Not really." Her voice quavered and suddenly she sounded much younger than her nine years. "I want you to come get me."

"Oh, sweetie, I can't. I'm in New York."

"But I need you to come get me," she whined in a shrill little voice.

"Your dad will come get you. Did you call him yet?"

"I can't," she wailed with a panic that clenched my heart like a fist. "He'll be mad at me. I just need you . . ."

But I can't help you . . . I pressed my eyes shut in desperation. My daughter needed me and where was I? Peddling my wares, three thousand miles away.

40

Bad Mommy! Bad!

I paced down the aisle past ghoulish horror covers, contorted houses and bleeding skulls. Trapped. I couldn't help Becca right now, and I hated that.

But part of me, my responsible mommy conscience, wagged an imaginary finger, reminding that it would all be okay. Her father was there. I hadn't abandoned her. "Listen, honey," I spoke slowly, sympathetically. "Whatever's happened, you need to call your father."

"Miss Z already called him," she said, gulping in a breath. "But she said I could talk to you, too." Miss Z was short for the unpronounceable Znarozinski, the school office manager who also served as the principal's first lieutenant on the playground battlefield.

"That's good. He'll be there soon, and you can tell him the truth and he won't be mad." Unless, of course, you did the wrong thing. "What happened, anyway?"

"Do you remember Ethan Snyder? That boy who's always chasing Madison and me?"

"Um-hmm." The apple of Suzie Snyder's tree.

"Well, Madison and I were playing Four Square with two other girls, and he was hanging around near us, only he said he didn't want to play."

"Mmm-hmm?" I'd clenched my teeth through Becca's typically long-winded setup.

"Ms. Barton says everyone has to be included. But he said he didn't want to play. He just stood there holding his lunch bag. Lunch was over, but he said he had a really good snack that he was saving. He kept telling everyone that. Madison and I thought he was just being a jerk. We tried to ignore him, like you always say to. But then, he took something out of the bag, and it wasn't a snack at all. It was your book, Mom."

My heart sank. "Some boy was reading my book on the playground?" This sounded like grounds for running me out of West Green, condemning me to live in a less fortunate area, a town without a lake or a country club or town square with manicured gardens. "Which one?"

"*Chocolate in the Morning*. It was a West Green library book. He climbed up on the bench like it was a stage and started reading, right there by our Four Square game."

"Oh, no!" I could just imagine which scenes he'd dog-eared.

"Scout didn't mean to punch him—"

"Yes, I did!" Scout wailed from the background. It sounded like she was underwater. "Is that Dad? Is he coming?"

"No, it's Mom," Becca snapped, gaining composure with Scout in the room. "And I'm talking to her now."

"Tell her I meant to punch him," Scout said, "but I didn't think I'd get suspended."

"Scout got suspended?" I asked.

"We all did," Becca said levelly, "but Ethan Snyder really deserves it. You wouldn't believe the words he was reading on the playground—"

"Tell Mom it was her book!"

"She knows it was her book," Becca told her, then returned to me. "I can't believe you put bad words like that in your books, Mom."

"He said the 'D' word out loud," Scout chattered. "I couldn't even say it when it was in my story, in Mrs. Piggle-Wiggle."

"He said a lot of bad words," Becca said. "Are those words really in your books, Mom?"

"It's adult stuff!" Scout yelled. "That moron isn't supposed to be reading adult stuff. Not on the playground."

"Is your father there yet?" I was beginning to worry that Jack would overreact to all this or turn the blame to me for writing racy novels. Maybe I could intercept him on his cell . . .

"He might be in the office," Becca said. "Miss Z let us come into the Health room so we didn't have to look at Ethan Snyder's latte-head. Scout, go see if Dad is here."

"No, you go see!" Scout retorted.

When Jack finally got on the phone, I immediately caught the amusement in his voice. "Quite a drama unfolding here," he told me. "A few twists worthy of *Law & Order.*"

I breathed a deep breath of relief. "I'm glad you can see the humor in it."

"Hey, I might have lost my mind," he said in a lowered voice, "but I haven't lost my sense of humor."

In that moment, I knew the girls were in good hands. Jack would soothe the girls and treat them with respect. His old salesman charm and finesse would kick in, and he would sort through this colorful dilemma with the school staff. As for Ethan and his parents, well, they might never "get it," but I felt sure that Ethan Snyder would not be wandering in the adult section of the West Green library any time soon.

"It's all good," Morgan told me that night at dinner as we went over Condor's new offer for a two-book contract. The money was significant but Morgan thought she could get more. "But here's the thing about signing a new contract," Morgan said as she topped off my glass of champagne. "You may want to put off signing the contract, or even signing a two-book deal if you and Jack are going to get divorced."

I choked on a clove of garlic in my wedge salad.

"I hate to be the one to push the bad news, but Jack is entitled to half of everything you make while you're married."

I nodded. "Of course. I haven't been thinking along those lines, but you're right." I took a sip of champagne and let the bubbles pop in my mouth. Divorce was such a hard word for my lips to form. It sounded like something that other people opted for, something that happened to movie stars and tragic characters in soap operas. "I need to figure out where we're going with this. I mean, why am I holding on? Jack made the decision for both of us. Case closed. The marriage is over, but . . . sorting out the debris is so awkward."

"I'm sorry!" Morgan's eyes filled with rue.

"No, don't be. You're right. I need to get this straight before I forge ahead."

"That's the business end, but all the laws in the world can't account for your feelings. You still love him, don't you?"

The minute she said it I knew it was true. "I do." I'd been looking forward to seeing Dash tonight, I'd even been planning my future without Jack, but for all his whirling energy Dash lacked the weight, the gravity of a man like Jack. "Damn him, I do."

I thought of the recent glimpses of the old Jack . . . dressed up in the M&M costume, rolling on the floor with Taffy, and just today, taking the kids' schoolyard calamity with good humor. The old Jack was still there. The problem was, he was no longer mine.

Morgan broke off a crust of bread. "As I said, there's no accounting for feelings. I've started seeing the Professor again."

"Really? I thought that was over awhile back?"

"He's a big beef jerky at times, but I missed him. Now, whenever he acts like a moron, I call him on it." She popped the crust into her mouth and brushed her hands together. "It's only been two weeks, but so far it's working for me."

"That's good news." I lifted my champagne flute and clinked glasses with Morgan. "Here's to someone for everyone."

"Two stars crossing," she said. "Let's hope we don't all collide."

41

Aruba, Jamaica . . .

"You'll need to be quiet," the man in black jeans and shirt told me after he checked my name on a list at the stage door. "The show is still going on. We should be doing the curtain call within"—he checked his watch—"ten, fifteen minutes."

When Dash had told me to meet him backstage at the Vivian Beaumont Theater, he'd neglected to mention that the bowels of the building were a dark, ancient pit. I sat down in a folding chair offered by the stage manager far back in the wings and marveled at the series of pulleys and ropes that could change a scene or make Peter Pan fly. From back here, without the smoke and mirrors and illusion, I saw a lot of dust bunnies and cracks in the walls.

I could hear the pit orchestra vividly, though the actors' voices were a bit garbled by the sound system. One of the last songs began as the *Billy* crew moved quickly and efficiently backstage, resetting for the finale. Actors were peeling off the stage, and there was Dash, joking in the wings with another actor, the older man who played his father. He turned and saw me, his face lighting up.

A little thrill shuddered through me. It was fun to make someone's day, even a ham like Dash. I jangled my fingers in a little wave.

A second later he was beside me, pulling me out of the chair and into his arms.

"I couldn't wait to see you," he whispered into my ear.

His thick makeup was a bit scary, but I closed my eyes as he pressed himself to me for a breathtaking kiss.

A moment later he stepped back with one finger to his lips in a shushing gesture and quickly dashed back to the wings and onto the stage.

That was when I realized that the cast and crew backstage were staring at me.

The woman.

I gave them all a little wave and sunk back into the chair, rubbing the pancake makeup from my chin. How had I ended up dating an exhibitionist actor?

After the show, Dash brought me out the stage door into a crowd of squealing fans.

"Hello! How's it going?" Dash asked as he stopped to sign their programs and chat. "So kind of you to wait all this time." The show had ended nearly an hour ago, but these enthusiastic "Dashers" had stuck around for an autograph and a close-up peek at his winning smile.

After a few minutes Dash graciously told them we were late for a train and escorted me into a shiny black limousine.

"That's a trip, seeing all those happy faces. Do they wait for you every night?"

"Every night." He fell back wearily against the seat. "The Dashers are a loyal breed."

"So where are we taking a train to?"

"Nowhere. We're actually just taking the limo around the block to Joe Allen's. The train ruse is one of many ways to make a graceful departure."

Walking down into the heated hub of Joe Allen's had the feel of walking into a speakeasy during the 1920s. Chatter and spirits were high, the lights were low, and the exposed brick walls and votive candles seemed to take the edge off the chilly night. Although I had been there before and had even spotted celebrities—Nicole and Tom, when they were married, were my highest profile sighting—I had never dined there with a celebrity. When I told Dash, he replied that he hadn't either, until tonight.

"You laughable, lovable man," I said. Champagne and Chardonnay had loosened my tongue, allowing my thoughts to flow without the usual paranoid censor.

He grinned, turquoise eyes flashing. "He's laughable! He's lovable!" He lowered his voice. "May I quote you? I've got that actor's ego to feed, and every little bit helps."

"I'd think the Dashers would keep you stoked, swooning from the first few rows and greeting you every night at the stage door."

"Yes, of course, we all love the über fans." He leaned in and put his hand over mine on the table. "But all the fans in the world will not keep you warm on a chilly November night."

"Dashiell Gray, was that a proposition?"

"Only if the answer is yes, as I don't cope well with rejection."

I laughed. Was I really going to go through with this? "Yes," I told him, and he twisted around in a clownish mania and motioned for the check.

"I haven't done this for a long time," I admitted as Dash trailed kisses along my neck. "I have to admit, I'm nervous."

"It's like riding a bicycle." Dash ran his fingers under the neckline of my velvet blouse, soothing my fears. "You don't do it for years, and yet, once you start pedaling, you're fine."

"I still have a scar on my knee from when I fell off my bike. Age five," I murmured, unbuttoning his shirt.

He grinned. "I'll try not to let you fall."

To my surprise, being with Dash was different and yet the same. Why had I thought there would be some elusive secret to lovemaking that the rest of the world was privy to?

Afterward, as we lay in Dash's king-sized bed, plush white pillows tucked around our heads, he pulled me against him and pressed his chin into my shoulder. "You're a lovely person, Ruby Dixon. I'm going to sweep you away to a tropical island and make love to you every day."

"Mmm. Can we sip froufrou drinks with little umbrellas?"

"Froufrou drinks would be a requirement, yes."

The fantasy had great appeal, but I knew it was a fantasy. Dash couldn't leave New York while his show was running, and I had three children waiting for their mommy at home. Two of whom were earning notorious reputations as schoolyard rabble-rousers.

"Somewhere in the Caribbean, perhaps," Dash went on. "Or maybe the West Indies, wherever that is. Would it be west of India?"

"I'd have to Google it," I murmured drowsily.

"Aruba, Jamaica, ooooo, I wanna take ya," he sang.

I laughed. Dash had a fabulous singing voice, but California surf music was not his forte.

"Are you laughing at me?" he asked.

I adjusted his hand on my waist, loving the feel of being held in a man's arms. "*With* you. I'm laughing with you."

"Funny, but I wasn't laughing."

The next night I went to see a show with Morgan. The night after that I hooked up with Dash again at his theater. This time we skipped the restaurant, went straight to his place and had Italian food delivered. He had me sign a book for a Christmas gift for his mother, I asked him for house seats to *Billy* for my parents. All so civilized and merry.

Is this dating? I wondered as we made arrangements to meet at Harrison's party after his show. Is a real relationship developing here? Things had never fallen into place this easily when I was a twentysomething trying to make my way in Manhattan. Even Jack, whom I'd felt certain was my soul mate, had resisted the big changes, phases he'd so affectionately named: the horror of shacking up, the ball and chain of marriage, the nightmare of kids. But hanging with Dash was easy—suspiciously easy.

"What kind of a man would admit to enjoying a woman's company?" I asked Gracie as we tried to coordinate our arrivals at Harrison's party.

"Oh, I don't know," she teased, "would that be a mature man? Ruby, once a guy gets past thirty his focus changes. It's not all about impressing the other guys anymore."

"I'm just not used to this much adult companionship. I'm afraid I'll try to hold Dash's hand crossing the street or ask him if he needs to go potty."

Gracie laughed. "I would love that! Hey, do you want to come with me for my ultrasound? You could see the baby on a cartoon screen and meet Dreamy Dr. Levin."

I would have liked to meet the man of Gracie's dreams, but I had a signing at the same time. We agreed to meet at Harrison's bash.

The barrage of questions and smiles came at me like cards slung in a poker game.

"Ruby! How's the book tour going?"

"We caught you on *The Lolly! Show.* Is it true that Lolly is a first-class bitch?"

"Whatever possessed you to move out to the woods? How do you stand all that rain?"

"Is it true that one of the characters in your book is based on Harrison?"

I took a breath, not sure which question to address first, but Harrison jerked my hand, pulling me away from the gang, who didn't seem to be waiting on my answers. Perhaps they were rhetorical questions. "Great to see you all again!" I called as we moved across the rooftop toward a row of manicured trees in giant yellow bowls.

"Harrison, do I actually know those people?" I asked, struggling to keep up in the devastatingly high-pitched heels I'd forced myself to wear.

"Who?" He glanced back, his eyebrows shooting up to his forehead. "Oh, you remember Jennifer and Stephanie. They're soccer moms now, just like you. Well, you in your alternate life."

"Thanks. But what about that girl in the pink faux fur? And her friend in the boots?" The tooled red and gold Western boots looked like they belonged in the Cowgirl Hall of Fame.

"They could be residents of the building. Technically, we can't bar them from the party if they live here, and, believe me, when people heard that this was a party for Ruby Dixon, everyone wanted in. You're a hot ticket!"

"Who knew." I rubbed my arms against the cold. Heat lamps had been judiciously placed on the rooftop, but at the moment they were populated by gangs of guests I couldn't recognize in the wavering light of the lanterns strung along the trellis and low brick wall at the edge of the roof. Gracie wasn't here yet but I spotted Morgan near the bar, chatting with Goldberg, who seemed to be moving into his role of Harrison's partner with grace and alacrity.

"Now let me look at you." Harrison's eyes went over me, head to toe. "The shoes are great . . ."

"The shoes hurt," I admitted. "Another half hour and I'm kicking them off."

"And walk barefoot on a New York City rooftop that's a harbinger of germs and bacteria?" He bristled. "Yucky. But tell me about the hair. You've lost your highlights."

"I went back to my roots," I said, "minus the gray, of course. I looked around one day and decided I didn't want to look like every other West Green yoga mom."

"But no one suggested Sarandon Red? How about Bullock Eggplant? Maybe it's the light, toots, but to me it just looks very . . . *brown.*"

"Brown is not a dirty word," Morgan said in my defense as she handed me a glass of wine. "And I like Ruby's hair."

Harrison pressed a finger to one cheek. "I like it. I do. I'm just not sure it's *Morning Show* worthy."

"Oh, that's what this is about," I said with a groan. "Here I thought you were worried that I wasn't a stylin' chick, but all along it's Harrison the publicist worried about public image."

Harrison held up his palms, as if to stop me from speaking another word. "Three hours with Ari. Ari Otani! You know him! He's a miracle worker."

I blinked. "Oh, now I need a miracle worker?"

"I like Ruby's hair," Goldberg said, joining in the conversation. "I think it suits her well."

Harrison rolled his eyes and touched Goldberg's arm gently. "You, my dear, are a banker. You're allowed to advise Ruby about mutual funds and e-trading, not hairstyles."

"This is so sweet," Morgan said cordially. "It's so sweet that you care so much, Harrison. Ruby, when is your *Morning Show* appearance?"

"Friday."

Morgan nodded. "The day after tomorrow."

Harrison let out a small gasp. "Oh, my God, I don't even know if I can get you in by then. Let me call Ari." He flipped open his cell phone and turned away.

"I am not going blonde again," I told Morgan and Goldberg and two other old friends that I recognized from my days at the insurance firm with Gracie. "Not that I have anything against blondes, but I am so over that."

"I hear ya," said Jerrilyn, whose hair was now a silvery gray. I remembered that she'd been one of the youngest actuaries at the firm, but that had been quite a few years ago. Had she stuck with the party scene all these years—more than a decade?

"How is everything?" I asked her, hoping for a real answer. "Are you still at the firm?"

She nodded. "It's going well. They made me a supervisor last year." She flashed me a superwhite grin. "Of course, not as well as your fast track to fame."

I wanted to remind her that I'd written more than thirty books before anyone sat up and took notice, but I knew it would seem petty.

This was my party; I had better behave.

42

Party Girls

"I think it's the French onion soup I had at lunch," Gracie told me. "I just feel a little off. Indigestion."

"Is it like heartburn?" I adjusted the cell against my ear, walking toward the stairwell where a string of jolly colored lanterns cast a glow on the brick wall. Harrison had assembled all the fixings of a rollicking party—delicious finger foods, elegant wines, a breathtaking venue and romantic decorations. Missing one crucial element—the right people. "Gracie, you might be in labor."

"No. I'm still two weeks away from that, and you know first babies are rarely early."

"Not every case is textbook," I said.

"But last week when Dr. Levin checked me out he didn't see anything going on. Something about the baby being too high. I'm just going to put my feet up and drink my milk and go to bed early so I'll be fresh for work in the morning." She sighed. "I'm sorry I'm missing your party. Is it fun?"

Making sure that Harrison was a safe distance away, I lowered my voice. "Not really. It seems my old New York friends have a new respect for me now that I've hit the best-seller list. Some of them seem to want my fame to rub off on them. Nora and Jerrilyn are here."

"I suppose Jerrilyn told you about her big promotion?"

"She did."

"Supervisor of nothing," Gracie said. "She's got one other woman in her department. Management just didn't know what to do with her; she's such a drone."

"Do you remember Weird Sonia? She actually hugged me, as if we were old friends."

"Pain in the ass."

"Makes me glad the Oregonians seem totally unaware of my best-seller status. At least they're dealing with me as a person." I thought of the people back home, the way Eric and Jan next door had warmed up to our family, the support from Ariel and Lexie and Daphne. I would rather be just another mom in West Green than the toast of the town at a Manhattan party. What did that say about me?

"So when am I going to see you? You can't leave without rubbing my Buddha belly."

We made arrangements to meet for an early dinner before my evening signing the following day.

Reluctantly, I returned to the party, where a crowd was forming by the stairwell.

Dash.

He was surrounded by guests, as if they'd all assembled to hear him deliver a speech. At first I thought he was giving something away, but on closer inspection I saw that people were just pushing forward to shake his hand.

Nora and Jerrilyn held their ground at the front of the line, Dash-ers at heart.

Weird Sonia snaked through the crowd and performed an odd, veil dance around him. With pursed lips and an odd sort of peacock strut, she seemed to have stolen Mick Jagger's choreography.

Switching into publicity mode, Harrison found his way to the front and soothed the savage fans by turning the press into a delightful Q&A. Watching Harrison moderate for Dash, I admired their skills, their energy, their quick comebacks—all of which I lacked. There was a reason I chose writing.

After ten minutes or so, Harrison thanked everyone for their interest and reminded them that the drinks were still flowing, the food still hot. Most of the crowd moved off toward the bar and dance floor. Only the true suck-ups remained.

I pushed forward, hoping to say hello to Dash, but Jerrilyn grabbed my arm, her cold, bony fingers a pincer.

"Aren't you going to introduce us?" she asked, her eyes on Dash, her face lit up like Times Square. "We're Ruby's friends."

"We used to work together, all of us," said Nora.

If I recalled correctly, Nora had not been a friend; she'd been an isolated drone, refusing to join us for lunch or drinks after work. I wondered if she'd come tonight for the free food or to meet Dash.

"Gracie's still with us," Nora added, "but not for long." She lifted her chin, as if she was above it all. "The mommy track."

"Gracie's planning to go back to work after she has the baby," I inserted.

Jerrilyn nodded sagely. "That's what they all say."

I felt offended that Gracie would be dismissed out of hand, but the conversation had already moved on to Dash's role in *Billy* and—God help us—Nora's experience in community theater.

Meanwhile, Weird Sonia was still dancing at the perimeters, circling in a tightening coil around Dash.

She worried me. Sonia Wimbledon had been a member of our party group when we were in our twenties. Sporting a descendent-of-the-*Mayflower* reputation, she'd portrayed herself as a straight-laced, penny loafer yuppie and had risen to upper management in a corporation based at Rockefeller Center. I'd always avoided her, mostly out of boredom, though her star was clearly on the rise. Then, a few years ago, she'd suffered some sort of breakdown. She'd quit the corporation, lived on the streets for awhile, then joined an ashram in Upstate New York. The last I'd heard she'd been picking berries and milking cows at the compound . . . and now here she was, performing some sort of ritualistic dance on Harrison's rooftop.

I pulled Harrison aside. "Where did you dig her up?"

He shrugged. "She found us. Someone must have forwarded an E-vite to her."

"Do ya think?" I scowled. "I'm not sure she's got the presence of mind to navigate e-mail."

"Ruby, love! There you are!" Dash called. His face was lit with a smile, but I read the message in his eyes. *Help. Bail me out of here!*

"You look like you need a glass of wine," I said, taking him by the hand.

"I could use a case," he muttered through a frozen smile.

With the center of her universe removed, Weird Sonia shifted her homage to the potted trees, draping her veils over the tender branches. Nora and Jerrilyn stood back, regrouping their siege on Dash.

"Your timing was perfect!" Harrison told Dash. "We have to be out of here by midnight, so you added that last burst of excitement to the affair."

Dash lifted his glass of wine in a toast. "My pleasure," he said. That was Dash: he could deal with kooky, crazy Dashers, as long as he had access to recreational beverages.

When the party ended we went with Harrison and Goldberg to a place called the Supper Club, where Rat Pack impersonators roamed the dining room. Dash had worked with one of the actors, the Sammy Davis Jr. impersonator, and after Dash had a drink or two Sammy had Dash on his feet, imitating Peter Lawford.

Harrison touched my shoulder and said: "Oh, this guy is a keeper."

I wasn't so sure about longevity, but right now, Dash fit into my life perfectly.

It was after three when Dash and I made it to my hotel room. I was feeling a little tipsy from wine, but Dash was positively spinning, singing "You Made Me Love You" Dean Martin–style, with a mimed cigarette and a Southern drawl.

"I think I'm going to have to put you to bed," I told him as I tossed my killer shoes into the closet.

He plucked a jar of nuts from the basket and used it as a microphone. "Ladies and gentlemen, she's killing the act here. Can we hear a round of applause for the lovely and talented Ms. Ruby Dixon." He took my hand, held it high for the audience, then swept me into a passionate embrace.

Curtain, please.

*   *   *

A buzzing insect woke me. It persisted every few seconds, rattling against something on the dresser, and in my haze of sleep I wondered how a giant Egyptian scarab beetle could sneak into a nice hotel like this.

When it buzzed again in its rhythmic way, I sat up in bed and realized it was my cell phone.

The middle of the night. The kids!

I tripped on the edge of the sheet and landed on the floor, but managed to crawl on my knees to the dresser and rip down my purse. My hands found the phone in its handy pocket and quickly flipped it to my ear.

"Hello?" I said quietly in the dark.

"Oh, my God! How fast can you get here?"

"Gracie?" I blinked, trying to orient myself in the dark hotel room. "You're in labor?"

"I am going to die in childbirth," she said in a very controlled voice. "Just like women did in the old days. This pain is going to kill me. But not before I take out the OB nurse who keeps yelling at me for not paying attention in Lamaze class. I swear, she was a former guard in a Russian gulag."

"Oh, honey. Can't they give you anything for the pain?"

"I *paid* attention," she ranted. "I *went* to every freakin' class. I *know* the breathing. I simply choose *not* to do it, especially when . . . Aaugh!"

Not wanting to wake Dash, I had groped my way to the bathroom and flicked on the light to discover I was embarrassingly naked. I grabbed one of the fluffy white robes from the back of the door and slipped into it.

Much better. It was hard to take myself seriously when surrounded by my naked reflection in wall-to-wall mirrors.

"I am with you on the breathing thing," I said. "They think that's going to distract you from the pain? It never worked for me. How dumb did Lamaze think women were?"

"Give me drugs!" Gracie wailed. "I want an epidural!"

"Gracie?" I held the phone with my shoulder and turned on the water to wash up. "Gracie, hold on. I'm on my way."

There was no answer, only a scuffling sound and barking voices.

"Gracie?"

"Mrs. can't talk now. Cell phones are not allowed in the hospital."

"Who are you?"

"I must turn it off now."

She had to be the gulag nurse. "Wait! What hospital?"

When she told me the name of the hospital and clicked off, I spun into action. Within five minutes I was washed up and dressed and wondering whether I should wake Dash. Is it cool to abandon a man while he's sleeping in your hotel room?

His face was buried in the pillow, his bare shoulders gleaming in the blue light from the bathroom. Considering his late-night schedule, I couldn't stand to wake him.

His breathing was steady and relaxed as I grabbed my purse and coat and stole into the brightly lit corridor, closing the door behind me. I'd left him a message on the hotel notepad that said:

> *Dash,*
>
> *Gone to deliver Gracie's baby.*
>
> *—Ruby*

43

Presto! Baby!

When I got to the hospital labor and delivery ward, I was annoyed to find that no one was manning the desk. Granted, it was after four AM, but try telling that to a crowning infant.

Down the hall, a woman in a navy lab coat was emptying items from a cart to a supply closet. I managed to sweet-talk her into helping me track down Gracie, who was standing alone in an examining room, her feet planted on the floor, her back against the wall.

"Gracie!" I gasped. She looked weak, her face pale and beaded with sweat. "Don't you want to lie down?"

"I keep getting sick." She nodded at the exam table.

That was when I noticed the mess. "Oh, I was vomiting with Becca. Can't they give you something for it?"

"Nurse Irena says the medicine is coming. She also went to get an aide to clean up here. I guess it's not in her contract."

"Unbelievable," I said as I pulled latex gloves from the box on the wall and got to work. I was a mom; I'd dealt with much worse. The paper on the table tore off easily. I gave the vinyl surface a quick cleaning with soap, warm water and paper towels from the sink, then stretched clean paper over it for Gracie.

As I worked, she told me that dreamy Dr. Levin was on his way, supposedly. She wouldn't put it past Nurse Irena to lie. She'd already criticized Gracie's breathing and told her she should try to make it through labor without pain medication.

"Thank you." She curled onto the table with a whimper. "I was ready to keel over."

Just then a woman in a pink lab coat trudged in with another woman in tow. "What? What's going on here?"

"I want a new nurse!" Gracie moaned.

"No, I am your nurse. And who clean up?" asked the nurse. Her nameplate said *Irena*.

"I took care of it." I pointed to the trash can. "You may want to remove that." The aide took it and ducked out of the room. "And she's serious about getting another nurse." I faced Nurse Irena squarely. "You're just not working out for us."

"You can't just pick and choose," she said.

I put my hands on my hips and got in her face, feeling the old New York etiquette surging back. "Watch me."

My act of courage was rewarded with a nurse named Elizabeth, a doughy woman with long red hair and a friendly freckled face. She started by taking Gracie's blood pressure and timing her pains. "Your contractions are pretty close together. We'd better get a resident in to examine you. Do you need some help with pain management?"

"Thank you, God!" Gracie whispered.

As fickle fate would have it, Gracie's painkillers kicked in right around the time dreamy Dr. Levin arrived, so Gracie quickly traversed from a state of suicidal panic to googly-eyed euphoria.

"How's it going, Gracie?" Dr. Levin leaned over the bed and got right in Gracie's face, so close I thought he might kiss her. But no, he just squeezed her forearm.

"Dreamy Dr. Levin," Gracie oozed, as the pain began to slip from her features. "I mean, it's just peachy, Dr. Levin." She giggled. "I'm sooo much better now."

"Glad to hear it," he said. "But I'm still going to need you to work with me. You'll have to work really hard and push when I tell you. Got it?"

"I am so on it," Gracie assured him.

* * *

"It's a girl!" Dr. Levin announced with pride.

Holding Gracie's hand, I watched in astonishment as he lifted a tiny, squealing body, a new person. Like magic. Presto, change-o! And you have a baby!

"A girl?" Gracie laughed. "But the ultrasound technician told me it was a boy!"

"She's a beauty," the anaesthesiologist called from the corner, where he was doing a quick exam of the baby, assisted by the nurse.

"You want an exchange?" Dr. Levin asked Gracie. "I deliver all babies with a money-back guarantee." He laughed, as if to reinforce that it was a joke.

"Oh, no, no, no! I'm so glad." Gracie squeezed my hand. "It's a girl, Ruby. It's a miracle."

"And she's perfect." Elizabeth brought the baby over and placed her in Gracie's arms.

Gracie rolled her head toward the little pink baby in the space-age foil blanket. "Hey, you. I've been so worried about teaching you baseball and shopping for jock straps." The baby squirmed, nearly knocking away the edges of the blanket. "Okay, I might have to teach you, anyway. We'll get you some lessons. A coach. A team. Look out, George Steinbrenner."

The baby squinted at Gracie, assessing. Her tiny pink lips and nose reminded me of the uncanny perfection of my own children. I remembered watching in awe as each child raised a fist or yawned. I'd been in her place less than three years ago, watching Dylan open his eyes cautiously or nuzzle his doughy face against my breast.

"Have you picked a name for her?" asked dreamy Doctor Levin.

"I've been agonizing over boy names." Gracie outlined the baby's smooth chin with one finger. "But a long time ago, when I hoped for a girl, I was thinking of naming you Josie or Cleo."

"Those are nice names," Elizabeth said. "Not something we hear every day."

"I'm thinking you look like a Josie," Gracie spoke softly to her daughter.

"Josie Hallinan," I said. "I think it fits her."

"You are just so sweet!" Gracie crooned. "Okay, I *will* teach you baseball. And how to balance your checkbook. How to pick the perfect cantaloupe and talk to boys and apply makeup. But don't even think about breaking your curfew," Gracie warned. "I'm a very strict mommy."

"I suspect that little cutie will be breaking lots of curfews," Dr. Levin said. "At least for the first few months."

"Look at you!" Gracie cooed at her baby. In the dim light of the birthing suite, the baby's eyes gleamed, and she seemed to smile back at her mother.

I loved it all. I imagined myself morphing into an octopus so that I could reach out and hug everyone in sight—the maternity nurse, dreamy Dr. Levin, the anaesthesiologist, the woman pushing the squeaky cart down the hall, and Gracie and her baby. I wanted them all to feel the love, to know it was real, but then the room was so thick with positive energy, I knew it was a moment ripe with hope: here was Gracie's future, a brand-new individual on our spinning planet.

Why hadn't I been cognizant of all this potential when I had my own children?

"We need to finish up with Mom here." Dr. Levin turned his thoughtful, intelligent Tom Hanks eyes on me. "Would you like to hold the baby, Ruby?"

I nodded. The nurse pointed me to a chair and brought the small bundle to me. I folded my arms into the oval of a cradle. You forget so many of the details of taking care of children, but most come sailing back to you when you need them.

"Hey, little one," I said softly. "We weren't expecting you so soon."

She pressed her lips together, and I suspected that today's events were equally surprising to her.

"Hey!" I nearly shouted into the phone when Jack answered. "How's everything going?" I felt exhilarated by life, by the traffic and pedestrians and pushcarts selling pretzels and bentos outside New York Hospital. A window to life had opened for me and I wanted to share it.

"Things are great," he said. "How's the tour going?"

"The tour is fine but I've got better news. Gracie had her baby—a little girl—and I was her coach. It was awesome, Jack. It's so different when you're not actually having the baby."

He laughed. "I'm sure it is. Mother and baby are doing well?"

"Perfect."

"That's so great," he said with true enthusiasm. "It really brings you back, doesn't it? Those birthing rooms . . ."

I laughed. "Oh, yeah. It comes rushing right back. Speaking of kids, can I talk to them?"

"They're still in bed. I wasn't planning to wake them up for another hour. You usually get them up at eight, right?"

"Oh! It's only seven there?" My mind had blanked out on reality. "I'm sorry."

"Actually, I was up. I've got an interview this morning, and I wanted to be prepared. I was just going over my pitch."

I flashed back to the days when Jack had run every pitch by me. I had played devil's advocate, shooting off questions and problem scenarios. We'd made a good team.

"What's your pitch?" I asked, then caught myself. "What's the interview about?"

"It's for a job here in Portland. Another affiliate, but a different corporation. Based out of Los Angeles."

"Oh." This was all new to me, hard to process. "Really. But the job's in Portland?"

"Yes, it is. I thought it would be good to make a fresh start, break the ties at Corstar. The thing is, it's over with Dez. It's been over for awhile."

"Really," I said dully, moving through the city street that now seemed surreal, a kaleidoscope of color. The bright green Starbucks sign, the line of vehicles waiting at a red light, the blue steel newspaper-vending machine on the corner. I gripped the edge of it, needing a bolster.

"I've missed you and the kids. I was going to talk with you when you got back, but, well, now you know," Jack said quietly. "I want to come home, Rubes."

44

Girls' Night In

"It's not that easy," I said. "You can't just move your stuff back into the closet and pretend nothing ever happened." The words came automatically, as if I'd been possessed by a personal manager. In my other-worldly state the composure surprised me, but it was my voice, the true thoughts of the new Ruby.

"I know. It's never simple." He seemed wounded.

"Jack, I don't know if I can trust you." I needed accountability, remorse, repentance. And would that be enough? I knew I could forgive him, but could I forget? "I don't want to be blithe and stupid again."

"You were never stupid," he said. "You didn't do anything wrong."

"You sound like my therapist. Even if I was blameless in the scenario of our marriage, and I really doubt that, I can't go back to what we had. Your favoritism of Scout, resentment of Dylan. My superefforts to fix everything for you and the kids. Not to sound petty, Jack, but toward the end, I even sensed that you were jealous of my success."

"Probably true," he said. "I think they're all valid issues, but they can't be fixed overnight."

"No, they can't. But I won't repress the issues. Not anymore."

"Hurray. You were beginning to remind me of the old lady. The new Mattress Queen."

I pressed a hand to one temple. "Okay, now you're really scaring me."

"Look, we can't accomplish much in a ten-minute phone call. Can we take this stuff up in couple's therapy?"

I felt a shiver of hope. Or maybe just exhaustion. "We could try."

"And if I get the job here, I'll find a place nearby. A rental. I'm done with hotel living."

"Debbie Tory knows the rental agents for the West Green Point. They're cute little bungalows on the lake."

"That would work," he spoke softly, sounding hopeful.

"The kids will be happy. Especially Scout. She's been heartbroken since I gave her the news."

"I know that. It really tears at me."

At last, he was taking responsibility for his actions. Maybe Jack really had hit rock bottom.

I sagged against the blue newspaper box, then noticed some sticky goop on it and sent myself walking back, toward the hospital. This was too much to solve now, too much to even absorb. "Can you have the kids call me before school?" I asked. "I think they'll get a kick hearing about Gracie's baby."

"Will do."

"And thanks for weeding through the curious incident of the obnoxious boy reading inappropriate materials on the playground."

"Yeah." He laughed. "One of the moms came up to me yesterday after school. Said her name was Daphne?"

"Daphne Sweet. She's Kevin's mom."

"Well, she says the mom of the instigator seems kind of clueless. Refuses to acknowledge that her little darling has some problems."

"That would be Suzie Snyder," I said. Suzie had shown her colors when she went toe to toe with Ariel on what to include in the auction back in September. Suzie no longer wanted Ariel to sponsor a book party based on *Chocolate in the Morning*—once Suzie had read the book she insisted it was inappropriate. "Oh . . ." I said aloud. "I get it. Now I know how Ethan Snyder got wind of the 'inappropriate' material." I filled Jack in on the back story.

"That kid's got balls, checking your book out from the library," he said.

I sighed. "At least I have a fan in Ethan Snyder."

"I gotta check this book out. And I notice you only have, like, *fifty* copies on your shelf."

"You can borrow one," I said, "as long as you promise not to read it aloud in the schoolyard."

"Oh, my God! I feel so exhilarated!" Gracie cranked the bed into the upright position and plucked a bran muffin from the hospital tray. "Ruby, get me my sneakers, I'm going for a run. The New York City Marathon. No, wait, when is the next Olympics? I'm officially in training."

I laughed. "Sounds like the endorphins have kicked in." I was feeling the effects of a night with two hours of sleep. My brain felt muddy, my clothes seemed to stick to me in all the wrong places and I didn't even want to think about my limp hair. A wiser woman would have returned to the hotel and come back later, but I hung in there, attracted by the Gracie-and-baby magnet.

"Hormones." She peeled the paper from the muffin. "I'm a hormone-crazed woman. Do you want some eggs? How about my applesauce?"

"Eggs are sounding good," I said, feeling as if I'd run a marathon of my own.

"Come on, then." She scooted to the side of the bed and flipped down the covers so that I could climb in beside her. "Just like old times."

"The sleepovers." I climbed in, sinking into the crisp whiteness.

"It's Girls' Night In," Gracie said with a chuckle.

Back in the old days when we'd both been "insurance specialists" dreaming of underwriter salaries, we used to have Girls' Night In, a slumber party at one of our apartments. We'd hang out in our pajamas, give each other a facial and pedicure, trade books, rent sappy movies and spend half the night talking in bed. "This feels so good," I murmured, tucking a pillow behind my neck. "I might fall asleep head-down in your applesauce."

"And that would be okay. Your work here is done, Ruby. Until they bring Josie in and tell me I have to feed her or change her or make her stop crying or something. Then, you're on," she said, dropping part of the muffin top into her mouth. She chewed contentedly, then gushed, "She is just so deliciously adorable, isn't she?"

"She is."

We sat there in quiet tandem for awhile, me spooning cool applesauce between my lips, Gracie nibbling on two muffins and three slices of Canadian bacon. As she shifted beneath the sheets, I thought of how much I loved Gracie Hallinan, how I wanted our lives to be forever intertwined, our children to play together, the two of us to grow old together like kooky spinster sisters once we'd outlived our loves.

"This is great," Gracie said with such gusto I was sure she was talking about the Canadian bacon. "So great. Thank you for being here to help me."

"Help you?" I rolled my eyes. "Believe me, you did all the work. Although I guess I did a good job of warding off Nurse Ratched."

"That and . . . everything. Sometimes you just need to know you're not alone in the world."

A little lump formed in my throat at the thought of Gracie being alone. She'd always been so independent, quick to give orders, confident when it was time to buy a property or fire a housekeeper. "Remember," I told her, my voice catching, "I'm just a phone call away."

"I know." Her amber eyes sparkled mischievously. "But a phone won't share your eggs in the morning. Sometimes it's nice to have the real person."

"I'm afraid I'm going to have to fire you, Doc."

I must have dozed off. When I opened my eyes, Gracie's obstetrician stood at our bedside, his arms crossed defensively. He didn't seem miffed that there were two people in the patient's bed; only that he'd been sacked.

"What?" The dreamy doctor blinked, a catch in his voice. "Is something wrong?"

Gracie nodded. "I like you. I mean, I *like* like you. And I know you're a guy of high standards. You would never date a patient. So as of today, now that you've safely navigated little Josie into the world, you're fired. No longer my doctor."

I yawned, not wanting to move too much and draw attention to myself. This was clearly a private moment and I should have left. But it was all too interesting and I was still sort of groggy.

"Oh." His face softened, a smile pulling at his mouth. "Wow, you don't mess around."

"No, I don't. I'm thirty-three years old and a single parent now. I don't have time to play the dating game anymore." She adjusted the collar of her robe, smoothing it down. "I think you're great, and I'd like to spend more time with you."

An embarrassed smile consumed his face. "You're great, too. I'm just in shock. I've never been fired before."

"Would you rather resign from my case?"

He shrugged. "That sounds better. And for the record, I like you, too. It's been a pleasure being your doctor."

"But . . ." she coached him. "Don't tell me you're secretly married. In love with someone else? Gay?"

"No, no, none of those things. I just . . . I'm a little miffed. I never had a woman go after me like this before."

Gracie shrugged. "I guess you've never met the right woman. Not that you'd meet too many candidates as an OB."

"That's exactly what my mother said." He smiled. "So I guess I'm free to say that I like you, too, Gracie. I *like* like you. Like you said."

Hard to believe a guy so cute and successful could be such a social dweeb.

"Okay, then. I'm stuck here for two more days, but then we could meet for lunch or dinner." Gracie folded the edge of the sheet neatly over her lap. "My schedule is flexible at the moment. Unpredictable, but flexible."

He smiled. "How about if I bring you coffee tomorrow morning? Decaf? I mean, if you're breast-feeding . . ."

"A decaf skim latte would be great," she said.

His beeper sounded. "I have to run. But . . ." He reached forward and extended his hand. "It's been a pleasure being your doctor."

"It'll be more fun being her friend," I piped up.

When his cheeks reddened, Gracie added, "Ruby can vouch for me. She's known me for years."

"Well, good," he said. "Glad to hear it."

"And one more thing," Gracie said, "can you give me the name of a decent gynecologist?"

45

The Lady Is a Champ

"I didn't know you had a medical degree," Dash said when we spoke on the phone that day. "A writer and a doctor, too. So many things I don't know about you."

I laughed. "What are you talking about?"

"Sneaking off during the night to deliver a baby."

"My friend Gracie had her baby and I went to be with her." I wanted to say that I'd witnessed a miracle, but somehow that sounded trite and syrupy, not at all like the real explosion of life I'd felt holding baby Josie in my arms.

My departure from the hospital had been hurried along by Harrison's frantic call, saying he'd made the appointment with his stylist person—"The Ari Otani!"—and where the hell was I? He almost forgave me for being late when I told him about Gracie's baby—almost. "Just get yourself over there and I'll flog you with a wet noodle later."

So many demands. Didn't these people realize that every moment mattered?

It was my new mantra, my new lease on life.

"I don't quite understand," Dash was saying. "Couldn't the surgeon manage without you?"

I smiled at his Britishness. "He's not a surgeon, and Gracie was the one who wanted me there. For moral support. She doesn't have a husband."

"Ah, yes, the immaculate insemination. So how about tonight?" he asked. "Your place or mine?"

"I've got the *Morning Show* on Friday. I have to be at the studio at five thirty AM."

"How very unpleasant. When can we get together, then?"

With my weekend schedule packed with appearances at book-stores and colleges, there would be no time to see Dash until Mon-day night—my last night in New York and Dash's day off.

We met at the Peninsula, a grand hotel trimmed in gold, smiles and richness. The pedestrian traffic in the lobby had such an air of wealth I half-expected the floor to be covered with hundred dollar bills. Although this was the New York I'd never kept pace with, I thought myself worthy of walking on money in my designer heels. No one else had to know they were borrowed.

Of course, Dash was a regular customer at the Pentop Bar, a lovely space at the top of the hotel.

"What shall we drink tonight, Ruby?" he asked, rubbing his hands together.

We had reached the bar in time to watch the sun set over the city, and though it should have been romantic and elegant, I was still hav-ing trouble warding off the chills from a blustery November wind that had blown in that morning. Snowflakes had actually floated amid the cavernous buildings at Rockefeller Center as I arrived there for a signing.

"I hate to be a buzz kill," I told the bartender, "but I think I need to start with some coffee to warm up. Decaf." I grabbed a handful of peanuts and tossed a few into my mouth. I'd missed lunch and I was feeling a little worn down.

"Well, that's no fun at all," Dash said. "Make hers an Irish coffee. And I'll have a Chivas on the rocks."

The bartender nodded, then told me, "I'll see if we can get a little heat up for you."

Dash was already off on a tale of a new show that was supposed to be coming to Broadway, a musical, with a part that would be perfect for him. "Except the producers don't even want to think of me, since I'm contracted to stay with *Billy* through the next year."

I waxed sympathetic, but my words seemed to be background noise to his continuing lament. The producer was in town with the playwright. "Out and about at this moment," he said. "I was hoping to run into them in the lobby, but my spies are out. I expect to get the call any minute, and we'll close in on them." He smiled. "How would you like to meet Arthur Smeltzer? Wouldn't that be wicked excitement?"

I forced myself to brighten. "Well, sure." Though I wasn't sure I knew Smeltzer's work. Was he the producer or the writer? I was too embarrassed to ask, and it clearly didn't matter to Dash, who was fixated on his way into their show.

"Dash." I stopped him. "I thought you enjoyed doing *Billy*. You've gotten great reviews, and the show really highlights your talents."

He grinned. With Dash, flattery could get you everywhere. "It's been grand, but that show wears thin quickly. I'm bored. I need something new, Ruby. Something to test my talents."

We were halfway through our drinks when the call came. Still on his cell, Dash tossed some bills onto the bar and motioned for me to get my coat. The chase was on.

Fortunately, Arthur Smeltzer and his entourage didn't move too quickly. We caught up with them at the Supper Club, where Dash's friend the Sammy Davis Jr. impersonator was on the floor. He finished singing "The Candy Man" as we were seated, and made a fuss about having a celebrity in the house.   •

"One of Broadway's best, baby," Sammy said. "And he's not just any star. Take it from the Candy Man, here, this guy is one cool cat. Ladies and gentleman, Mr. Dashiell Gray!"

Graciously, Dash tossed his napkin onto the table, took the microphone and launched into "What Kind Of Fool Am I?"

Although I'd been hoping to order—the Irish coffee was churning in my empty stomach—I folded my hands in my lap. I'd never cared for this song, but Dash sang it with such sincerity, I made myself listen to the words. With a flash of turquoise, his eyes projected pain, the disappointment of a man who could not fall in love. "Why can't I fall in love . . ."

Listen carefully, I told myself. This was Dash's Achilles' heel. Kind, fun, jolly Dash could not get beyond himself to place someone else first. It didn't make him a bad person, but I was beginning to understand what drove his beloved Sara away.

Two people at the table beside us gave him a standing ovation. "He's a young Richard Burton," said the woman with a fur-trimmed jacket.

Two couples . . . Was this the Smeltzer entourage?

Ah, yes . . . There went Dash, shaking hands and kissing cheeks. And did they want to meet his friend Ruby Dixon?

"The author? Is she here?"

I raised one hand, jangling my fingers. Was this how it felt to be the wife of a politician? I was happy to help Dash score some points, but couldn't we just get a basket of bread? Some appetizers?

"Next round is on us," one of the men at the producers' table said as Dash waved me over. "Bring your writer friend over!"

I pressed my hands together, determined to jump on the back of the next passing waiter. One more round and Ruby Dixon would be a stream-of-unconsciousness writer.

An hour and one delicious plate of ravioli later, Dash was performing again. His friend Mike had joined me at the table. Mike played Frank Sinatra in the show, and he struck me as a great overall guy. Sliding me his card, he'd explained how he moved to Vegas to get into the impersonator scene. His current goal was to put together a Rat Pack tribute that could run every night on a Vegas stage. "Steady work near home, that's all I'm looking for."

When he sang the song "The Lady Is a Tramp," he replaced the word *tramp* with *champ*. That struck me as endearing, though the songwriter probably wouldn't agree.

"Ah, look at him work the room, sweetheart," Mike said to me in his uncanny Sinatra voice. We stared, spellbound, as Dash showered turquoise magic on the Smeltzer table. "He's a pro."

The words *professional suck-up* came to mind, but I restrained myself. I couldn't begrudge Dash wanting to stay on top, keep his edge, land the next big part. It just wasn't the way I'd planned to spend the evening.

"Our man Dash loves to win them over," the fake Frank Sinatra said.

"He sure does." It was a big part of Dash's psyche. Keep the people happy, win them over, make a lasting impression. Rave reviews and photographers snapping your photo on the street.

Not my world.

When it was pushing midnight and it became clear that Dash was ensconced with the Rat Pack until the Supper Club closed, I decided it was time to call it a day.

"Leaving already?" Dash seemed shocked.

"I have a commitment in the morning." *It's called breakfast in bed, my last day of room service.*

Dash swept me into his arms and dipped me back dramatically. "Till we meet again, my love." The producer's entourage giggled, highly amused.

I kissed Dash good-bye, pulled on my coat and went outside to catch a cab.

"Hey, Ruby!" Mike appeared, a penguin in the cold night. The street lamp gave the white trim of his tuxedo a surreal glow. "You need a cab? Dash is a little preoccupied at the moment."

"Thanks, but I can handle it." Now that I was a visiting dignitary in New York, people seemed to be all over the transportation thing. "Watch." As three yellow taxis came careening down Forty-sixth, I stepped to the curb, thrust my fist in the air and yelled: "Taxi!"

Two of them snaked over to me.

Mike chuckled. "The lady is a champ. Make sure you look me up if you ever make it to Vegas."

"Will do. I hope you get your show off the ground."

He patted his heart. "Thanks, kid. You have a nice life."

As I ducked out of the illusory night and into the cab, I realized that I already did.

46

Jack: Redemption

Every morning I watch the sun rise. It's my new thing, my hope therapy.

Today I get up from the big bed I used to share with Ruby and throw open the plantation blinds. The sky is dark, but soon the horizon beyond the fir trees will stir with an infusion of pink and orange. Sunrise. Dr. Ep told me I need to focus on positive things that I can count on.

The rising sun is pretty damned reliable.

"You can redeem yourself," Dr. Ep told me, "or at least you can try."

Redemption. I hadn't thought about that word since second grade at St. Rose of Lima when the nuns worked so hard to get us all ready to make our first communion. Actually, second grade was probably the last time I felt any chance of redemption. If you listened to my parents talk, we were all going to Hell. Oh, they did the mass thing, but I don't think they believed any of it, and that lack of faith got passed on to the rest of us.

"Our parents gave us no moral grounding, no foundation, no sense of security," Gia told me. "It's a marvel that you made it as far in your life as you did without snapping. I lost it years ago." It's great to have a sister now, though a little weird to be close to someone studying psychology when you're in the throes of a crisis. "You'd make a great case study," Gia tells me all the time. "We have a juicy past full of dysfunctions."

So that's my excuse. Sort of. But it gets worse.

Dr. Ep's interpretation of why I picked Dez to act out really bothers me. Dr. Ep thinks my mother and Dez are both somatic narcissists. Stuck on physical appearances, sort of in love with their physical selves to the exclusion of everything else. So I picked a woman like my mother, to recreate the same insanity I had at home.

Is that sick, or what?

It didn't end well with Dez.

Thank God she didn't get pregnant. Apparently, a baby was part of her master plan, a way to lure me away from my family and claim me for her own. If she only knew what a lousy father I really am, that I'm carrying this dysfunctional baggage around and subconsciously inflicting it on my own kids. Then again, Dez has a few scary dysfunctions of her own.

When I was packing to leave her place, going through some drawers in the closet, looking for my stuff, I came across two framed photos. One was my corporate mug, the company photo, obviously downloaded from Corstar's website. The other photo creeped me out because Dez and I stood beside each other and everything around us was clipped out. It reminded me of the kind of collage Scout would make for school.

"What is this from?" I asked aloud.

That brought Dez in from the living room, where she'd been crying on the couch. Her face went taut with fury when she spotted the frames in my hands. She snatched them away and scowled. "Those are mine! What are you doing in my stuff?"

"I'm just trying to get my things and get out," I said quietly, trying to keep the weirdness out of my voice. I sensed she was ready to snap.

I was right.

She tore the photos from my hands, pressed them to her chest and wailed, "How can you leave me? How can you do this? How can you? How can you?"

Revulsion curled through me. I hate melodrama.

I hated it when my mother whined that we didn't appreciate her. When she made a scene because I'd spilled my milk or tracked mud into the house. The way she'd moan, like someone was sticking a knife in her belly . . .

That was how Dez sounded.

She sat rocking on the edge of the bed, hugging the photos like you'd hold a baby. "I won't let you leave me!"

"Stop it," I growled, turning back to the closet to finish packing. The sooner I was out of there, the better. "Stop it now."

"I won't! You can't leave me."

"Watch me," I said under my breath.

Suddenly something flew from the bed. It hit the side of my head first, then smashed into the closet door.

My ear and head burned. The frame had cut me, blood dripping down my neck. "Dammit!" I took a T-shirt from my duffel bag and pressed it against the wound.

"Oh, no! Oh, baby, I'm sorry." She gasped, falling to her knees at my feet. "I'm so sorry! I didn't mean to hurt you."

Ignoring her, I picked up the frame at my feet. Through the spider cracks in the glass, Dez and I smile at the camera like zombies. Most of the background had been cut out, but over our heads was a bit of greenery with gold ribbon. Boughs of holly.

That was when I recognized the photo. It was from Christmastime, the Corstar party back in New York. Dez had cut out Ruby on my right, and God knows who from the other side of the photo . . .

If that wasn't the sickest thing.

So I'd been a target? How long had she had these photos in her apartment, staring at them, staring and planning?

I needed three stitches that day. There's still a small chunk missing from the edge of my ear and a scar on the thin skin behind it. My hair covers most of it, but I catch myself fingering the scar, a warning, a reminder.

Once I walked into the valley of destruction . . .

And somehow, I found my way back home.

I'm not sure how much of this I should share with Ruby. I've always told her everything, but I don't want to hurt her any more.

"Tell her what she wants to know," Dr. Ep says. "Don't lie to her, don't withhold information, but don't offer it all up. She is not your therapist."

I guess in the past, she did that for me, too. Well, not anymore. I want back into the relationship, and I want to do it right. No more screwups. My head is on straight now, and I want to keep it that way. For myself, for my kids and for Ruby.

I've done my damage here. Becca is angry with me. She goes off to bed at night without kissing me, without the tuck-in ritual she used to demand. If I let her, she would spend all of her time at Madison's house. Nine years old and she'd like to run away. She reminds me of myself when I was a kid, when I would bunk in with Tommy McGee and pretend to be just another face at the table. My escape.

Is Becca's life so horrible she needs to escape?

No, I think it's just me. She's mad, but she'll get over it. I'll show her that I've changed, that I'm back to being her Dad.

On the other hand, Scout's gotten a little manic. She's all over the car thing, as if a new BMW is the way to my heart. Every time I take those FOR SALE signs out of my car, she makes new ones and tapes them onto the back windows. Weird, but a year ago I'd have thought a new car would do it for me. My midlife crisis car.

If I could have just gone with a Beemer or a Corvette. That would have saved a lot of grief.

Every night after dinner, when I sit on the couch to watch the kids' DVDs, Dylan crawls on my lap. He puts a hand on my knee and pulls himself up until he can rest against my chest, the top of his head tickling my chin. Such a simple act, a kid climbing into your lap, but it got the message home the first time he did it. He trusts me. This kid loves me. Despite the fact that I've been an absentee father to him, despite the fact that I've been a prick to his mother.

Love is definitely blind.

I'm learning to get some satisfaction out of the little things. Wrapping Dylan in a towel after his bath. Pulling a splinter from Scout's fingertip. Teaching Becca how to crack an egg. As I move through this house, relearning its blueprint, I realize it did become my home. This is the place on the planet where I belong.

I hope Ruby can take me back. The kids are stuck with me, but Ruby has a choice, and here's the kicker: informed love isn't always blind.

The sun has leaked over the horizon now, the sky dusky cobalt. I go into the walk-in closet Ruby and I used to share. My side is nearly empty but for a suit hanging from the rod and a few sports shirts and jeans on the shelf.

But it's Ruby's side I go to, her clothes hanging like a wall of colorful cheer. I press into them, the stubble of my chin bristling against soft sweaters. I take peach and red and periwinkle cotton sleeves by the fistful and cling to them. Her scent lingers, her spirit, that perennial smile.

I soak it up until tears sting my eyes, then I pull back. It wouldn't do the kids much good to wake up to their father sobbing in the closet. That would be good for years on the couch, and I'm hoping my children can avoid the psychological scarring I endured.

Touching the scar behind my ear, I grab a pair of jeans and head out of the closet. Time to start the rest of my life.

47

50 Ways to Heal Your Marriage

Twilight lingered as I took my seat on the plane, and for once I was glad for the five-hour flight to Portland. You can sort through a lot of thoughts and feelings in five hours, order and reorder them. The time gives the harsher ones a chance to soften, the quiet ones a chance to bloom.

Flight therapy.

I could just imagine the commercials we'd see if the airlines got ahold of that concept. They'd have customers extending their stays in the air just to buy time to meditate.

As the plane strained to become airborne from the runway, I realized that I was now a very different woman from the mommy who'd left New York City with three children less than a year ago. Back then I couldn't stomach the notion of divorce. My lower lip would pout at the notion of single-parenting. If you'd suggested that I'd indulge in an affair with a Broadway actor and not even feel guilty about it, I would have wagged a finger and laughed in your face.

So much had changed. As we banked and soared over a gleaming turquoise bridge over the Hudson, skimming a lit-up Bronx multiplex cinema and heading west toward the fading sun, I realized I'd grown comfortable in my new skin. I was prepared to deal with divorce and raising my children on my own. I had learned to be my own person without a husband to define me.

And now, with all those plates successfully spinning, came the finale of my new cirque de mama act: Did I *want* to proceed on my own . . . or did I want to reengage Jack?

Flipping open a women's magazine, I thought of the message I'd retrieved during the limo ride to the airport. The voices of the kids, eager to see me at the airport.

And Jack, steady and humble. "The new job in Portland is a go, so it looks like I'm moving back. But don't worry. I put some money down on a rental. Got it through Debbie's friend. I'll be here for the kids, at least, and you, if you want. I know there's a lot of work to do. Relationship work. God, I hate that psychobabble, but I want to make it work again. To make *us* work. I miss you, Rubes. But I won't push. I'll stay out of your hair for as long as you want. I just . . . Okay, is this, like, the longest message in the history of broken relationships?"

Replaying the message in my head, I savored each word, relishing his sincerity, his self-deprecating humor.

God help me, I still loved him.

Not the smitten variety of steamy attraction referred to in the magazine in my lap. After fifteen years together, 6 SIZZLING SEX TIPS were not going to mend our riff. But I didn't want to throw the relationship away because *the zing* had *zonged* from our relationship, or because Jack had failed the 9 WAYS TO TELL YOUR MAN IS CHEATING ON YOU test.

Yes, Jack had behaved badly. He'd been an ass, but I wasn't without flaws. Who was? And what were the chances of my next relationship working out any better? Magazines and self-help books were so quick to tell me to cut him off. Cut your losses. But was there no hope for the bleeding patient, the wounded relationship?

Doctor, save the arm! Save my head and my heart!

In a world of evolving couples, where were the headlines crying for a bandage? A medic?

Why didn't any of these headlines talk about healing a relationship, steering it back in the right direction when a marriage runs off track? I leaned back into the seat and imagined the stories I would write.

KRAZY GLUE YOUR RELATIONSHIP!

MEND YOUR MARRIAGE WITH INDUSTRIAL DOUBLE-STITCHING
IN 4 EASY STEPS!

Of course, I knew nothing of sewing and I had taken a single psychology course in high school.

I pressed my cheek to the cool window and stared out at the darkness. A few rows ahead of me, the light from the wing blinked blue, a beacon in the night. Such a small light for an enormous aircraft, and yet, it was enough.

I could navigate these waters with Jack. At least, I was willing to give it a try.